Ministry of
Bombs

NELSON LOWHIM

Also By Nelson Lowhim

The Struggle Trilogy

CityMuse

Tree of Freedom

When Gods Fail (I, II, III)

Alternative Book Press
2 Timber Lane
Suite 301
Marlboro, NJ 07746
www.alternativebookpress.com

Originally published in electronic form in the United States by Eiso Publishing.
Library of Congress Cataloging-in-Publication Data

Nelson, Lowhim, [date]
Ministry of Bombs/ by Nelson, Lowhim.—1st ed.
p. cm.
1. War—Fiction (Fiction). I Title.
PN3311-3503.L69M565   2014
813'.6—dc23
2014933619

ISBN 978-1-940122-11-3
Printed in the United States of America
10 9 8 7 6 5 4 3 2 1

Ali walked to the street and looked down at the cafe, rustling awake in the morning sun. He could feel his muscles wrapped tight around his bones. And he could smell coffee in the air. But this was no time to think of his one addiction. He nodded at the young man beside him. The young man, Abdul, dripped in sweat, his eyes darting back and forth.

"Don't worry. I'm going to be here with you the whole way," said Ali. He stroked a scar on his jawline. It went deep. Old wounds from a war on the other side of these desert sands. In the mornings his jawbone would pulse with pain, shaking his skull.

He walked first, to scout the cafe, which was now filled with Western tourists. All had that vapid look that Ali had come to associate with them. He scowled at a handful of women with skirts on.

As Ali walked past, he pulled his cellphone out. "Abdul, it's clear. Get a coffee and do it."

Ali didn't look over his back. When he turned the corner, he jumped into the front passenger seat of the car. The street here was busier. That gave them more cover. Horns honked, and car exhaust wafted into his nose. He waited. A few minutes later Abdul came around the corner. He smiled. Abdul jumped into the back.

Ali pulled out a remote control. He handed it to Abdul. He'd done this hundreds of times, and it never got any easier.

"Your turn," said Ali. "When I say so, press the button."

The young man nodded and grabbed the remote, a little too easily for Ali's tastes.

The car drove forward and the cafe came into view. Ali saw some kids playing soccer in front of the cafe.

"Not yet," Ali said. He placed a hand on the driver's forearm. "When Abdul presses the button you move away slowly, like there's nothing wrong. Got it? No driving fast."

Ali watched as the cafe owner drove away the kids with a broom. He noticed the red skin of a tourist who seemed to see him.

"Now."

The flash and corresponding shock wave traveled through Ali, and he felt the warmth of the explosion. Then the car alarms and screams. Smoke and mangled debris was all that remained of the cafe. They drove slowly around the corner. A few streets over people were going about their business. None of them seemed to know what was going on only a few blocks away. Near a pile of garbage, Abdul threw the remote.

Soon they were on a highway leaving the city. They stopped when they finally came to a mountainside house. It was their safe house. The government didn't have much control out here.

But Ali knew that his day wasn't over. There was a meeting with some of the local tribal leaders in the evening. But first he was going to have to talk to his bosses. He told Abdul to relax and drink some water.

Ali walked into his office and saw his two bosses: the head of Al Qaeda in Maghreb, and the liaison from Al Qaeda in Afghanistan. Ali didn't much like either of them. They were too grand, and never liked to hear about the minutiae of the local political movement. But they brought in recruits and money, so Ali didn't have a choice.

"Please to sit down," said Ali. "Drinks?"

The two men shook their heads. The liaison was a tall and lanky man. He claimed to have fought the infidels in Afghanistan. But Ali didn't believe that since the lanky man, Mohammad, looked too good, with skin too smooth to have seen a battle. Not any kind of battle *he* knew about. Ali in charge of the Maghreb, Laith, was a short and stout man. He'd blue eyes and red hair, though he was born in the sands of Algeria.

"How can I help you?" the man said, sitting back in his chair.

"How did the operation go, Ali?" Laith asked, his eyes gleaming.

"Let's see," Ali said, massaging his jawbone. It was always

aggravated when these two came here. He switched on the TV and turned to the news channel. There was the cafe, with emergency services pulling people out of the rubble.

Laith and Mohammad giggled with glee. Ali forced a smile, though he didn't like the way these two men seemed to love the sight of destruction. It only served to highlight how much they hadn't done anything on the ground. How they hadn't had actual blood on their hands and clothes and how that blood hadn't infiltrated their dreams.

"It says ten dead, twenty injured, good job," Mohammad said.

"Thank Abdul," Ali said. "He was the one who carried it out. His first."

"He's a soldier," Laith said.

Ali didn't say anything. Only deskmen would dismiss a soldier's job. "What do you two want?"

"Just wanted a discussion of where your team was going. The next few missions," Laith said.

Ali let out some air and filled them in on the next few attacks planned, and the local political situation. The two men's eyes glazed over. Ali dived further into the situation, trying to cause them some pain. Finally, Laith raised his hand.

"We also wanted your opinion on something."

"Please," Ali said, suppressing a smirk and preparing himself for a grandiose idea that he'd have to shoot down.

"You know the great Dr. Noklar?" Mohammad asked.

"Of course, who doesn't?"

"Well we have been in correspondence with him," said Mohammad.

"Really?" Ali said and leaned forward. He never imagined these two to be that competent.

"Yes. We may have convinced him to finally come out and help us."

"Come out?" Ali said. "The ISI watches him like a hawk. How can he come out? And even if he did, the Americans and the Israelis would have him killed in a heartbeat."

"You think too small," Mohammad said. "Too risk-averse. We

8

have good word that he'll soon be with us, and that when he is, we'll finally have what we always wanted."

"Is *that* so?" Ali said. "And what amazing nuclear facility will he be working at?" He leaned back. He did not like these two, and he especially hated their foreign accents. It only proved that they didn't care for the local situation anywhere and would forever be grasping at magical solutions to mundane problems.

His comment shut the two of them up, but after a few glances they seemed to regain their composure.

"You think too small," Laith said, shaking his head. "The doctor will soon be helping us. And then we shall be unstoppable."

"Well, I *must* think too small," Ali said. "What did you say to him that brought him on board?"

"We explained how he could help the cause."

"And what did he say?" Ali asked.

"At first he claimed we had no cause. But we think our last letter convinced him."

"Why?" Ali asked.

"We told him to think of the bigger picture."

"Ah, ingenious," Ali said, wondering how long before he could kick them out of his office. He wanted to drink some chai. Then he wanted to talk to the local leaders about money for some water.

"It is," said Laith. "We want to draft one more letter..."

"And you want me to?" Ali said, not hiding his annoyance.

"Yes. We need you. You can tell him some stories and help convince him about our cause."

"All right. I will," Ali said.

When the two men left he shook his head and wondered what letter he could possibly write to someone as smart as the good Dr. Noklar. He would finish it later.

And as he walked out of the building, a prickle ran up his skin. He looked up at the sky. The distant sound of a jet engine hummed. Just like any other day. As he watched the motorcade with Laith and Mohammad leave, he suddenly knew what was going on.

A few other men were milling about, and Ali yelled: "Missile!"

Most of the men stared at him like they thought he was mad. But Ali knew what the drill was and ran to the rocks a few hundred meters from the building. He dove into them as the sky was filled with a horrid swooshing sound. And in the middle of his dive Ali twisted in the air as his world went black.

Dr. Noklar leaned back on his window ledge when a loud series of horns, odd even for Karachi, forced his eyes over to the street. He was on the outskirts of the city, and the tree-lined streets here were filled with hawkers of all wares. Outside his house, in two black cars, were a handful of men in aviator glasses and gray suits. They occasionally glanced up at him and nodded.

They were there, according to the Pakistani government, for his protection. But he also knew that they were there in place of his prison bars. Protection, in Dr. Noklar's life, had always meant less freedom. He sighed as he lit up a cigarette. He'd started smoking ever since stooges in his government collaborated with the Americans to make his life a living hell.

In his other hand he held a crumpled piece of paper. He knew its contents by heart. And he knew no one else could ever read it. Using his matches, he set it on fire, opened the window and watched as the paper turned to ashes and smoke.

The men in suits glanced at him, but they didn't seem to react. The air outside was cool and refreshing, and Dr. Noklar admonished himself for picking up this disgusting habit. But he couldn't stop from taking another hit of nicotine.

And what was he going to do about the request in the letter? He could feel his intestines crawl up to his heart, and his heart pushed blood to his brain, and he was overwhelmed. He took in another drag. The sun was setting fast, and swallows came out to eat the insects rising in the shade. He didn't know what he was going to do. He stared at the men in suits. They would see him the moment he left. Or was there another way?

Dr. Noklar threw out his cigarette and pondered his choices.

Soon dinner would be ready, and he'd go downstairs and eat with his wife and her relatives. He didn't mind them, really, their deferential respect towards him always allowed him some room to breathe. But none of them would be willing to help him with this. In fact, it'd be better if they didn't know about this at all.

But the boy who brought him the letter, he would be able to help, wouldn't he? How to reach out to him?

His wife's voice sounded off the marble floors, and Dr. Noklar slowly made his way down the stairs and to the dinner table where everyone stared at him. He raised his hand and everyone dived in to eat. He chewed his food, not tasting the lamb, though the clove curry spices that hit his nose made him wonder why not. No, his thoughts were with the letter he'd just burned. The more he dwelt on it the more it seemed that these people in front of him were strangers.

His wife placed her hand on his wrist, a concerned look flashed on her face. He forced a smile. But inside he was annoyed. He just wanted to lay with his thoughts, the letter, and the emotions it stirred up inside him.

This idea made him feel bad, and he placed his other hand in his wife's and smiled again, staring into her big brown eyes. She had, after all, been the one to stand behind him. Especially when he'd been arrested, forced to live in a house, never to see the light of day. He tilted his head at her. She nodded and went back to eating. He returned his eyes to his own plate, feeling that if he concentrated on the food in front of him no one else would notice his cogitation, and perhaps he could even forget the damn letter.

It didn't work. He focused on each grain of rice embedded in the pilaf. A piece of clove. And still the letter's contents wouldn't leave his mind be. He pushed his food aside, half-finished and left the table. He could feel everyone's eyes piercing his back. He walked around the corner and opened the bathroom door, shutting it loudly. He could hear a few murmurs from the dinner table. It didn't matter. The sweat on his forehead, and the feeling of a vice on his heart. He had to leave. There was no other choice. He headed to the servants' room. There was still one who stayed after dinner.

11

The servant, Karim, looked at him like he didn't care for the intrusion.

"Can I help you?"

Dr. Noklar stopped to take in this bold servant. The newest of the lot, and the most rebellious. Normally the doctor's wife would've said something, but even she seemed to know better. There was something about Karim that didn't seem to accept authority, and whatever had led him to become a servant, it didn't seem strong enough to make him a loyal dog.

"I know this is your dinner time, but I wanted to talk to you," Dr. Noklar said. He tried to keep his eyes on Karim's almost black eyes. He failed and his eyes darted to the scar that ran down Karim's dark forehead, denting the nose, then across the lower jaw and disappearing on his neck.

Karim put down his plate of food and pointed at his bed. It was a small room, with a jail-like window, a three-legged stool that Karim sat on, and an army cot with a blanket on top. The whole room stunk of dirty feet and a hint of perfume. Dr. Noklar knew the house rules didn't allow the servants to have any guests of their own, but Karim seemed impervious to such rules. That it was a woman Karim was violating the rules for, made the doctor like him.

Dr. Noklar sat down, the cot creaking to greet him. He stared at his hands because staring at Karim's eyes, those incisive things, would make his inner turmoil worse.

"Well?" Karim said, casting a glance at his unfinished plate.

"You know the young boy who came by the front door today?" Dr. Noklar said. He could clearly smell perfume and sweat rising off the sheets. He suppressed a smile. And for the first time in hours he relaxed.

"Abdullah? The one with the message for you?" Karim said.

"Yes," Dr. Noklar replied. He took a second to hold Karim's stare, but those vacant-yet-sharp black eyes forced him to look elsewhere. He settled for the wall behind Karim. Peeled paint, and a cockroach running into a crack. What was it about Karim's eyes that seemed so scary? After all he, Dr. Noklar, had dined with plenty of military men with time in and around Kashmir. Men who'd fought battles at twenty thousand feet.

What was it about Karim's eyes that seemed harder?

"What about him?" asked Karim.

The doctor wasn't certain what to ask. Instead, happy to not think about the message, he was thinking that Karim, even with the suited men outside, was the kind of person to take a slight and murder an entire family. The doctor had heard stories like that and thought it impossible. Not with the kind of servants he'd had before. But with Karim... "He's a street child, isn't he?"

Karim stood up a little taller. "So am I."

"You're no longer a child."

Karim half-grinned, showcasing his browned teeth.

Dr. Noklar let out a sigh of relief. For a second he'd thought his last sentence went too far. "Do you know him well?"

"I knew him before I had this job. He's smart..." Karim trailed off. Something about his demeanor suddenly seemed unconfident.

"I know he is." The doctor had only talked to the boy a handful of times, but it was easy to see his intelligence. Dr. Noklar had seen that in a smart remark that had all the suited men laughing with him. That was a few weeks ago. Little by little he'd let the young boy buy things for him. Abdullah always knew how to evade the men in suits.

"And you want to talk about Abdullah, why?" Karim asked. His face had contorted into a snarl.

The doctor was confused for a second before he realized what Karim was insinuating.

"No. No," Dr. Noklar said. "I am not like that."

Karim nodded, but his face remained hard.

"Do you know how he got the message he gave me?"

Karim shook his head. "I can ask him, if you want."

The doctor paused to think. Would including Karim in his scheme be foolish? Perhaps the hard man only saw him as a way to get money. Perhaps the first chance he got he would stick his master and take his wallet. But the doctor knew he was going to have to risk it. He picked up the blanket and smelled it. "A woman of yours?"

Karim clenched his jaw.

"I don't mean anything. I think having a woman is important. The

13

greatest thing in the world."

"What I do is my business," Karim said.

"Of course. I just want to make sure I understand a little about you."

"Why? You pay me to wait and serve you. What do you care what I do?" Karim said.

The doctor glanced at the door. He got up, checked the hallway, and shut the door. He stood in front of Karim. He could see the young man's fists balling up.

"I too have a secret," Dr. Noklar said. "That's what the message was about."

Karim's forehead furrowed, his head tilted like he was confused, then his face lit up and he grinned. "Oh?"

"Can you help me keep them?"

Karim leaned back and smiled. The odor of an unbrushed tongue hit the doctor and forced him to hold his breath. Dr. Noklar had not thought it possible to see the young man's face and eyes go soft, but they did.

"I will tell no one," Karim said and pointed at his blankets. "The servant girl from across the street comes in at night. I leave my window open and she comes in almost every night."

Dr. Noklar smiled. "It's good... a woman."

"Yes. And secrets," Karim said, holding up his finger. "Nothing is more important than being able to share secrets with someone."

Dr. Noklar nodded his head, though he was in no mood to share what was in the message. "I need to leave. And I need to do it without any one else knowing. Abdullah seems to know how to avoid them."

"We can manage."

The doctor wasn't certain how the poor young man in front of him was so confident, but he liked it and didn't want to burst the elated feeling that gave him.

"And where do you want to go?" Karim asked.

"I want to get out of the country."

Karim chuckled, then looked at the doctor with narrowed eyes. "Out of the country? This will not be easy."

"I'll pay," said the doctor. "But it must be done right away and—"

"I know. No one must know."

"Right," Dr. Noklar said. Now that doubt was creeping across Karim's face, his hopes were crashing. "This can be done, right?"

"It can."

"You ever try something like this?" the doctor asked.

Karim's eyes darted about the room. "Yes. On the border to Afghanistan. But that's easy if you want to be in Afghanistan."

So the young man was fighter on top of being a street kid. Dr. Noklar could feel his throat tightening. "And?"

"It can be done. I will talk to Abdullah tomorrow—"

"No. Tonight. Get him tonight."

"Okay, okay," Karim said, smiling. "It will happen."

The doctor stared at Karim for another half second before he turned to the door. "Let me know if you need anything."

"I will," Karim said, his smile almost too nice now.

As Dr. Noklar made it up the stairs to his room, his hands started shaking. How foolish could he have been to place his trust in someone like Karim? The young man was a street kid, a violent one. He would turn the doctor in, or kill him for his money the moment he had a chance. Dr. Noklar's stomach rumbled and he pulled out a bottle of whiskey. It was a gift from decades ago during his time in Germany. He'd barely touched it, but tonight he needed something. He made sure his door was locked before he took a sip. After today he would make peace with his past. He could finally say that he had won.

The doctor awoke, lurching up and staring at darkness. His heart was beating fast. After a few seconds he made out a form beside his bed.

"You're awake," Karim said.

It took a few seconds for Dr. Noklar to remember what he'd talked about with the young man only a few hours ago. He rubbed his eyes, picked them with his fingers and removed the crust between them. Even though his bed called him, made him want to sleep and forget this ever happened, he pulled his feet out of bed and waited for Karim to say something.

15

When nothing was said. When in fact all he could hear was Karim breathing, he wondered if Karim had woken him up, or was he just sitting here watching the doctor sleep? Perhaps he had made a mistake. But as the young man's chai-infused breath infiltrated the doctor's olfactory senses, he decided that the young man was here to help.

"Did you find Abdullah?" asked the doctor.

"I did," said Karim.

"I'll be meeting with him?"

"We leave now. Pack what you need."

The doctor flinched. He instinctively looked to see if his wife was in bed, but they'd stopped sleeping in the same room ever since she claimed that he snored years ago. Patting the sheets he felt some regret for leaving without telling her. He walked to his dresser in the dark and pulled out the bag he'd packed. He tried to remember what was in it. He put on a fresh change of clothes, then his shoes. He made sure his wallet was full and in his pocket.

Karim grabbed his hand. "Now."

Before he could protest, the young man pulled him out to the hallway. They went down the steps so fast that the doctor was sure that they'd fall and be found out. But the young man was sure footed, and even though the doctor tripped twice, and pushed on the young man's back, he didn't fall.

Dr. Noklar found himself in Karim's room. The window was open, and Dr. Noklar was certain that there was someone on the bed. The smell of saffron was strong. He didn't say anything when a form beneath the blanket stirred. Karim pushed him to the window.

The doctor pulled himself up and over the window and into a small section of the garden he'd never seen before. A cool night breeze hit his face. There was a high wall with glass scattered in the cement on top. Karim, now beside him, pointed at the wall. "I hope you can climb," whispered the young man.

Dr. Noklar looked around. There were no windows facing this part of the house. He wondered how big of a security threat that was. He walked over to the wall and looked at Karim. Now that he had to climb it, it seemed impossible.

Karim grinned, a garlic smell now spewed from his mouth. Dr. Noklar wondered how it changed so quickly. But before he could think of that, Karim got down on all fours and indicated that the doctor should climb on his back. At the same time Karim handed him a piece of cloth. He indicated to the doctor to wrap his hands in it. The doctor did so and stood up on Karim's back. It was less stable than he thought and he fell down. The second time he secured his balance with the wall and reached up over it. Even with the cloth to protect his hands, he could feel the glass pushing into his skin.

And he used all his might to pull himself up. But his muscles weren't used to this sort of exertion. He pulled himself high enough that his chin rested on the top, and he could see the small street that greeted him. For some reason it didn't seem familiar.

He felt a push on his ass, and he used it to pull himself over. He could hear his pants ripping on the glass shards. When he fell, feet then ass, on the other side, there was a momentary pang of relief. That was soon replaced when Karim didn't come over.

Lying there on his back, he stared at the cloud cover highlighted by the city lights. He could sense the freedom that leaving the house afforded him. The air was almost lighter. It was as if he knew the men in suits could no longer touch him.

But the longer it took for Karim to come over—where was he?—the lighter the air grew until the doctor couldn't breath any more. And then the warnings the ISI and their men in suits gave him tickled his brain and increased in volume until they were yells in the silence of the night. He thought about the warnings they'd given him. That in fact there were trained American and Israeli assassins in the streets who were after him. And now he'd given up protection, for what? To trust a street kid who may well have still been a terrorist?

He could feel his chest tighten.

"Doctor?"

The doctor opened his eyes. "Where were you?" he asked. He knew that trusting Karim with his life was foolish. But what else could he do?

"I heard some noise inside the house, and I had to make sure no one knew you were gone."

"Where to now?" the doctor asked as he got up and brushed himself. Karim pointed at a white Korean van on the street.

"In there," Karim said and handed him a passport.

The doctor looked inside. There was a picture of him. Again his mind started to run, and his chest tightened. How could a street child get such good forgeries? In so short a notice? It could very well be that Karim was working for the Americans or someone else…

They drove in the van for a few minutes, pulling further and further away from the city. Dr. Noklar wanted to ask Karim what the plan was, but with his thoughts in such a jumble, he couldn't.

At a corrugated tin shack by the side of the highway, Karim hid the van in plastic siding then pointed to a car. The air out here was clean, crisp, and crickets chirped in the distance.

The young man opened the trunk.

"No," said the doctor; he hated closed spaces.

"You have to," Karim said. "There will be checkpoints up."

The doctor wanted to run, pee, but in the end there was no choice and he climbed in. The trunk shut tight, inches from his face. He looked for an air hole, or a crack, but couldn't find anything. The car started up and started to toss and turn through a bumpy road. What bumpy road? They were next to a highway.

Dr. Noklar's heart started to race. The darkness of the trunk seeped into his mind. He never wanted to be back at home as badly as he did now. He pushed at the trunk and yelled. The trunk wouldn't budge. This was a mistake, and he could feel it through his bones. He yelled again. In response loud music was turned on. Dr. Noklar knew that Karim wasn't what he pretended to be. How he wished he were with the men in suits. He could smell something sweet in the trunk, and realized that it was blood. He kicked again and his whole world, nothing but black, fell in on him.

The doctor woke up when the car hit a bump, and his head was launched into the top of the trunk. He took in a couple of breaths before he realized that he was cold. Very cold. What had he gotten himself into?

His heart dropped into his stomach. He wondered where he was going to find himself. Perhaps in some alley somewhere? Would Karim hand him over to some thugs, or terrorists, or agents who would be more than willing to finish his pathetic life? He thought of his wife and how they hadn't been getting along, and yet he still would prefer her presence.

He rolled forward in the trunk as the car screeched to a halt. He could hear loud voices. He thought he heard a child's voice as well. Was that Abdullah? The doctor realized that his teeth were chattering. He hugged himself and rubbed the sides of his torso.

The car drove slowly. A few minutes later it stopped. He could smell garbage. But all was silent as the car engine cut off. The sound of footsteps crunching on gravel. The doctor realized he had to piss really badly.

The trunk swung open. The light blinded the doctor. As he raised his hands to fend off the light, a hand grabbed his shirt and pull him. He tried to twist, but his hips and knees were frozen in place. He had been unable to move for too long.

He opened his eyes and saw Karim grinning at him. Next to him was Abdullah who held out a bag of sweets.

The doctor, feeling the pain in his legs, and his joints, pushed Karim. "What is the meaning of this?"

"No," Karim said and raised his hands. "We had to get you out of Pakistan. And we have."

They were in an alley with several cement buildings around them. Dr. Noklar noticed that the script on one building was Farsi. "Iran?" he said. He could feel something tickling his bones.

"That's right, Iran," said Karim, beaming.

"Eat something," Abdullah said.

Dr. Noklar took a few of the sweets from the bag and ate them. "We got past the border," he said, curling his toes and trying to sense that his body was getting back to normal.

"We can't go to India. And we don't want Afghanistan," said Karim.

"Karim was there," Abdullah said with a smile. "He was a soldier."

Karim didn't seem to like this: "Don't bother the doctor too much.

He's tired from being in the trunk all day. Let's get you a good breakfast, right?"

As they shuffled out of the alley, a splendid desert-moonscape appeared, created from a dark sand Dr. Noklar'd never seen before. The horizon was marked by guard towers and barbed wire.

"Was it hard?" he asked.

"No," Karim said. "We paid the guards. I don't think they're looking for you."

"Good," Dr. Noklar said.

They sat down at a roadside diner that was an old cement building that doubled for a storefront. It was from this wide window where they ordered their breakfast of chai and eggs. The chairs directly outside, covered with a thick layer of dust, weren't comfortable, so they ate standing at the window.

When he finished, the doctor looked at Karim. Dr. Noklar was surprised that the young man hadn't asked him what this was all about. And he remembered the men in the suits, and he now knew that they were too far to ever be able to touch him.

Then he noticed that Abdullah was staring at him.

"What is it, little one?" Dr. Noklar asked.

"Why did you want to leave your wife so badly?" Abdullah asked.

Dr. Noklar couldn't help but laugh. Karim joined in.

Abdullah didn't look pleased. "What did I say?"

"Nothing," the doctor said and rubbed the little boy's hair. "Nothing at all."

"Then why laugh so hard?" Abdullah asked.

"Leave the doctor alone," Karim said as he wiped food from his mouth. "We had better get going."

They shuffled towards the car. Rust ate away at the edges, while the rest was a peeled-white color. Karim handed him the keys. "You're driving."

"Where?" Dr. Noklar asked staring at the keys. Since his house arrest and subsequent watching he hadn't driven a car.

Karim reached into the glove box and pulled out a map and pointed: "This town."

The doctor squinted. He realized that he'd forgotten his reading glasses. What a thing to forget. "Qal eh Shahi?" he said as he leaned backwards to read the name of the coastal town.

"I have friends there," Karim said, getting into the passenger side. "If you need help wake me up. Otherwise." He pointed in the direction they were to drive.

"All right," Dr. Noklar said. He jumped in and stared at the stick shift. He was sure he would remember. He pressed the clutch and started the car. It whined to life. He stuck it in first gear and released the clutch. Too quick. The car lurched forward and stalled.

Karim opened one eye. "You can driver, doctor?"

"I can," the doctor muttered, feeling the sting of embarrassment on his cheeks.

"Let me drive," Abdullah said, leaning forward from the backseat.

"Shut up and sit down," Karim said. "Little boys don't drive."

The doctor started the car again. And this time, though the car lurched, it managed to stay off stalling. Soon they were on a single lane highway, driving at a top speed of 50km/h. The doctor looked over at Karim, who was now snoring. The road opened up straight ahead, small puddles of sand obscured it here and there. Dr. Noklar was finally at peace, the aroma of gasoline and body odor taking over his thoughts. He stared at a doll jiggling on the dashboard. He wasn't sure if he'd seen that before, though the dress on the woman reminded him of Pacific Islands. And he inhaled and for a second it was as if he could go to all the places he'd wanted to go in his life. The woman started to shake faster. He slowed the car down, but the windows started to rattle.

Karim shook out of his slumber. "What?" A wind buffeted the car.

A helicopter landed in front of their car. The doctor couldn't breath. *They had caught him.* How foolish he was to think he could escape a government. Men in fatigues and rifles raised jumped out of the helicopter and came running at them. The doctor closed his eyes as the car came to a complete stop. He wasn't going to defeat them after all. He could feel a cold draft on his insides. Life wasn't worth fighting for anymore.

Nelson Lowhim

Ali screamed as he felt his legs on top of his head. Was he broken in half? He couldn't feel them. He tried to open one eye and it wouldn't budge either. He was certain that he was blind. He shook his head. What would a life be like without sight? He prayed to Allah, hoping to find a way through this. His nostrils were filled with an odd chemical burning. Underneath that was the smell of metal and flesh burning. For some reason his mind went back to the cafe. Had he been tracked since then?

A child's cry pierced his skull. He twisted his torso. And his legs moved into place. A light tingle ran through his body as he realized he could feel his legs. He smiled again when he realized that his arms were moving. He wiped his forehead, pulling back quickly when he felt a sharp pain. Slowly, he raised his hand to his blind eye. He could feel flesh. He lifted it and almost cried when he realized he could see. He tried to stick the flesh back to where it belonged. But it wouldn't stick.

Another cry from a child. Ali wasn't certain if he should head out from his cave of rocks. It was known that the American drones would hang around for a few more minutes to kill any stragglers walking around.

He peered out to the now charred compound to see a child stumbling, shocked and staring at a body without limbs. Ali knew then that he could walk out because the Americans would have blown the boy by now. He stepped out, one hand to his forehead. The boy looked at him.

Ali walked up to the boy and placed his hand on his shoulder. He had never seen the boy before.

"What are you doing here, child?"

The boy looked up at him. There was a dried trail of tears on his cheeks. "My…" the boy pointed back to the highway.

Ali walked with him and came to a car, burned beyond recognition. A man and woman were burned in front and two children were in the back, both half crawled out of the collapsed window. A sharp pain stuck Ali's heart. He shook his head. His heart now pumping pain to the rest of his body.

Ali looked down at the boy who was staring.

"My family," said the boy. "I was peeing."

Ali hugged the boy and walked him away. Further down the highway Ali could see the motorcade of his now dead leaders. The boy in hand, he decided that they needed to run away from this place. He knew where a safe house was in the city.

They walked past the motorcade. Ali couldn't recognize any of the bodies. They walked on until they came to a farmer's hut. There the farmer took them to the city.

It was midnight when Ali walked into the safe house. There was no one there, and there was no phone. But that's the way it was built. No way someone could electronically survey the place. Well, limited at least. It was a building near the center of the city. Thus there were neighbors all around, but all of them knew to keep quiet.

Inside, the house, dust prevailed, and Ali could hear mice scattering every time they entered a room. Cockroaches too. The smell of feces pervaded his senses. Ali took the boy to the kitchen and fed him some chicken and rice. The fridge was stacked, and that was good.

But he didn't want the boy to sleep inside. The air was too stuffy to be any good. And Ali was developing a fever. He had to attend to his wounds soon.

He walked up to the roof with a few blankets and told the boy to get some sleep. The boy stared at him like this wasn't an order he'd follow.

Ali didn't push the kid. He'd been through enough for even a man. The boy hadn't talked once since they walked away from the destruction. Ali wasn't certain if that was good or not. But he didn't want to push the boy.

The flutter of pigeons, all in cages, tickled Ali's spine. He had to do one more thing before he succumbed to exhaustion.

"You have to get some sleep," he said to the boy. "You've been through a lot." He ruffled the boy's hair. He remembered that he would have to send this boy to someone who knew him. "Do you have any family?"

"No," said the boy. "They were in the car."

Ali wasn't certain if the boy understood. "I mean uncles or cousins or grandparents."

24

"No," said the boy.

"All right," Ali said, deciding that perhaps asking the boy when he was less traumatized and sleep-deprived would give better results.

"Why did that happen? It was the Americans, wasn't it?"

Ali wasn't sure he could answer the first part, and he had to give some context for the second. "Yes, Americans. They were trying to kill that car in front of you," he said.

"What's your name?" the boy said, scrutinizing Ali.

"Ali. You?" Ali said, a little embarrassed that he didn't think to introduce himself to the kid. It was just that he was so at one with him.

"Laith."

Ali wondered if this was a sign from Allah. Surely Laith was a common name, but what were the chances that he would find a boy who survived the attack that killed his former boss Laith?

"That's a good name," Ali finally said.

The boy nodded then lay back on the blanket. He was soon sleeping.

Ali wondered what the boy was going to do with that information. He knew that the likes of Laith and Mohammad were lurking everywhere willing to take such a young boy and change him. And though Ali despised Laith's, his former boss, ilk, he knew that this boy didn't have much of a choice.

He walked up to the cage with pigeons and pulled out a lock box next to the opening gate. The pigeons all tried to fly away from him. But they were in small boxes and though they flapped their wings, they couldn't fly. Ali wrote a small note and pulled out a pigeon, tying the scroll to its leg. He released it and watched as it flew into the night sky. He took a few moments to observe a patrol of police walk by below. He was tired, and sweating from his fever. Tomorrow morning help would come. He sat down next to the boy.

The cogitation from before was evaporating, and he was feeling angry, perhaps on the boy's behalf. He remembered the letter that his former boss had told him to prepare. Ali wondered if the men higher up knew about this plan. It would escalate things, but it would also help protect them from this American oppression. That was the reason he had fought. He remembered watching his relatives dying in an errant bombing raid. It wasn't an American pilot, but those were American bombs.

Feeling a surge of energy that would prevent his sleep, Ali went back to the box and started to formulate his letter to the doctor. He now knew what was needed.

"Spare some change?"

Justice broke out of the hedge of his thoughts and stared at the homeless man in front of him. The homeless man's skin was covered with grime, and he smelled like sulfuric mold. Justice didn't normally give to the homeless; he knew that many of them were undercovers, but he fished his pockets for some change and handed it over.

"What're the stocks looking like today?" asked the homeless man.

Justice, staring at the rooftops of midtown New York brought his attention back to the homeless man. He wondered when the last time he looked at a stock ticker was. "No idea, why?"

"Just asking," the homeless man asked, then hobbled away.

Justice wondered what made the homeless man want to live his life like this. He didn't appear to be nuts. What about choosing another city to panhandle in? New York had to be high on competition. Justice knew if he were homeless he would go and live in the forests, live off the land and not let anyone disturb him. He inhaled and the exceptionally-warm-for-spring air heated him up.

He walked by a kiosk, shaking off the strings that pulled his eyes towards the cigarettes. That was a habit he'd rather not pick back up. Though with the kind of job he had, he wondered why he cared.

At the corner, a man handing out leaflets stared at a beautiful woman passing him by. Justice was next to him, and the man tapped him. Pointing at the ass and licking his lips he said: "Perfect, huh?"

Staring at the woman's perfect, almost loud proportions, made Justice think about his woman and *her* perfect flesh. "Ain't nothing perfect," Justice said.

The man let out a hyena-laugh. His long roped body bent back, and his white teeth lit up the sidewalk. "Ain't that the truth."

They clasped hands and Justice tried to keep up with a handshake that morphed into what seemed like hand wrestling. The man's bright eyes forced a grin to spread on Justice's face. There was something about the man's ways that made Justice feel better about humanity. They embraced, and Justice walked on.

Now the shining tower that was the Freedom Tower appeared. It filled Justice with an immense pride. This was the reason he had his current job: to stop something like 9-11 from ever happening again. And though it'd taken a long time, there was finally an emblem for his fight. He walked on.

Buzzing the door, he stepped into a marbled lobby, slid his card through a slot and waited for the retina scan. Coworkers told him that studies had shown that the retina scans caused premature glaucoma. And so what was his attitude. The door buzzed open, and Justice stepped to the next door. Here he punched in a code.

"State your name," a raspy computer voice said.

"Justice."

It took a few seconds before the door opened and Justice walked through.

He remembered how he loved doing this when he first came to work, how exciting it was to be in such a secure building. How important. And for a second he felt a similar excitement.

Next he placed his palm on a touch screen and waited for it to scan. Another door slid open. Justice walked through that. Finally he walked by a desk where three security guards sat and talked to each other.

"Gentlemen," Justice said.

"Justice," they all said in unison. "How's it going?"

"Not too bad," Justice said.

"ID," they said. Justice handed them his ID, and each of them took several minutes holding it up to the light.

When they handed it back, they buzzed open a door and Justice walked through and to a wide-open hallway. No one was around.

Justice's wingtips echoed as he hurried down the hallway. He turned left, then finally came to a large door with a brass title that read: "Head Officer In Charge."

Justice knocked.

"Come in," the voice on the other side said. He entered and smiled at a redhead with a scar running down her face.

"Julie," Justice said, trying to keep his eyes off her screaming cleavage, and glass eye that never followed the real one.

"Mr. Justice," Julie replied, giving him a once over that he was by now used to.

"Drail in?"

"Hold on," Julie said as she picked up the phone. "Mr. Drail? Yes, Justice. Yes. No." She looked up from the phone as she rolled her eyes. "Go in."

Justice headed in as Julie muttered something on the phone. Walking into his boss' office always gave Justice a head rush. The room smelled old-school, like cigars and wood. While the walls were covered in plaques and pictures of Drail shaking hands with various Presidents and other heads of state. Justice knew the power his boss had—and his boss' bosses—but to come face to face with visual representations was always overwhelming. When Justice first walked into the office several years ago, he had hoped he would be able to collect a few pictures of him self alongside some head honchos. That hadn't happened yet.

"Justice," Drail said, his large hairy hand sweeping at the chair in front of the desk. "Sit down."

Justice sat down. When he hit a bump in his work, when he wasn't getting the promotions he wanted, he was ready to hate Drail. But he learned that he couldn't help but like Drail. The large Greek looked dangerously Arab, though he'd bristle at any such statement, almost as bad as calling him a Turk. Justice learned that on his first day of work when he assumed Drail spoke Arabic. Justice was lucky to keep his job then. Drail forgave faster than most. During those tough times when Justice was ready to quit, Drail kept him focused on the job.

"Drail, how's it going?"

"It's busy as usual," said Drail, running his hand through his thick, black hair, that always seemed to stand up. "How was your vacation?"

"Great," Justice said, scratching his shoulder where his skin peeled from sun exposure. "Costa Rica hit the spot."

"Nice women?"

"Went with my girlfriend," Justice said. He wasn't certain if he could call her that. Not after the fight they had. Not when in the wake of every silence between them his heart dropped. And as he thought of the possibility of losing his girlfriend, his heart sunk once more. But such topics he'd learned to keep away from work. And especially away from the likes of Drail, a former spec-ops officer.

"So… nice women?" Drail said, and laughed with his chin back before Justice had time to answer.

Justice smiled. "I'd say so."

"You should stick to Miami. Best pussy anywhere in Latin America."

"Next time," Justice said. Though he'd developed a habit of leaving the country whenever he was on vacation.

"You're probably wondering why I called you to come in early," Drail said, and interlocked his fingers in front of his face. All his gold rings matched up in a perfect row. Justice wondered why he never got such rings.

"I suppose. I thought I was going to Yemen to work at the embassy," Justice replied. He thought about saying something to save his vacation days. He had a couple weeks worth coming up, but he wasn't going to be able to use them up. And if he didn't use them up they would be discarded in the next week. Perhaps they'd be set aside. He decided not to say anything. His eyes shifted to a breast on the large *Les Demoiselles* replica behind Drail. It was something his boss enjoyed boasting about. He got the painting from a curator friend who claimed that it was impossible to tell the difference between it and the real deal hanging in the Museum of Modern Art in New York.

"You were. But now there's a change in plans. We need you elsewhere. And it's a Tango-one mission. Just for you." Drail raised his eyebrows as if waiting for Justice to start thanking him profusely.

Of course, Justice's heart jumped, and a giddiness come over him. He had never been given a Tango-one mission before. It had been above his pay-grade. "Tango-one?"

"That's right. Remember how I told you if you just stuck to your guns you would be rewarded. Well this is it. Your moment."

"Thanks," Justice said. He didn't know what else to say. He wanted to ask about the raise that came with such a job, but he didn't know if it would sound unappreciative.

Drail picked up a piece of paper and stared at it, narrowing his eyes and curling his top lip upwards. "You know anything about a Dr. Noklar?"

"The Pakistani?" Justice asked, shifting in his seat. The smell of cigars, strong, was making his nauseous. His chair, a hardened plastic reject from Sweden, wasn't helping.

"That's right." Drail looked at him as if he wanted to hear more.

Justice wasn't a fan of these moments where he was expected to recite all he knew. Reminded him too much of his times in school: teacher waiting with a ruler in hand as he stood in front of the class naming capitals on cue.

"Father of the Pakistani bomb. Helped numerous rogue states in their quest for nuclear weapons. Arrested and charged, though he never had anything more than house arrest. And even that was lifted a few years back. He can't leave the country, if I remember correctly, but he's free to go where ever he wants within Pakistan."

"Damn horrid sentence if you ask me," Drail says, shaking his head. "How anyone wants to live in those countries is beyond me." He opened and shut his desk draw, staring as if something was really bothering him. "You're missing one thing. He wasn't free to go around. The Pakistani intel, ISI, followed him like a hawk. Nothing intrusive, just that they didn't want any more crap on their faces."

"Of course," Justice said. "So what's the problem?" He wanted to say something about Drail's comment on Pakistan's status as a country to live in, but knew better.

"Well, you know our relationship with those Pakis is a little off. Especially with Geronimo and all."

Justice nodded.

"And well, we were given a copy of a letter that Dr. Noklar received a few weeks ago." Drail adjusted the rings on his fingers. "A pretty bold letter to send to a man like that." He shook his head.

"And?" Justice asked.

"He flew the coop a few days ago. ISI just told us, and gave us the letter, the bastards. Now we need to find him before things get out of hand."

"And I'm the man to do so?"

"Well... There'll be others, but you'll be our head man in charge."

"Who else?"

"Work alone."

Justice shifted in his seat again. His rushed morning breakfast of coffee, cereal—no milk because he'd just returned from vacation—and more coffee had just been released from his stomach and was doing a number on his intestines. "Alone? Isn't this mission kind of big for one man?"

"Some other agencies will be working on it, but don't worry about them. We need to find Dr. Noklar, and we need to do it as quickly as possible." Drail leaned forward, placing his hands palm up on the desk. "I'm risking a lot by giving you this mission, Justice. You've got to show me results."

Justice nodded. He could feel the gravity in Drail's voice, but he didn't like the sound of this mission. It may have been a promotion and a once in a career chance, but something was amiss.

"We're trying to get it done with as little fanfare as possible. The Pakis don't want noise, and neither do we. If any terrorist groups get a wind of his escape, they're going to piss themselves trying to find him."

"And the letter?" Justice asked.

"The letter?" Drail cocked his head at him. "Oh yes, the letter. I'll let you read it in the file. But first you have to let me know if you're in."

Justice hated this trait of Drail. He always loved withholding information from Justice. Justice supposed that it came with the territory of being a boss. He stared at the breast's brush strokes again.

Drail turned to see what Justice was looking at.

"So you like it, eh?" Drail asked. "You know it's not real. Not that you..." Drail paused to make his point. "Would know the difference. Only a handful of people would know the difference. But unfortunately it's not a real Picasso." Drail turned back to Justice, his face expecting a reply.

Justice knew better than to point out he already knew about the painting, that in fact most people in this building knew about the painting. "That's great. What a find."

"That's," Drail said, tapping his temple. "What counts in this world. Those who can use their brains can make their dollar go a little further, you know?"

"True," Justice said. He'd blown all his money this past vacation, so he was in no position to understand this truth.

"So what's your answer?"

"Of course," Justice said, shaking off the feeling that this was wrong.

"Great," Drail said and leaned back. "This will take your career far, trust me."

"Good. There's a promotion, right?"

Drail's face turned as hard as stone. "Well you know about the budget cutbacks, don't you?"

"I do," Justice said, a lump forming in his throat. "I just thought that this mission, Tango-one, was only for those with a higher pay-grade. So shouldn't I be bumped up?"

"Oh, don't worry about that," Drail said, waving his hand in the air. "That's a matter of paperwork. The main point is that you have the ability to get this done. Don't you?" He pounded his chest.

"Of course I do," Justice replied.

"Budget cut-backs, Justice. We all have to sacrifice, don't we?"

"We do," Justice said, feeling admonished. "I also have some vacation days. If they don't get used up, they're going to go to waste."

"Justice. You can't take time off," Drail said, shaking his head like he was talking to a child.

"I know that," Justice said. "I-I mean if you could, you know, let me keep them and use them for later."

"Justice, you know the rules. If you don't use them, you lose 'em."

"I know," Justice said. "I haven't had chances to use them."

"You know the job, Justice."

"Sacrifices?"

"That's right. Sacrifices, Justice."

Justice shifted in his seat. He lowered his eyes.

"So what's the budget?" Justice asked.

"That's the fun part. Over two million," Drail said. He picked up a thick manila envelope and handed it over to him. "And all you need to know is in there."

Justice held the extremely slight folder in his hand. He couldn't remember a folder being smaller. He shifted through the contents. A printout of an email and a blurry photo of a man with a crooked jaw and twisted smile slipped out into his hands.

"This is it?" Justice asked, confused. It seemed that he would find more information on Wikipedia.

"Yep. That's why the budget's so big."

"Can I request more information?"

"You could, but you won't get much."

"Even about him? His history?"

"Not really. He wasn't a priority before this."

Justice let out some air, though he tried not to be loud about it. "So no information on him?"

"That's why your budget's so big," Drail said again, nodding like that was all that needed to be said. "We want results, of course."

Justice stared at the picture because he didn't want to look at Drail at the moment. "So it's the letter that got him to jump ship?"

"That's what we think."

Justice looked over the email. The sender's email was number1alqueda@mail.com. "They sent him an email? I thought he was being watched like a hawk?"

"Well, he was. But they were sneaky."

"Sneaky with this email name?"

"Well, the algorithms weren't built to catch something like this."

"Makes sense," Justice said. "And we think he's going to meet them on account of this letter?"

"Yep."

"And I'm to stop him from reaching them?"

"Well, if things are that bad. Yes. Stop him. But we'd rather you find him, and bring him to us alive, or call us and we'll send someone else to pick him up."

Justice's blood flowed faster. This *was* an important mission, he thought. So what if he wasn't getting a raise. He signed up to defend this nation and now he was being handed the most important mission of his life. No more being a cog in the intel machine, crouching on his hands and knees, sifting through sewage to find something that would get churned into a supercomputer. No, now he was finally doing something substantial. He smiled.

"I see you're looking forward to this, aren't you?" Drail asked with a grin. "That's the spirit. I knew you'd be up to the task. You'll go far. I know you will."

"Thanks," Justice said, his chest swelling. "Well I'll be off then. Need to get souped up on some gear."

"Of course," Drail said and stood up.

They shook hands.

"I'll see you in a few?" Justice said.

"In a few. Give me updates whenever you can."

"Got it," Justice said and took one more look at the painting. It was a rather nice piece, though Justice was never one for modern art.

"Too bad you're going to be busy," Drail said.

"Why's that?"

"Have a party in a few days. But you won't be able to make it."

Justice wasn't certain if Drail was asking or telling. "Of course. What's it for?"

"Oh, I got a raise. Been a tough few years of work, you know?"

"I know," Justice said, sensing an odd feeling in his fists.

The phone rang and Drail picked it up. "Yeah? I've got my best on it." Drail's face hardened.

Justice perked up at the sound of "my best". Surely that meant him?

"Don't worry about it. We'll get him," Drail said and looked up at Justice, covering the mouthpiece. "They're pretty worried about him."

Justice knew who *they* were. The heads at Washington. The most powerful men in the country. He grunted affirmatively.

"They want you to get him as soon as possible. They think there's going to be a mushroom cloud in DC if you don't."

Justice wasn't certain if Drail was kidding, but he seemed to be serious. If the mission was this important, why only him? When Drail nodded, Justice turned and walked out of the office. Julie, sitting on her desk with the phone to her ear, winked at him and slapped his ass as he walked out.

Justice headed down the hallway to the elevator. He pressed QM button and touched the sensor with his ID card. There were no numbers on this elevator. One had to learn what the letters meant. QM was where he could get some gear, and hopefully some information on Dr. Noklar.

He entered the large laboratory where several men and women in lab coats hovered over circuit boards and mechanical parts.

"Justice!"

Justice couldn't help but smile at the fairly young, but ultimately unattractive woman who greeted him. "Sasha," Justice said and hugged her.

"You've come down for some toys?" she asked, beaming. She was a cauldron of energy. An MIT student who was kicked out for hacking the university's mainframe, she was immediately swooped up by their agency.

"I might need some, though I'm not certain what," Justice said.

"No?" She cocked her misshapen head. She was about a head shorter than Justice, with a furry lip and barrel body. Her half-Asian-half-unknown background hadn't lent her a single ounce of exotic characteristics. No, her gift was her brain.

"Well, the boss gave me an odd one," Justice said. "Tango-one."

"Ooooh, Tango-one," Sasha said. "Does that mean that someone got a raise? You should take your girlfriend out somewhere nice."

Justice felt warm. Silence broke out across the lab.

"Well, what's the mission?" Sasha asked, her voice quiet.

"To find someone. You have any good searches on Dr. Noklar?"

"You got *that* mission?" Sasha blurted out, then covered her mouth.

Something about the way she said that made Justice uncomfortable. He shifted his feet. "Yes," he said. "That's the one. Dr. Noklar. Why?"

"Oh, nothing," she said.

He looked at her face, hair sticking out from her bushy eyebrows. He forced himself to look away. Still, why had she seemed shocked that he was the one who got the Dr. Noklar mission? Did they not expect that much out of him? When she didn't break the silence he decided to let it go.

"What do you know about him?" he asked.

"I heard... That he's someone we can't have on the loose."

"No we can't," Justice said. "Anything else?" He expected more from the eyes and ears of the country.

"Not really."

"Anyone have any idea where he is?"

"No. No one."

"Can you hack ISI comms?" Justice asked.

"That would violate international protocol," Sasha said, her eyes beaming like red dwarfs.

Justice raised his eyebrows.

"But that's just what I needed for the morning!" she said. With another hand she pulled out a small white bottle and popped the top. Three small tablets swallowed and she started to shake her feet. She offered the bottle to Justice. "Any magic pills for you?"

Justice raised his hands, palms out, and shook his head. "No thanks." He knew the lure of slow-release amphetamine salts in this business, and so far he'd managed to stay away from them.

"You sure? This *is* a Tango-one," Sasha said, shaking the bottle. "To date no one has successfully completed a Tango-one without these little helpers." She rocked her head from side to side.

"Really?" Justice asked. She seemed otherworldly, and he wanted to leave.

"Oh, yes."

Justice paused.

"Here," she said, and grabbed a large white bottle sitting on the desk next to them and shoved it into his chest. "Just take it. In case. If you don't need it, fine."

Justice was certain that this was how drug dealers pushed product. He took the bottle and kept it to his side. "And what about ISI? You think it'll take long to hack them?" he asked.

"I can tell you in a few hours."

"Also I want all his relatives and friends and close associates," Justice said, knowing they had access to all the cell phones in any area.

Sasha nodded. "Of course. Looks like you're getting the hang of Tango-one."

That helped. "Anything you get, let me know."

"I will. Anything else?"

"Yeah, I'll need some equipment to take with me."

"What are you planning on doing?" she asked, her face turning into a frown.

Justice was an operator, and he knew he didn't have the certificates to go around doing whatever he wanted. Drail's words echoed in his head. It took a few seconds before he realized that Sasha was looking at him, expecting an answer. "I guess I don't know. Some basic surveillance equipment won't hurt."

"You're going to have to take him in," Sasha said. "We can also give you something to neutralize him."

"That sounds good," Justice said. He tried his hardest to make it seem like he wasn't lost, because right now the pressure was rising, and he wondered if he had the talent to pull this off.

Sasha leaned in, her legs twitching, squirming. "Isn't this exciting? You're going after the most wanted man in the world." She smiled. "And the stakes have never been higher. You're going to save millions of lives."

Justice's heart jumped. He always liked Sasha, but this new level of energy was downright sexy. "I will," he said and couldn't help but grin back. She smelled of a hospital and roses. His imagination started to take over, and he stepped back. He had a mission to do. Besides, he had a girlfriend, even if they were on the rocks.

Sasha stepped back, her face slack. "Well let's get you all the things you need."

"And if I need something enroute?"

"We can help with that too," she said. "Here. This will be your new cell phone," she said and handed him a normal looking smart phone.

"What does it do?"

"Everything!" she said and handed him a manual 200 pages long.

"I have to read this?" Justice said, his heart dropping. He was hoping that she would show him.

"You've been promoted to a higher pay-grade. This is the manual," she said, her voice almost scolding him.

Justice wanted to correct her point on his promotion, but he felt small enough as it was. "And I can call you on this?"

"Of course." She reached under desk and pulled out a black, hard plastic case. "This is your start up surveillance kit," she said. She opened it and pulled out a manual. This one was at least 500 pages.

Justice leafed through it. "Christ, it's long."

She walked to another desk and pulled out an even bigger black hard plastic case.

"I'm not g—"

"And here is your snatch kit," she said.

"What?"

"To pick him up, silly." She wagged her finger at him with one hand and handed him a monstrous book with another.

"Manual?"

"Of course… wait," she said and pulled out a chart. "You'll need this to make sure you don't kill anyone."

"Thanks," he said and stared at dismay at the chart and book. Was this a mistake? Perhaps he could walk to Drail and say he's too tired? No, it's too late he scolded himself, and besides, this will be good for a future promotion. "Isn't there an app for this?" He looked at his phone.

"And this is your kill case," she said, rolling out a black hard plastic case that looked like a small European car.

"Is that to bring the bodies back in?" he asked.

"No," Sasha said, her face dead serious. "This is everything you will need for protection." She handed him two large hardcover books. "Manuals."

Justice stared at all the cases. "Can I get someone to help me carry all this to the prep room?" he asked.

"Come now, Justice," she replied, shaking her head. "This is why they pay you extra."

"I know," Justice said, biting the inside of his cheek. "You'll let me know if you find any more information?" he asked.

"Of course."

Justice piled the cases one on top of another, and, with one case in one hand and the rest on top of the kill case, pulled them out to the hallway. His wrists started to tighten, and he clenched the cases tighter. Before he got to the elevator his grip gave up and the case fell on the floor.

"Justice!"

He turned. Sasha was running towards him. He half-smiled. Maybe she had a crush on him, he thought. Maybe she was going to help him, he hoped. She had a good heart.

"Here," she said and handed him a tablet. "This will help with communications as well as searches. It's new. She handed him a manual.

"Does it come in a case?" he said.

"Come now," she said. "You know you're ge—"

"The big bucks. I know," he said and took it from her. She walked off, and he stuffed the tablet down his pants.

He got on the elevator, punched in the code and the letter P.

Half way up, and the elevator stopped. Justice stepped aside to make room for whomever was going to get one. The door opened and Drail stepped inside.

"I see you're getting started," Drail said, rapping the kill case with his knuckles. "Don't waste any time now. This man is dangerous."

"Of course," Justice said. He was a little annoyed at the insinuation that he would be wasting time.

"You're getting the big bucks now, remember that," said Drail.

Justice took in a deep breath. He stared at the kill case for a second and, after finding some strength, he stared at his boss. Was he serious? Nothing on Drail's face gave any indication he was joking.

"You mean it's a sacrifice," Justice said.

"Of course. We're all sacrificing, Justice," Drail said, his face adorned with scorn.

"I know," Justice said. He wasn't sure what just happened, but his heart dropped. Drail got off a floor before Justice's.

It took a few minutes of the elevator closing on him, to get all the cases out of the elevator. He faced another desk, manned by an over weight man who rested his hands on his belly and peered at Justice over his bifocals.

"Prep room?" the man asked.

"Yes, please," Justice said.

"Mission?"

"Tango-one," Justice said. He puffed out his chest.

"Oh?" the man said. "One second." He picked up the receiver on a phone next to him, and he mumbled a few words. After a few minutes he hung up. "Just a minute." He picked up a book and started to read it.

Justice nodded, and strummed his fingers on the black kill case.

"Please," the man said. "Quiet."

Justice could see that he was reading an erotica book.

"Sorry," Justice said. He stared at the cases and thought about reading the manuals. How long would it take? He didn't mind this waiting, however. It was providing a brief respite from over thinking this mission.

"Hey Justice."

Justice straightened himself up to the cooing voice as she came around him. Today she was wearing a suit that hung to her curves.

"Natalie," Justice said. "So good to see you again." He wasn't sure if that was the right thing to say. He always tried to deny that he liked her, but now that things with his girlfriend weren't looking so good, that lie didn't seem necessary. His eyes agreed, and they involuntarily jumped to the lip of her ass as she stood in front of him talking to the man at the desk.

When she was done talking—she didn't need any phone calls to get through—she turned to Justice. "So I heard you got a Tango-one."

"That's right," Justice said, smiling and feeling his face flush. "First one."

"Well," she said, patting his head. "I'm sure you'll do well."

She was a regular Tango-one operator. She'd hardly talked to him before. He tried his best not to stare at the two mounds jutting from her chest, nor that perfectly chiseled face of hers. His heart wasn't listening, but he tried his damnedest to make his eyes listen. They moved to her lips. "Thank you," he said. His vocal chords were even rebelling. How could he expect to handle a Tango-one mission on his own, when he was falling apart in front of a beautiful woman?

Her green eyes twinkled, as if she could read his thoughts. "Is the

41

mission solo?"

"It is," he said, his voice cracking.

"That's great," she said.

He didn't know if she was humoring him now, because her eyes were dancing around his face as if they were laughing.

"It is, thanks," he said, almost whispering because he was too scared to talk out loud and risk another crack.

"I bet you love the promotion," she said and tapped his arm again.

"Yeah," he said, not sure if he had it in him to lie to her. She was, of course, the woman that every male operator talked about. No one had ever heard of a man who stole her heart. Or even got close to the security system. The fact that no one had her, made Justice like her even more. His eyes rebelled and fell to the mounds on her chest. He was certain they turned upwards.

She saw.

"And how's your girlfriend?" she asked. She seemed disappointed.

"Oh, okay," he said. "Just got back from vacation with her."

She nodded, not seeming to be that interested. "And what is the mission, if you don't mind me asking?"

"Dr. Noklar," Justice blurted out. He paused and wondered why he said anything. These missions were supposed to be need to know only.

That seemed to shock her. "He fled, right?"

"That's right."

"And you're going after him. Solo?"

It wasn't a question, and Justice knew what she meant when she hardened the syllables around "you're".

"That's right," he said, feeling a spike of anger at her for doubting him. Immediately, whatever fantasies his mind was playing as background music halted, and he realized that she didn't think much of him—not when he had the control of a child. "Solo. I have to get going," he said. He turned to the man at the desk. "Listen, if you don't let me through I'm gonna get higher involved." He was surprised at how low and gruff his voice was.

The man looked up from his book. "All right. What room you want?"

"The biggest one you got."

"Here," the man said and handed him a key.

Justice snatched it as hard as he could. "Thanks." He had half a mind to ask what he was being made to wait for, but thought better of it.

Grabbing all his cases, he dragged them through a set of automatic glass doors.

"You need help?" Natalie asked.

Still stinging from her previous sentence, Justice shook his head and pretended to be more focused on his cases than was really needed. He heard her disappear into a room, and he dragged his gear towards the main room at the end of the hall.

Halfway there and his forearms gave out again. A case went tumbling to the ground.

"Hey there, Justice," a tall man with gelled up hair and a Hell's Angels leather jacket peered from another room.

"Geoff," Justice said. He could have done without seeing Geoff today, or any day for that matter. "How's it going?"

"Not bad. Just trying to see what all the noise is about. You planning on starting a carnival out here?"

"Sorry for the noise," Justice said. He didn't care to hear Geoff's jokes. "I'm trying to get all my cases into my room." He pointed to the doors at the end of the hallway.

"Uh huh. You sure you don't have too much to handle?" Geoff said, grinning broadly.

Justice didn't reply and picked up his littered case.

"Man, sure hate to have to carry all that down the hallway, all by yourself," Geoff said. He raised a martini glass to his lips and took a long, loud slurp.

"Are you working in there?" Justice snapped, wondering since when was alcohol allowed in the planning rooms. He had gone through initial training with Geoff. Geoff had never done well at any of the tasks, but he knew how to make the trainers laugh—usually at Justice's expense—and he had somehow found favor with the bosses, Drail included. That meant he was promoted before Justice was.

"Oh heavens no," Geoff said. "I'm just preparing for vacation."

"You're using agency support for personal reasons?" Justice said, almost shocked, but then again, this was Geoff.

"That's right." Geoff took another sip of his drink. "You get a promotion?"

Justice took in a lungful of air. He was calm again, and made sure the case was firmly in his grip. "Can you give me a hand?"

Geoff backed off. "Don't think I can, Justice. Too busy. Besides, this is a solo mission, right?"

Justice nodded slightly, though he wondered how Geoff already knew this.

"Gotta do it all on your own, otherwise there's no learning. You earn the big bucks now."

Before Justice could reply, Geoff slammed his door. Muffled laughter drifted into the hallway.

A few minutes later, Justice was in his room. It was a large room, with no windows, empty except for a large desk in a corner with a computer on it. He was changing his anger into focus on the mission at hand, so that he could wow his boss, get a promotion and silence all the hecklers. *That* would be the sweetest revenge.

He laid out all the cases and opened them. Seeing the manuals sent a nausea through his body. It was going to be a long day. And he had no clue as to where to go after it was done. He would have to wait for a phone call from Sasha, and that made him antsy. What if no phone call came? He could go to the other agencies, but they wouldn't like to have an outsider come in and try to take information from them.

In fact all this gear was nothing without some good intel.

He opened each case and looked inside.

Dr. Noklar stared at the men as they shouted and pointed their guns at them.

"Show them your hands, doctor," Karim said.

The doctor raised his hands, surprised that they didn't want to move. He could feel his heart beating fast enough to make him sick. And he wondered how he could have been so stupid as to think he could avoid the long arm of a nation. Or numerous nations.

A soldier came to his window and yelled, the barrel of his AK47 only inches from the doctor's face. He could feel his urine trying to escape his body. It took the doctor a few seconds to realize that the soldier was yelling in Farsi. And that the flag on his shoulder was the green white and red of Iran.

"Pakistani," the doctor said and pointed at himself.

The soldier scrunched up his face in response. With his rifle he indicated that they should step out. The doctor opened the door. He was again surprised to realize that Karim and Abdullah were both out of the car, their hands on the hood. Was he that focused on the barrel and his possible death that he didn't notice this?

He walked to the hood and placed his hands; nothing appeared real. The other soldiers went through the car, ripping out things and throwing them out on the sand nearby.

Dr. Noklar could smell his own sweat, strong and full of fear. He looked over to Abdullah who seemed to be humming a tune in his head. The doctor wondered if the boy had been through this before.

A soldier came by and searched through each of them. Finally, all of the soldiers stopped and started to stand and talk and smoke cigarettes. The sun was midway up the sky and the doctor could feel its sting on his neck and head. He needed some water.

A motorcade of army trucks came rolling by and halted. The soldiers flung out their cigarettes and stood tall. A man from the lead truck came out. He seemed to be the officer in charge because everyone half-bowed to him.

One of the soldiers ran up to him, saluted and pointed at the doctor. The officer waved the soldier away and walked up to the doctor. He seemed young, perhaps too young for even secondary school.

The officer beckoned the doctor to walk to him. Dr. Noklar did so and the officer said something in Farsi.

The doctor shook his head and said, "I don't speak your language, I'm sorry." He was frightened that this untested young man might be unhinged. Dr. Noklar hadn't lived much of life on the edges, but he knew what untested men tended to do.

"Oh, you speak Urdu?" the officer said and smiled.

"Yes. I'm from Pakistan," said the doctor, feeling a little more at ease. The officer's skin was very pale. But there was a mole on his lower chin that stood out. The wind blew and a hair on the mole waved.

"Welcome. What is your business here?" the officer asked.

"We're here to see the coast," said the doctor wondering what reason he could possibly give to travel here. He was well aware of Iran's desires to know how to create a nuclear bomb. And he knew even more about his own abilities to help them achieve that goal. But helping the Persians wasn't his goal. Nor would it ever be.

"Oh great!" the officer said, beaming a smile so white Dr. Noklar had to squint.

"Thank you," the doctor said, not sure if that was the right thing to say. He wanted to be as nice as possible because he didn't want the officer to dig deep enough to find out who he was. If the officer did find that out, the doctor knew life as he knew it would be over.

"Of course. Sorry about all this," the officer pointed to the soldiers who were now playing a game of soccer with a rusted tin can. Karim and Abdullah had joined in. "We're getting a lot of smugglers on this road, so we're trying to clean up."

"Not a problem," Dr. Noklar said.

The officer gave a terse nod and walked to his truck, yelling at the soldiers who all were too involved in their game to look up. The doctor stared hard at Karim and Abdullah. He didn't want to test their luck by staying here. They seemed to sense his apprehension, and they ran to the car when he started to throw their belongings back inside.

Soon they were on their way.

Several hours later, the sun setting in his eyes, the doctor drove through some hills and was met with the expanse of the sea. Both of his travel partners were asleep. The smell of salt water tickled his nose and his lungs opened. A few seagulls cackled in the distance. There was the smell of grilled fish somewhere.

Karim awoke and rolled down his window. "We're here, right?" he asked, rubbing his eyes.

"This is the town," Dr. Noklar said.

"They told me it would be beautiful," said Karim.

The doctor wanted to ask who "they" was. "Where to from here?"

"We'll have to see. Let's get some food first."

But as they drove down the first street with people, Dr. Noklar noticed how they stared with vehemence at his car. He saw a few soldiers walking down the street, and they too stared at the car.

"Are you sure this is the town?" the doctor asked.

"Trust me, it is," said Karim.

The doctor ground his teeth, the heat generated in his jaws only making him angrier, though less nervous. He knew the risk he was taking, but coming to a town like this didn't seem to make sense.

"Where are we going to?" he asked.

"You still don't trust me?" Karim said and shook his head, spitting out the window.

"The people here don't seem friendly. That's all."

"You don't trust me," Karim said. "People like you are all the same. You rule our country and you don't even care for the people in it. You would probably like to get rid of us, no?"

It stung being coupled with the politicians who had helped run his country into the ground. "I am not like those who run our country," the doctor said. "And I do trust you."

"You're putting up with me," said Karim. "Because you don't have any other choice."

"That's nonsense," the doctor said, sensing that his lies weren't being bought.

The car fell into silence, and Dr. Noklar could feel the young man move away from him. When Abdullah woke up, he could feel the air relax.

"Are we going to eat?" Abdullah asked.

The doctor smiled. As did Karim.

"Of course," said Karim. He pointed to a handful of shacks on the outskirts of the town. "We go there. And we eat."

Though the shacks didn't exactly look appetizing, but it seemed like it would be better than the main town where the people were staring hard at their car. The doctor knew that people who lived in shacks wouldn't stare.

The shadows had stretched over most of the road by the time Dr. Noklar parked the car behind the shacks. The ground was uneven here, and puddles dotted the area. The shacks, with mud walls and corrugated tin as roofs, were built with random leans, daring gravity to take them down. Gravity had taken that dare and the rubble of a few still dotted the neighborhood. Some were closer to the others, while a few stood dangerously near the coast.

The doctor stepped out and stretched his legs. Pain shot through them as his joints cracked into place. His two companions jumped out. Dr. Noklar allowed the crash of waves to sooth his mind. He was thinking about the message and the words that so easily moved his heart. He then sensed what it meant to be human. To be tied in to his fellow man. And he felt more trustful of Karim.

"I have never seen the sea so beautiful," said Abdullah.

"It is gorgeous," said Dr. Noklar. There were people by the shore, some fishing, some staring—though it didn't seem hostile. The sun was low and reflecting polygon shapes of yellow white and now orange in the millions. The waves, small and rolling, pushed through this mural of infinite shards and tickled the folds of the doctor's brain.

"You can't be a doctor here," said Karim, sternly.

"Fine," said the doctor. He didn't like that Karim seemed tense again.

"What's your name, doctor?" Abdullah asked.

Karim hit the boy over his head.

"I'm Nasar," said the doctor. "Should I use my real first name?"

"That's fine," Karim said. A group of boys, some in their teens and some younger, all without shirts, was eyeing them.

"Do you know who you're meeting with?" asked Nasar.

"I do," said Karim, looking around confused.

"I'm hungry," said Abdullah.

"Be quiet," said Karim.

The oldest two boys came up to them. They were dark skinned and had curly hair. And they both had scars across their chests.

"What do you want?" asked one of the boys. He had an ear missing.

The doctor tried not to stare. But he was also wondering how the boys knew Urdu.

"I'm looking for Shan," said Karim.

"There's no Shan," said the boy, narrowing his eyes.

"Get me Shan, little one. Or else I'll make sure he deals with you.

"I'm no little boy," said the teenager. "I will slit your throat open if you talk to me like that one more time." He pulled out a knife and moved it within an inch of Karim's face.

Dr. Noklar flinched and could feel his weak heart fluttering.

Karim grinned. "Where did a little boy like you get this toy? You want me to go get your mother?"

The doctor moved in to intervene. He could see that Karim liked this, but it didn't make sense. But he held back because he figured Karim knew what he was doing, and the knife looked a little too sharp for Nasar's tastes. The young man also smelled like strong cologne and for some reason that made the doctor even more hesitant.

The young man moved the knife from side to side. "I told you once. You think I won't open your throat? You think we haven't buried bodies all over this place?" He gestured in a circle with his other hand. "You think the police care who we kill? Especially if they're Pakistani scum?"

"Oh. Are you going to wet your diapers?" Karim said.

Nasar noticed that Karim, for all his smiling, never took his eye off the knife. There was now a crowd of onlookers. Adults smiled and pointed at them; none of them seemed to care. Nasar didn't know if he was to take it lightly that they didn't want to intervene.

"I'm warning you," said the boy, his voice almost cracking. "I'll cut

49

you up—"

"You'll do no such thing," said a booming voice.

A large man, bald, with no shirt and a gold chain clinging to his body hair, stood with a woman beside him. The woman was resting a baby on her hips. The man, barefoot, stepped over a few puddles and came up to the young boy with the knife.

"What did I tell you?"

The young boy was visibly shaken, and started to lower the knife. But he seemed to realize something and raised it back up.

"Bashir?" Karim asked, his eye still on the knife.

"Karim?"

"Yes."

"Come with me. Your friends must be tired," Bashir said.

"He goes no where. Not unless he wants to leak into a puddle," the young man said.

Nasar could see that no one in the crowd was intervening still. And yet the big man, Bashir, paused as he looked at the knife.

"Come," Bashir said. "You want to hurt my guest?"

Again the young man flinched, but he pushed the knife up to Karim's nose. "But this mutt tried to walk over me. And now he'll pay."

"He's not even from this country. He doesn't understand our ways. Why don't you show some mercy?" the big man said. He finished and gave Karim a widened eye look. "He didn't know, right?"

Karim seemed to consider this, then seemed to realize that he might have the knife under his nose for longer than he would like. "I didn't know. This is how we do it in Pakistan."

The young man seemed to hesitate.

"He's right," Nasar said, stepping closer to the knife. His heart beat fast as his intestines wind up. "We don't know any better. After all, we're Pakistanis." He gave a smile and the young man with a knife smirked.

"And," the doctor continued, "we're all Muslims here, aren't we?"

The boy lowered his knife. "We are."

Karim stuck out his hand, and the young man shook it and walked off.

Bashir led them to a shack with a couple of goats tied to stakes

50

outside.

Nasar pulled Karim to him. "Why did you mock that boy? He'd a knife."

"He wasn't going to do anything."

"How do you know?" asked Nasar.

"When you survive as long as I do, you know."

Nasar wasn't sure if Karim was posturing, but he let it go.

"Welcome to my house. There's not much room, but it's a good night to sleep under the sky," Bashir said. "Business still good?"

"Always. We're selling to the Indians. A line right to Mumbai," Karim said and rubbed his thumb against his fingers.

"*We're* hitting the workers in Dubai," said Bashir. "We can't sell enough of it."

Abdullah looked at the doctor and smiled sheepishly.

Bashir narrowed his eyes at the doctor.

"My good friend Nasar. He has to get to the other side of the world."

"We can get you as far as Musqat. That's it." Bashir stared at the doctor.

Nasar's feet shuffled. He didn't know what the stare meant. Bashir had lucid green eyes, and they didn't seem to like him.

"We eat in an hour. We slaughter a goat and celebrate," said Bashir.

Nasar, his stomach rumbling and the lack of sugar making him dizzy, watched as Karim and Abdullah played a game of soccer with a group of local kids. The old tattered ball with string holding it together bounced erratically. Karim and the boy with the knife from earlier avoided each other. Karim dribbled past two boys, cut back, sending another boy flying, and shot past the goalie. The ball ricocheted off the rock goal posts and Karim took off his shirt and went running in the other direction. He claimed the mantle of Messi. The other boys whined in disagreement, but it had been the most Messi-like play of the day.

Nasar smiled. In the distance, Bashir slit a goat's throat. The bleating of the goat grew higher in pitch, gurgled out, and gave way to the kicking of hooves. When the goat was bled out, Bashir stepped aside

51

and women cut up the goat.

The sun was almost down and a cool breeze kicked up. A ripple ran through the doctor's skin. He rubbed his shoulders. For the first time since he left Pakistan he was homesick. Or perhaps it wasn't that. But there was a hole in his heart when he thought about the place he grew up, and this hole dripped an acerbic liquid onto his guts, and he felt sick all over again. His brain tightened and his thoughts circled on Pakistan. The men in suits. His wife.

Karim once again dribbled passed two kids. A one two with Abdullah and he burst past the last defender. He toyed with the goalie, dribbling around his outstretched hands and tapped the ball over the goal line with his head. A chorus of cheers arose from the onlookers. Again Karim claimed the mantle of Messi. This time no one argued with him, though the kid who had the knife was glowering at Karim.

"Why don't you play?"

Nasar looked up, surprised to see that Bashir was right behind him, cleaning his butcher's knife with his pants.

"I'm too old," said Nasar, rubbing his knees to show the reason.

"So am I," said Bashir and rubbed his large belly.

"There comes a time when watching is preferable to playing."

Bashir nodded and stared at Karim, who was now playing keep away from two of the local boys. They finally got the ball away from him.

"And how do you know Karim?" Bashir asked as he sat down next to Nasar. The large man now had a clean white-collar shirt on with two bloody forearms sticking out. He was smoking a cigarette and offered it to the doctor, who refused.

"We know each other from work," said Nasar. He could smell sweat and the remnants of the goat's fear on the man. It was a sharp ammonia aroma and made Nasar's mouth water. Made him want to vomit.

Bashir tilted his head back and laughed. "I'm sorry. But you don't look or sound like the kind of person who would know Karim from work." Bashir waved the knife in the air, then seemed to think better of it and threw it into the ground in front of them. It stood stuck halfway into the ground.

"That's the way it is," he said. He tried to focus on the game.

"You're too smart to hang out with him," Bashir said. There wasn't any malice in his voice. "And you're too smart not to think of a better story."

Nasar decided that not reacting would be the best thing. Bashir's eyes searched Nasar's face. Seagulls squawked.

"How do *you* know Karim?"

"I don't know him except through an intermediary friend."

"And what does this friend do?"

Bashir furrowed his forehead. "I thought someone who worked with Karim would know." There was a teasing tone to the big man.

"I don't," said Nasar. For some reason Nasar's head was unwinding, like he was a free man. If there was ever such a thing.

"Karim helps me smuggle goods across the borders. Sometimes it's easier to get things from the tribal areas of Afghanistan to Pakistan then here. Better than coming straight from Afghanistan. The police and army watch that border too closely."

"We were stopped. A helicopter landed right in front of us," said Nasar.

"That's no good," said Bashir. He rubbed his head and looked at the game. The darkness was pulling players away from the game. Now a few were juggling the ball with their feet, seeing who could get the most. Karim was talking to a young woman on the sides. The small waves rolled onto the rocky shore, each crash was more balm for Nasar's senses.

"He's nothing like Messi," said Bashir.

Nasar laughed. "He isn't. No one in this part of the world is that good."

"We don't have the infrastructure," said Bashir. "Our leaders would rather spend their money on stupid things."

Nasar, knowing how things at the government level were done just nodded his head slightly.

"Helicopters?" asked Bashir.

"One. And a few trucks. They searched our car thoroughly."

"They will never leave us be," said Bashir.

"Who?"

"The Iranians."

"Aren't you Iranian?"

"Only in name. They treat us like second class citizens."

"Why?"

"We're not the right kind of Muslim. That's why. We're forced to live here in these shacks. We used to have buildings in town. But those were taken from us."

"How—"

"They said they were illegal," said Bashir. His eyes darted off to the twinkling lights of the town. "And when we find a way to make money they come with police raids," Bashir said, shaking his head. "You know it's impossible for one of us to work in the government?"

Nasar kept his eye on a purple flock of clouds. The sun was gone and he felt sad.

"They take taxes but give us nothing," Bashir said and spat onto the ground. "It's the same for the poor everywhere in this country."

"In most countries," said Nasar. Though he didn't agree with Bashir, it said something that the man was willing to complain to him.

"Do you know what they would rather spend their money? On nuclear power," Bashir said and shook his head. "What will that do for us?"

Nasar glanced over. The large man was peeling him with his eyes. Nasar stayed silent. The young boys had all gathered around the fire and some were dancing with the women.

"The world revolves around power, unfortunately. One cannot escape that. One never can."

"Smart," said Bashir.

They sat silent as more waves rolled in.

"Your face…" Bashir said and wagged his finger in Nasar's face. "I know you."

These words, which seemed to come out of nowhere, sent the doctor's thoughts into a tailspin. Nasar shifted his weight.

Bashir placed a hand on the doctor's thigh. "I'm sure a man who has escaped his country doesn't want himself to be known. You must

54

trust me."

"I trust you," Nasar said, though he didn't and he wasn't certain if Bashir knew.

Bashir stood up and shrugged. "You're the Savior of Pakistan, aren't you?"

Nasar could feel the world closing in on him. He looked around unsure as to whether to be happy or scared that they were alone.

"No, no," said Bashir. "That's not anything I care about. But you are *him*, aren't you?"

Nasar nodded his head. His mind raced to the possibility of Bashir telling the Iranian authorities. Of him being hauled off to Tehran, a prisoner forced to do their bidding.

Bashir waved his hand in front of Nasar's face. "You all right, doctor? I'm not going to tell anyone."

Somehow Nasar didn't believe that. "Let's walk," he said. He wanted to suck in some air and stop his mind from racing. They walked away from the festivities into further darkness.

"It's an honor," said Bashir. "What your government did to you was horrid."

"There was pressure," said Nasar, not wanting to relive the pain of his own government holding him hostage.

"Smart," said Bashir.

Nasar wasn't sure if the man knew what smart meant.

"Our government would murder for your knowledge," said Bashir.

Nasar's throat tightened. "Many governments would." He saw how precarious his situation was. All the goodwill towards the large man melted.

"I'm not threatening," said Bashir. "I already told you how worthless I think our government is. How little it cares for its people. How it would rather control them than help them. Giving them you would only increase the pain for us."

There was contempt in Bashir's voice.

"No. Your secret is safe with me. Where are you going anyways? You're not going to help Wahhabis, are you?"

Nasar was still trying to judge the man's sincerity so he shrugged.

"Not that it's my business. But be careful. There are many other governments who will kill you on sight."

"I know," said Nasar. "You won't tell anyone?" he asked, though he knew it was a silly question.

"Of course not," said Bashir. "And you can trust my word." The large man banged his chest.

"Thank you," said Nasar. Perhaps he trusted too easily.

They walked farther from the shacks. There were yells that punctuated the quiet around them, but mostly it was the small waves nudging the land that filled the air with a certain regimentation. Nasar absorbed it. He always liked it when things he observed looked like they could fit into a mathematical equation. There wasn't much trash here, as they jumped from rock to rock. Puddles of water released their salt fumes into Nasar's nose. Those fumes ran through his brain and a very certain and strong feeling, one he hadn't had in decades—he was sure of that—passed through his body. He was at one with Bashir, everyone. "Funny how the world has turned, isn't it?"

Bashir didn't say anything.

"We're here, masters of our destiny. More so than we've ever been in history," said Nasar.

Bashir snorted then laughed. "Smart. Forgive me, doctor, if I don't agree. You're a scientist... But the problems we face are bigger than ever. Do you know how much oil Iran sits on? And yet even here there are shortages."

Nasar kept quiet. He wasn't sure what the large man was getting at. He'd never heard of shortages in Iran. If that was the case, then perhaps it was the fault of the Iranians and not science. Some night bird swooped nearby. A mosquito landed on his skin. He didn't swat it away and immediately regretted it when the bite started to itch. He remembered a military colonel using that as an example of why violence was always needed.

"And I'm sure you consider yourself a great man... You *are* a great man, and perhaps I'm just being jealous. But what good is it to have nuclear power when our people are going hungry? I don't care about those things. I *do* care about my children eating and finding a good life.

You can point out all the bad the Americans and their Zionist friends have done, but it doesn't help in the end. I have to care for what I see. Not what some person on the TV tells me might exist, and only in his head at that. What can I do with these crazy ideas? Tell me?"

Nasar could hear the big man breathing heavily, though he could barely make out his form in the darkness. Nasar'd never been confronted with an argument like this. Everyone he'd ever met had told him what a good thing he'd done. How he was the savior. He'd always told himself that he didn't believe it, but now he could feel anger inside him. And he wondered if he did believe that. And if he did, then why? He searched his mind for something worthwhile to say.

"It's not like the Americans have left us alone. You're old enough to remember the Shah, aren't you?" Nasar huffed.

"I do. He was bad. He tortured many people... Tell me how many less people the Ayatollah has tortured?"

"But—"

"Surely you know that your country has always been in bed with America."

"That has been a relationship of convenience," said Nasar. "No country can be perfect."

"All right. I'll admit, that's true. But what about the poor in your country? When has India ever invaded you?"

"Need I remind you of Bangladesh? The Indians helped them break away from us."

Bashir scoffed again. "Let's not forget about all the people you slaughtered. And for what?"

"They were *our* country. It was only Indian meddling that helped them to break away." Nasar's blood pressure rose, he didn't like the insinuation Bashir was making. And besides, it seemed that attitudes like this would only lead to his nation being weak.

"I'm sure the Indians are saying the same thing about Kashmir and Pakistan."

Nasar's hands clenched. "How can you say such a thing? Kashmir is a Muslim nation. Why would they ever be under Hindu rule?"

"All right. But blaming foreigners for meddling is never correct. Let me remind you that we're Muslims. But because we're darker, we have African roots, Tehran thinks of us as inferior. And even though we're Muslims we are outsiders and treated like dogs. And when we complain they tell us not to make trouble. And if we complain more, suddenly they are certain that we are being paid off by American agents. Don't you forget that, when you talk so easily of killing people for country."

Nasar bit his inner cheek. "It's tough when you're in charge," he said.

Bashir muttered. "I'm sorry doctor. For too long I've heard of foreign interference, when they want to take money away from us and to pay for a nuclear project that will never help. When instead they *could* pave more roads and help us. And I know what will happen if I say just that."

"Well—"

"And how can you take their side when you know if they saw you they would take you to Tehran as a prisoner?" Bashir said.

Nasar heard him thump his chest, though he wasn't sure why.

"So will the Americans. So will the Israelis. They would kill me in a heartbeat," said Nasar.

"You assume I'm on *their* side."

"You have to pick a side. That's how life works," said Nasar.

"Do I? Can poor people eat uranium?"

"Yes, they can eat it. They will have pride in their country and they can eat it all that they want. You just have to tell them."

Bashir spat on the rocks and grunted. They stood in silence. The waves crashed in and some foam hit Nasar's shoes. He decided not to antagonize Bashir any more. After all, he needed him to get out of the country.

"Let's head back," Bashir said after some time.

Nasar followed his footsteps. He hoped Bashir's silence wasn't anger. He could see the light of a fire and shadows of people around it.

"You will enjoy tonight," Bashir said.

"Thank you again," Nasar said.

The flames of a fledging fire, where the soccer game had been held, now rose a meter high.

"You like goat?" asked Bashir as they arrived at the fire.

"I do," said Nasar. He was still feeling perturbed from Bashir's earlier comments, but he reminded himself not to bring it up again.

"You will love this. We soak it in spices and cook it up. My wife makes the best pilaf in the world."

Bashir beckoned Nasar to sit next to him. There were some women, spherically shaped, who were sticking pieces of goat meat to sticks and placing them over the fire. Nasar sat down, the smell of charred meat forcing his mouth to water. He could see Karim and Abdullah trying to learn a dance from the young men and women. The young man, with whom Karim had jostled earlier, was now jovial and happy. All this noise pulled a happiness out of Nasar.

That evaporated when a young and lean man, without a hand, came up to Bashir. He gave Nasar a dark look and whispered something into Bashir's ears. Nasar stared at the man's pockmarked face. It was ugly. But at the same time it was almost a masterpiece of art. Life perhaps. Nasar turned towards a chorus of yelps. A man had walked in front of the fire. He had a tall drum and he started to beat.

Bashir leaned in. "The boat leaves at midnight. Eat. Have fun. And be gone."

Nasar nodded. The drumbeat was intoxicating. The man's hands were a blur as he banged out rhythmic trance. His eyes closed. Nasar wondered what Bashir meant by "be gone" but again he told himself that it didn't matter. In the background he could still hear the sea. Smell it too, as the wind shifted.

"That's our drum," said Bashir. "It was invented here."

"Really?" said Nasar. He didn't believe him.

"It was. We were the first people with drums. That's why we're the best. See?"

"He *is* good," Nasar said. He couldn't help that his feet were tapping the ground.

The wind shifted and the smell of roast, and some burnt, goat meat filled his nostrils again. His stomach protested its emptiness. A score of shirtless young men started to dance in front of the drummer. It was a winding gyrating dance. Karim joined in. He fit in perfectly.

59

"And here. The first bagpipes were ours," said Bashir.

Nasar didn't know what he was talking about until he saw an older man holding a kidney shaped bag with pipes sticking out of it. The man started to belt a sordid tale with the instrument. At first the notes grated against Nasar's eardrums, but soon it started to sing to his heart, and he was overcome with sadness and happiness at the same time.

The old man removed his shirt. He was older and the creases and sags on his body were pronounced, but he moved well with the instrument, and the young men made room for him.

"It's beautiful," said Nasar. The old man started singing in a tongue Nasar never heard before.

"The best," said Bashir.

Some of the older gentlemen joined the group of youth. They danced slower, in more measured steps, but they too had the gyrations down, the smooth thrusts of the hips.

When the goat was done, it was placed on a large tray with pilaf. They served the doctor first. Then everyone else.

Nasar realized that he was happy here. But there was something worming its way through his gut, telling him never to rest. He wished he could've changed Bashir's mind about power. But he knew that such things would never happen.

The festivities subsided and people started to pull away. The fire dropped into a low ember, and the smell of marrow and sea made Nasar tired. He closed his eyes.

"Doctor?"

Nasar looked up. The stars overhead were brighter than he had ever seen them, like he could touch them.

"Doctor?"

He looked over and could make out the faces of Karim and Abdullah.

"I told you not to call me that," he said. His cold, he realized that he had a blanket over his body.

"No one's here."

"What?" Nasar said.

"Let's go," Karim said. He helped him up. It was very cold without the blanket.

"Where?" asked Nasar. The sea still crashed in. It seemed quieter now.

"There," said Abdullah. He pointed to a small light further down the seashore.

They walked over the uneven rocks and puddles. Nasar slipped on seaweed a few times. But finally they made it to the light. It was Bashir holding a lantern.

"Hurry," he said in a gruff voice. "The tide will shift soon and it will be too late."

They climbed on to a small dingy. Its sails were down. The man with the pockmarked face was staring at Nasar.

Nasar turned to say good-bye, but Bashir was walking away with his lantern. Something was wrong.

The pockmarked man pushed off the rocks with his oar and silently paddled.

"You should help," said Nasar to Karim. The young man leaned forward. But the pockmarked man shushed them and kept on paddling.

Something *was* wrong. And in the distance Nasar saw a boat with a searchlight coming directly for them. There was nowhere to hide and he couldn't swim. He closed his eyes. He knew his journey was over. He just hoped that his captors wouldn't mistreat him.

Ali woke up. Laith was asleep, but the sun was out, so Ali shook the boy. He still hadn't figured out what to do with him.

"Wake up."

Laith opened his eyes. There was still a calm aura about the boy. Ali wasn't certain if this was normal. Shouldn't the boy have been ready to mourn? Still the boy couldn't stay here with him.

"Do you go to school?" Ali asked.

The boy nodded his head.

It was weekday. Perhaps Ali could talk to the boy's teacher and figure something out. He grabbed him, and they walked out to the street.

It was almost noon, so he bought a small lunch for the boy. Then they walked down a dusty and almost abandoned street. Only a few cars drove by. Ali realized that the boy didn't have a curiosity. He wanted to know if the boy had always been like this, or if the bombing had made him that way.

A heavy feeling came over Ali and he realized that they were close to the cafe he'd bombed the night before. He saw some men in military fatigues lounging about. He held the boy's hand and walked on. A bad feeling arose inside him about what he'd done. He reminded himself about the reasons he was doing it. And he also reminded himself about the things that were done to him in the first place. To innocents.

After a few minutes, the sun growing stronger, they reached the school. The white building, with a wall around it, and a guard at the entrance, seemed new. Ali liked that.

It was lunch and many of the boys were playing in the all-dirt yard.

"May I help you?" asked the guard. He had an AK-47 propped behind him.

Ali was going to ask after the boy's teacher, but the gun caught him off guard. "Why a gun, friend?"

"It's to keep the Wahhabis away," said the guard.

Ali ground his teeth. He knew that meant him. But when had they ever attacked a school? He nodded his head so that the guard wouldn't know. He asked the guard to call the boy's teacher. The guard told him to go inside and find her himself.

Inside an empty classroom sat a woman correcting papers. She had a hijab on and the most beautiful brown eyes in the world. When she smiled, Ali tried not to quiver.

"Is this your student?" he asked.

"Yes. Laith. Where have you been?" she asked the boy. Laith squirmed.

"Let us talk," Ali said. Laith ran outside.

"Are you a relative?" she asked. Her scrutinizing eyes warmed Ali's skin.

"I'm a stranger…" He didn't know what else to say. "Laith's family was killed in a drone attack yesterday."

Her eyes widened. "Oh no. Oh no," she sat back on the chair, her face in her hands. "How?" She shook.

"A mistake," he said. He could feel something sharp pushing through him. "But he tells me there's no one else in his family. Perhaps you know of someone who was close to them? Who might be able to take care of him?"

"I don't know, " she said.

Ali shuffled his feet. "Maybe you could take care of him then?"

"I…" she said and looked at her hands. She wiped her eyes dry. "I could."

"Then do it," he said. When she jumped he realized that he was speaking in too curt a manner. "Please."

She nodded her head.

Ali thought of saying something else. Instead he turned to leave.

"And your name?"

"I'm Ali," he said. "You?"

"Nadia," she said.

"Very well." Silence shifted between them, and he wasn't sure why her look stopped words from coming out properly from his mouth. "I will check back soon."

"Good. That will be best," she said. She smiled. Ali's heart raced.

"Do you have a mobile?" she asked.

"No," he said. "I can't have mobiles."

Another silence enveloped them.

"Good-bye." He left before he could hear an answer.

In the yard he waved good-bye to Laith, but he was busy playing a game of soccer.

When he was back at the safe house, Ali went to the roof. A pigeon had arrived. He ate some more food from the fridge and swept the house. The dust filled his nose, and him sneezed for several minutes. Finally, with the dust somewhat rearranged, he went to the front and waited.

Two men arrived on foot. They each had a large man with them. These were the important men from high up in the group. He wondered if their ideas would be as foolish as the ones he'd heard before.

They sat on the roof, as the dust inside was too much.

The men refused to give their names. They were both fat, with oily skin. One had on aviator glasses on, and the other had a crooked nose.

"Tell us what happened. Exactly as you remember," said the one with the crooked nose.

"No names?" Ali asked again. This was very odd, almost as if he were being interrogated.

"No names," said the one in aviators.

Ali thought that was silly. Then his mind flashed with images of their faces. These two men were very dangerous. And very wanted. "I think I have seen your faces before," he said. "You two are very big in headquarters. Right?"

"Well," said the one in aviators. "We don't like to boast."

"Didn't you help with the two bombing in the Green Zone," said Ali, referring to a hit in Iraq.

"That's right," said the one in the aviators, smiling so wide his face look split in half. "I'm called the Saladin of today."

"Don't talk rubbish," said the crooked nose one. He leaned forward, trying to get into Ali's view. "I'm the Saladin of today."

"Says who?" asked the other fat one.

"Says everyone. Just ask."

"You'll say anything. I'm the Saladin," the one in aviators said and pounded his chest. "What did you do in Iraq?"

"My masterpieces were in Afghanistan, and you know this," said the crooked nose one.

"How is that—"

"You heard them call me Saladin. You heard them, and you took the name for yourself."

"I never. What do you think?" the one in aviators asked his bodyguard. His bodyguard shrugged.

"See?" the crooked nose said. "Tell him I'm Saladin," he said to his bodyguard. His bodyguard shrugged. The two fat men turned to Ali. "What have *you* heard?" they asked.

"I...I think of you," Ali said and pointed to the man in aviators.

"As the Saladin of Iraq, and you as the Saladin of Afghanistan."

The men mumbled, looked at each other with narrowed eyes, then turned back to Ali. "So," Saladin of Iraq said. "What did you see?"

"Nothing," Ali said. He tried to think back. He couldn't remember why he ran away from the building and to the rocks. Had he heard something? It all seemed a blur.

"Laith and his friend came over. They discussed a letter to Dr. Noklar—"

"What?" Saladin of Afghanistan asked. "A letter to who?"

"The Savior of Pakistan. You know him, right?" Ali said.

"I do," said Saladin of Afghanistan. "I'd even call him the Saladin of Pakistan. But why a letter?"

Ali paused for a second, wondering what their obsession with the Saladin name was for. "The idea was to convince him to help us build *the* bomb."

"That's crazy," said Saladin of Afghanistan.

A jet flew overhead and each of the men flinched.

"So you don't remember anything?" Saladin of Iraq said.

"I don't. The explosion blacked me out," said Ali.

"Because I find that suspicious."

"I don't know what else to say," said Ali, feeling angry that he'd survived this attack and was being held in suspicion because of that.

"What my friend means," Saladin of Afghanistan said. "Is that we're trying to piece together information on signs that an attack is impending. So anything will help."

"*That's* what he meant," said Ali.

"Of course."

"I think we were too undisciplined about using cell phones. That must have been a big thing," said Ali. "I no longer use one myself."

"How can you not use one? Have you seen mine?" Saladin of Iraq said and pulled out a shiny phone with a huge screen. "See?"

Saladin of Afghanistan shook his head. "I have the same phone it's amazing."

Ali looked at them, trying to see if they were joking. "Isn't it an American phone?" he asked, trying to mask his anger. He couldn't believe that after a drone attack by the Americans they would be holding on to such phones.

"Oh no. This one is South Korean," said Saladin of Afghanistan.

"Aren't they allies of the Americans?" Ali asked, hoping to push these Saladins to the same conclusion.

"They are. They are. But they're also a people with a long history of being colonized. In a way they're like brothers to our cause."

Ali waited for a qualifying statement, but the two Saladins played with their phones. He coughed and they put them away.

"Well, I'm going to make sure that we don't use cell phones anymore," said Ali.

The Saladins looked at each other and rolled their eyes. "Very well," crooked nose said. "But pigeons can't fly everywhere."

Ali took a deep breath. He'd hoped that this meeting would result in a reaffirming conversation, but he was feeling more and more depleted as it went on.

"And another thing," said Saladin of Iraq. "You're being promoted to head of Arabia." He grinned. Between his teeth a brown substance leeched out.

"Me?"

"Yes. You're a regional officer now," Saladin of Iraq said.

Again Ali tried to penetrate their faces, looking for a crack. He got nothing. But he did smell burnt meat wafting off them. He held his breath.

"Wasn't I just a suspect only a moment ago?"

"Yes Of course. But that's standard," said Saladin of Iraq. "Now that we've talked to you we can see you're one of us."

"Well," Saladin of Afghanistan said. "You may be a little crazy about this whole mobile phone thing, but sometimes you need to be crazy for this job."

Ali nodded. This would make implementing all the ideas that he'd been cycling through very easy. "I'll have to set up a cell from scratch. I will need a new building and a new fund," Ali said.

"We'll get you that," said Saladin of Iraq.

"Good. And our region will no longer target innocents. We will only go after heads of state."

The two Saladins tilted their heads, then glanced at each other.

"What do you mean—"

"Surely this is a joke," Saladin of Iraq said. "You understand that we are terrorists, right? That's what we do. We kill people." he raised a finger." But it's for a good cause."

"No," Ali said. He remembered the look on Laith's face and gathered strength from that.

The Saladins flinched.

"I am certain that this will be the way. We must not fight the people who will protect us. That is foolish. And what have the people done to us? And aren't they the ones who we are freeing? No, we will only target the leaders who cause this misery," Ali said.

"Please, come on," Saladin of Afghanistan said. "Surely you joke. If you only go after the big men, the reaction will be worse. They will make life hard."

Ali wasn't sure he heard that correctly, but he decided to ignore it. "We will go after the American Embassy first. Then we'll pick larger targets."

The two Saladins shook their heads. "You've been through a lot. I'm sure you need some rest—"

"I know what I need," Ali said. Things were coming in focus. He would never be someone who could wipe out a family. Never again. "I will also keep writing to the doctor," he said.

"That's better. You will have our full support for that," said Saladin of Iraq. He seemed to release air and relax. Ali smelled rotten eggs on his breath. He didn't say anything.

Ali watched as the two men left. He would have to start recruiting men. He would aim for jobless adults. But he would tell them the real reason they were fighting. And he would make sure they were fearless. He walked over to the American embassy. It was heavily guarded. Ali took a few mental notes of all the barriers. It would be hard to attack this place. Then he saw a dark truck leave the premises. That's where he would get them, he thought. He would get them outside their fortress. Sooner or later they had to leave.

Nelson Lowhim

Justice took out everything from each case. Not bothering to look at them, just checking the manuals' first few pages to see if the case contents matched with the list on the pages. Everything was there. He'd hoped that touching everything would help him familiarize himself with the items, but his mind was still blank. He felt tired and he stared harder at the items. Then he wondered if the room had a security camera. He glanced at the foam tile ceiling and couldn't see anything sticking out. Well, he thought, it's probably hidden.

His normal phone rang. It was his girlfriend. He wasn't supposed to take calls in here. A twitch inside his chest told him that he should answer. Even if they were fighting, he missed her and wouldn't be able to see her for quite some time.

"Hi baby," he said.

"Justice."

The pause, and the manner with which she used his name struck him as odd. "How are you doing?" he asked.

"Not bad."

A voice inside his head told him to apologize. "How's work?" he asked.

"Same old," she said. She worked at a small startup that dealt with rich clientele with large art collections. They digitized everything and helped them find the value and keep an eye on the pieces as they moved from museum to museum. It was a job he'd wanted to do at one point in his life. "You?"

"They've got me with a long project. Overseas," he said. He'd never explained his job to her. With the amount he traveled he told her he was a businessman, but he could never be too specific. He didn't like lying to her. But that lack of specificity was the source of their latest fight and many fights before that.

She sighed and he knew that this wasn't going to be mended. Not now, not over the phone. Yet how could he tell her that this was something important he was doing?

"I know you don't believe me," he said. "But you have to. I'll be away for a while. I'll try to call. I promise." He knew it was a promise he couldn't keep, and that if he broke it this time he might never see her again.

"I believe you," she said. "I just want to know more. Is that too much to ask?"

"It isn't," he said. "We have to chase a client in Europe."

"For?"

His mind raced. "Corks. He's looking to find someone Stateside to deal with his corks."

Silence.

"Okay. When can you call?"

"I'll try to every day. Sorry, no promises."

Silence. And though all he could hear was static on his phone, he knew she was hurt. "Sorry," he said again.

"It's fine," she said. "I just feel like there's this wall and I can't, no matter how hard I try, break past it."

Her voice was tingling his nerves. He'd hurt her. "Sorry," he mumbled.

"It's always you who's sorry. What about me?"

He wasn't sure what she meant. He sensed a verbal trap, so he didn't say anything.

"I love you," she said.

"I do too," he replied, hoping she could hear how sincere he was. He tried to think of how he could salvage the relationship. Nothing came to mind.

"Call, if you can."

Before Justice could reply she hung up. He stared at his phone. Just wait for the promotion, then you can find the time to apologize to her.

His picked up the manual for the phone that Sasha gave him. It was long. He flipped through it. How to track using phone. How to search databases. He stopped at that page and stared. It was simple. He picked up the phone and went through a few menus. He searched Dr. Noklar. The search started. A minute later it was only 0.05% done.

"Christ," he muttered to himself and put it aside. He tossed the manual in a corner. The phone, unlike most electronics this agency purchased, seemed pretty self-explanatory—outside of the search. He stared at the tablet manual. It seemed identical.

His phone started to ring again.

"Hi, Justice?"

It was his mother. She always answered with a question. He wondered what she expected every time she called him.

"Mom, how's it going?"

"Not too bad. You doing all right? We haven't heard from you in a while."

"Just busy, sorry," he said.

"How was the vacation?"

"Good."

"How's Carol?"

"Good."

Silence. "Are you at work?"

"Yes."

"You work too hard."

He didn't retort with how they were the ones to instill this work or else ethic in him. "I can't help it." His mother and father knew about as much about his work as Carol did.

"Ask him if he got a promotion," his father said in the background.

"You ask him yourself," his mother said. Some discourse followed and Justice held the phone away from his ears.

"Your father wants to know if you've got a promotion yet."

"Not yet ma."

"You know you should ask. If you work this hard they should give you one."

"I'm close. That's why I'm busy," Justice snapped, feeling immediately bad for doing so.

"He's stressed," his mother said, off the phone.

"Tell him to ask for the promotion. They shouldn't work him this hard," his father yelled from the background. A tussle ensued.

"Justice?" his father asked, his voice loud and deep.

"Hi dad."

"You know you can't let them push you around like this."

"I know dad," Justice said, glancing at his watch. He didn't mind talking to his parents, but he hated it when they talked down to him.

"Just let me handle it."

"He'll handle it," his father said, off phone. There was a tinge of pride in the way he said it.

That helped calm Justice's annoyance some. He loved his parents and especially loved it when they talked about him with pride. He wondered if he would ever be allowed to tell them about what he really did. "I need to get going. Sorry."

"That's fine, son. We're proud of you; you know that? We're just... getting old. You should visit more often."

"I will," Justice said. "Try," he added as if an afterthought. They still lived in the same house north of Chicago. He didn't have fond memories of the place, and he regressed too much into childhood when he returned, but he felt guilty if he stayed away for too long.

"Love you," his father said. "Love you," his mother said.

"Love you both," he said.

A knock sounded on the door. Justice hung up and opened the door. "Yes?"

Drail's face was stern. "You using an unauthorized phone in here?"

"Yes, I am. I—"

"You know that's not allowed."

"Sorry," Justice said, and decided not to mention that he did in fact know.

"I'll have to ask for it," Drail said, placing his hand palm up.

"I won't do it again," Justice said. He was loathe to give the phone to his boss. Not when Carol might give him a call.

"Sorry, gotta take it," Drail said.

"In trouble already?" Geoff said. His head was peering around his slightly opened door. He wagged his finger. "You've got to watch for this one."

Drail didn't seem amused. "Get back to work Geoff!"

Justice was thankful for Drail's reaction, so he handed over the phone. He could use the other phone to call Carol and explain things.

"How's the work going?" Drail asked.

"You know. Slow but steady," Justice said.

"Well, don't let it get too slow. You know what's at stake."

Justice shut the door and alone again stared at the phone searching the database. It was at 1%. He shook his head and looked through the surveillance case. There were several sheets of stickers. He examined them closely. They were each the size of a paper hole. Reading the manual he saw that each was activated as a listening and tracking device.

"I'll be," he said. He pulled one out and stuck it on the wall. His phone beeped. He stared at a map of New York and a blinking red light. "Damn," he said. And the word Damn came up on the phone. Transcription. He smiled. This would be useful. He wasn't certain how, but he would use them as much as possible.

On his phone he pulled up a notepad. D23s=tracking device, he typed.

He stared at what else was in the case of surveillance goods. More sheets. Plastic sheets. These were thicker, coin battery size. Cameras. He broke the plastic stick attaching the camera to the sheet and placed it in a corner. Again another light, this one green, came up. He clicked on it and there he was, a video stream on his phone.

"Amazing," he said. The words came up on his phone. He was going to like these Tango-one missions. He'd never had this kind of equipment before in his life.

The rest of the surveillance equipment was powder for marking, some edible trackers, as well as mini drones. These were the size of a quarter. He smiled.

He played with the drone for an hour, controlling it through his phone, before he realized that he was famished. He headed down to the cafeteria for lunch. He wanted to eat as fast as possible and get back to work, but when he had his tray he saw Sasha waving him over from a corner. He sat down next to her, this time with an appreciation for the work she did.

"How's it going?"

"Amazing," he said. "Just getting a hang of all the equipment," he said. Feeling a little better about himself.

"Good," Sasha said and took a bite out of the sandwich she was eating, sauce dripping down her chin.

"And you? Any information?"

"Not yet," Sasha said; a sigh released from her that seemed to be asking him to ask her questions about her personal life.

Justice stared at his mixed gruel food and took a bite as he wondered whether he should ask her anything personal. That was the rule here, wasn't it? That amongst the workers you kept out the personal details of your life.

"You've other projects?" he asked. As soon as he said it, and heard her stiff pause, he knew it'd come out wrong.

"I'm putting all my effort on *yours.*"

The way she said Justice, emphasizing the "s", made Justice think of the way Carol said his name during the last few days of their vacation. It were as if, with that emphasis, they were trying to change his personality. Or perhaps he was just being paranoid. "I didn't mean it like that," he said.

"Don't worry about it," she said, waving her hand. "You're under a lot of stress."

He wanted to tell her that that shouldn't be an excuse, but he decided not to. He thought about bringing up what Geoff was doing, then thought better of it since it sounded like he was ratting Geoff out.

He focused on his steamed carrots and brown gruel that had pasta mixed in somewhere. It tasted like beefsteak, not bad. He looked up for a second and saw Natalie bouncing across the room. Or rather her body was gliding while her secondary characteristics were bouncing.

"She's gorgeous, isn't she?" Sasha said.

Justice shot his eyes around the room, as if he were observing, down to his plate, then up at Sasha, hoping that she would be fooled.

"Don't worry," she said. "She's something that *should* be looked at."

Not sure of what to say, Justice, stared at his food even harder. Burned into his retina were Natalie's parts. Think about the way Carol spoke to you. The mission. He had to focus.

"You know she's a lesbian?" Sasha said.

Justice glanced up. "Who?"

"Come on," Sasha said.

Justice was intrigued to think of Natalie as a lesbian. "How do you know?"

"Everyone knows," Sasha said, waving her hand.

"But how? If it's just a rumor then that's all it is."

"My, you're defensive."

"I'm not. Just wondering," Justice said and took the moment to steal another glance of Natalie as she approached the food line.

"Well, rumor has it that she has a string of lovers, all women, across the world."

Justice, hearing the cooing in her tone, now took in Sasha. She was slightly red on the cheeks, but she was definitely ogling Natalie.

"Wait. Are you..." he said.

"I can appreciate," Sasha said, not once taking her eyes off Natalie.

"It's fine if you are," Justice said. "I won't tell anyone."

"That's what everyone says," she said, rolling her eyes. "You should see how easily rumors get started."

"I can't imagine," Justice said, going back to his food. His mind was lost in the crunching of his jaws and food. It took a second longer than normal to register Natalie's subtle, almost fading, peachy perfume, covered with sour sweat.

"Mind if I sit here?" Natalie said.

Justice looked up, and as nonchalantly as he could manage, he nodded and raised his eyebrows.

"Of course," Sasha said, bubbling with energy. Natalie sat across from them. Justice stared at his food and ate it, paying attention to each bite as it came to his mouth. His discipline lapsed, and his eyes moved up to the shadow that Natalie's breasts cast on the table in front of her.

"You two been busy?" Natalie asked.

"Yeah," Justice said. "Trying to get all my equipment down."

"Well, you can't learn it all in a day," Natalie said. She smiled. Bright and glorious. Justice didn't smile back, and he must have sent a look, because she qualified her statement: "Well, that's been my experience at least. Spend a few hours with it, but get out there and start talking to people."

"That's so right," Sasha said. "Those manuals are horrendous, totally written by politicians. Best to just try out the equipment while on the mission."

Justice was certain that Sasha hadn't said that about the manuals before.

"That's *so* right," Natalie said and reached across the table to touch Sasha's hand.

Sasha turned bright red.

Justice kept quiet as a conversation formed between the two. Feeling somewhat left out, he ate his food quickly.

"Good bye," he said. They nodded, while staring into each other's eyes.

He made his way back to the room. Then, staring at all the equipment, he started to fill a suitcase, from the kill case, to take with him.

That's when the phone rang. He picked it up.

"Good news," Sasha said.

He could tell that her voice was calm and relaxed. His mind jumped to what possibly could have transpired between her and Natalie. When he left that table the electricity between them had been burning his ears.

"What's that?" he asked.

"We finally found a lead."

"Awesome, where is he?"

"Well… it's not him. That's still up in the air. But he has a cousin."

"A cousin?"

"Closest thing we have. ISI's interviewed the doctor's entire family and has nothing."

"A cousin," Justice said, more to himself than her. "Where is he?"

"That's the good news. Right here in New York."

"That's great," Justice said, though he didn't think that it was all that great. "Where?"

"I'll send you the details."

"Great."

"Oh, and you've read the letter right?"

Justice almost hit his head. He'd forgotten about what had started this whole mission.

Sasha seemed to read into his silence. "You haven't read it yet, have you?" she said. "You'd better get on it."

"I will. Thanks," Justice said. As soon as he hung up, he looked for the manila folder. He'd forgotten about the entire thing. And a few minutes later there it was, under the kill case. He cursed, reminding himself that he needed to focus or else a mushroom cloud would appear over the city.

He pulled out the letter and started to read it:

Dear Dr. Noklar,

I do hope that this letter finds you in the best of spirits. Of course, one can never be in the best of spirits when they're living in a virtual prison. I'm sure it's a sore subject for you, but I must say that, like many other Muslims, I find that your country can restrict your movements, condemn you, to be nothing short of ludicrous. Of course, if your country's leaders were more than lapdogs for the American scoundrels, then we wouldn't be having this conversation, would we? They would have stood up for someone who is nothing more than a hero to Muslims around the world.

I should say that, should this get to you, it's of the highest honor to be able to reach you, to talk to you. I hope that this letter is the first of many.

Let me get down to the point of me writing. As you may know, I'm a wanted man. Ever since our fearless leader was shot, illegally, by American pigs, we have been looking for something to help hold our group together. There isn't much I can say. Of course I'm next in line, so the Americans will be gunning for me. I'll never give up, of course, I'll fight them until my last breath, but I'm not being over dramatic when I say that I'm living on borrowed time. I have been lucky one too many times, praise to Allah.

So before it's too late, let me try and find a way into your heart with respect to your many talents. Dr. Noklar, I have studied you closely. As I've said I'm nothing more than impressed with what you've done in your life. You are someone every young Muslim should try to emulate. It is true that nothing but the best will come from learning, and you are a

77

first-class example of this.

And the reason for the letter, you ask? I'm asking you, imploring you to share your talents with us. Before you decide to toss this letter into the wind, remember that we are on your side. If we were in charge, you would have statues being built to commemorate your deeds. If you're still thinking that perhaps these are the ramblings of a madman, I will implore you not to believe the lies that have been told about our group. Remember we are only fighting a resistance against the oppression of the Americans. The reason you are under lock and key. They have distorted your image. Imagine what they have done with us! And trust us, we have merely been fighting against their evil since day one. These are the days where they've killed our women and children in the street. You must believe me. I hope you believe that we were never responsible for any of those acts. All done by America agents, trying to stir up men for their futile war.

It's my hope that you have not fallen for these lies of theirs. If they tell you we are going to use your talents to kill innocents, think of all the innocents you will save! We will finally use such power to build a better world, instead of allowing them to piss wherever they want. Think of the greatness that could be the new world! Think of no more American or Zionist intrusion. Think of your own freedom and your legacy. Think of the freedoms that will be uncovered around the world.

My friend, I hope that this letter has convinced you to at least consider my proposal. We shall meet again. And until then, I will await your reply.

The letter wasn't signed. Justice read it over again. He chuckled, when he got to the part about ramblings. The man must have been scared for his life. So whatever the American military and intelligence was doing, they'd better keep it up. But as he read it the second time, he wondered how it was that someone like Dr. Noklar could be persuaded by such an incoherent letter. The doctor had been a homebody for most of his recent life. What in this letter made him get up and go? What made him risk possible death, either at the hands of Al Qaeda or American drones? Was it the part about the statues? Was every man driven by some secret desire for immortality?

Justice sighed. Well, perhaps he could talk to the cousin and see if he knew anything. His phone vibrated, and he browsed a few pages before he saw that Sasha had sent him mail. The cousin was at Columbia University. His address on 125th street was given. Justice had never been to this part of town. He checked his watch. It was two. He packed a few sheets of surveillance-tabs and checked the kill case contents for something good. There was a small laptop with a gun hidden inside, as well as a remote controlled drone the size of a golf ball. He grinned and grabbed both and left.

Their building was in midtown and it only took half an hour to make it up to the building. He had to double check, for the building was a dorm, nestled amongst the brick buildings outside Columbia's main campus.

He flashed a fake NYPD badge so that the security guard at the desk would let him through. Up the elevator and to a narrow, claustrophobic hallway. Smoke billowed out from a community kitchen, but a man, dressed in his underwear waved away Justice's concerned look. He wondered what would happen in case of a fire in here. Most likely pandemonium and death.

Justice knocked on the door.

"Yes?" a voice, a man's, asked from behind the door and muffling sheets.

"Mr. Agha? I'd like to talk to you for a second." Justice knew better than to claim his authority. That usually sent the other person running, or calling a lawyer.

"Who is it?" the voice asked again, this time right behind the door.

"I'm Mr. Justice from the NYPD. I just have a few questions for you." He flashed his badge to the peephole.

"Justice?" the person asked, his low voice almost squeaked. "Is this a joke?"

"I assure you it's not, sir."

Some shuffling occurred. "Just a second."

Justice knew that here on the eighth floor, the man was stuck. These buildings had no fire escape. Just stairs in the middle with hoses to keep them cool in such an event.

The door opened and Justice came face to face with a slim, handsome young man with a shaved face, but with one of those beards that always threatens to bush out.

"Justice."

"Ben," the man said. The door was half open, and it was obvious he didn't want Justice inside.

Justice shook his hand and noticed that it was wet. He looked; the man's brown forehead glistened in the hallway light.

"Worried?" Justice asked. He noticed that the man had a perfect American accent. Justice hadn't been able to read his file before coming up here, because there was no file. Sometimes he wondered about his agency and their ability to not gather information in a time of web crawlers.

"No," the man said, his eyes darting around the hallway.

"Can I come inside?"

"It's a mess. We can talk elsewhere."

"Please, let's talk in here," Justice said. Though the man was acting squirmy, there was something kind underneath him.

After a few seconds of deliberation, the man opened the door wide. An aroma of sweat, cologne, and mold hit Justice.

"Can I ask you what this is about?" the man asked.

"It's about your cousin."

The man's face whitened. "My cousin?"

"Dr. Noklar. You know him, right?"

"Dr. Noklar? From Pakistan?"

"Yes, you know him?"

The man's face visibility relaxed. He shrugged. "I know *of* him. But I don't know that side of the family well."

"Can I come in?"

"Okay," the man said.

Justice stepped inside and almost tripped on some books and food wrappers on the floor. Or what he assumed was a floor because books were strewn all over the place, with clothes in between for good measure. Otherwise the room, a small box, held a bed, desk and closet, without much hanging on the walls.

"Your real name Ben?"

"No, it's Bashir, but Ben works better for getting jobs."

"You a student here?" Justice asked as he sat on the chair that Ben pointed to.

"Yeah, but will graduate in a few."

"What do you study?" Justice asked. This part of the job he didn't mind. Liked it, actually. Find out more about the person. Relax them with questions about their life, see how long they take to answer, and then hit them with the harder questions.

"History."

"Bachelors?"

"Yup."

"Going to graduate school afterwards?"

"I want to work."

"Where?"

"As a teacher."

"Don't you need a masters for that?"

"In this school."

A muffled click came from the closet behind Ben. Justice froze and reached for his suitcase. "Something in there?"

"No," Ben said without looking.

"Open the door," Justice said. The hair on his skin shifted, and he could sense that someone else was in this room.

"I swear, there's no one."

Justice held Ben's stare. He wondered what the young man had to hide. Finally Ben stood up walked to the closet. Justice took his turned back to place an audio sticker under the desk, then he placed the camera on the corner of the desk leg. It would be noticed if Ben looked closely, but in a mess like this he might never notice it.

"Get out, you idiot."

Justice stood up as a man came tumbling out of the closet as soon as the door was opened. He looked a little like Ben, except instead of a sculpted face, he was chubby and wore cargos with a t-shirt, while Ben's tight jeans and jacket made him seem that much more put together.

"I told you to be quiet," Ben said, standing above the man and shaking his head.

The man's belly protruded from below his t-shirt. He stood up and glared at Ben. His eyes were blood shot.

"So you're here to take me away?" Ameer asked Justice. He didn't seem scared.

"You are?" Justice asked.

"Sorry, Justice. This is my cousin, Ameer. Ameer this is Justice."

"Your name is Justice?" Ameer asked, raising his eyebrows. He let out a laugh. "Did they give the job on account of your name?"

Justice didn't take kindly to digs on his name. He stiffened up, then remembered he was here for information.

"And are you a prince?" Justice asked, half-smiling to himself. When neither of them reacted he took a second to adjust his shirt. He stood up and put out his hand. When Ameer didn't make an effort to shake hands, Justice nodded his head. "And what were you doing in the closet?"

"Who are you? If you're here to take me away, then do so."

"I'm only here to talk to your cousin. Though if you can help me that will be great."

"I'm not helping anyone, who are you with?"

"I'm of the NYPD," Justice said. He noticed that Ameer had an accent, and it was stilted. And he also noticed that he was defensive, like a man who had something to hide. "Why was he in the closet?"

Ben looked down at his feet. "He's not legal," he said.

"What?" Ameer gasped. "How could you turn me in? I can't believe this."

"You're the one who messed up. What, now you're going to drag me down? I told you not to—"

"Wait," Justice said, raising his hand. "I'm not here to take anyone away for immigration problems, all right? Just help me, answer my questions and I'll be on my way. Got it?"

"Got it," Ben said.

Ameer stared at Justice. Ben elbowed him. "All right," Ameer said. "I'll help. You're asking about the great Dr. Noklar?"

Justice could sense the sarcasm in his voice. "Yup. Have either of you had contact with him in the past few weeks?"

"No, not recently," Ben said, a little too quickly for Justice's taste.

"When's the last time you talked to him, or heard from him?" Justice asked.

"He's not interested in talking to us," Ameer said, with disdain in his voice.

"Tell me," Justice said.

"He's so high and mighty," Ameer said.

"Don't talk about your cousin like that," Ben said.

"Oh, you and your family just love kissing his ass, don't you? He's nothing but a stuck up goon."

"Now you're going too far," Ben replied. "He's been through a lot."

"Been through so much he can't talk to his family? Our side of the family? You know they always looked down on us, and once they were famous they never bothered to even send a letter," Ameer said.

"What are you talking? He never was bad to us."

"Don't point your finger at me."

"Don't act like a spoiled child," Ben said.

"Gentlemen," Justice said, raising his hand, hoping to silence them.

"Who are you calling a spoiled child?" Ameer said. He squared off his round body to Ben.

"You," Ben said and jutted his finger into Ameer's chest.

"You're just like his side of the family, always thinking you're better than everyone else."

"I? I helped you. You let you stay here after they kicked you out of college."

"Oh yes, thank you, and you'll never let me forget it."

"Of course I won't. Especially when I told you not to go making trouble, that they would kick you out if you did. You were a guest and you didn't know how to act like it. Of course, now that I've lived with you, I can see what kind of guest you are."

"There you go. Telling everyone what I did. I know it was you who told my father. Wasn't it?" Ameer said.

"I did nothing of the sort. Why keep blaming me?"

"Who else could have told them?"

"I don't know," Ben said, raising his hands.

"Gentlemen," Justice said, stepping close enough that they could see them. "Let's not start a fight here, all right? I don't care what he's done."

"Why not?" Ben asked. "He protested with that crazy Palestinian group. They vandalized some of the campus, and he was kicked out for it. What kind of idiot goes to a country, invited, and trashes the place?"

"You are a dog," Ameer said, his finger now in Ben's face.

"Me? How dare you."

"Oh yes, let's accept everything that this country throws in our face."

"I told you to just start a blog. That's what people in this country do, they write in blogs. They don't waste time in the streets. That's what third world people do."

"What the hell is a blog going to do? You talk nonsense, you know that?"

"Hey!" Justice yelled, his voice box almost stretched and cracked. "I want you both to calm down for a second." He couldn't quite believe that they were at each other throats. How could they live together? "You," he said and pointed to Ameer. "Sit on this chair. And you stay right here."

Ameer sat down, eyeing Ben.

"I'm here to find out about your cousin. Dr. Noklar. All right? Any issues you have between yourselves, can you push it aside?" Justice asked.

"Oh, right, the stuck up cousin. We have plenty of those," Ameer said.

"See?" Ben said, pointing to Ameer while directing his talk to Justice. "This is what I'm talking about. He's an ingrate."

"Don't you dare call me that."

"That's what you are. You've always been an ingrate. Always blaming others for your problems. Always thinking the world is out to get you, when all you should be doing is focusing on doing what you should be doing."

"You're a dog."

"And you were in a terrorist group. That's what happens. They kick you out."

"It was a student group," Ameer said, pleading.

"Hold on," Justice said. He now wanted to know. Though Ameer seemed a little angry, he didn't seem to be so much a terrorist than a young man with too much energy. "What happened?"

"They carried out a terrorist act, and were kicked out," Ben said.

Justice raised his hand. "Let him speak."

"We were a student group. So we decided to take over a room to protest the college's backing of Israel with statements it had made."

"Were there people in there?"

"No. We went in at midnight," Ameer said.

"This was at Columbia?"

"No, I went to Fordham."

Justice was certain that Ameer was withholding some information about how he got kicked out.

"All right," Justice said. "I'm sorry about that, but those are the breaks sometimes."

Ameer nodded, his eyes fell to the ground. "I know."

"But I'm here about your other cousin. So please, let's stay on topic." When Justice stopped speaking, he looked at each of them. They seemed to be listening. Of course, he didn't like that he was pleading, but they seemed like reasonable men.

"All right," Ameer said, waving his hand in front of his face.

"And keep all opinions to yourself," Justice added.

"We will," Ben said. "Why are you so interested in him?"

"He's left Pakistan and no one knows where he is," Justice said.

"Wait, I thought you were NYPD," Ameer said. "What do you care about Pakistan?"

"We have an overseas division. New York is the most sought after target by terrorists," Justice said. A swell of pride filled his chest.

Ameer squinted his eyes, staring Justice down. "You from Pakistan? You look a little—"

"My mother is," Justice said. "She moved to the States when she was young." He could feel them visibly relax, and he wondered why he hadn't mentioned it earlier. "So we think your cousin is talking with terrorists. That's our concern, and it's the concern of the ISI."

"Oh, *those* thugs," Ameer said. And Ben seconded this with a huff.

"Well, they're who we have to work with," Justice said, annoyed at the opinions. "He received a letter from the terrorists, and a short time ago he disappeared. We think out of the country."

"Of course you would think he's with the terrorists," Ameer said. "Have they brainwashed you too? He was a hero, and instead of being treated like a hero, America made our government treat him like a criminal. A common thief."

"He was caught breaking the Non-Proliferation Treaty," Justice said, a little angry. "Why do you think we have these international laws? So anyone can break them?"

"Give me a break," Ben said. "I don't normally agree with my cousin, but he's right. He was a hero and your country made him a villain."

"He broke the law," Justice said. He felt angry with these two men. Why wouldn't they just cooperate?

"Oh, and the US hasn't? Who's breaking the law with India, our enemy? And that's okay, isn't it?" Ameer said. Ben nodded his head vigorously.

"I'm not here to discuss politics. The fact is we're looking for him, and if you have any clue where he could be, I would appreciate some help," Justice said.

"They're always ready to bully others," Ameer said to his cousin while pointing at Justice.

"I know," Ben said, as if it was a part of life he hadn't got used to.

The two cousins stared at each other. Justice was angry, but it was good to see that they could come together on at least one issue.

"Well?" Justice asked. "Are you going to answer the question?"

"Listen, we've told you. We don't talk to him. Never did. Just because we're related to him doesn't mean we know," Ben said.

"Yeah. They would never stoop so low and talk to us. Our side of the family is the rejects. We get kicked out of college," Ameer said. He seemed sad now.

"He's right," Ben said, "about them looking down on us. I went to a reunion once, and all I heard was disparaging remarks about how none of us have amounted to anything."

"Was Dr. Noklar there?" Justice asked.

"Oh, he was. I think that's the only time I ever saw him. I was young. But he was full of himself. You could see from the way he walked. I, of course, was enamored with him. The famous cousin. But now…"

"I was there. He was looking at us through his nose, just like everyone else on his family. Dr. Noklar this, and that. And I got hit if I didn't call him doctor," Ameer said. "Maybe it's good you got him under house arrest."

"Anything else you can tell me about him?" Justice asked.

"This was before the charges were laid against him, but after the world knew that Pakistan had a bomb. So he was really full of himself."

"He kept saying that America was trying to be a neighborhood bully, but their time had come."

"Is that a fact?" Justice said. This was something new.

"He's right," Ben said. "He was saying that no one should listen to America. That they were trying to bully the world so that everyone was poorer than they. After all, they were the only nation to misuse a bomb, so why should anyone listen to them?"

Justice's head spun with anger.

"Everyone in the world was saying that about America," Ameer replied.

"Everyone?" Justice asked, not wanting to believe such a statement.

"Yeah," Ben jumped in. "His view was common. You ask a single non-American at that time and they would've said the same thing."

"Listen," Ameer said. "Even when your twin towers fell. Everyone thought it was sad, but there wasn't a person who didn't say that America deserved it. Or that the other people had a point."

Justice's hands clenched together. "I said," he said loud enough that the two of them jumped. "I'm not here for political discussions. You two think you can slime this country while you live here? I won't put up with that for a second."

"Sorry," Ben said, looking down. "We were only trying to put things into perspective."

"That's a load of bull," Justice said, pointing his finger in Ben's face. He liked it that the young man shrunk back from the finger. Justice decided to let it be and keep pursuing the doctor. "What else can you tell me about him?"

"That's about it," Ben said. "Everything else is hearsay through the family."

"Like?"

"He was getting depressed about the house arrest. Then he was kind of angry about the ISI always following him," Ben said.

"I think he was angrier at the Pakistani government than the Americans," Ameer said.

"And did he ever talk about hurting the governments for what they'd done?"

"Oh no. He wasn't like that," Ben said.

Justice focused on Ben's facial features. He'd said that too quickly.

"He wasn't?" Justice asked.

"He always talked about how the terrorists were zealots who only made the country look bad," Ben said.

"He's right. He'd never be on their side," Ameer said.

"Then where do you think he disappeared to? It's not easy for a normal person to defeat surveillance and leave the country," Justice said.

"No idea," Ben said.

Justice glanced at Ameer who shook his head as well.

"None?"

"Did he have any friends outside of the country?" Ben asked Ameer.

Ameer shook his head. "His family is in Pakistan. I've never heard of him having many friends."

"Wait a minute," Ben said, his forehead creasing. "I might remember someone who knew him better than us. Remember Uncle Abid?"

"Oh, yes. He would know more. He talked to him a lot," Ameer said.

"And where does he live?" Justice asked.

"Here," Ben replied.

"In…"

"In New Jersey, right?" Ben said to Ameer.

"I think so."

"You've never visited him?" Justice asked, somewhat incredulous.

"He's not too talkative. But we have his number. We were only supposed to disturb him in an emergency only."

"And he knows Dr. Noklar?"

"That's right."

"Let me see the number," Justice said. "And address."

Ben walked to his desk and fished around in the top drawer. He picked out a piece of paper and copied an address and phone number down. "Here," he said and handed the slip to Justice.

Justice stared at the number. Another lead. A smile crept across his face. It was all falling into place, he thought to himself.

A knock on the door made Justice turn.

"Who is it?" Ben yelled.

"Yo, it's Sammy," a voice yelled from the other side. "You coming to play soccer with us or what?"

"Come in," Ameer said.

Growing slighted, after all he was conducting an interview, Justice he decided to let it be. A tall, lanky, brown man who Justice took for South Asian as well walked into the room.

"Hi," Sammy said, leering at Justice.

Justice decided to play the tough guy, so he stared at the young man until the man turned to Ameer. "Who's this douche?"

"This douche," Justice said, angry. "Is an officer of the law. You want to get arrested?"

Sammy looked at Justice with a smirk, before glancing at Ameer. "He serious?"

"Sammy," Ben said, stepping between Justice and the lanky newcomer. "This is Justice. He's with the NYPD."

"Wait. Justice?" Sammy said, curling his nose as if he smelled something off. When Ben and Ameer gave him an angry look he straightened up. "Sorry. I'm Sammy. What's going on?" His eyes darted to Ameer.

"Nothing. I was just asking them questions," Justice said. He was about to turn to tell the cousins not to say anything when Ameer blurted out:

"He's here because of Dr. Noklar—"

"Ameer!" Justice said, his voice low and grating. "Don't mention a single word about what we've talked about."

Ameer raised his hands, as if to surrender.

"Oh, Dr. Noklar?" Sammy asked. "He's left the country."

"How did you know that?" Justice asked, wondering if Sammy had been listening.

"The Internet," Sammy said.

Justice shook his head. He'd never liked what the Internet allowed, and now he felt vindicated. This was supposed to be a need-to-know piece of information. Journalists had no respect for the limits of information.

"We playing soccer or what?" Sammy asked after a long silence.

"Are we good?" Ben asked Justice.

Justice looked at his watch. He could get going to the uncle's place and be there in an hour or two. He was some ways from the nearest authorized helo-pad. But first he had to authorize it.

"Justice?" Ben asked again.

Justice realized that he'd been silent for almost a minute. "Where are you from?" he asked Sammy. Though the young man's accent was implacable, it was a touch too perfect.

"I'm from New Jersey," Sammy said.

Justice noticed the curved tube of a vein on the man's forehead. "Remember who I am. Where are you from, originally?"

"India. Bombay."

Justice grinned. "It'll always be Bombay to you?"

Sammy shrugged. "That's what it says on my birth certificate. *They* can call it whatever they want."

"And you're okay having two Pakistani friends?" Justice asked. He wanted, for some reason, to push these three into a confrontation. This was, of course, a result of his job training, but sometimes it would come up unneeded: Poke people to get them emotional, then grab information.

Sammy shrugged again. "Why does that matter?"

"They think you're the enemy," Justice said and smiled at Ben looked shocked.

"See? They're always trying to divide and conquer. That's how the British got us all," Ameer said, as the other two nodded, though almost imperceptibly.

Justice shook his head. "So that's what *we're* doing now? Like things between your two governments aren't bad enough on their own?"

"It's other people butting into our business that makes this worse," Ameer said.

"You kidding me?" Justice said, though in fact he knew he hated it when other countries interfered with America's business.

"He's not," Ben said; he seemed to be gaining courage with his friends in his room. "That's the difference between us. Our countries at least have the sense not to interfere with others and abuse the world like yours."

Justice had no clue where that false comment came from, and he wondered if his own tone had been too weak.

"Hello?" another person knocked on the half-open door. "Are we going to play soccer, or what?"

"Lee," Ameer said. "Come in. We're almost ready. Right?" He directed the last word to Justice.

"Oh, of course. We were just talking about the horrors *my* nation has committed in trying to protect itself," Justice said, hoping his sarcastic tone would send the young men scurrying.

"Ah," Lee said. "American insolence." He too was tall, perhaps six-three, with glasses so thick, Justice wondered how he planned to play soccer.

"Excuse me?" Justice asked, glowering.

Lee studied him then the other three men. "What? America is acting out of hand, that's fact." His accent was heavy without the r's.

Nelson Lowhim

Justice shook his head. "You're Chinese, right?"

Lee nodded his head.

"And you're lecturing us on what's to be done with human rights? What about Tibet? Your citizens?"

Lee puffed out his chest. "That's to protect our stability. And those monks burning themselves are nothing but terrorists."

Justice couldn't argue with that, so he pointed at Sammy. "And don't let me remind you about Kashmir. What's *your* government doing there?"

"We're protecting our homeland against terrorists," Sammy said and pounded his chest. "You saw what they did to our Parliament. How do you expect us to react?"

Justice raised his eyebrows, hoping they would understand where he was coming from. "And what are *we* doing but protecting ourselves?"

The men all glanced down at their shoes.

Justice didn't want to admit it, but they seemed to be reasonable men; even if some of their views were outliers. "Well. I'll be going, and you can get back to your soccer. I'll reach you if I have anymore questions," he said to Ben, who kept staring at his feet.

Outside, the weak winter sun cracked the air with surprising force. Justice called up Drail.

"I need a helo. Get me the closest one."

Drail laughed. "Easy there, boss. What for?"

"I have another lead to follow up on, but it's in New Jersey."

A pause. Justice didn't like that Drail was ready to second-guess him. He heard another voice whisper. Was he on speakerphone?

"Did the cousin talk?" Drail asked.

"He gave me all the info he could. But he didn't know much."

More silence and whispering in the background.

"How far did you push him?"

"Pretty far," Justice said.

"What methods did you use, Tango one?"

Justice bit the inside of his cheek. He heard the condescending tone used for one.

"Nothing tough, huh?"

"No." Justice, admonished, grasped at something that would save his reputation. "But I'm sure he's telling me all he can. This is *my* mission, right? That's my call," he said and stopped. The static on the phone was so dead silent that he knew he was saying the wrong things. "He's telling the truth."

"Justice. You do understand what happens if you're wrong? A city in America goes boom. This isn't a game. We have to make damn certain that he's telling the truth."

Then off to the side Justice heard: "Send in a team to snatch the kid and find out what he really knows."

Justice remembered to swallow.

"Justice. I'm sending in a team. I don't want to do it again."

"Got it," Justice said. He couldn't believe that he was being so foolish about something he knew was serious. "The helo?" he asked, hoping that would make him sound in charge.

A few minutes later, Justice was flying above the waves of buildings, then into the gleaming canyon of the Hudson. His phone vibrated, but he switched it off. Even though he knew how serious this mission was, he didn't want to think about what was happening to Ben, that nice young man doing an immense favor for his cousin. Justice filled out the report on the phone and sent it in.

He landed a few miles from the uncle's house and Sasha sent him a message saying that the uncle worked from home, and there was a 90% chance he was there. A small car waited for Justice at the pad. He grabbed the keys from a guard who seemed confused and drove off.

It was a large forest of large houses. The streets were tortuous, with tranquil nouns on the road signs, and large vehicles everywhere.

He parked in front of a rectangular mansion, shining from a new coat of paint. The lawn had no trees and seemed to match the drab house in lack of adventure.

A man who had some of Ben's looks, though he was rounder in the middle, answered the door.

"Mr. Abid?"

"Yes?" the man asked. His accent was heavy; American fricates fighting an insurgency in his foreign accent.

Justice flashed his badge. "FBI, can we talk?"

The man blinked. "Yes, come in."

Justice walked into a house with enough littered electronics that he knew teenagers lived here. It smelled like air freshener and spices. Abid led him to a living room full of flower print sofas.

"Do you want anything to drink?" Abid asked.

Justice sat down on a love seat. He was famished, but it was against the rules to take food or beverages from a suspect. Drail had told him plenty of stories about agents taken down because they decided to let their guard down while talking to a suspect and ate poison. Justice's stomach and parched throat tried to tell him that he had never read of any such stories, not on the list of lost agents, but it was best to follow procedure, especially after Drail had just dressed him down. "No thanks," he said and told himself to remember to grab a drink on the way back to the helo pad.

"How can I help you then?"

"I'm here to ask questions about Dr. Noklar," Justice said and with one hand he swept at the seat next to him. He didn't need Abid standing over him.

"I'm sorry, I didn't catch your name," Abid said.

"Justice."

Abid blinked twice. "Mr. Justice... With the FBI?"

Justice nodded slowly. He wasn't going to be able to bowl over this man. He was in control of his emotions, and obviously knew an interrogation was about to hit him.

"*I'll* need a drink then," Abid said and walked over to a cabinet with glass doors and liquor bottles behind that. "You sure you don't want one?"

"I'm fine."

"Of course," Abid said, pulling out an aged whiskey. "Have to have a clean mind, don't you?" He poured three fingers worth into a tumbler, and dropped a couple of ice cubes into it. He sat down across from Justice.

Now, the light from a lamp directly above the man, Justice could see covered scars on his forehead, and cheek. Yet the rest of his epidermis glistened from daily moisture and oil massages. Another look around—at the ebony African statue, the Picasso-esque mask, and post modern painting next to that, with brush strokes so precise that Justice wished Drail could take a look—and Justice knew that this man was wealthy.

"You like the painting?" Abid asked.

"I do. It's… It's inspiring."

"The wretched coal. By some poor West Virginia boy. Saw it by luck. Such talent, eh?"

"That's clear," Justice replied. The swirl of colors reminded him of a sand storm, but with Appalachian fall leaves and coal and blood. It was possibly hopeless, but hopeful as well.

"He's doing better now. When I saw him he had nothing."

"You bought all his art?"

"Most of it. And he's started up a proper art store near Fayetteville."

Justice nodded. He and his girlfriend had always tried to find paintings by some unknown, but it was too hard.

"A little like a madman's cubism, don't you think?" Abid asked.

Justice nodded again and sat up straight. He wasn't here to talk art. Abid was trying to get inside his head. Justice had to maintain control of this interrogation.

"Where are you from, Mr. Abid?"

"I'm from Pakistan. Karachi. Moved here twenty years ago."

Justice thought about mentioning Ben or Ameer, then he decided that with what was about to happen to the young man, he was better off not saying anything. "And how do you know Dr. Noklar?"

He's in my family. A nephew, but only by the need for familial labels. We're more like brothers, really. Or were."

Was that last qualifier something Abid was saying to protect himself?

"Were?"

"When we were younger we were quite close. He always talked about his engineering, while I my business schemes."

"And recently, have you talked to him much?"

"Not much at all," Abid said.

"When's the last time you talked to him?"

"A few months ago. Why?"

"I'll ask the questions here," Justice said.

"Fine," Abid said and sipped his whiskey, closing his eyes. "You should really try this. Aged fifty years, from Ireland. Never liked whiskey until I tried this. Man," he said leaning his head back and staring at the ceiling. "This is what life's all about."

Justice felt like reaching over and seeing what the man was talking about, but he decided not to.

"Perhaps," Justice said. "What did you talk about last?"

"Nothing. The same. He was annoyed about the virtual house arrest, but he had finally learned to laugh about it."

"Virtual?"

"Yeah. Well, he was free to go where he wanted, just the ISI watched his ever move. Damn shame, that. He is a hero. He shouldn't be treated that way."

"You think he's a hero?" Justice said.

"He is," Abid said. The finality with which he spoke made it sound like he didn't think this was up for discussion.

Justice pulled out a piece of paper and scribbled something. He pointed at the tumbler. Abid leaned over and handed it to him. Justice, thinking about how he was going to have to call in the team on this man, took a sip. The whiskey hit his mouth, burning his throat as it went down. It settled in his stomach. A fire in its trail, then the oak flavor tickled his tongue, slowly fizzing out. Justice closed his eyes.

Abid chuckled and slapped his knee. "What did I tell you? Marvelous, isn't it?"

"That it is," Justice replied, and opened his eyes. The taste, of oak, perhaps cherry as well, lingered in his mouth. In his stomach, a rumble, a fist. This was what it was all about. But it wasn't the life Justice chose. Stay strong, Justice said, squeezing a hand tight. This was about the mission, don't let him win you over.

"Mr. Abid."

"Call me Abid."

"Very well. Abid. You know what Dr. Noklar has done?"

"No…"

"He's disappeared. We have reason to believe he's with terrorists. Al Qaeda, Abid. A.Q." Justice studied Abid's face and he could see a wave of disbelief come over his face. "And it's no joke that he did this disappearance came shortly after he received correspondence from A.Q."

"Mr. Justice. Can I call you Justice?"

"Of course."

"I know you Americans want to think that any brown man, especially any brown man from a problematic country," Abid said and pointed at himself. "Is up to no good. Is, in fact, a terrorist just waiting to break out of his normal brown skin, but I can assure you that no one in our family cares for the terrorists. You have to understand, if Al Qaeda ever came into power, I would be the first kind of person they would drag into the streets and shoot. Same with Dr. Noklar."

Justice had heard enough terrorist apologies for the day that he brushed off what Abid said. "That may be what you think. But there's always the opinions, which I want you to keep to yourself, and the facts. The facts tell us otherwise. In fact, A.Q. Holds your brother in great esteem."

"To get what they want," Abid said, raising his finger. "They only want to destroy."

"Do they have a good reason?" Justice asked. He wanted a reason to take the edge of the guilt he might feel for calling in the team to put the screws to Abid.

Abid shrugged. "I would argue no. Though some people might argue."

"And who would those people be?"

"I don't know. I'm sure you have more experience with them, Mr. Justice."

Justice raised the tumbler to his lips, sipped, then handed it back to Abid who did the same.

"So what are your theories, on this disappearance? Did he ever give you any indication that he might run?"

97

"No. I mean, where would he run to?" Abid stopped, as if he remembered something and took a gulp that almost finished the whiskey.

"And…"

Abid stared at the tumbler and with another gulp finished it.

"Mr. Abid."

Abid held up his hand.

Justice watched as lines formed and disappeared on Abid's face, cracking across his forehead. The man's eyes stilled.

"If you know something, I'd recommend you not withhold it."

"I do know," Abid said and shook his head. "I just don't think it would help you."

"Leave that to us."

"Well. There might be one place he's at."

"Where?"

"France."

"Why France?"

"You should know that he did some work in Europe."

"That's right."

"Well, he came to like visiting the south of France. And he came to know a woman," Abid said and stared at the tumbler in his hands. "I promised him I would never tell anyone. But… this won't be used as blackmail, will it?"

"It won't. We just want to find him. It's more for his safety than anything else. If A.Q. knows where he is, you can be sure they'll be after him."

"I know. Those bastards," Abid said.

Justice didn't believe the man's tone. "Tell me more about the woman."

"She lives in the South of France. He had a long relationship with her. He never wanted the family to find out."

"How strong were his feelings for her?"

"The strongest kind. Several times he talked of going to live with her."

"Do you know where she lives?"

"I'm sorry. He never said. I think her name was Francois. In Nice?" Abid said, his eyes rolled up and to the left.

It seemed unlikely that the doctor would leave his country and risk getting kidnapped for a woman. And why not have her visit Pakistan? No, this was something Abid was throwing to pull him, Justice, off the scent. Then what was the real scent.

"And do you know anything else that could help us?" Justice asked.

"I'm sorry. I don't."

Justice pulled out his phone, his hands shook.

"What's that for?"

"Just registering that you don't know anything."

Justice called in the team. In five minutes.

"Well, that will be it," Justice said and got up.

Abid nodded, staring at the tumbler.

"Abid. If there's anything else... you *have* to tell me."

Abid nodded slowly.

"Well, good day."

"This isn't right. Taking the things men hold dear and ripping through them for a nation's vice."

"Don't worry about that," Justice said, though he was sure Abid was rambling because he was scared of being caught. After all, wasn't it settled that the things any men hold dear don't matter when it comes to nations? To think otherwise was to undermine his own reasons for doing his job.

Outside, two black SUVs pulled up. Men in black suits and black glasses nodded at Justice as they ran by. The men lined up and broke down the door, even though it was unlocked. Justice stepped into his car and heard a gunshot. Did they kill him? He ran back into the house. On the sofa where Justice left Abid, the men were gathered around Abid's body. A hole in the back of his head.

"Did you shoot him?" Justice yelled.

"He did it himself," one of the men said.

"Dammit," Justice said and typed up a quick report, taking a photo of the man.

On the helicopter back to the City, Drail called.

"Looks like you're getting closer."

"How do you know?" Justice asked.

"Why else would he have shot himself?"

Justice didn't know if that logic worked, but he stayed quiet. "And how's Ben doing?"

"He's pissing himself," Drail said with a laugh. "And that cousin of his."

With a tinge of regret, Justice reminded himself this was a job. And many more lives were at stake. "And what did they say?"

"Oh. Nothing. Your report was spot on."

Justice was hit with a mix of relief for being right and anger that this had to be done.

"Awww, you worried about them?" Drail asked in a mocking tone.

"No," Justice lied.

"Don't worry about them. They're not citizens, and we've got them on other crimes, so they'll be getting kicked out. They won't be an issue anymore."

Justice bit his tongue. "Fine."

"Oh, and we'll search about this French girl. Though I think it's a red herring."

"Fine."

"You angry, Justice? You worried about the kids?"

Justice didn't know to reply. If he admitted it...

"It doesn't bode well for you to get so weak-kneed. You need to man up."

"I'm fine," Justice said.

"Good. Keep at it. By the way. Next time take the suspect to the team and hand him over. We don't need another suicide."

"Got it."

"Damn brownies. Always giving up on us."

"I know." Justice tried to think of something to put his mistake in a better light. "I tapped their room."

"Oh, the devices? We really don't need those. We have access to all electronics these days... you know that?"

"Oh. Why do we have them?"

"To keep R&D busy," Drail said, annoyed.

Back in the City, Justice walked to Central Park. The trees were darkened by the sun's low rays. Pockets of warmth, gave out to the chilling wind that picked up by the second. Few people were braving the weather. Justice liked that. In this silence, rare on the island, he could think.

For some reason Abid's dead body was lingering in the recesses of his mind. What else could he have done? And wasn't it Abid's fault for dying? No, that wasn't it. Justice had seen plenty of deaths, dead bodies, and had never given them much thought. The painting, figured back in his memories. The one on Abid's wall. What had been so great about it? Blood. Abid's last act had sprayed blood on that beautiful work of art.

Justice's phone rang again. He checked it. It was Drail. Justice picked it up after a few rings.

"You still in country?"

"I was waiting to see if Sasha had anything on that French girl."

"What did I tell you? It's a game; Abid was trying to play on you. He probably couldn't handle the guilt. That's why he blew his brains out."

"You sure?" Justice asked. It didn't sound all that plausible.

"Of course. It's what I'm sending up for higher. That's how you get the big bucks, Justice. You have to learn the ropes and how to think outside of the box."

"But…" Justice thought better of what he wanted to say. This *was* probably why he wasn't promoted yet. He needed to think like this. "Okay."

"You were going to say something?" asked Drail.

"I said okay."

"Good. I need you up here. You can't be waiting for anything, Justice. You have to be proactive."

"All right. I'll get on it."

"Well there's something for you."

"Send it."

"No, you have to come in. Besides the shrink wants to see you."

"In the middle of a mission?" Justice asked, surprised. The shrink was the agency's therapist. Whenever something extreme happened, he was there to make sure an agent or operator didn't snap. But he was usually there only for follow-up after a mission.

"That's right. New protocol. Agents have been offing themselves at a remarkable rate recently. So new regulations from Washington is that the shrink checks up on you whenever something bad happens."

Justice sighed. "I thought that was soldiers dying."

"That's a different wing, Justice. We're agents. We're worth more. Soldiers are a dime a dozen."

"All right, I'll be there in a few."

He hung up before he had to hear anything more from Drail. The dim sunlight peered from behind the tops of skyscrapers. To the south a new building arose, hard, skinny, and gleaming. Justice followed it through the winding paths of the sidewalk he was on. A few fully covered runners sprinted by him, legs shaped by pants. He could smell pine trees, dog shit. Abid's painting came back to him, full blast. Why did the man kill himself? Surely there wasn't something he wasn't telling Justice?

Ali pushed his ear against the wall. He could hear the American talking to the young man.

"Come on now. I know you want to help us. You've a sister in France, don't you? She wants to go to college in America, doesn't she? Then help me help you. Tell me where they are."

Ali could understand English a little, though not at the rate this American was talking. Luckily, the translator's Arabic was impeccable and he could easily understand that.

"I-I will," the young man said.

Ali knew who the young man was, and it hurt him to hear that he was willing to help the Americans. The pressure in his skull rose. What to do with this man? A flush went off somewhere in the hotel, and the pipe above Ali's head dripped a brown water that stunk of fecal matter. Ali wiped his head and drew deep breaths through his mouth. He had to stay quiet here in this crawlspace that the Americans apparently didn't know about.

"Don't toy with me, Yasar. You don't want to see me angry."

"I'm not."

"Then give me something. Who's the head?"

"Ali."

Something gripped Ali's heart. He'd recruited Yasar only a few weeks ago. The young man was, of the whole lot, the most promising. He was bright and picked things up easily. He was too smart to be a soldier and Ali had reserved a place for him by his side. He'd treated him with nothing but kindness, so what made him come here to the Americans and turn him, Ali, over? It was weak people like him who were betraying the movement.

"More, Yasar," the American said.

"He's from here," Yasar said. There was a tension in his voice.

"What about his training?"

"In Iraq. He learned there."

"With who?"

"He never says."

"And now?"

"He says no one."

"Don't lie to me, Yasar. I know he's Al Qaeda."

"No. Yes."

A slap. "Which one is it?"

Ali held his breath; the young man was going to spill all the secrets out. More water dripped on him. Now he could smell urine.

"He officially works for them. But he says he's only using them for money."

"So he's a whore?"

The young man didn't say anything. Ali felt sorry for him, and the thought crossed his mind that this young man was being suckered into this. Perhaps the security forces had a family member in one of those prisons. Perhaps they were blackmailing him. But still, it didn't excuse this complete capitulation. And in the end, Ali knew it was his neck on the line, *his* room that would get a missile screaming through it.

There were some murmurs.

"All right, I want you to go back, and I want you to keep your ears open. Got it?"

"Y-Yes."

"And I will call you when I want to see your filthy stinking self again. You will only call us when an attack is about to go down, all right?"

"Okay."

"You did well," the American said, his voice softer now. "And just keep your wits about you and everything will be all right. Your sister will be proud of you, especially when she learns that you helped her get into America—"

"Don't tell her," the young man said.

The American laughed. "I won't. As long as you do everything that's needed here."

More murmurs and the door creaked open. Ali listened as everyone shuffled out. He waited a few more minutes after that before he slid sideways out of the crawlspace. He climbed down a ladder and found himself in a closet. He closed the trapdoor he had just stepped out of and pushed the closet door open. There was no one in the hallway. He walked out of the hotel, through the back entrance where the cleaners were sitting around and smoking cigarettes and left without acknowledging anyone. It was sunny outside, but surprisingly there wasn't any dust in the air. The warm air compounded with the swirling feeling in his chest and his skin went dark, and he felt like he was burning up. He stepped into the back of the car. Two men were in front.

"Do we get him now?" the man driving asked.

"No, wait," Ali said. His body was calming down, and he wanted to hear something from Yasar about why he did this.

"Did either of you know him?"

The two men up front, twins with the same lazy eye problem, shook their heads vigorously.

"I never trusted him," said the driver. "He always seemed too uptight for his own good. Like he was never one of us."

Ali could sense the glee in his voice and he didn't want to see him gloat. But he needed these men.

"Move up a block and let's see what he does," Ali said.

They moved and waited, Ali feeling like he was on the verge of vomiting. He'd never had to deal with a mole before, but with the drones he had to be more vicious. He wondered who the mole could have been with regard to that drone attack. Perhaps the mole was killed in it.

"There," the driver said.

Yasar walked out of the hotel alone. He didn't seem to be concerned. He was a tall young man, with a huge Adam's apple and a crooked back, and he sauntered down the street away from them. Ali drew deep breaths. He couldn't appear weak in front of his men. When he fought off a wave of nausea, he pinched his skin and wiped the sweat off his forehead.

"Pull up behind him. No one mention a thing about what we know. Do you understand?" Ali said, as forcefully as he could manage. "And act happy," he said. The twins seemed to be brooding.

"Yessir," they said.

The car slowed down behind Yasar and Ali jumped out.

"Yasar?" he said.

Yasar spun around fast, his face drained of color.

"Ali?" he said. It was spoken so softly that Ali wasn't certain what was said until a few seconds later.

Ali did not like the guilt on the man's face. He walked up to the man and embraced him. Yasar smelled like sweat. Sweat tinged with fear. For some reason that calmed Ali down. He reminded himself about the drones. About how this man was about to kill him.

"So what are you doing here? Come on, we were driving from a meeting. Let's drive you back to the safe house," said Ali.

Yasar stared at the yellow rusted car belching black smoke with the twins inside.

"N-No. I'll walk. I have to meet some friends."

"Oh, who?"

"F-friends from my neighborhood."

"No, come have lunch with us first," Ali said. He took Yasar's hand and led him back to the car. Yasar slid in. Ali slid in after him.

"Hi Yasar," the twins said, beaming.

"Hi," Yasar said. He was sweating profusely now, and his breathing picked up.

Ali didn't want to torture him. "We were talking about the market and which stalls have the best goats to buy," Ali said.

The twins didn't miss a beat: "Yes, yes," they chimed in. "You know the stalls there, Yasar? We're going to have a feast."

"Really?" Yasar asked, his voice cracking. "When?"

"Next week," Ali said. His nervousness had evaporated, and he no longer felt sorry for Yasar. "What days work for you?"

"You know I am ready whenever," Yasar said. He too was relaxing; his breathing was now normal.

Ali now saw treachery in everything the young man was doing. And this infuriated him.

"Of course," Ali said. He could feel his voice growling. "And what were you doing in that part of town?"

"Nothing," Yasar said. He held Ali's stare. "Why?"

"No, it's not a part of town I expected *you* in."

They were pulling into their first safe house, the one Ali slept in the first night. They now had five houses all across the city. The point was to never establish a headquarters and to keep moving, so that a drone strike would never hit them all. Ali had recruited fifty men in the past few weeks. And with the raging war in the countryside and lack of jobs, it was too easy to find young men willing to do his bidding. There were levels, of course, and he would have to explain that to the two Saladins who would be here in a week.

They walked inside the safe house. It was empty, though cleaner now.

Ali wasn't certain if Yasar knew he was in trouble. His face appeared cheerful, and he cracked a few jokes.

Ali, who now carried a handgun, check to make sure that it was in his pant's pocket.

"Where are you going?" Ali asked, as Yasar veered away from them.

"Why are you acting like this?" Yasar asked.

Ali let out some air. He pointed to a room. "Come," he said.

Yasar looked at the twins who were grinning.

"What is it?" Yasar asked, his face draining of color again.

Ali didn't like it when Yasar was scared. It made his job that much harder.

"Tell me what you did today, and don't leave out anything."

Yasar gulped. "I went to the market and stared at the foods. I knew I couldn't afford anything. Then I met an old friend. I talked with him. And that's when I saw you."

"What foods?" Ali asked.

"They were selling rice. It was mostly rotten, but it was cheap."

"And the friend?"

"He was… a friend from school," said Yasar.

"He's from Yemen?"

Yasar stared at Ali. His face looked like it was ready to crumble.

"Come," Ali said. There was a feeling like a hundred knives in his chest. He didn't want to do this, and he didn't want to see the twins gloating.

Yasar walked into the room. It was an empty room, with dirt in the corners, where the new recruits hadn't bothered to clean. When Ali first saw Yasar, he was sure he saw a leader because Yasar had been such a fastidious cleaner.

Ali pulled out his handgun. He could feel his hands trembling. Yasar was shaking too, except more pronounced.

"Ali," Yasar whispered and turned around. He was crying. "Ali."

Ali aimed for his head and pulled the trigger. Yasar collapsed and Ali walked out of the room. He stared at the twins who also appeared to be in shock. "Clean it up," Ali said to them.

He tucked his handgun in his pants and walked outside. He tried to control the spinning of his head, but failed. He looked to make certain no one was around and he vomited on the side of the house. A stray dog came by, wagging its bony brown behind. It licked the vomit.

Ali leaned up against the side of the building, trying to ground himself. He couldn't believe that such a promising young man would be so willing to help those American neo-colonialists.

He wondered how Yasar's sister was doing in France. Then he wondered how he was going to be able to put together a good enough team to do the high value hits that he needed. Most of his other men were like the twins. What was he going to do with that? If the Saladins had it their way, they would strap each one to a bomb vest and have them walk in a different direction. This lack of imagination was something Ali had come to hate.

Just as he was trying to put together his thoughts, a motorcade with three cars drove up the street. Ali knew who it was and walked in the house. The twins were staring at Yasar's body.

"What are you waiting for?" Ali said, making sure that he didn't stare at the body. "Clean it up. We have guests. I'll be upstairs."

He walked before they could ask the questions that appeared to be on the tip of their tongues. At the top he sucked in as much air as he could. He sat on the ground and placed his head between his knees. He didn't want the Saladins to see him so weak.

He heard the commotion downstairs. Then the slow trudging of footsteps up the stairs. He reminded himself about the drones, how Yasar would have only helped to rain down misery like what had happened to Laith's family. He reminded himself to head out and see

Laith. It would be good, and he could see the teacher as well.

"Ali!" Saladin of Iraq said, his arms outstretched as he embraced Ali.

"Saladin of Iraq," Ali said and touched the man's cheek. He nodded at the bodyguard from before. There was a contingent behind with at least five men he hadn't seen before. Ali nodded at them all.

"*I'm* Saladin," said Saladin of Iraq.

Ali nodded. "Of Iraq," he said, though the look on the leader's face was somewhat angry.

"No. I'm the only Saladin," he said.

Ali, not really caring what he was named and figuring that the other man must be gone for this trip, shrugged. "Saladin of Afghanistan is not here?"

"He's no more," Saladin said. "He was hit by a drone." He shook his head mournfully. "These drones are going too far."

Ali looked up to the sky. "They're everywhere. They hit a house outside the city a few days ago."

"Ours?"

"No," Ali said.

"Thanks to Allah for that."

It's what every one of his new recruits had said as well. And though Ali was no fool, and understood that such tragedies were good public relations and recruiting tools, he didn't like to feel good when innocent people suffered.

"Two families, three generations each, were killed. There's no need to thank Allah."

"Oh," Saladin said and wagged a finger in Ali's face. "We cannot question how Allah chooses to work."

"That we cannot," Ali said, realizing that he really didn't like these meetings. "And I suppose we cannot question him when he chose to take the other Saladin."

Saladin's face darkened. "Surely you're going too far. He was killed by Americans."

Ali, not sure what Saladin was saying decided to change the subject. "Where did he die?"

"Near the border. Where they all die."

"Well, we shall try to avenge him."

"Oh yes," Saladin said and clapped him on the back. "So I see you're still the hard worker."

Ali didn't believe that, but he had to say something. "I work for Allah."

"Of course. I saw the man downstairs. He was an informant for the Americans?"

"Yasar? He was."

"Weak man," Saladin said.

"No," Ali said, despite himself. "He wasn't. That's what made it so hard."

Saladin, his eyes bordering on dry stared into Ali's eyes. "You liked him?"

"He was smart," Ali said. He was surprised, and pleased, that his body wasn't reacting in a negative way to the thought of Yasar.

Saladin leaned in, his hand landing on Ali's shoulder. His breath smelled like cloves and cigarettes.

"You're really a tough one, Ali," Saladin said.

Ali, not really feeling tough, didn't answer and instead stared into Saladin's lizard eyes.

"But, as tough as you are, you shouldn't have killed that young man." Saladin turned and looked at his entourage and with a jerk of his head, they left.

"What would you have done? Let a traitor live?" Ali said. His voice was close to trembling.

"No, and yes. Perhaps for the first one it's good to send a message out that you're not willing to brook any dissent. But in the future you would be wise to keep him."

"And what?"

"Many things can be done. You can keep him at a distance, where he won't know your whereabouts and just serves as a vessel for misinformation. Or you could have used him to find out things about the Americans. This way, you would have known the spy in your midst. Now, we have to assume that the Americans have, or will have someone else. And it won't be so easy to find out, will it? And with all the drones killing us. It's good to know where the Americans get their information, isn't it?"

Ali could feel his face burning with embarrassment. For as little as he thought of Saladin, the man was right. He wondered why *he* hadn't thought of that on his own.

"Your words have wisdom," he said.

"Thank you," Saladin said and grinned. "Though you shouldn't be so hard on yourself. Your men will respect you and be your dogs now that you've done this. Trust me. It does wonders for your name."

Ali pictured the words that the twins had and the look on their faces and he didn't like it.

"And you were right about the cell phones. The story is that he got a call from some relative in America, and the next thing a drone hit him," Saladin said.

"Allah remains," said Ali.

"Allah remains," Saladin said. "But don't mock the deaths of our brothers."

"I won't," Ali said, feeling bad. "And I'll save the next rat."

Saladin laughed. "You have a horrible sense of humor, Ali. I like it."

Ali, not aware that he had made a joke, smiled.

"And I have great news."

"What's that?"

"The great Dr. Noklar has escaped. And we know where he is."

Ali's heart stopped. "This is certain?"

"Of course. Our intelligence is the best in the world."

Ali couldn't tell if Saladin was joking around, but he decided to take it at face value. "So where is he?"

"We're not sure. No one is. Even the ISI is worried. He just disappeared. It could be that the Israelis kidnapped him and buried him deep somewhere. They couldn't stand the idea of a scientist who was Muslim," Saladin said and snapped his fingers.

Ali felt confused. "Perhaps he listened to my emails."

"Oh yes, the unauthorized emails," Saladin said, peering at Ali with one eye half closed.

"A regional leader can't speak to a great Muslim with words from his heart?" Ali said, offended.

"I'm joking. You must relax. If he is listening to your message than we must act quickly. We may never get a chance like this again."

"We must. But then we should also be careful."

"We've sent him another email. Using yours, of course."

"Mine?" Ali said. He didn't like this.

"Of course, don't worry, we know what we're doing."

"But you didn't even want me to email him."

"Well, what's done is done," Saladin said, wagging his finger in Ali's face again. "We'll let that be."

Ali, seriously wondering if Saladin was crazy sighed. "What did you tell him?"

"It's top secret. You can't know," Saladin said.

"But—"

"We're sending him somewhere where he can be of the most use to us."

Ali jerked his head as a jet flew overhead. He could smell car fumes, for some reason. He realized that he needed to write out what it is he heard the moments before the drone strike. He was getting too nervous, even with Yasar dead.

"One must be careful," Saladin said, squinting up.

"One must," said Ali. "The doctor. I will still write to him."

Saladin stared at him. "Very well. Don't interfere," he said. "We are working on this very hard."

"I won't," Ali said. Lost in thought, he walked to the cages of pigeons. He could hear Saladin shuffling next to him. He liked it better when Saladin was quiet, but he reminded himself that the man was his boss, and the only reason they had money here.

"Did I ever ask you about to start writing for our magazine?" Saladin said.

"Inspire?" Ali asked. He was thinking about how secure pigeons were.

"Yes. I think your writing could really help the magazine. It's been suffering under a conservative editor lately."

"You want me to be the editor?" Ali asked. "I don't have time—"

"No. We want you to write. We can influence the editor to get you a column, but it will help."

Ali nodded. He wanted this conversation to be over. He couldn't imagine Saladin coming over just for this.

Another jet flew overhead.

"Another one," Saladin said and chuckled.

Ali could feel his stomach rumble and his head tighten. He wasn't sure if it was from the man next to him, or the possibility of another drone.

"You're a quiet one," Saladin said. "You have a writer's demeanor."

"Thank you," Ali said. He realized that he didn't like it that Saladin had co-opted his letters to the doctor. But, the last time he checked, the doctor hadn't replied.

The pigeons fluttered in their cages. One dropped feces next to Saladin. The big man shook the cage.

"Don't frighten them," Ali said. "They're sensitive creatures."

Saladin wiped sweat off his brow. "And what are the new recruits looking like? The ones that you haven't shot?"

Ali, not liking the joke, felt sick. "We have over a hundred recruits."

"All local?"

"Most. We have a few men from USA and UK."

"Oh," said Saladin.

Ali, sensing some disappointment in his boss' voice pushed a finger into the pigeon cage.

"What's wrong with those men?" he asked.

"Oh, nothing," Saladin said. "I've never trusted them entirely, though they're good people to get money from."

"And why?" Ali asked. "They've always fought well. I haven't tested the ones here, but in Iraq, where I fought, they were fine."

"I know, I know. They're our Muslim brothers. But something about them turns me off. Especially the ones who were born there. I feel like they're always trying to make up for being born in non-Muslim lands."

"Awlawi was born there."

Saladin didn't say anything. Ali knew the sensitive topic it was. Awlawi wasn't officially working for Al Qaeda. His death had been a first in the drone wars.

"Where are these men?" Saladin asked after more moments of uncomfortable silence.

"Spread out. It's best not to keep them here. Some are training in the mountains. Some are here helping us gather information."

"Any great ones?"

Ali wavered his head to indicate that the men weren't that good.

"The only good one you shot," Saladin said.

"That's the case so far."

Saladin shook his head. "I'm not going to tell you how to get your job done, but these men might be good for only one thing. And that's suicide bombing. Think about it was our cheaper version of drones."

"I told you how I feel," Ali said, clenching his jaw to expend some anger. "I want to go after the head of the snake. Enough of hitting the low men." Ali could see that the man's face was not convinced. "You don't believe me."

"I don't. These men. The best thing you can do for them is send them on to the next life. You can try to train them, but they won't be able to do these high-level missions you're so fond of."

"I will train them."

"For how long? And how long before a drone strike takes out your training camp? Then what? You start all over again? This way you'll never be able to finish any attack."

Ali, from the force in Saladin's voice, could tell that the man wanted attacks, and he wanted them now. This was the real reason he was here.

Ali, now regretting that he hadn't yet written out his reasons so that he wasn't floundering here, scurried to think of a reason.

"You do have a point to all this? You're not wasting money, are you?" Saladin said. "I hope the drone attack and seeing that family burn didn't spoil your appetite for Jihad, did it?"

"It didn't," Ali said. "But you remember Iraq, right? You know how much good it did to just hit the restaurants and the innocents, right?" He knew he was on thin ice here, telling a major leader of Al Qaeda that their strategy was all wrong, but he knew no other way.

"You mean when we hit Zionist collaborators?"

Ali sucked in air. Was convincing this man possible? "No. When we hit marketplaces for no reasons."

"No reasons? Those people were helping the Americans in a Muslim land. What could we do?"

Ali nodded, making sure he didn't cross a line. Even regional commanders were shot and dumped if they thought too much.

"I mean," Ali said. "That it didn't help."

"How can you say that?"

"The Americans," Ali said. "Were not weakened by that, and neither were the Shiites."

"We never fought against our Shiite brothers. Only the collaborators," Saladin said raising a finger in the air.

Ali, who knew the ground truth and the official truth wanted to slap Saladin. "I mean that the Sunnis there turned against us. And…" He didn't say what he wanted to say: "With good reason."

"The Americans left because of us. We made them bleed," Saladin said.

Ali nodded. He would not be able to get through this man's thick skull. Especially if he didn't want to accept the facts of the ground. "We could have done it quicker if we'd struck the head of the snake."

Saladin poked his finger through the cage wire and shook the cage again. The pigeons fluttered and their feathers fell to the ground.

"Well, just remember that you have the cheap bombs in front of you. And we pay for results only."

"I know," Ali said. He was now thinking of how to get rid of this man as quickly as possible. He wondered if a drone strike wouldn't be so bad.

The warm sun heated Nasar's face. They were in the city of Muscat, Oman. A city perched amongst crumpled brown mountains that seemed to be pushing it into the sparkling sea. The buildings all seemed well kept and old. There was a strong sun out today and a few tourists amongst the traditionally dressed locals.

Sipping on chai, Nasar wondered what was taking Karim and Abdullah so long. They were supposed to be finding a man to drive them across the Arabian peninsula. The boatman who brought them here and dumped them on the docks had sailed away without so much as a word.

"Nasar," Karim yelled from across the street. The locals eyed them with disdain. Though Oman wasn't the same country as the rich Gulf States to the north, it still had its indentured servants from South Asia. Thus people like Abdullah and Karim were looked upon with disdain.

Nasar waved back, though he didn't like being stared at like this.

Karim sat next to him. "We found a driver."

"Good," said Nasar. He really just wanted to sleep. Seeing Karim and Abdullah so full of energy at this stage in their journey made him hate youth *and* wish he was there again.

"Abdullah, you will wait at the steps of that fort for the man." Karim pointed up to the fort. It stood on top of a hill, its edges crumbling.

Abdullah looked at each of them and with a sneer on his face, trotted off.

Nasar could see Karim staring down some of the locals. He wondered how Karim had managed to stay out of trouble in Iran. It didn't seem in his composition. But something else was bothering Nasar. These deals Karim was making were being done very quickly.

"How did you know Bashir again?" Nasar asked.

"Why?"

"You can't answer?"

"We smuggle drugs across the border. Bashir and his... tribe, they help to sell them in Iran."

"And so this was a matter of work?"

"What's so bad about that?"

The smell of a roasted sewer hit Nasar and he held his breath. This place was odd, in that it looked cleaner than Karachi, but was painted with singular smells that were much worse than anything he'd smelled in Pakistan. His mind drifted back to Bashir and what he'd said that night about nuclear power. How righteous he'd sounded, and now it came to light that he was no more than a drug dealer.

"All his braying about the police and the Iranians bothering him… of course they did," said Nasar.

Karim turned to eye Nasar. His lips formed a snarl. "And you're so pure? You have never been forced to make such choices? You think people like Bashir and me want this life?"

Nasar didn't want to back down. "There are many honorable choices in life. And don't you mock me for what I've done. Surely I should be afforded a little respect."

They were interrupted by a call to prayer cackling over the loud speaker. It was only one loudspeaker, which was odd. Nasar listened for a second, his thoughts on Bashir and the talk on the beach.

"And doesn't Bashir deserve respect? Don't I? Where would you be without us? Bashir helped us with great risk to his life. Isn't that something?"

Nasar was stung by Karim's rebuke.

"Very well, and I thanked him, as I thank you," he said, hoping to end that argument. "But what is done by you two is against all decency."

"And your friends in the Army, they don't also do the horrible?"

"What do they do?"

Karim waved his hand, and rolled his eyes. "What don't they?"

"They keep you safe," said Nasar.

"You haven't been to the west, have you?"

Nasar thought for a second that Karim was talking about Europe, then remembered the Wild West. "Oh, I forgot." He wasn't certain what to say on that front. He didn't like, as everyone else in the country, the fact that America was being allowed to blow things up there with impunity. On the other hand, what was to be done with such unruly people? "What about it?" he said, regaining some of his bravado.

"They allow the Americans to do these things. You know this!"

"It's more complicated than that." He knew the elements that were fighting with each other there.

The call for prayer seemed to sparkle back to life before the loudspeaker cut out.

A long period of silence transpired between them. Nasar knew that he'd have to be sure to keep on Karim's good side. Why was he engaging in these horrid arguments anyways? He couldn't remember another time that he'd done so. All the people he knew agreed with him. Perhaps it was because they were so smart. Yes, he was going to have to stop arguing with people like Karim.

"I need the Internet," he said.

Karim scrunched his face up. "Why?"

"Email."

Karim shook his head. "You understand that many people in the world are looking for you right now, right?"

"I do," Nasar said and sighed. He wanted to get in contact with a few people. He stared at the road and watched as a couple of cars drove by. The passengers stared back.

"There is a way," Karim said.

"And how is that?"

"Tell me your email. I'll get someone in Pakistan to write back what it is."

"This is doable?" Nasar asked. "No one will find out?"

"This is how we talk to each other about shipments. There's a shared account. We type up messages in drafts and made up of codes. From there someone from an Internet cafe will check up and carry out the order."

"Really—"

"We do email, or sometimes twitter. Either way, it's fool proof so far."

Nasar handed over his account and password, and Karim disappeared.

As Nasar waited for his companions to return. He watched in dismay as a pair of boys kicked around a tattered soccer ball. They looked at him and one muttered something in Arabic, sticking out his hand as if to ask for something. Nasar shook his head, hit by a pang of guilt; he searched through his pocket before remembering that he didn't have any of the local currency. The boys stared at him and muttered angrily before running away with their ball. Nasar felt better, for some reason, and he listened to the sound of the road as the cars drove by. For a capital, this was very calm.

A few minutes later Karim returned, grinning. He handed a note to Nasar.

"This is your email."

"All ready?" Nasar asked. He expected this method to take several hours, if not days.

"Of course. It only takes a few minutes. There's someone constantly checking these things."

Nasar read the message. It was in the pre-approved code. As he read the message, his hands started to tremble.

"Is everything all right?" Karim asked.

Nasar couldn't speak. A sickness was growing inside him. "Can you get a message back?"

"Of course," Karim said. "What did that one say?"

Nasar didn't answer. He started to write down the message that needed to go out. It took half an hour. He double checked the code, then handed it to Karim.

Karim stared at what seemed to be gibberish. "You won't tell me what this is?" Karim's face darkened, then looked hurt.

"I'm sorry," said Nasar. "You of all people must know that this is something sensitive… must be kept to as few people as possible."

Karim nodded his head, smiling. "I know. I know. Things that are important must always be kept secret. In Pakistan, and Afghanistan, we were told to do crazy things. Like attack a school. Or kill families. But we could never know why. This is what makes us good soldiers," Karim said and thumped his chest. "I am a good soldier."

"Of course," Nasar said. When the young man was gone, Nasar started to wonder if it was true that the way the world was required soldiers to be quiet and do as they were told. If that had happened in Bangladesh, wouldn't have Pakistan never lost that part of their nation?

And when he'd run labs, wasn't it best, with a doctoral student, to have the ones that didn't ask questions? He decided that it was best, and that Karim was on the right track.

Karim came back a few minutes later, breathing hard, and sweat beads on his forehead.

"Let's go," said Karim.

They walked past the stores on the main street, and past a littered dirt lot behind that. Soon they were walking through winding small streets between cubed mud huts. Kids darted in and out and didn't seem to pay them any attention. It smelled like baked rotten food here, and Nasar had to hold his breath.

Karim seemed to notice this. "This is how the common people live, doctor," he said.

Nasar didn't reply. He was certain if these people tried, they could do better.

They moved above it all, on the base of a hill, and the footsteps of a fort. There Abdullah awaited them. There was a large man, with one eye, standing next to Abdullah. With a turn of his head, he indicated that they should follow him. They walked to a small road with an SUV waiting for them. The large man climbed into the driver's seat.

"Do you know him?" Nasar asked.

"No," said Karim. "But people I know know people he knows."

"Where is he taking us?"

"Driving us to the Red Sea," said Karim, as if that was obvious.

Nasar got in the back with Abdullah. The boy fell asleep as soon as the car picked up speed on the highway. The sleep was infectious, and as the landscape turned into cragged desert, Nasar too fell asleep.

He wasn't sure how long he was asleep, but when he woke up, He startled back when he saw the bottom of a ravine outside his window. For a second he was sure they were about to fall, but the car lurched away from the edge.

"Where are we?" he asked.

"We're near in Yemen," Karim said with a smile.

It was still daytime.

"Is that possible?" Nasar asked. How could they have travelled so far? At the rate they were making it past these switchbacks, there was no way that they would be able to have travelled anywhere. "I don't believe you," Nasar said.

Karim laughed. "Do you know how long you were asleep for?"

Nasar decided that he didn't have to doubt everything. He did completely well rested. He looked over at Abdullah, who was still asleep. "Then how come he's asleep?"

"He's a kid, what do you think?"

Something shook the air.

"What was that?" Nasar asked. What ever it was had moved the very air inside his lungs.

"Artillery, Nasar," Karim said, with a smile. "You know what's happening in Yemen?"

The large man grunted.

"See?" said Karim. "It's a war."

"And we're driving through it?" Nasar said. He was starting to sweat because he knew about the American drones that hovered around this place.

"Of course," said Karim, and he turned around and winked. "We'll be safe. Besides, there are no other routes. The sea is filled with pirates. At least here we have a chance. They *usually* don't hit innocent cars."

But what if they found out about him? Nasar thought. This wasn't going to turn out well. "I need to piss," he said.

The large man grunted.

Nasar wasn't sure if that meant that he was going to pull over. Five minutes later, Nasar assumed no, and he started to look for bottles in which he could piss.

The truck lurched to a stop. The large man grunted and stepped out.

They were on the top of a small hill. All around were waves of brown mountains. Nasar stepped to the side of the truck, the ravine before him howled with wind, and he pissed. When he was finished, he watched as Abdullah ran up a small mound of rocks.

Karim came over.

"Does that man talk?" Nasar asked, pointing to the large man who was now checking the engine. On top of the SUV were several jugs of gasoline that Nasar hadn't noticed. So he *had* been asleep for a long time.

"Why would you want him to?"

Nasar grinned. Sometimes, just when he thought Karim was stupid, the young man managed to redeem himself. "I suppose not. So we have a boat in the Red Sea?"

"We'll see," said Karim and patted the doctor on his back.

Just then a drone cut through the sky. As it grew louder, the two men looked at each other. The large man slammed the hood shut and Nasar could see his eyes widen.

A speck in the sky appeared, and the sound now vibrated inside Nasar's head.

"What..." Nasar said.

Karim shook his head. The large man came over to them and placed his finger on his lips. Nasar wondered how being quiet was going to help. His heart was pounding very fast, and he felt weak.

The large man gurgled to Karim.

"He says there's no place to hide, so we need to act normal."

Nasar nodded his head. The jet or drone or whatever it was, was so far away it was hard to think that it was a threat.

And like that, his heart stopped. Abdullah was on top of the mound pointing a stick at the plane.

"What's he doing?" Nasar said.

"Oh, it's just a stick," said Karim.

But the large man was shaking his head.

Nasar didn't get to think anymore. A screeching sound filled the air, and his insides churned. And a flash burned his skin. The ground started to move. Everything went black. All Nasar could hear was a loud air splitting sound. And his own screams.

Ali watched as the man stepped into a truck. He jotted down the time. When the man had driven away from the embassy, Ali walked away. There would be others to write down more information on the man's route. The good news was that *this* man didn't appear to change his route. That would make hitting him that much easier.

Ali made his way down a narrow alley. Everything seemed sinister today. He'd woken up this morning, sweating, a nightmare slipping out of his hands. What was going on with him? None of the men higher than him, Saladin especially, was willing to listen to him. They thought his plan to attack higher targets was a waste of time. No matter how much he yelled this is what they thought. And the drones were getting worse. Every time Ali heard a jet engine, he would flinch. He was certain that his men saw this and snickered behind his back. But he had no time for that. He wanted to go and see Laith, and see what he was up to. His mind relaxed as he neared the school. He would still have to make his case to Saladin. After all, the man had been in Iraq. He had to have seen the logic in Ali's thinking. Of course, none of this was helping Ali's confidence. In the back of his mind gnawed the thought that perhaps he'd been through too much war. That perhaps there was more to life than the fight he was fighting. That perhaps the last drone attack was too much and he was finally broken. How else was it that everyone thought his ideas to be too far out?

He walked past a group of old women sitting around in an alley, fanning themselves, flies darting between them. Ali stopped for a second when it seemed that they were talking to a Westerner. But when the Westerner smiled at him, he decided to let it be. For some reason he could smell sandalwood soap here. That was funny, there were no clothes hanging anywhere. His mind returned to the men in his organization whom he was trying to twist to see his view on the war they were fighting. Why was it that people would always rather just pick a group and its views rather than work for new views? That was the problem in Iraq, and now that he knew *how* it was a problem, he *had* to spread his knowledge.

He walked past the school's gateman with a nod. The gateman grinned at him and waved. Ali felt his heart beat faster. The kids were out enjoying lunch. He was going to get to talk to Nadia on his own. He hadn't seen her in some time. He walked through the dusty hallways. It seemed more run down than he last remembered it. Then the strong smell of feces knocked him out of his ecstatic state. He saw a dog, back curved up, in a corner. As it strained, brown logs crept out and stuck to the floor.

"Get out, you!" Ali yelled and moved to kick the dog. The dog leapt out of the way and jumped through a bar less window in the wall, a piece of feces hanging out its anus.

Ali stared at the shit in the corner. Flies were buzzing around it.

"Leave it alone."

Ali looked up and saw Nadia. He opened his mouth to say something, but nothing came out. He smiled. He could smell her, though the odor of feces was still strong, and he walked towards her, almost tripping. When he was next to her, his mind was a blank slate, and he couldn't think of what to say. His feet stopped moving.

"Come in," she said and pointed at her empty room.

Ali's mind moved to doing lustful things, and he scolded himself as he entered the room. He had to be nice.

"So what brings you here?" she said, closing the door behind her.

He remembered that he had brought her a gift, he reached into his pocket and pulled out the plastic bag and as he handed it to her, he realized that it was soft. He pulled it back and stared at it. The chocolate had melted. How stupid could he have been?

"I…"

She moved forward and took it out of his hand. "For me?"

"That's right," he said. "I'm sorry. It's melted," he said.

"That's all right," she said and pulled out the chocolate bar. "Let's break bread." She smiled at him. Ali didn't know how, but somehow this woman made him of two minds: like he couldn't breathe, excited to the core, and yet calm to death at the same time. She tore a half-melted piece off. She ate it, licking her fingers. She handed him a piece. He took it, savoring the touch of her finger, and ate the sweet chocolate.

"Thank you," she said. She sat down on her chair. Dust flew and the chair creaked loudly. Ali wished that he could help her get a new chair, but didn't know how.

"You're welcome," he said. He felt giddy. Like this was the best dream possible. He wondered how he would be able to get away from this life and live with her.

"So what did you come here for, Ali?" she said. With a sweep of her hand, she offered him a seat to sit on. But he knew he was too flustered for that. But in a second he decided that a seat would help him conceal a new issue.

"I was wondering about Laith."

"Oh, Laith? He's doing wonderfully. Thank God. He holds not a single bad bone in his body. He just works and works. So bright."

Ali nodded. He was glad that the boy was returning to normal. Saladin had wanted to use him as a poster child of what the drones were doing. And though Ali wanted some sort of revenge for the boy, he also wanted the boy to live a normal life. He knew what would happen if Saladin got his claws in the boy. The boy would be turned. Saladin could talk almost anyone into strapping on a vest. And then what would Ali be able to hold on to?

"Has there been anyone else to see him?" asked Ali.

"No," she said.

Ali relaxed. "And he's doing well in school," he said.

She nodded her head. There was something sly about her look. Ali started to feel uncomfortable again.

Then silence enveloped them both and Ali knew that something was wrong.

Nasar came to. He looked over at the truck. It seemed fine. The large man was dusting himself off. Karim lay beside him. Nasar shook him.

"Karim?"

Karim groaned. "What is it?"

"You alive?"

"No. You?"

Nasar touched himself. There wasn't anything but dust on his body. He looked up to the sky and saw that there was no trace of the drone that had been there a moment ago. His fear was slowly replaced by awe. That had to be one of those American drones. It had been so far away that he'd barely seen it. And yet it had been able to see him clearly. The level of technological expertise that was needed to achieve this was nothing short of amazing. He wondered if Pakistan would ever be able to achieve that. That was the issue, wasn't it? That the colonial power that was Britain, and her derivative, America, were still more advanced than they were. Even India was moving ahead of his nation. Anger bubbled up, and Nasar's mind started to shift over to what could be done to start a program that would help with accuracies of weapons.

"Are you okay?" Karim asked. He was up, and with one hand he gripped Nasar's shoulder.

"I'm good," Nasar said, standing tall and stretching. His joints hurt a bit, and even his head, but overall he felt fine.

Such accurate weapons. Then his mind flashed the last moment he'd seen Abdullah.

"Abdullah," he said.

Karim jumped up. "Abdullah?" he yelled.

Both of them ran to the pile of rocks and boulders that Abdullah had been standing. All that remained was a crater.

The large man came over. He whispered something into Karim's ear. In a spiral route from the crater they started to look for signs of the boy. Not seeing any blood, Nasar held hope that the boy had managed to get away. Then he saw a shoe. The foot was still in it. He picked it up. The ankle was charred. Karim came over.

"I should have never taken him with us."

A tear rolled down the young man's face. Nasar was surprised that the tough man was shuddering. More tears rolled down his face, and Nasar moved to embrace him. As he felt Karim's hand on his back, Nasar wondered why it was that *he* wasn't crying. The thought that the boy who'd been so happy, was gone, drove needles through his heart. But Nasar wasn't sure if it was sadness, or if it was something else, for tears still didn't pour forth.

"It's not your fault," Nasar finally managed to say.

"Those damn Americans," Karim said, pulling away and wiping the tears from his eyes. "Damn them. He was just a child."

Nasar knew plenty of trigger happy, boastful men in the Pakistani Army, and he knew how men of war could be, so he kept quiet and just nodded.

The large man came over holding a leg and arm. With a jerk of his head, he walked away.

They followed him and came to half a head, sitting between two rocks. The boy's tongue hung out, a stew of brains and blood and flesh pooled beneath it all. Nasar had to look away to keep from vomiting.

"At least he died quickly," said Karim.

The large man was nodding.

"When the bomb hits right on you, you rip apart. When it doesn't, it just throws you," Karim said.

Nasar's intestines wound up. There wasn't anything that he'd done in life that he cared for anymore. Well, except for one more thing.

Karim and the large man started to dig a hole with their hands. Nasar got down on his knees and helped them.

The ground was hard and full of rocks. By the time they'd dug a deep enough hole, all their fingertips were bleeding. They placed the body parts in the hole and filled it up. They piled up rocks on top, since they had nothing else.

They stood silent for a long time. Nasar felt the tightness in Karim's body, and he wondered if the young man was going to be the same again. He wondered if *he* would be the same. He could hear an insect buzzing, and he imagined that something would sooner or later eat up Abdullah's body. Again he felt a sickness inside; this time it was for his life's work. He wondered why.

They walked back to the truck in silence. Surprisingly the truck started and the large man cracked the gearbox and they were off. Nasar wanted to say something to Karim, but the young man didn't look like he was in the mood to talk.

When the sun set, they slept on the side of the road. The whirring of insects, and the smell of rocks crept into Nasar's body, as his mind was ripped between making more accurate weapons and making peace, though he was certain both routes required a fastidious use of science.

Ali wondered if he'd any right to be here, interfering with this schoolteacher and her students. "Well," he said and stood up.

She seemed hurt by this. "What's wrong?" she asked.

"Nothing."

She looked down on her hands, then looked up.

His skin crawled. Perhaps she wasn't as nice as he'd thought. Her eyes stayed fixed on him.

"Is it true you're…" she said. "A fighter?"

"What?" he asked. His heart started to pound; his fists clenched.

She seemed to lose her patience. "Is it?"

His felt his cheeks warm.

"I am," he said, looking down at his hands.

She seemed angry. "So why are you coming here?"

He flinched. "To check on Laith," he said, his words came out quieter than he expected. Why was he being so meek? Perhaps he *was* a broken machine. The young him would never have backed down from something like this. She smiled and walked over to the window.

"Why?"

"I care for him," Ali said.

"And do you care enough not to come here again?"

"I…" He didn't expect that. His insides churned. "I'm not sure what you mean."

"You and I both know very well the reason why Laith's family is dead."

"It was the Americans," Ali said, growing furious.

"Yes, it was. And it was you too. Or someone like you." She was still staring out the window.

"What do you mean?" He wondered if she was an agent.

She turned and looked at him for a second before she looked back out the window. "I'm not faulting you. Not entirely. But it was the presence of fighters that killed Laith's family. And now, you, a fighter, are willing to walk here to a school full of innocent children. And for what? To put them all in danger? The Americans won't hesitate to kill everyone here."

His armor was up, but a sliver of what she was saying cut through him. He wasn't sure why. "So it's my fault what the Americans have done here?"

"No," she said, her voice still calm.

A dog barked outside. Ali could smell her perfume, barely overpowering the dust and cement of the school. And he stared at her, as everything else went blank. His anger dissipated. Her face seemed distraught, and her breathing shallow. Talking like this must have been hurting her. He bit his tongue.

"I'm saying, like it or not," she said and swatted a fly buzzing near her head, "your presence increases the likelihood of a missile coming through this window." She glanced over at him. "I want to see you again. But not here."

The dog in the distance stopped barking, and the children stopped yelling. His stomach churned and he felt foolish.

"I understand," he said.

"Iraq?" she asked.

"I was," he said.

"What—"

"Horrid," he said. He'd never spoken about Iraq like that before. In his line of work it was always a positive thing, and though his heart was never in it, he always tried to pump up his experience there. It was the ultimate trump card in most arguments.

"What did you learn there?" she asked.

He thought about his attempt to convince Saladin. But then he realized that he had never truly thought about his time there.

"Let's talk later," she said jolting him out of his train of thought.

He nodded slowly.

She gave him her address. "I live alone," she said, as if stating a fact.

"Your parents?"

She didn't answer and he felt foolish again.

"I'll see you soon," he said and walked out. Even though he was walking out on his own accord, and he knew that she was right. He walked through the gate, and wandered aimlessly around the city. No one recognized him, and no one seemed to want anything from him. He both liked and hated that.

In an otherwise abandoned alleyway, he noticed a man crumpled over in a heap. Ali walked up to him. The man didn't smell of alcohol, or of qat, or any other drug. In fact he wasn't even dirty.

"My friend. Are you all right?" Ali said and shook the man.

The man stirred. His rags, mostly blackened from smoke and dirt, emitted such a smoky stench when he sat up, that Ali's eyes watered.

"What?" the man said.

Ali noticed a heavy accent and peered closely at the old man's face. Though it was cracked with old wrinkles, and his face was almost black with dirt, as well as his hair, Ali could see a few strands of red hair, and red rather than brown skin. Ali had met two people with red hair when he was in Iraq. One was called 'The red' and was actually born in Iraq. Some people joked that somewhere down the line a Greek or a Brit had inserted themselves into his lineage. No one dared to say such a thing to his face, though. The Red was much too crazy to make fun off. He made his name in Western Iraq by putting out the best videos of head chopping, and would lend his services to whatever insurgency group wanted to improve their image.

The other red was actually an Irishman, who fled his country when he realized that he was a relic. Betrayed, he called it, by weaker souls. He was an expert in bomb making and was hit by an American missile.

Ali walked to a nearby young boy who was poking at a dead goat with a stick.

"Where can I get some water?" Ali asked.

The boy, shielding his eyes with his hand, looked up at Ali. "What for? Him?" he said and pointed at the man in the alleyway who was leaning over to one side with his penis out. He started to piss.

"Why?" Ali asked, annoyed that the boy was looking down on the man just because of his poverty.

"He's no good," said the boy and went back to the goat.

"You shouldn't play with the goat," said Ali. "It may have diseases."

The boy ignored him, and Ali lamented that even his own soldiers wouldn't listen to him when it came to some level of hygienic. "What has he done?" Ali said.

"The goat? Who knows? He was living one day, and dead the next.

One can never tell with the way life is here."

"I mean the man," Ali said, somewhat surprised that the boy suddenly sounded well spoken.

The boy stopped his poking to examine Ali. Ali felt uncomfortable under the boy's gaze. It was filled with wisdom. He now saw why his elders had always preferred him to be silent and to behave.

"Shouldn't you be in school?" Ali asked.

"Shouldn't you be at work?"

"Where did you learn to talk like that?" Ali said, wondering if he should pull the boy by his ears to see his parents.

"Who do you think taught me? The dust and the goat," said the boy.

"Do you have parents?" Ali asked.

The boy peered at him, a snarl developing on his lips. "Why would I be poking goats if I had parents?" he asked.

"What about relatives?" Ali asked. The old man in the alley started to cough. Ali was feeling very helpless, though he wasn't certain why. He could very easily walk away from all this.

The boy spit on the dirt and returned to poking the goat. A cloud of flies rose up and settled back away from the stick.

"Then tell me what the old man did," he said, his throat growing dry.

Once again the boy stared at him, pissed that he'd been interrupted from his goat poking. He pointed at Ali's face. "Did you get that scar in a drone attack?"

Ali shook his head.

The boy examined him some more. "You walk funny. You sure you weren't in a drone attack?"

"I was," Ali said. "But that's not why I have scars and a limp."

The boy seemed to like this, and his demeanor changed to that of a child. "So you were in Iraq? You speak a little funny. And you don't look like you're from the hills." His eyes widened slightly.

"Yes."

The boy nodded. "Did you kill anyone?"

"You shouldn't ask that," said Ali.

"How about any Americans?"

"Does it matter?"

"It doesn't. But it does."

"You should be in school," said Ali.

"And I should also have parents. But I don't." The boy's harsh demeanor cracked for a second. "The old man doesn't disturb anyone. But he's always pulling out his penis to pee. He never goes to a corner. There's a store there." He pointed. "And next to it is a pump for water."

Ali nodded and headed over to the store. He bought a small plastic cup from the owner and filled it up. Walking back, balancing a full cup of water made him feel stupid, but he knew he was doing something good. He wondered what the red headed man was doing here in Yemen.

When he returned, the man was gone. The boy, still poking at the goat, looked up. "He left. He always leaves."

Something sad lingered in the air after the boy said that. Ali stared at his half full cup of water. "Do you want water?"

The boy didn't reply. Ali drank down his cup. "You should be in school," he said. But the boy didn't pay him any attention. Ali felt even sillier than before. He walked away. When he looked back he saw that the boy had some how severed the goat's head and was now joined by two kids kicking the head back and forth. Ronaldo, one yelled, and the others jumped on him, kicking and punching until he took back his claim.

It was evening, and as the air buzzed with swallows and call for prayers, Ali found himself in another neighborhood he'd never seen before. As the sun settled on the horizon and the air changed its smell from baked dust and cement to thrown out soap water—from every family finishing the day's wash—Ali was tired. He sat down on a stoop, in a darkened alley where clothes on strings swayed in the evening wind. He remembered how Saladin had turned down his plan. Perhaps he should just ignore him?

"Ali?"

The voice cut through his thoughts and jumpstarted his heart. "Nadia?" he said as he stood up. "Hi?" He hadn't expected to see her here. Then, realizing that she was standing in an open doorway, he knew he was in front of her house. Had he walked here on purpose? He was certain that he'd been wandering aimlessly.

"I didn't think you'd come," she said.

He noticed a strand of hair breaking free of her veil. He stared, then reminded himself that this was rude.

"Come in," she said. Her smile blinded him and he looked down.

He stepped inside. It was a sparse living room with a burner in the corner, incense burning in all four corners, and several mats in the middle. The smell of incense would have been overbearing if he couldn't have smelled her through it all. There was a single dark doorway with a curtain hung over it.

"That's the bedroom... Laith," she said. "Come out."

Laith burst through the curtain. He squinted then yelped: "Ali!"

Ali had assumed that the young boy had moved on. But the greeting was welcome.

"Laith." Ali hugged the boy and rubbed his hair. "What have you been up to?"

"I scored twice," the boy said, his voice bubbling with energy. "Now, it's homework time." His voice fell flat.

"Well," said Ali, not sure what to say about the football. "It's important to study. We need you to help build this country, don't we?"

Laith shrugged.

Nadia clapped her hands. "Finish your work, then dinner will be ready," she said. She walked to the corner with bags of grains and beans that surrounded the boiling pot on the burner.

Ali was only then aware of the lentils and chili cooking. His stomach rumbled. He was supposed to do something with his men tonight, but he figured that could wait. "Do you need help?"

"No. Make yourself at home," she said. "Chai?"

He would've died for some good chai, but seeing that she was busy, decided against inconveniencing her. "I'm fine."

He sat down, the mat emitting fumes of trapped dust and farts. He tried not to watch her. It was a feat of great discipline, and as he examined the carpet, and the walls, he noticed that there were no prayers anywhere. He knew there could have been another explanation, but his heart sank. She was smart, and he liked that about her. But did that mean that she was another secularist?

He noticed a handle on the floor. His hand swopped over to the metal grooves, and he noticed the outlines of a trapdoor.

"That's where I keep the books," she said.

He looked over, but Nadia still had her back to him, stirring the pot. "You can open it," she said.

He lifted the door and peered in. There was barely enough light to make out the shelves of books on either side of a ladder. He saw several Qurans and felt much better.

"You can go down if you want," she said.

He leaned over, the dust still swirling in the trap door. A lot of the titles were in English, and though the Roman script was something he'd learned in Iraq, he hadn't used it in some time, and it hurt his brain to try and make sense of the combination of random sounds that ran past his eyes.

"Have you read all these?" he asked.

"Of course," she said. "They're my father's collection."

He'd forgotten if she'd mentioned her father before, so he just nodded. There was a book with "tales" written on the spine. He leaned in and pulled it out. Inside the book several glorious pictures of blonde and blue-eyed royalty shined through. He ran his finger over them before remembering that picture books were something that Saladin had banned. It'd started when too many potential terrorists were shirking their duties because they enjoyed reading, or looking at Western magazines with pictures of pretty women on them. Saladin had been furious, though Ali less so. He'd seen the effect of escaping for a foot soldier in Iraq. It could be vital for them to fight on. But he'd always seen himself above it. He shut the book, angry that it had only blonde and blue-eyed people in it.

"I loved that book as a child," Nadia said. She was standing right behind him. He could still smell her through the chili and lentils. He opened the book to focus on it.

"Tell me about it," he said.

"The story? You know. Imprisoned princess, who's at the mercy of some dark and sinister force. And prince serves her by slashing all that lays before him."

He flipped through the book and looked at the pictures. The lightly colored ones at the beginning, to the darker ones later on. Then the red stained ones celebrating the death of the dark creature holding the princess, then the end. Love lives on. He wanted to spit, mock the book, and at the same time it spoke to something deep inside him. He too wanted to live this way.

"They really set themselves up, don't they?" he said.

"What do you mean?" she asked.

He placed the book on the floor trying to think what he did mean. "Do you think one can tell a lot about a culture from the stories it teaches its kids?"

She scratched her chin, looking over at the pot. "Where does that leave us?"

For a second he thought she meant the two of them and his heart twitched. Then he realized. "We all look for heroes."

"Life would be better."

He had a feeling that she was talking above and beyond his intellectual level.

She looked up. "Laith! Aren't you supposed to be studying?"

Ali looked up to see Laith's head disappear as the curtain moved.

"You should talk to him. He looks up to you," she said.

"He doesn't study?" Ali asked.

"Not always. It's hard for me..."

"I'll talk to him," said Ali and headed to the room.

"Don't…"

Ali looked over. Nadia was wiping her hands on a towel.

"Don't what?" he asked. There was something distant about her.

"I mean. I don't want you putting ideas in his head. About other things he can do."

A sharp twinge pushed through Ali's chest. Anger swelled in his blood, then he remembered that all she knew about men like him was what she read in the government newspapers. "Why do you think I brought him to the school? To use him?"

"No"

"Then?"

"I'm just…"

"I'm not here to recruit him."

"I know," she said, still looking down. "What do you do if he asks you to join?"

"He already has," Ali said. He realized he was only a foot away from her and whispering. It would mean the world to him to have her believe him. "And I said no."

"Are there other boys with you?"

Ali had heard of younger boys being used, but so far he hadn't done so in his group. Perhaps as couriers but surely that was admissible?

Her eyes were now pecking at his face. "Fine."

He walked back to the curtain. There was only one other room here. Hunched over the floor, with a book spread out, Laith stared up at him. A naked bulb hung from a long wire that rose to the ceiling.

"How are you?"

Laith's eyes were grim. "Were you fighting with her?"

Ali, sensing anger in the young boy's voice, smiled. "Only talking."

Laith turned back to his book.

"What are you reading?"

"Math. I hate it," he said.

"Well, it's important," Ali said, though he wasn't all that great at math either.

Laith sighed. Ali felt his heart go out to the boy. He wondered if he cried for his family. He remembered the stoic look on the boy's face while the car next to them still crackled in the fire.

"Dinner!" Nadia called from the other room.

They sat and ate in silence until the chai was served.

"I want dessert," Laith said, staring at his feet. "We always had ice cream at our house."

Ali, caught between twin thoughts of admonishing the child and soothing him, looked at Nadia who flashed a pained look. Ali realized that he never asked the boy about his family. What they did or anything.

"I'm sorry," Ali said. "But unfortunately that's how things go in life sometimes. We must make do."

"Why do we always have to make do?" Laith said. "I watched a movie yesterday and no one was making do."

"That's a movie," Ali said, his voice turning low and angry. "Not real life."

"No. Walid says that in America that's how they live. Why can't *we* live like that?"

Ali sipped his chai. The boy was ripe for rebellion. Nadia was right to worry about him. "Life's not fair," he said. But he could see that his words hadn't helped and that the boy was bubbling with emotions he couldn't handle.

"So? Why can't it be unfair for others?"

Ali shrugged and looked at Nadia who was staring at the boy with a distinct pain. "It's the way of life," she said.

Laith scrunched up his lips like he believed neither of them.

"What did your parents say about the matter?" Ali asked, hoping that he could maintain some continuity with what *they* wanted. That's what he would want.

"What does that matter? They're dead." Laith said and leaped up.

Ali half expected the boy to punch him, but instead he ran into the room.

Nadia looked at her hands.

"Does he always do this?"

"He does it a lot. He's been through a lot."

"I know. Does he blame me?"

Nadia shook her head. "He looks up to you. He's only worse when you haven't seen him for so long."

Ali swallowed. He felt lightheaded. "Does he just need time?"

"This is the kind of thing that time doesn't heal," she said.

So the boy was mixed in with the same hate as he was—that same virus and stench that wafted into Ali's nose every day that he woke up. Ali shifted his legs, trying to think of what to do, then got up and walked to the room. It was dark outside now, and the light was out so it took a few seconds for him to see the form of a lump in the corner.

"Laith?"

"What?"

Ali kneeled next to the boy. "How are you?"

A stifled cry cracked through Ali's ears. He placed his hand on the boy's hair and rubbed it. It was soft and emitted the smell of hard soap. "I'm sorry. I really am."

"Why?"

Ali took the boy's hand and patted it gently. It was soft, innocent. "You shouldn't have to go through that."

"What does that matter?"

"Sometimes…" Ali trailed off because he'd heard all the pep speeches in his time in Iraq and he wanted none of that here. Not for Laith. "It's tough to lose loved ones," he said. "…Live for them."

"What live?" Laith said. "All I want to do is kill everyone. Everyone." The boy trembled and started to cry. "They should all feel what I did."

Ali had always seen such emotions and helpful, but he now realized how harmful it would be for the boy to take these bombs with him as he walked into manhood. "No. You shouldn't. You can live in peace."

The boy reached up and hugged Ali. Ali held him tight, his tears dripping down Ali's neck.

"Are you living in peace?" Laith asked.

Ali knew there was no use lying.

"No. But... I'm pushing them there."

That seemed to suffice and the boy lay down. A minute later, Ali could hear Laith's heavy breathing.

In the distance artillery shelling the mountainside shook a handful of molecules. He walked out to see Nadia putting away the dishes.

"He's asleep."

She smiled. Then took his hand. It was unexpected and his heart jumped. They walked outside. It was dark now, and a blinking light flew far over head. They walked up stairs on the side of the house. The air chilled Ali's bones. She pointed out a pair of chairs. He sat in one and she settled next to him. He was truly stilled with her around. He wondered if this was love.

"Is what you said true?" she asked.

She must have listened to him talking to Laith. That was understandable. "Yes." He wasn't entirely sure if it was true, but thinking that way was making him feel better. Or was it just doing something that she liked?

His mind flashed to a gutter in Iraq where the blood swirled down the gutters like rain in his childhood. His insides churned. "That I'm pushing others towards peace?"

She stared at him. He was certain that she could smell his lie. He tried to think of something to say, but he couldn't. What *could* he say? Though he didn't want Laith to walk down his path, he didn't know how to prevent it. He'd been so full of anger, and he'd never known what else to do with it.

A satellite flew overhead. It blinked as it hustled through the sky.

"Americans," Ali said to make a joke. "They're watching."

She didn't say anything. He was wondering now what she was thinking. He could sense heat and cogitation from her body. He swallowed. What could he tell her about his life?

"Whoever's satellite that is, it's not *ours*."

The way she said it, he was sure she was blaming him.

"And what about that?" he said. "Am I to build satellites? Is any of us to do so when they bomb us daily?"

"We bomb ourselves too. Not just them," she said.

Her voice was calm and very measured. He was certain that she had been thinking about all this for a very long time. And though he would normally launch into a diatribe about how wrong she was and how the Americans had done all this, he wanted to show her more, maybe convince her with words and not some sense of loyalty.

"And I don't just mean us Yemenis."

He knew what she meant. His head felt warm as he tried to think of a way to answer her. It wasn't just a matter of phrasing. Or a matter of putting into words something that he'd thought long and hard about for years now. It was a matter of taking all his thoughts and hopes of the past and creating something cohesive. He was certain that all his words would be nothing more than the ramblings of a mad man. After all, these thoughts had been the result of mad acts, or thought of when he'd been close to madness. How can he explain this?

"Would you have us stand by while they blow our children apart?" he heard himself say. He wasn't certain why. The outline of the neighboring mountains stood out in the dusk. He stared at them until he lost the border between the mountains and night sky. He realized he was tired. Perhaps he was tired of his work. He could hear her breathing, or perhaps it was her chest rising and falling and pushing on her clothes, or maybe he was just sensing her. Whatever it was, perhaps she was trying to convert him, change him from being the man he was. Was he that man?

"No," she said softly. "But what are we building for them?"

That cut. He watched as the satellite disappeared over the horizon. She was right. No one here was able to build that yet. He'd met so many engineers who were willing to fight. But what about building something other than bombs? He contemplated the history of the Caliphates and how civilizations stayed afloat. Better to fight and only think about survival. Deep down, however, he knew that to focus on fighting alone was a fool's errand as he was aware of what history thought of men who fought for too long. Even the Mongols ended up enjoying the fruits of civilization and settling... Perhaps all these thoughts were a result of him fighting the tide. Perhaps he was old and tired.

"Nothing right now," he said.

"Oh, there are plans for future building?" she said. Her voice was caustic. It hurt.

"No plans. Not immediate," he said. "But." He raised a finger. "There are committees meeting to make sure that the plans will be planned."

She chuckled, then stifled it. He turned and lapped up the remnants of her smile.

"This isn't a joking matter," she said, her voice excessively firm.

"I know. But when you say that Americans aren't to blame, you're wrong."

"We're not doing this to ourselves?"

"If you knew how much they've infiltrated every part of the intelligence services and the government with their money, then you wouldn't speak like that."

"I *know*," she said, somewhat exasperated.

Below them a throng of teenagers walked by them. They were chanting something about a soccer game.

"And what do you tell them when they have nothing to do?" she said pointing at the teenagers. "When they're old enough they no longer come to school. That's when they come to you."

He couldn't argue with that. Most of his soldiers were young men. "And what else are they to do?"

"Build something for them," she said.

He could feel the strain in her voice. He took several deep breaths and wondered what it was that he could build for them. Nothing came to mind.

"You know that without education we will just be some dusty villagers the Americans bomb?"

His insides churned some more. "What does it matter who they bomb? They don't care. Do you think they stopped for a moment to think about all that history they were willing to destroy as they turned Baghdad into a smoldering ruin?"

She seemed to shrink, but her eyes remained steady. Another satellite blinked up above. She was right. And he had to talk to Saladin about this. But he didn't like feeling weak.

"You think that they don't destroy the fabric of our country when they bomb us? Just because we won't submit like sheep, doesn't make us the problem," he said. He sighed. The aroma of grilled lamb wafted up in the wind. His mouth watered. He tried to think of the last time he had some really good lamb.

"I'm not saying they're not," she said softly. "But when our young men die, it helps no one."

"I've argued the same thing," he said, melancholy spreading throughout his bones. "I have always said that. Why waste our young men with suicide vests—"

"And why do you?"

"They don't listen," he said.

More silence. The cold seeped in.

"How long were you in Iraq for?" she asked.

"Several years."

"In Baghdad?" she asked.

"Only a few times. We worked west of Fallujah."

She gasped. "I'm sorry. Were you there for the massacre?"

"No. Fortunately," he said. His head was swirling with thoughts and emotions. How to make sense of any of it? It'd seemed like something of the utmost importance when he had done it, and yet right now he saw how irrelevant it was.

"Why did you go?"

"There was a cry from our brothers, wasn't there? The Americans were killing them off. And so I went to help. Only in the end did I realize that it was better to come here to help at home. We have our own problems."

"Did they want you there? I know Iraqis don't like outsiders."

"Some did. Towards the end more didn't," he said.

"Why?"

This he had been thinking about for ages. What went wrong? There were still a few fighters streaming in, especially lately, but most had left, or been killed—betrayed. He smiled because there was nothing else to do. "The Iraqis are an interesting people."

"I've heard," she said.

"We, my group, we never did what the others did. The car bombs. The market places," he said. "Even if the Shiites were traitors who worked with the infidel."

"Traitors? How can anyone trying to feed their family be considered a traitor?"

"Not all of them were just trying to just feed themselves." His head almost hurt with the memory of how many different people were fighting each other in Baghdad.

He could hear her shift in her seat. A mosquito buzzed by his ear. Again he tried to make out the outline of the mountains.

"But did you stop those who did?"

He fidgeted with his hands for a second, peeling at some scabs on his knuckles. He wasn't exactly certain where he got them from. Worming through and decimating all his neural matter, were past memories, and the harsh acidic emotions they'd created or pulled up in him made him feel weak. He swallowed thinking about all his doubts. Her words, her simple whispers and questions were not only bringing these old memories and their friends back to life, but they were providing them energy. His initial instinctive reaction was to assign her some sort of nefarious goals; in the back of his mind the idea of her being a witch even surfaced, but in the end he knew that she was merely asking questions and not thinking about the results of her actions. After all, he could end this conversation any time he wanted. Yet he'd rather have her comfortable with him. The thought of that settled him. "No," he said.

"Why?"

Of course why was the question he'd asked even himself. "What can you do? Murder the man next to you?"

"If they're murdering innocents, then yes," she said, her voice raising in pitch.

He swatted another mosquito on his hand just as an itch started. "Don't think I haven't thought about this," he said.

"Thought doesn't matter if it results in the same reaction."

He raised his hand to indicate that he wanted to talk. He wanted silence, the memories were back in full force, and yet he didn't want to leave her. "We only hit the heads of government who were hurting the people," he said, remembering the squad he'd started out in, then finished as the head of, when everyone above eventually died. He trembled as he remembered seeing the first leader they killed, his head chopped off.

"What about here? If the same group and leaders are here, then you're saying innocent people will die. Why would you want that on your mother's land?" she said.

He could feel her turn. She was staring him down. "I'm making sure we don't do that," he said.

"There—"

144

"I can't be responsible for every single person who claims to be a terrorist. I want to make sure it's all clean, but there will be collateral damage."

"You sound like an American," she said.

"We are nothing like them. We don't lie. We don't kill children and laugh. How can you compare us?" Anger filled his fists and he clenched his jaw, torn between wanting to punch her or himself. The anger was leeched by the realization that she was right about this. He'd always mocked people who hadn't fought the infidels around them, but with her, it was different.

Another mosquito buzzed by his ear. "There are lots of mosquitoes," he said. "We should head in."

"I'm fine," she said. "What is it like to fight on foreign soil for reasons that don't exist?"

"Are you saying we had no right?" he said.

She sighed. The mosquitoes whined louder, and Ali stared at another satellite flying far above him.

"I'm not saying that. I'm wondering what it was like for your friends to die in a foreign land. Where the people didn't want them there."

"They wanted us there," he said, louder than he intended. "They were lied to. And they believed those lies."

"That you killed innocents?" she said.

"You can't based your assumptions on the newspapers. Remember who they work for."

"Should I listen to your magazine instead?"

He never liked the idea of their own magazine, though he knew why it needed to exist. "Perhaps not that either."

"Then tell me," she said.

His heart beat hard in his chest. How to tell something that you had yet to formulate? How miraculous that the Prophet had been able to formulate all those thoughts, and in such perfect language too. If only Allah would reach down and help him.

He felt her warm hand on his. Somewhere a truck's transmission whined and groaned as the vehicle's suspension pitched and rolled. He looked at her hand; it seemed so perfect compared to his, so small.

Fragile. His mind made a connection with the fragility of her and the fragility of the people he'd killed. Not that she was one in the same, just that the powerful kill the weak, and if that was the case who was going to help her? He'd always pictured himself as the protector of the weak, but he was no longer sure. Not with her around. But he swore to himself then that he would change. Was that ever going to be enough?

"What about the suicide bombers?" she asked.

He should have expected that, but it still surprised him. "They were different. The ones going in always seemed scared, but there were ways to make them do what was needed."

"Like what?"

"Pray. Over and over. We would joke—"

"In front of them?"

"No, never. When they were gone we would joke that they were robots."

"Horrible," she said.

"We were revolted and amazed by what they could do," he said. All the ways the suicide division had learned how to infiltrate the enemy's defensive posture: he'd been amazed, and for a while thought that it'd work, that it would win the war for them. But in the end, he couldn't see a way to win. Not when just killing and no building was the way. It was partially the reason that so many Iraqis had turned on them. And he couldn't help but see the latest bout of bombings in Iraq as an affront to his own tactics.

"How did the leaders say it was all right?"

"There's an excuse for everything," he said. He sensed the evil in what he'd done. What he was doing.

He swatted a few more mosquitoes. He wiped the smeared blood on his skin. He was exhausted from all this thinking. "What would you do?"

"Never go to Iraq," she said.

"No. Here, now. What would you do?"

"In Yemen?"

He looked over at her; her eyes reflected the limited skyline of Amman; a generator nearby started up, more diesel fumes filled the air.

Saladin's words, the loud breaths that the man took as he thought, all ran through Ali's head. Wasn't he allowing the same thing here?

"Where else?" she said.

"We're trying to change things. We'll start up an entirely new way of doing things," he said. But he felt scared because he didn't want people like Saladin in charge of his land. He'd seen what they did for a village in Iraq. That wasn't the way, whatever propaganda they spewed. It hadn't been the way of the caliphate and it wouldn't be the way here.

"Will it work?"

"It'll be better," he said.

"That's said by anyone," she said. "Who wants power."

"It is," he said sadly.

Ali could smell more diesel fumes. He looked around, though he wasn't trying to find anything. She sat perfectly still. He needed to find an answer.

Nasar stared at the back of Karim's head. The truck's gearbox whined as they drove up the side of another hill. It was getting tiring, watching all these peaks of brown mountains. The dust was also driving Nasar crazy. He'd seen dust before, of course, but never this much and never for this long, and never the type that just burrowed its way into his lungs and nostrils and every single open pore. The two men up front had been quiet all day. They were supposed to arrive at the coast, avoiding the capital where all the police and law resided, and take a boat from there. Karim had said this gruffly when they woke up in the morning. Nasar was sure that he still blamed him, Nasar, for Abdullah's fate. After all, the child wouldn't have been here if it wasn't for Nasar. But Nasar was certain that he'd never wanted the child to come along. Hadn't that been Karim's call? A fly flew into the cabin, large and black; Nasar let it be.

The biggest thing was to pray that the truck even made it to the coast. Karim'd said something about how the blast had shook something loose. The gears in the engine whined again. Nasar wasn't an expert in engines, not car engines at least, but this one sounded like it was dying. There were a few pieces of shrapnel in the side. He could see the light lines poking in.

Abdullah. Nasar's heart sank as his brain involuntarily moved to the young boy's laugh, then his remains. Such a change. These were the results of war, something he had to admit he'd never seen, even when Al Jazeera would show the Israeli's attacking Gaza there hadn't been *this* much... flesh. He thought of all the times he'd seen representations of war: Goya's drawings; the frayed art from post World War I, artists who'd seen too much; the flash media of the day. Nothing had prepared him for the shock. He wondered again if perhaps those representations had been nothing but weak lies. After all, wouldn't the real art have been pushed away for being too true? He tried to think of Abdullah whole. His mind wouldn't bend. It wanted to see Abdullah in pieces.

Blood, flesh, bone; liquids and solids. That's what it was in the end. And he, as a scientist, couldn't cope with this simple organic fact. Why? He'd end up the same thing. But this wasn't the same, and he knew it. This was so sudden. This switch from youth with hope to a frayed piece of flesh. Nasar felt warm and hot. He unbuttoned the top of his shirt. This ride, it may well be his last. It sure was for Abdullah.

He thought again about his final destination. The exact steps they were going to take at the coast. A boat, again. He wondered if it was going to be possible. He considered asking Karim a question, but the man was too engrossed with the road in front of him. And the silence was still hostile.

Again Nasar's mind drifted to Abdullah. The scientist in him had to admit to being impressed with what the Americans had been able to create with their drone warfare. Pakistan's military was decades away from it all. Hell, even the Chinese were. That was what he was trying to create, wasn't he? Some parity in the world, so that the Empires like America, probably India soon, couldn't push their way through the world and raze to ashes cities at their whim. This was what it was all about. Nasar remembered his conversation with Karim; how Karim had dared to confront all this. But how did he ever expect to create anything? He thought of the Iranian. But that man, as friendly as he'd been was an outcast. One of the destroyers of the world, and having been born in the shadows of his nation he was destined to remain there. Like the multitude of poor in Pakistan. Why allow any of them to take control of a nation? Isn't that what came close to happening in the USSR?

Nasar sighed, feeling a little better. They drove by a young boy with a handful of goats. The boy seemed to stare off the cliff, without noticing them.

That was right, thought Nasar, if they ever hoped to be more than goat herders, they had to build machines better than other Empires. Empires like America simply had to be taken down a few notches. That was all there was to it. Feeling better, Nasar closed his eyes and thought of his cool, soft bed. He wondered if he was going to be able to contact the young man who'd emailed him. He wished he had a pen and paper to solidify his thoughts in an answer to that man.

A droning sound picked up, or a distant jet perhaps. He felt the truck lurch to a stop.

"Out!" Karim yelled.

Nasar stared on for a second. Both the men up front were outside, running to an outcrop of rocks.

Nasar opened his door and stepped out slowly. He could see an object in the sky. The Americans in the drone could probably see him clearly. He stared on. That was impressive. When would they get a machine like that?

"Here," Karim said, almost whispering, his hands beckoning Nasar over.

Nasar, seeing the fear in Karim's eyes, smiled. What did he expect was going to happen? If the drone thought they were a target it would kill them all. Nasar pulled out a cigarette, lit it, and inhaled. He sat up on the hood. Would they be able to start up the truck again?

Another object appeared in the sky, then another. They were impressive, these drones. He wondered what kind of lenses they had to be able to see so far. And what sort of intelligence. He sucked in a lungful of smoke and held it until it warmed his insides. He realized that he didn't care if the drone did fire on him. It was his life's work, and he didn't care about any of the consequences of that life.

One still couldn't notice the drones unless they squinted. Nasar watched as they appeared to circle a place below them. He tried to scan the horizon to see if there was a target. He could sense Karim sitting next to him on the hood.

"Someone's going to die," Karim said.

"Yes. And no one has any choice about it," Nasar said. He wondered what that meant. Of course he felt the injustice of an outside power being able to murder as many people as it wanted, all the while covering it with beautiful prose of fighting for freedom. That was what he hated the most: the ability for the Americans, just like the British, to be able to cover their actions with beautiful prose.

Perhaps Karim did have a point. He shook his head. This was the way it'd always been. From the moment that humans were able to take advantage of their environment, they crushed all those without an environment to take advantage of. If it happened that he and Pakistan, and Muslims, were the ones being picked on, then maybe he was just becoming sentimental in his old age. But oh, to place a black eye on the powerful. Karim *was* right.

"What is it, old man?" Karim asked. There was no more hostility in his voice. "You've been very quiet."

"Thinking. You?"

"Only feeling like a fool."

"Same here."

"And when they rain destruction there shouldn't be any blowback?" Karim said.

"I don't know," Nasar said.

The driver grunted.

And like that the three vulturing drones spat fire. That was when Nasar noticed the flock of buildings nestled between two peaks, no more than a few miles away. A line of smoke reached out from the drones and licked the villages with fire. Flashes lit the land, followed by earth shifting booms. The rocks in front of them spit up dust before settling. Dust enveloped the village.

Nasar glanced over at Karim who was mumbling. The explosions lit his face, a small warmth reaching Nasar's chest. Karim started to mutter "Allah Akbar". Nasar stared at his lips moving and couldn't help but keep staring because the young man's words were calming him.

The explosions continued and Nasar looked back at the flames that engulfed the village and the dust that rose further into the sky and flattened and fell back to the earth.

The drones hustled out of the sky. An eerie silence fell across the waves of brown dirt. Nasar held his breath. A whining sound echoed in his head. There was beauty in this: the land, the flames and the dust cloud now settling. Nasar could smell his sweat, pungent and full of fear. Karim continued to mumble his mantra. Nasar wondered if Karim was mumbling for what the Americans had done. Or for whom they'd just killed. Why wasn't Karim more used to this? After all, he must've seen plenty of drone attacks there.

The beauty was ripped away when cries and wails echoed across the landscape. Nasar's heart cracked. It bled a harsh acid onto his guts, and the sickness expanded yet again.

"There," said Karim.

Another drone appeared in the sky. It spat out one last puff of smoke. The people didn't notice, and when they did it was too late. All froze and another flash hit the village.

As the dust fell back from where it came, the flames flickered, and on the crumbled concrete and mud left behind small masses could be seen moving or crawling. Some raised their hands to the air. Nasar tried to say something to alleviate his spinning head, but in his throat something stuck and he coughed, but it didn't help. He'd read about Serbs using artillery to decimate Muslim villages appeared. The world had been shocked then. Horrified. Nasar had been proud of humanity's reaction afterwards. He hadn't thought it possible, and perhaps he'd ignored the Iraqis' plight. But now, with the destroyed village before him, Nasar held tightly to a truth he'd known before but hadn't wanted to entirely believe: that a nation was only powerful once it could kill without consequence. And here he was seeing just that: a nation that knew it was powerful and willing to kill because it could. Only the weak nations had to watch what they did.

Karim stopped mumbling. Nasar understood then that it was his job to give more power to the likes of Karim and Pakistan. There wouldn't be a day of rest with the knowledge that the brethren of the colonialists could easily take over if they cared to.

The driver grunted.

"This is horrid," Karim said.

Nasar nodded.

"This must be avenged." The young man clenched his fist.

Nasar placed his hand on Karim's shoulder. "Of course it will. We will become strong and strike back."

The driver gave them curious looks. "That's what you believe?" he said.

That the driver could speak, surprised Nasar.

"Of course," Karim said. "What do *you* believe, taking it like a dog?"

"Never," the driver said. "But I know what the likes of you pray for."

"And what's that?" Nasar said, suddenly angry.

"The death of innocents. How is that better?" said the driver.

"Collateral," Nasar said.

"Then you are no better," said the driver.

"You'd have us lie down like dogs," said Karim.

The driver didn't seem perturbed by them. "Of course, that's the call of every tyrant in the world," he said. "Murder more innocents. At least look the child in the eye and call him a fool for wanting life."

After the shock of embarrassment, Nasar gathered for a defense. "So take no sides then, and that's the same as lying down like a dog."

The driver scoffed. "Take sides. I take sides with the truth. And that's all Allah has ever said. He has never said slay innocents, has he?" The driver puffed out his chest.

Nasar had the feeling that what the driver was saying was either right or mad. Nasar wanted to say mad because all he knew in life was opposite of what the driver was trying to say. As he tried to formulate a reply, the smell of smoke and some harsh chemical filtered through to his nose. He needed to get away from all this.

"In every battle, side with the innocent," the driver said. "Always. Protect and defend and fight for them. Picking sides is for Satan."

"You are quite the philosopher," said Karim, letting out an angry laugh. "But you don't talk sense."

The driver walked to his side of the truck and stepped inside. Nasar and Karim did the same. Inside, the car smelled fresh. The car started and they drove off. This time they headed downhill. Nasar stewed in the silence. He hated the driver now, but only for trying to make him, a doctor, the savior of Pakistan, look like a fool. A fly landed on his shirtsleeve, and he watched it flicker out a feeler before flying away.

Nasar looked at the back of the driver's head and reminded himself that the man was not smart. That made him feel better. Of course the simple man would say such a thing. That was the wish of child to be on the side that which was never evil, to have one's hands clean. But that wasn't how things worked. You had to pick a side and see it through until the end. That was the only way that you survived in this world. And if you were willing to abandon your tribe, your chosen side for a few actions, then what were you but a coward? Yes, thought Nasar, this was only way to live, and for the driver to think otherwise was an indication of how disturbed he was. Imagine that, trying to live life without backing a single evil act. Nasar let out an ugly life.

Ali walked into the newest safe house. It was late and he was sure that no one would be awake. In the living room lay several mounds of dark shapes. Coughs and snores filled the room. This was where the foot soldiers slept. It smelled of rank body odor and possibly feces. He'd asked for working plumbing, but that might have been too much. In the kitchen he found several bags of ready made military rations. They had American flags. He stared at it. Besides them were brown paper bags with old shawarmas.

Though he'd left her house in a cloud of silence, Nadia had been right. There was something that even *he* knew about Iraq, that she'd simply felt. For all his sacrifices and fights, there was the need to come out of *that* foreign land with something more important than just heads of enemies. No, they had to build towards something. He thought of Laith and the nation he'd be leaving behind for him.

Upstairs, he saw a light on. He ate his food, a stale shawarma, and listened. There was a TV playing, and hushed whispering filtering down the stairs. Ali swallowed his food and headed up. His mind absorbed the beats of his heart. He noticed that there was blood on the stairs. He thought about Yasar. The poor kid. He formed a stronger regret than ever before—a young man died—and Ali wasn't even sure why that made him sick. When he reached the second floor there was a door with light streaming from its edges.

He knocked; the television was on a news channel.

"Come in," said a familiar voice.

He pushed the door and walked in to see Saladin with a hookah pipe and the TV on.

"Sal—"

"Shh," Saladin said and pointed to the TV screen. The scene was one Ali was very familiar with. There were police shepherding people away. In the back burned spidered hulls of cars. Women wailed. Ali knew this city too. He'd been part of such terror, and he was certain that whoever did this could be traced in one way or another to him, or people he knew.

"Baghdad," Saladin said, clapping his hand with glee. He smiled. His face sweaty, his teeth brown, his eyes full of joy.

Ali realized that he hated the man with all his might. Why did he insist on coming here? For a handful of seconds, Ali prayed that a drone found this man and a missile was heading for them. He would gladly die if he could be assured that Saladin would die with him. How could the man laugh at such things?

The TV zoomed back to the reporter who was mentioning the people who were responsible were most likely Sunni extremists.

"See? They thought we were beat, but we still have it in us!" Saladin said, clapping. Our Iraqis are good. You know that they freed almost a thousand of us from the prison?"

"Really?" Ali said. He was no fan of prison, and he knew how bad the conditions there could be, so a twinge of happiness for the prisoners passed through him. He wondered if there was anyone he knew.

"Yes. You know how they did it?"

"No," Ali said, wondering how he would carry out such an attack. He'd a strange feeling in his stomach telling him that Saladin was about to tell him off.

"Suicide bombers. How else?"

"Of course," Ali said, knowing that his earlier complaint against such operations would possibly be used against him.

"They sent the suicide bombers first, then after that breached the initial lines, they blew a hole in the wall and tore through the prison!"

Ali nodded. He had to admit that the tactics were solid. "It's impressive," he said, a lump forming in his throat.

"These other bombs," Saladin said, pointing at the screen of more burning cars. "Were just to help overwhelm the security forces. Once they were focused on putting out fires and securing areas, they were overrun," he said.

Ali stared at the TV because he didn't want to deal with Saladin's grinning face. He wasn't sure what to think. It was a victory, and he knew that the Sunnis they'd worked with had all been spurned because of what the Baghdadi government had done to them, but he had hoped, deep in his heart, that with the Americans gone that the Iraqis would see peace. Of course there was a level of selfishness in that, and he knew it. He would never want his own nation to burn for so long without peace for mothers and children. He wondered how one stops such things.

"It's the Persians' fault. They're the ones who tried to push us too far," Saladin said and pounded his chest. "Now they will pay. You know they made deals with the Americans?" He shook his head, disgusted.

Ali kept his eyes on the TV. Saladin's stare burrowed through his face.

"Listen," Saladin said. "I know you're against the bombs. I know they aren't easy. Nothing in war is. But it must be done. What else do the Sunnis have?"

"I know," Ali said. Still, one reason he didn't like Saladin's flippant remarks concerning the suicide bombs was that the man had never really participated in a proper attack. At most he'd met the people carrying them out, give the usual pep speech about saving lands from infidels. But he'd never had it truly weigh on his conscious. Everyone that Ali knew who had a hand would sooner or later develop nightmares. Even the makers who never saw the aftermath. They would feel horrid about themselves.

Ali had heard about the American Army's suicide rates. He wondered why no one bothered to see the same undercurrents among their ranks. Or perhaps he was too soft. This *was* war. And he should've known better. And perhaps having a general like Saladin, unaffected by the choices he made was the only way to win the war. But it still rubbed Ali the wrong way, and he continued to stare at the TV.

"They have nothing. They can lie like dogs to wait for the Persians to kill them, or they fight back."

Ali nodded.

"This is all we have as well. We cannot afford to train people to the level that you want. Some of them are only useful as suicide bombers," said Saladin.

Ali heard a rumble in his stomach. Anger bubbled into his throat. "Maybe," he said. "Maybe both." He hoped that those words would shut Saladin up.

"Very well," Saladin said with a sigh. "Try it. But I'm telling you." He wagged his finger. Then he pointed at the hookah. "You want some?"

"No," Ali said. He could smell his own body odor—strong with ammonia—and he could smell the stiff cologne wafting off Saladin.

Saladin laughed. "That's what I like about you, Ali. You're very serious about being a good Muslim. But this is war. And sometimes you're permitted a little leeway." He handed the pipe to Ali, raising his eyebrows.

Ali knew it would be a breach of decorum to not do as Saladin wanted, but he hated smoking and had, unlike most he'd ever met in Al Qaeda, never touched it in any form. He wanted to quote the Quran and put some shame in Saladin, but Saladin had to be placated.

Ali took the pipe and huffed it. It was smooth, at least, but he still coughed.

Saladin laughed and slapped his thigh, spittle flying out of his mouth when he did so. Ali sat down next to him. The TV soon spit out images from Yemen.

"Ah. Now your fight," Saladin said and patted his back.

"Yes," Ali forced himself to say. He felt better for some reason.

The TV blasted some tripe about another government victory over some decrepit foreign terrorists. Ali shook his head. "The media are the real terrorists," he said.

Saladin nodded and took the pipe out of his hand. "You're liking it too much."

Ali ignored the comment. "The suicide bombers," he said slowly.

"Yes?" Saladin replied, apprehension apparent in his voice.

Ali thought for a second. His mind drifted to Nadia's soft voice and the truth she'd forced him to see. Ali knew better than to mention her to Saladin, but *something* had to be said. A mosquito buzzed in Ali's ear and he swatted it.

"Where does it leave us? If we beat them?"

"You sound lost."

"I'm not. I will fight until I bleed on my own land," Ali said and pounded his fist into his open hand. "But... what do we build with youth who are primed to kill themselves?"

Saladin grunted, shifted to one side, and cleared his throat. "What else do they have?"

Ali didn't know.

"We must fight with what we have," Saladin said. His voice was soft now, as if he wasn't really sure either.

Ali didn't say anything else. He now realized that he didn't like being unsure, and he really didn't like Saladin being unsure either. If that was the case, what use was it to ask all these questions?

The TV moved to some drone attacks in Pakistan. A lump formed in his throat. Machines in the air looking to kill him and all his kind. "The Americans have really made this war like a book."

"They kill without remorse," Saladin said. "We must be the same. Do they flinch when they kill children?"

Ali didn't say anything, though he was thinking about the children who'd died at their hands.

His silence must have tipped off Saladin.

"Of course if we had the technology that the Americans did, do you think we would try to hurt the innocent? We would never. It's only because we have no choice that we do what you do. With the Americans, you know they are trying to kill every last one of us."

Ali nodded, though he was sure that someone on the other side was having the same conversation as this.

The TV zoomed in on a pair of size 2 shoes, torn, burned and bloodied.

"Doesn't it seem like war is only getting worse?" Saladin said and shook his head. "One day it will burn the world."

Ali wagged his finger. "It doesn't affect them. Why should they care?" He was thinking now on the American press conferences, always full of lies.

"We must take it to their streets," Saladin said.

Ali nodded. For all he hated the murder of innocents, seeing the people who caused this feel the same as they had, warmed at least a part of his heart. His brain tried to argue otherwise. Ali took the hookah pipe and inhaled, holding the smoke in his lungs. He blew it out, a white wisp streaming out and clouding up and out of view. "We should," Ali said.

Finally some football images blasted up on the screen. "Where are our teams? You know they keep them out on purpose," said Saladin waving his hand at the screen. "Besides, we shouldn't have our young men waste time on such frivolous activities."

Ali inhaled again. He wanted to see the score. He wanted an Arab country to make it to the World Cup and not embarrass themselves.

Saladin placed his hand on his thigh. Ali, feeling odd, thinking that he should shift away, didn't.

"The doctor was last seen in Iran."

"What?" Ali said. He hadn't received any emails lately. And he was certain someone had caught him by now.

"You know. The Savior of Pakistan. He was last seen in Iran."

"With who?"

"Some smugglers. People think he's dead."

"Smugglers?"

"You know how they are."

Ali did. He'd worked with them in Iraq. Always asking for money, never caring about the struggle. Of course he couldn't complain because they did, in fact, do what was needed, but they were still horrid at times. Once he heard they were smuggling in some new recruits when they saw American forces. They dumped the cargo in a canal rather than risk arrest. They claimed the Americans did it, but Ali knew better.

"When was that?" Ali asked.

"A week ago. I think the Iranian mukhabarat killed a few of the smugglers."

"Do you think he's dead?" Ali asked.

"Of course not. They're not stupid. But I think if a Zionist gets in their graces they will sell him off for a pittance."

Ali mapped the doctor's travels. "Is he coming here?"

"I don't know what's in his head. But let me tell you something," Saladin said and with his hand gestured at Ali to move in closer. "We have big plans for him. We do believe he's trying to find us. That he's sending us emails."

Ali's heart dropped. He couldn't imagine the doctor talking to Saladin. "Really?" he said.

"And he will help us make a makeshift bomb." Saladin leaned back and smiled.

"But urani—"

"Congo. We have people there who know how to get the material."

"It's a war—"

"I know. But you know these zunjees."

Ali didn't like that word. "And we build it with his help."

"That's right," Saladin said, his grin cutting his face in half. "And then." With his hands he indicated an explosion, and he stretched them as high as he could. "We bring the war to them."

Ali wondered why he didn't, in fact, smoke harder substances, or at least start a qat habit. His mind churned.

"Quiet again?" asked Saladin.

Ali thought about hitting the Westerners in a place where it would affect them. That led him to wonder why it would hurt them: because screams amongst their weakest were all that mattered and it would affect them one way or another. But if that was the case, that bombs, shredded flesh, bloodied gutters, charred cars, and screams hurt them that much then the same could only be said for his own nation. "The suicide bombers…" he said. He felt immensely helpless and sad.

"What about them?"

"Let's try my way first."

Saladin didn't say anything.

"It will work better," Ali said, because he was certain hitting the puppet masters could only be better than hitting the puppets.

"How?"

"We hit the people they can't replace. That's all."

"All right. Show me."

Ali smiled. He knew that his way had to work. He didn't want to imagine the alternative too well. Build. They had to build. In a way Saladin was right, they could only build once the occupiers were gone, so some strike was necessary, but they do so in a way that left something to build upon.

"Come on in."

Justice entered the room and froze. Drail was inside with the therapist, a man Justice had only seen a handful of times, and never learned his name. But it was the painting to his right that kept him captivated.

"Isn't this—"

"Justice. Come on," Drail said, winking at him. "Let's not bother the therapist with the details of that painting's history, shall we?"

Something odd sat in Justice's stomach. What was Drail doing?

"Oh yes. Drail here told me he found this from a poor artist in West Virginia. Saved the boy's life by buying the thing. Amazing things we do here at the agency, don't you think?" the therapist said.

"Of course," Justice said, grinding his teeth trying to figure out what the feeling in his chest was. The painting, the one from the dead uncle's house did look good here. He decided to let it go.

"Let's get down to brass tacks. You were going to ask him some questions?" Drail said.

"You saw something traumatic, is that right?" the therapist asked.

"I suppose," Justice said, his eyes darting to Abid's painting.

"A man killed himself in front of you, didn't he?" the therapist asked, looking over at Drail with a half-mocking face.

"Well, I saw him just after he shot himself."

The therapist pulled out a leather briefcase and pulled out a booklet. "Protocol requires that you fill out this psychological questionnaire. Now," the therapist said as he handed the booklet to Justice.

"Now?"

"Now."

"Now," said Drail in a loud voice.

Justice opened the booklet. The first page was blank. So was the second one. The third and fourth were blank too. He looked up at the therapist who was observing and writing in a pad. Justice decided to stare at the booklet even harder. Perhaps he was missing something. The fifth page had the agency name. Then ten more blank pages. Then a copyright page. Finally, a page had a question: How do you feel? Ten being good, one being bad, please circle a number that best describes you. Justice circled ten. The next page asked: are you sure? Yes, No, Maybe. Justice circled yes. There were fifty more blank pages.

"Here," Justice said and handed it back.

The therapist thumbed through the book. Page by page, nodding his head.

"It's mostly blank," Justice said, almost wondering if he missed something.

"It's blank to you," the therapist said.

Justice glanced at Drail who shrugged.

"You sure you're okay?" the therapist asked after looking through the entire book. "This entire book is blank."

"That's what I told you," Justice said. He wondered if he was supposed to fill in the pages. But the therapist had said to answer the questions, didn't he? He hated these mind games.

The therapist wrote something else in his notepad.

"I never got your name," Justice said.

The therapist looked at Justice and wrote something else in his pad.

Justice's uncertainty morphed in to annoyance. "Well?" Justice asked.

"That will be all," said the therapist. He did a half bow to Drail and walked out of the room.

"What was *that* all about?" Justice asked, hoping someone would say it was a joke. He'd always been debriefed by the therapist— something bordering on the therapist lecturing about how no matter how traumatized they were, they couldn't relax by writing a journal or writing books.

"What do you mean?" Drail asked, his tone somber.

"I mean, what kind of test was that?"

"We've been doing this since before you, Justice. Let it go."

Justice started to bite his lip. "What did you want?"

"We think the good doctor is in Yemen. I want you there now."

"Now?"

"Here," Drail said and handed him a ticket. "You leave in an hour. Take the helicopter to JFK."

Justice glanced at the aisle seat in economy as he rubbed it in his hands. "What's the info on him?"

"You'll see, Sasha will send you something. We heard rumblings of a terrorist attack."

"And you think it might be him helping them out?"

"Who else?"

"Very well."

"Good," Drail said and hunkered over his desk, studiously scribbling notes.

Justice turned to leave, then saw the painting. A streak of blood was still visible, and had dried on it. That feeling that something was sitting in his stomach returned. Except this time it was more like a small beast clinging to his heart and pissing in fear on his guts. "Why did you take the painting?"

"Why do you care?" Drail asked, his voice crusty, angry, dominating.

Justice's throat tighten, but the little animal inside him didn't disappear. "Just wondering."

"He's not going to need it where he's from, is he?"

Justice still wasn't certain. "And we take his painting and his story, is that it?"

Drail put down his paper and looked up. "Don't tell me you're getting weak."

"I'm not," Justice said, suddenly aware that his promotion might slip away. "I was just asking."

"This is the job, Justice. I need to know if you can handle it."

"I can," Justice said, forcefully, angry that this had turned into a questioning of him instead of the painting.

"Good."

The flight to Yemen was packed. It had a layover in Zurich. Justice didn't even get an aisle seat. Instead he was sandwiched between two overflowing Americans. Both complaining about heading to Europe to see family.

"And the worst thing is there's no good food in Europe."

"Indeed."

"Well, you look like you don't enjoy food," they said to Justice.

Justice knew to keep quiet.

In Zurich the passengers were switched: whites for browns.

He landed in Sanaa, tired and angry. It was afternoon, and even though it was winter, the dust rising up made it seem hot.

An embassy clerk waited for him outside the plane.

"Mr. Justice," the young man with a chubby red face stuck out his hand. "It's an honor to meet you."

Justice wasn't certain if he was being polite or if he had a reputation as it was. "Nice to meet you Mr. . . . ."

"Rex."

"Rex?"

"Rex."

"Pleasure to meet you too. You're with the embassy?"

"That's correct," Rex said and flashed a badge.

Justice didn't see it. "And how far to the embassy?"

"A few minutes. But you're not going there. We have a place in a hotel."

"Is it safe?"

"We live there," said Rex.

Justice was going to point out that that didn't answer his question, and in fact that the city was filled with strife and terrorist attacks, but he decided that a night's rest was what he truly needed.

The hotel was five stories, painted white, with cracks making up most of the facade. Justice had expected a five star hotel. Then he remembered that several five star hotels had been bombed around the city.

"It's a dump, but they'd never think to hit it," Rex said.

"It's never been hit?" Justice said. There were no guards, and no barriers preventing a car bomb from taking down the entire thing. He was under the impression that such things would be carefully evaluated, but in the end, what did he know? He hadn't even been promoted yet.

"Damn straight," Rex said, nodding with pride at the hotel.

Inside an old man slept at the lobby. They walked up two flights of stairs to a room.

"This is yours. I'm across the hallway, in case you need anything," Rex said.

Justice wasn't sure but he thought Rex winked at him. Unsettled, it took him a few seconds to say what was on his mind. "Do you have any information on the good doctor?"

"Shhh." Rex placed a finger on his lips. "Not here. It's not swept."

"Oh," Justice said, somewhat confused.

Rex turned to his room.

"Rex?"

"Yes?" Rex said and turned back.

"What did they tell you about me?"

"That you were a top dog," Rex said.

Justice was now certain that he was being winked at.

"And that you had already caught some real bad guys. Threw them in the roaster without hesitation," Rex added with approval.

"Really?" Justice felt some sense of pride.

"That's right. I'll tell you one thing, sir. We need that kind of can-do attitude here. There're plenty of bad guys to roast. If you clean a few up, all the better."

"Indeed," Justice said, hoping he looked as cool and badass as possible. "Good night."

He walked into his small room. It was an only slightly redecorated prison cell. The toilet and sink were stacked next to the bed, a small twin, and a single naked bulb swayed to his entrance. He sat down on the bed. It creaked, screamed. Taking off his shoes, leather soft-soles, he inhaled through his nose and immediately regretted it when a hint of crusted urine made it's way to his conscious. There would be no forgetting that now. He lay down, staring at the light bulb, and trying to breath through his mouth.

Abid's painting, the feeling he had when he first saw it, then when he saw the blood splattered across it, then when he saw the painting in Drail's office, all hit him at once and he had an unpleasant sensation of sadness.

He slept like that, waking up to the urine, which somehow seemed to get stronger, though now it seemed more bearable, for the entire night.

"Justice?"

He looked at the door. It was half open and half of Rex's face blinked at him.

"Yes?"

"You all right?"

"Is it morning?"

"Yes. It's time to go."

He blinked again. He couldn't believe he was this tired. He stared at his backpack. Untouched.

"The door was open."

"The door was open?"

"That's right," Rex said, his eyes darting around the room as if he was worried about Justice. "You shouldn't leave the door open like that."

Justice was certain that he'd shut the door, though he couldn't say with any certainty now. "I didn't know it was open."

"Okay. We should go."

"Can I get a coffee?"

"And breakfast. There's a place nearby. We all go there."

Justice wanted to point out that this was another security issue, but he decided that he needed coffee before he could make any calls. The lobby was abandoned and there were two bullet holes in the wall behind the lobby desk that he was certain he didn't see the night before. It smelled like someone had soiled their pants in there: feces and cleaner.

"You know the guy who was here?" Justice asked.

"Of course not. Why?"

"No reason," Justice said, thinking that he really needed that coffee. He checked his phone, as they got in the car. Sasha hadn't sent anything. He sent her another message asking if there were any leads on the French woman. He would have rather been in France. When he had first been recruited for this job, he had pictured Europe. Ski slopes and hot women with loose morals. How wrong he was. He stared at the covered in black women and men on donkey carts as he passed them by. Rex was talking about something, but all Justice could think about was the dust that surrounded him.

"Here it is," Rex said.

Justice looked over to see a perfect cafe. Of course here, in a country simmering with civil hate, it was a perfect target. Though the awning was dusty, the chairs were laid out about the sidewalk looked somewhat new. There were a few men, locals from the look of it, sitting around and drinking from cups. Justice stepped out, and the aroma of coffee jolted him. He could see why Rex liked this place.

They sat down and ordered eggs and coffee.

"Best coffee I've ever had," Rex said.

It was soupy, syrupy, but Justice agreed.

"So is Justice a nickname... you know for all you've done?"

"No, it's real," Justice said, biting into the eggs and wincing as his teeth ground against sand.

"Oh, you have to watch out for the sand. The cook is an old bastard who never heard of the word clean."

Justice couldn't imagine how Rex was smiling, since all *he* was thinking about was how people in this part of the world didn't use toilet paper and if the old man out back had solid morning bowel movements.

He swallowed down the food trying not to taste it and they were off to the embassy. The dust veil lifted some with the sun, and brown mountains made themselves be known. Justice felt relaxed. He was never sure why, but the sight, or presence of mountains always relaxed him. And though these ones were crawling with Al Qaeda soldiers, the safety they offered all inhabitants agreed with something basic inside him.

"The mountains here are crap," Rex said.

"Why's that?"

"Make it hell to capture these terrorists."

Justice tried to react as sagely as possible. The embassy was thankfully surrounded by barriers and guards. Marines saluted them as they parked the car and walked in.

"The Ambassador's high energy. You'll have to watch out, but he likes how you work, so there shouldn't be any issues."

They walked down polished hallways that were a relief from the dusty outside.

"Ambassador Stones?" Rex said as he leaned into an open door.

"Yes?" a smooth voice replied.

"Justice is here."

A chair scraped. "Let him right in."

Justice entered a small shiny room. He could smell cigarettes and whiskey.

"Mr. Justice. Please, come in, sit down," the Ambassador pointed to a leather chair across his desk from him. "Rex could you get me a coffee, and close the door? You want anything?"

"Coffee is always good," Justice said.

"Same as the cafe?" Rex asked.

"Sure," Justice said regretting it immediately—why was he always trying to be compliant?

The door closed.

"I can't tell you how great it is to have someone of your caliber, of your style here. We've been inundated with State department pussies for the past few years," the ambassador said. He had the stature of a wrestler, with a round shiny head and a birthmark across his nose and forehead. His eyes seemed to be black holes, and Justice tried not to look into them. Yet he was well spoken enough that his straight back spoke more of good posture than military rigidity.

"Thank you," Justice said.

"I'm Frank, by the way."

"Justice."

They shook hands. Frank lit up a cigarette. "You want one?"

"Don't smoke."

This elicited a pause and a single raised eyebrow. "You're not a health nut are you?"

"No," Justice said, though he had no idea why Frank would care.

"Good. Don't need that shit in this line of work. And I'm sure someone like you appreciates that."

"Of course," Justice said; now he didn't like Frank.

Rex came in with some coffees, laid them on the table and stood behind Frank. Justice could taste the grinds as he sipped. But the bitter grounds were welcome in his mouth. He could feel the caffeine working, though he wondered if it was just his imagination. The three men concentrated on their coffees. A morning prayer broke out and seemed to add to Justice's introspection; he just wasn't sure what he should have been thinking about. After a minute of straight silence, Justice decided to talk.

"What can you tell me about Dr. Noklar?" Justice asked.

"They did a sweep of his house and hardware. Did you see the results?" Frank asked.

"No," Justice said, leaning forward in his seat.

"Nothing new."

"Oh." Justice bit his tongue. He wasn't certain if Frank had all his neurons firing properly.

"That's right. He's a clever one. If you don't find anything, that's when you should suspect everyone he's ever known," Frank said, while Rex nodded his head.

"Fair enough. But that doesn't help us here," Justice said, wanting to forget Abid's painting and anything to do with it.

Frank looked at Rex with a raised eyebrow.

Justice sipped his coffee, concentrating on the black liquid with more intensity than was warranted. He looked up into Frank's black eyes and his chest caved in.

"You all right?" Frank asked.

"I'm fine. Go on," Justice said without looking up.

"No. Your face looks pale."

"Jet lag."

"Where was I?" Frank asked.

"Evaluating lessons learned," Rex said.

"That's right. Your Mr. Abid was a sneaky one. The trick in such situations is to do what the Israelis do. You know what they do?" Frank said.

Justice had nothing but respect for the Israeli spy services. But he wanted to go on with his mission, not hear some remote outpost's ambassador tell him his view on the world. "No."

"Anyone commits a crime against them they go after the entire family. Throw them out on the streets. That's what they do," Frank said. When he finished speaking, he nodded his head like this was wisdom perfected. Rex nodded as well, his lower lip furled.

"I'm sorry. I think I missed something. What does this have to do with Mr. Abid?"

"It has everything to do with Mr. Abid," Rex said, stepping forward. Frank placed a hand on Rex's leg, stopping him.

"His family. We know he's up to no good. The lack of evidence proves that. He shot himself as an escape. Now we should go after his family. Interrogate every single one of them. Then kick them out on the street."

"Okay," Justice said. He really didn't care. He just wanted Frank to tell him where Dr. Noklar was.

"That is what has proven to work in history. Time and again. You want to uproot a cell, or a network. You go after everyone who's associated with it."

Justice, not wanting to add his words to this gave the slightest nod he could and sipped the rest of his coffee.

"That's why I'm glad you're here. You understand this more than anyone," Frank said, smiling a smile so wide that Justice could see a glint from one of his back teeth. He tried hard not to look at his eyes.

"And we *are* going to go after his family," Justice said, hoping to twist the conversation to his benefit. "Dr. Noklar."

Frank looked up at Rex who smiled.

"He understands," Rex said.

"Yes he does."

Justice returned his face to the empty cup and tried to lick the grounds at the bottom.

"And to answer your question," Frank said. "We have no idea if the good doctor is in this country, but we aim to find out."

"There was talk of a terrorist plot being hatched?" Justice asked.

Frank waved it off with his hand. "There's always talk of a terrorist plot being hatched. Where do you think you are?"

"I was led to believe that this was bigger than most," Justice said.

Frank's face creased up. "Is that true?" he asked Rex.

"Yes sir. Apparently the switchboards have gone silent, so we believe something big is brewing."

"Any clues?" Justice asked.

"We're working on it," Rex said, his tone defensive.

"All right…" Justice stared at his cup. Why the hell did Drail send

Nelson Lowhim

him here?

"Well it's why they sent you here, right? Any threat is a threat by the doctor," Frank said.

"How's that?"

"You don't see? He's clever enough to disappear, so he's clever enough to be where there's any trouble."

Justice chewed the inside of his cheek. He was growing tired, but perhaps what Frank said made sense. Besides, he reminded himself, he needed to get with this situation. "Fair enough," Justice said, his head tightening. "So what's the next step?"

"We're not certain, yet," Frank said, looking at Rex as if this were to be expected.

"No leads?" Justice asked.

"There *should* be some," Frank said, giving Rex an eye.

"We'll have to chase down a few," Rex said.

Frank examined his hands as if they weren't his.

"So no good ideas?" Justice said.

"Nope," Frank said, rubbing the back of his hands against each other.

"Well, I could head down to the prison and see what they've dredged up," Rex said.

"Our place?" Frank asked.

Rex nodded, and a darkness crept across his face.

"Let's ask the major if he knows what's going on," Frank said.

Rex rolled his eyes as Frank picked up the phone and asked for the colonel.

"He's a little edgy, but he means well," Frank said.

"That's fine," Justice said. "We have a few colonels around the agency headquarters."

"Doesn't everyone," Rex said.

And with that a large man stepped into the room. He had a perfect high and tight haircut, and his eyes grabbed whatever they were looking at.

"Ambassador, you called?" the man said in a low growling voice.

"I did. Have you heard anything about the switchboards going silent lately?"

"I do. I sent you a report yesterday morning. The one you told me good job on, remember?"

"I…" Frank ruffled through the things on his desk. "Ah, this one," he said holding up a thick file. "Can you summarize it?"

"Basically we're not sure what's going on," the colonel said.

"Nothing?"

"Nothing. They're sneaky bastards, these brownies," said the colonel and with that he glanced over at Justice.

Justice tilted his head at the large man but got nothing in return.

"Well these men are going to look for leads," Frank said, handing Rex the file. "You have anyplace for them to start? The prison perhaps?"

"I was there," the colonel said. "The new batch are exceptionally sneaky. They claim to know nothing. But you know how they are."

"That we do," Frank said shaking his head. "The colonel was in Iraq, and Afghanistan. He knows…"

Justice nodded.

"Is that all?" the colonel asked.

"That's all."

As the colonel's footsteps echoed away, Justice stood up. His foot was asleep. "So we should get started and look at this prison," he said. He wanted to get away from Frank.

Rex stepped forward. "Let's go."

"Oh, wait. First you have to sign a non-disclosure form," Frank said. "Right?" he asked Rex.

"That's right."

"What for? This is Tango-one," Justice said, realizing then that he really didn't know what Tango-one meant, or what gates it would get him through.

"Of course it is," Frank said, looking at him with pitiful eyes. "But this prison is still a need to know basis only. Everyone has to sign this. He pulled something out and handed it to Justice.

Justice stared at the paper, which was a print out of a PowerPoint presentations pointing out how useful the enhanced interrogations were, and the final page saying that nothing would be said about it, even if the interrogations weren't helpful.

Justice signed it on some blank space at the bottom. "Here."

Soon they were driving through narrow streets, with market stalls on all sides. They parked in an alley and walked through alley-corridors so narrow that at times they'd to walk sideways. The smell of dusty concrete covered with sewer water filled the air. Justice had a sudden need to spit.

"Is this our prison, or theirs?" Justice asked.

Rex placed a finger on his lips to tell Justice to be quiet.

Coming into a wider, dusty road, they walked past kids playing soccer with rags wrapped into a ball. When the ball bounced into Justice's path he juggled it with his feet and kicked it back at the kids. They yelped for joy. One kid, with a burn scar on his left cheek, and a curled up foot that could perfectly scoop up the ball gave him a thumbs up.

"Better watch out," Rex said. "You never know who's on your side."

"Surely they're harmless," Justice blurted out. Then he thought better of what he wanted to say and kept quiet. This was Rex's territory, which meant he knew the place better than Justice.

Rex gave him a stern look. "That's what they all say, until they realize that a thumbs up is a signal for someone to shoot."

Justice jerked his eyes towards the rooftops all around them.

Rex gave Justice a once over look. "This war would be over if we just stopped having rules of engagements. It's people like me who have to suffer, while the liberals in Washington make up rules for a game they've never played and don't understand."

Justice, sensing the hostility, and knowing that it could only come from hard experience, and not wanting to be part of the problem said: "I know. Sometimes I forget."

Rex walked on.

Finally, in another small alley, where old women sat on their haunches, and muttered to each other, Rex pounded on a steel door. An eye-level slit opened.

"Who goes there?" a muffled voice from inside asked. The pair of eyes in the slit ran over Rex, then parsed Justice.

Rex flashed a badge. "The midnight crow can't be seen. It's the dove that cries at night."

"And the midget at noon?"

"He cries for two."

"He may cry, but he weeps."

"And for what?"

A grumble arose on the other side of the door. The scraping of a metal latch made Justice shiver, but the door opened.

"Long," Justice said referring to the passwords.

"Security needs it. Can't be too careful these days," Rex replied.

Justice glanced at the old women who were staring at him.

"What about them?" Justice asked.

"Do you mean the women?" Rex asked, stepping inside and shook hands with a hunched over old man. "Don't worry about them, can't be too suspicious, can we?"

Justice stepped into the dark corridor. There was an open door at the other end with light blinding his eyes. "Hi," he said and stuck out his hand to the old man. The old man slammed the door shut and locked a latch. The wispy, white hairs on his head seemed frozen.

"Hi," the old man said. He had milky eyes, and Justice forced himself to look into them.

"I'm Justice."

"No need for names here," the old man said and slapped his hand away.

"Let's go," Rex said and they walked to an opening to an office, where a young man leaned back on his chair, and another larger man stood beside him.

"Rex, come in," the young man said. "What can I do for you?"

"We need the files on all your prisoners. How many are there right now?" Rex asked.

There was an odd smell in the room worming it's way into Justice's nose. A pine cleaner covered it, but not entirely.

"Only one. We just sent the lot of them to the locals."

"Dammit," Rex said. "Which one?"

"The uni."

"Can we see the one?" Rex asked.

"Two," the large man standing said.

"Two?" the young man said.

"That's right, two."

"All right, we have two then." He tossed Rex a chain with a key on it. "You know where."

Justice followed Rex through a backdoor and into a dark hallway. Here that smell that had crept into his nose stood out even more. There was something sweet, yet grimy to it. Justice could feel his stomach retch. He inhaled through his mouth.

"Yeah, the smell really gets to you here. It's these brownies, they're stinky by nature," Rex said, then gave Justice a once over. "Say, what are you, by the way?"

"American," Justice said, not wanting to get into his background, especially since it made him feel so out of place just thinking about it.

"Oh," Rex said. He pulled out a flashlight when it got too dark, and they made their way down stairs.

"Everything here is underground. Or the secret parts at least."

The smell was growing stronger, and Justice wasn't certain if he was hearing wails in the background, or if it was the grinding of metal doors echoing off the walls. His heart beat faster. Sweat leaked from his hands. He'd been to prisons before, but they never smelled like this. The air grew staler. Suffocating. He spat on the floor, wondering if he was getting weak.

"Here," Rex said.

They were at the bottom of the stairs. A large metal door in front of them. Rex twisted the handle and pushed. It screamed open. It was a pitch where Justice could feel the vibrations separating his bones and muscles.

Another room came into view. Two men sat on stools, reading newspapers. One was the old man from before, and when he looked at Justice, there was a certain hollowness to his eyes that moved Justice. He wondered how the old man made it here faster than they did. The other one was younger and seemed zealous.

"Hi you two." Rex threw them both a pack of cigarettes he fished out from his pocket. "To keep you satisfied."

"Rex," the old man said. His voice had the dual properties of being a whisper as well as with heavy bass. "What brings you down to the dungeon?"

"You know they've banned the use of the word dungeon. It makes us look bad," Rex said.

The old man hacked up some phlegm and spat at Rex's shoes, barely missing. "That's what I think about your ideas."

Rex let out a sigh. "How are you doing?" he asked the young man.

"I'm doing good. Grandpa here won't do the questioning anymore. Why the hell don't I get a promotion? I'm doing all the work."

"When you've been here as long as I have, you learn," the old man said.

Justice noticed that the old man was only old in spirit. There weren't many wrinkles on his face. He was just haggard. "I'm Justice," he said, sticking out his hand.

The old man hacked up some phlegm and spat at Justice's shoes. This time he didn't miss.

"Who's this idiot you brought down?" the old man asked Rex.

"He's from the agency," Rex said.

The young man looked at Justice. "My friend may not have manners, but he's right. We try not to use names here. Just call us the interrogators."

"I'm heading up to get some fresh air," the old man said. He folded his newspaper, placed it on his stool and headed up.

The young man shook his head. "See what I mean? He doesn't do anything any more. Claims he has too many nightmares. So I told him to quit, and he says he can't. Needs the money. Tell the boss that we need some new blood here. He's not cutting it anymore. He's talking with those old women up there and it's making him soft."

"I will," Rex replied. "The prisoners?"

The young interrogator stood up off his stool and walked over to the wall on his right. He pulled open a small case and pressed a button. Where Justice thought there was only a wall, part of it swung open.

"Follow me," the young man said. Rex and Justice followed him into a hallway small enough to be a closet. The young man opened another steel door and pointed inside. "Two of them. They don't like talking, but I've taught them enough lessons."

The smell that'd been bothering Justice all this time was now in full bloom. It was from the men. On opposite corners, were two men, naked, on the floor with one hand handcuffed to steel handles on the wall. The floor was clean everywhere except where the men were. Around them was a liquid-fecal mix. Justice dry-heaved, then remembered to breath through his mouth once again.

"Yeah, they're filthy," the young man said. "That one," he pointed to one of the men who was mumbling and staring right at them. "Claims to be a journalist. We found him on the compound where a terrorist cell was captured. He claimed he was only there for a story. That guy was a possible lookout for the terrorists." He turned without waiting for any questions and headed out.

Rex shook his head. "They really are the same where ever you go. Always stinking up a place."

"They get bathroom breaks here?" Justice asked.

"Of course not," Rex said and furrowing his forehead. "Let's talk to this one. He looks like he's asking for it." Rex walked over to the journalist. "What's your name?"

"Please," the man said, in an English accent that didn't seem to have any flaws.

"Please what?"

"I need some water. Food. They haven't given us anything. You must treat…" the man seemed to lose energy and hung his head.

"Treat you better?" Rex said. "Would you rather we send you right away to a Yemeni prison? You know what they'll do to you there?"

The prisoner trembled. Justice trembled.

"Good. Then perhaps you should start thanking us."

"I'm sorry."

"That's better."

"So tell us, what are your friends up to? Are they planning to attack America?"

"I already said. I don't know... Only a journalist."

"Come on now," Rex said, pulling out a flask from his pocket. "Tell me and you'll get a drink."

"Please... nothing... please." The man hung his head again and closed his eyes.

"Christ," Rex said, looking at Justice. "They *always* play these games."

Justice leaned forward, though he made sure not to touch the man. "Have you heard anything about a doctor helping them?"

The man's eyes opened. There was a flicker of recognition in them. "Maybe... a doctor."

"Speak up," Rex said, softly kicking the man's ribs.

Whatever this man had done, there was something in the way he seemed so defeated that Justice liked. "Go get some water."

Rex stared at Justice, his mouth half-open. "What?"

"Get some food and water for our friend here," Justice said. He winked, hoping that Rex would see this as a ploy against the prisoner, though in fact it was Justice trying to get rid of Rex. "Let me have that flask... Please."

Rex handed over the flask after a momentary pause, then he walked out.

Justice sipped the bottle. It was tea. "Here," he said and pushed the mouth to the prisoner.

"Oh thank you. Thank you." The man sucked a couple sips then stopped.

"So you did hear of a doctor?"

"Yes."

"Dr. Noklar?"

"Don't. Know."

"From Pakistan?"

"I think so."

Justice's heart jumped. A lead. "Where?"

"Jebel. Nabi. Suyad."

Justice pulled out a pen and wrote down the name. "And who did you hear this from?"

"Everywhere."

The man seemed to deflate, and he collapsed on the ground.

"Here," Rex said, holding out a box of crackers.

"I think he's sick," Justice said, grabbing the box. He tried to shake the man, but he wouldn't budge.

Rex laughed. "He's faking it." He walked over and kicked the man. "Get up."

When the man didn't respond, Rex kicked even harder, but the man still wouldn't move. "Well, let's check out the other man."

The other man wouldn't budge either. Justice checked for a pulse and only after a few minutes did he feel something.

"Guess that's it," Rex said and walked out.

Justice followed him all the way back up to where the old women sat. The old interrogator was there and he fell quiet; the crystals of a conversation hung in the air.

"Rex," Justice said. He grabbed his shoulder. "The journalist said something about a doctor at Jebel Nabi Suyad."

"He did?"

"You know where that is?"

"We can check it out. First, let's head to the Yemeni prison." Rex stopped for a second. "I need to get something. Wait here."

Justice watched, with a weird disappointment inside his chest, as Rex went back down.

Chatter sounded up again. Justice knew some Arabic. They were talking about an infidel. He glanced over. The old interrogator was pointing at him.

"What is it?" Justice asked. Any sympathy he had held for the old man evaporated.

"They think you're pretty."

"Thanks," Justice said, feeling his face turn red.

"That wasn't a compliment," the old man said. There was something about his face that only now made Justice's skin crawl. It was as if there were bumps and canals of an ancient landscape on his face.

A truck honked in the distance. Justice was aware of the exhaust in the air. It was a welcome change from the sickening smell inside. He spat out on the sidewalk. Then again.

"I can't stand the smell either," the old man said. He stuck out his hand. "Atropos."

"Justice."

"You can't stand the smell," the old man repeated.

"I guess not. It's a weird combination."

"It's hell is what it is."

"Maybe."

"I can't take it anymore. What we're doing down there is nothing more than a crime."

"Well, it's all for a better cause," Justice said, looking around for Rex. He didn't want to seem rude, but something about the old man smelled of failure, and he didn't want to be around that. Not when he was this close to a promotion.

"What better cause? There's nothing, I tell ya, nothing. We tear souls out of their fleshy home, that's what we do."

"I thought none of that was allowed. Not anymore at least."

"You think you can't figure out other ways to tear out a soul?" Atropos said. "We do it all the time. To whoever we want."

"Still better than how they treat their own."

Atropos looked at him and shook his head. "That's not the point, is it?"

"Then what is it?" Justice asked angrily. It was people like this old man who made America weak. He knew that much.

"The ghosts, man."

Justice looked at Atropos to make sure that he's not joking. The man was holding on to Justice's sleeve, and he didn't appear to be anything but serious.

"Ghosts?"

"Yes. I know you saw them too."

"I didn't see anything," Justice said.

"You didn't?"

"No," Justice said, half shouting.

"What?"

"I think you've lost it, old man."

The old man shrunk back, then he puffed out his chest. "You don't dare call me an old man."

"Why don't you go downstairs and do your job?" Justice asked.

"I c-c-can't. Besides the young man will handle it. He has no heart, and no head. So he'll be fine."

Justice had a feeling that the old man was dumping him in the same category as the young man downstairs. "You mean he's willing to do his job."

"I mean he's dumb enough to do his job, and lap up whatever else they throw his way."

Justice shook his head. "While you take breaks up here and he works? Sounds like a great moral stance for you. Why not quit?"

"I have a family. What else am I going to do?"

"Ask for a transfer," Justice said, getting annoyed at the old man.

"I wish. They've denied them all."

Justice wanted to say of course they would, especially for someone who doesn't do his job, but he remained silent.

"I'm not joking about the ghosts," Atropos said.

"I don't doubt that."

"There's a better explanation," the old man said, holding up a hand. "You need to see these people when they come in, full of life. Full of zeal."

"Terrorists."

"Let me finish... They're not terrorists. But we're making 'em that way."

"So you're the kind of person who blames his own country before he blames the problem. I have that right?" Justice said. People like this didn't understand history.

"I didn't say that," the old man said, angrily. "I said... Let me finish... I said that they come in. Young men. Full of life. And we suck it out of them. We take their humanity. But humanity doesn't just go away. It dies inside them and it excretes out of their pores. And it smells. It stinks. That's the smell you couldn't stand down there." Atropos shook a

182

finger at Justice. "And it infiltrates your pores. And it eats away at your DNA. It becomes a part of you. That's what happens. It gets so deep in you that it changes you. And it sucks the humanity out of you. Do you think people in the past didn't know this? It makes you a monster... It makes you something else. And that's what I'm saying. That we will change as a nation, all of us, from knowing this, and we will have no soul. We will no longer be humans."

Justice didn't like the way the old man was talking. He had some soft view of how the world worked, of history, of how sometimes bad things had to be done for good to happen. Some of it made sense. But he reminded himself that there was no way he made sense. The old man was lazy. He didn't want to do work. And he was nuts too. Whoever talked about ghosts had to be nuts.

"Well thank you for that insight, Kant," Justice said, throwing in a mocking tone, hoping to browbeat the man to leave him alone.

"Apropos... I know you think you're tough. But you're not. You're another spook doing his job. And you'll fall like the others when you realize that your humanity is gone."

"So what? That's our job," Justice said, now fully angry and no longer trying to paint it under a cool veneer.

The old man shook his head and walked back to the old women. Justice reminded himself about all the deaths that would occur if he didn't do his job.

Rex came up. "Ready?"

Justice followed him. Back through the alleyways they went. They brushed past an old man selling sculptures made from old coke cans on a split potato sack on the floor. Rex kicked a few of the pieces and grinned at Justice.

"Is that old man nuts?" Justice asked, smiling apologetically at the man who seemed shocked that his sculptures were kicked like that.

"Atropos? Did he talk to you?" Rex asked.

"Yes. He doesn't seem to like his job."

"Can you blame him?"

"The young one seems to like it."

Rex shrugged. "Who cares?"

Nelson Lowhim

Justice didn't know what to think. He was glad to be away from the smell.

They walked through some winding alleys and finally made it to a large concrete fortress with guards posted everywhere.

"We do exchanges with the Yemenis?" Justice asked, as he watched a group of guards beating a man at the front door.

"Of course. It's their country, isn't it?"

"But, I thought that…" Justice decided not to finish.

The guards acted like they didn't care that Rex was there, and they walked into a grand lobby with pictures of leaders all over the walls. They then headed down a shiny hallway. Rex knocked on an oak door that read: "Head of Prison."

Inside the office a man, whose perfectly tailored suit and hairy knuckles that reminded Justice of Drail, smoked a cigar.

"What can do for you?" the man asked. His skin seemed to glow.

"We need to know if you've heard anything about a Dr. Noklar," Justice said.

The man shook his head; loose flesh on his face jiggled. "No."

"What about any Doctor?"

The man laughed. "Every man with a professional degree trying to overthrow the government claims to be a doctor."

"Oh…" Justice said.

"I could point you to doctors, but there are simply too many to bother with."

"What about one from Pakistan?"

"A foreigner?" The man said, shocked. "Oh no. That's no good."

"Of course," said Justice. "It's atrocious how—"

"All non-Arab start trouble, I tell you."

Justice nodded.

"Doctors," the man said and shook his head, still perturbed by the whole situation. "Back in my day they only treated sick people. Now…"

"How's the terrorist situation here?" Justice asked.

The man scoffed. "Under control," he said, then staring at his desk, he seemed to reconsider this. "With your help, of course."

"Well, we're always there for our friends," Justice said, feeling like a proper diplomat.

The man stared at his desk again. He muttered as he adjusted the rings on his fingers. Justice was certain he heard something about Libya and Kaddafi, but he let it pass.

"Is the situation here getting out of hand?"

"It is," the man said and wiped his head. He was now sweating profusely. "I tell you, the Americans are the only thing that stand between people like me and those barbarians. They will have our heads on a stake."

"So no problems with our drones?"

"Oh, that's not something that goes on here," the man said, rubbing his hands vigorously. He grinned. "Why cry over criminals, eh?" He winked.

"Of course," Justice said.

The sounds of screams in the hallway filtered into the room and all three stood in silence. The man went back to shuffling through some papers on his desk. Justice glanced at Rex who shrugged.

"Wait," the man said. "We *are* after a doctor. Here at Jebel Nabi Suyad."

"Jebel Nabi Suyad?" Justice said, his heart beating fast. "That's him."

"I arrange for you to ride along."

A few hours later they were in the back of a canvas-covered pickup truck, riding with several soldiers who looked like they were high on qat. The head officer, Walid, sat next to Justice. Rex had closed his eyes and didn't seem to care where they were going.

"How do you like our country?" the officer asked Justice, his eyes gleaming and his teeth yellowed on the edges. His breath smelled like smoke and goat meat.

"It's nice," Justice said. What else was he going to say? That it was a dirt bowl of shit? That they all should pick up and move somewhere better? "The mountains here are... magnificent."

The officer's grin widened. "I know. I love the mountains. I hate that these foreign fighters are using them."

"So it's mostly foreigners?" Justice asked, his spirits perking up. He was still down since the old man had confronted him with his conspiracy. Though Justice was certain that the old man was nuts, the words he'd spoken were burrowing through his mind and playing on repeat.

"Of course," said Walid. "Who else? They think that they can push us out and do what they want with us."

"So you don't blame us?" Justice asked. He was feeling better now.

"Of course not," Walid said.

Blood rushed to Justice's cheeks as the officer furrowed his forehead. "That's good. I heard different from some of the locals," he said.

The officer dismissed that with a wave of his hand. "Oh, some people talk anything. If it wasn't for America these prisons wouldn't have been built. These men here would be without a job. I wouldn't have a job. We wouldn't have a way to fight back. Those terrorists would win."

"Indeed." Justice's chest had filled to the brim with pride, and he admonished himself for ever doubting what he was doing. That old man *was* crazy.

Justice nodded. He felt a burn on the side of his face and turned to see a soldier staring at him, with eyes narrowed.

Justice smiled. The soldier glanced over at Rex and sneered.

"What's his problem?" Justice asked Walid.

"Oh, he's probably hoping for some qat."

"All your men take qat?" Justice asked, wondering how the officer could trust any one of his soldiers who were high.

"Of course. I tried the other way, but they revolt."

"Addicts?"

"No," the officer said, shaking his head. "They're not that bad. But it's the only way they can do this job. Especially raids like this."

Not knowing what the officer meant, Justice closed his eyes and let the time pass by. The truck jostled back and forth, dust pushed in from the gaps in the canvas.

The officer, seeing Justice's reaction, leaned farther in. "This is how it's done here. We have many enemies."

"Oh?"

"Our history is long, though, and we will win."

Justice didn't know what to say to that.

"You have seen our museum?"

"No."

The officer seemed shocked and moved away from Justice.

Justice closed his eyes, trying not to feel bad.

A hard lurch to the right, and Justice opened his eyes to catch himself from falling. The officer laughed. Justice tried his hardest to stare at something that wasn't the eyeballs of a qat-high soldier. He focused on the sunlight, which highlighted a few strands of dust, crisp in the dark pickup.

The car came to a halt and the soldiers started to jump out.

"Wait here," the officer said. "You can watch from the back." He patted Justice's knee and jumped out yelling at his men to run forward. Rex didn't stir. Justice hopped out of the back and watched, his legs swinging on the edge of the truck.

The house in front of him was a two story, tan-colored building circled by a head-high wall. Justice watched as the soldiers stormed through the front gate. Gunshots went off. There was yelling.

The soldiers on the outside of the wall were angry and huffing. They harassed anyone on the road. Three of them swarmed around a man with a donkey. They pushed him to the ground. On the donkey were two sacks. It was dates. The soldiers stuffed their pockets full of dates. Annoyed, Justice stepped forward. The officer was nearby.

"Tell them not to rob," Justice said.

Officer's face grew stern, before he smiled. "No, not to worry. He's a terrorist."

Justice wanted to argue, but remembered that it wasn't his place to make any such comments. This was a young nation feeling itself out. America had done the same in its struggles.

An explosion ripped through the air. Justice turned to see the second floor burst into powder and mud bricks. Pieces of the building whistled by. Screams filled the air. The officer ran into the building. More shooting. All the soldiers outside returned to pulling guard. The tension turned the air into a heavy crunched material. The soldiers exchanged glances and asked each other questions with voices ready to crack. Justice empathized with them, and felt bad that he'd just been ready to yell at them.

The building went silent for at least ten minutes. Finally, Walid walked out and beckoned Justice in.

"There's one left. He's a doctor."

They'd found him! Justice followed the officer with great anticipation. The inside of the compound was a dirt lawn with rusted fingers poking from the ground. Two nothing-but-ribcage mutts licked themselves in a corner. Justice could smell sewage. There was also the smell of something sweeter, though he didn't know what.

"Did anyone get hurt?" Justice asked.

Walid didn't seem to be all that disturbed. "Oh, only them."

"The bomb?"

"One of my men shot at a shadow. There was a propane tank behind that." Walid grinned.

Justice thought he saw some blood in the man's gums, but didn't say anything. A few soldiers filed out of the building talking loudly. Justice followed the officer in. The door inside was too low and Justice had to duck to enter. He walked through a hallway. To the side, in a room, were a group of women and children crying. A small boy, just hitting his teens, looked up and glared at Justice. His hateful eyes shrunk Justice's chest.

Justice flashed a smile, but the boy turned away. A soldier, with blood on his sleeves, pushed the boy to the ground. The other soldiers laughed. One poked Justice, his face all brown and yellow teeth. "Good," said the soldier.

Justice forced his next smile.

"Justice," said Walid, his arms out.

Justice, shook his hands. "You and your men did well," he said, though he knew he had no experience in these matters.

"We got the doctor," said Walid.

At his feet lay a man, his clothes seem to have been ripped off, and his skin was smeared with blood. As Justice took a step closer, he realized that the man was arching his back in spasms, and that the blood wasn't smeared but flowing from his chest. There was a beard on the man's face, but he was no more than twenty and Justice knew immediately he wasn't the Dr. Noklar. Nevertheless he could have some information.

"Is there a medic around?" Justice asked.

"He's taking care of my men," Walid said, a sneer on his face.

"Of course," said Justice, feeling foolish. He tried his hardest not to look at the man's ribs poking through his skin, or his eyes, wide open and staring at the ceiling as if he were trying to fly through it.

"What happened?" Justice asked, trying to iron out all the worry out of his voice.

"This terrorist tried to kill my men. Didn't you?" Walid said and kicked the man's legs.

The man groaned.

"Where are you from?" Justice asked.

The man, staring at the ceiling seemed to stop breathing for a second. Then he returned to sucking in air like each breath was his last.

"Answer him," Walid said, lighting up a cigarette. He offered one to Justice. Justice thought about his attempt to quit; out here it seemed so silly. He took one.

"Answer him," Walid repeated. He poked one of the man's ribs poking out of his chest.

The man screamed, the last syllables of his plea ricocheting off the walls and inside Justice's head.

"Tun-Tun…" the man said after a few seconds.

"Tunisia," said Walid.

"Are you a doctor?" Justice asked.

The man shook his head.

"Don't lie," Walid said, raising his boot above the ribs.

"Bomb-maker. N-nickname," said the man.

"See?" Walid said. "Barbarians. They fill our people with dangerous ideas. And call themselves doctors." He shook his head and tapped a few ashes on the man's face. The man turned his head to dodge the embers, but a few landed on his cheek, sizzling out in his blood.

"Where did you learn to make bombs?" Justice asked.

"I-iraq," the man said.

For a second Justice was sure he saw pride pass across the man's face.

"Al Qaeda in Iraq?"

The man shook his head. "Helped... people."

Walid shook his head, growing agitated. "Liar." He threw his cigarette into the man's open wound. Justice made the mistake of looking and saw the cigarette sizzle out on a piece of intestine protruding from of the man's stomach. It made him think of that old story about the Vietcong soldier dying with his intestines out and the American soldier, out of respect, handing him his bottle to drink out of.

"Why are you here?" Justice asked. "What do you want in this country?"

"Fight America. F-f-f back."

That didn't seem to make sense. The only reason the US even cared about this dump was because of terrorists like him. Justice was annoyed that the man wouldn't look at him. "We've never done anything to Tunisia," said Justice. He could smell sweet blood and feces now, and he felt nauseous because the smell wasn't that bad, only the thought of the cracked open man being the source of the smell was bad.

"Sir."

Justice turned his head. The recalcitrant boy he'd seen earlier, now stood with a bloody face in front of a soldier, who had the boy by his hair.

"What is it?" Walid asked, lighting up another cigarette.

"We have a terrorist here," said the soldier and threw the boy. The boy fell, the sound of air wheezing out of his mouth made Justice wince. Walid stepped in front of the boy.

"Is that right?"

The boy, his face scared, looked over at the man on the ground, his ribs cutting air. The boy's face turned resilient. It was obvious he hated all of them.

For a second Justice thought that Walid was going to hit the boy, and he didn't want to see the boy harmed. He stepped between them.

"People like him don't have your best interests at heart," Justice said, pointing at the "doctor" on the ground.

"Like the missile that killed my father and brother?" the boy said in a slightly stilted English.

Justice could see the hatred in the boy's eyes. He stepped back. He wasn't certain if he'd seen anything so pure in his life. Yet he hoped that it wasn't real.

Walid grabbed the boy and slapped his face. "Silly boy. What do you know of the world and how it works?" said Walid. He glanced at Justice. Justice nodded. The boy knew *nothing* about the world, and men like this doctor were fooling him by offering him easy answers to the pain he'd endured.

"We'll teach you," said Walid and raised a fist.

Justice didn't know what to say. He'd rather not see the boy beaten. Some soldiers came into the room and grabbed the kid. Justice tried to remain stolid. After all, these soldiers were his only protection. It wouldn't make sense to get on their wrong side.

Walid stepped up to Justice. "These village boys, they know only one thing." Walid held out a fist. "Talking doesn't help."

Justice, not wanting to answer that, walked over to the man. "Did you know that boy?"

The man moved his head up and down; Justice barely noticed it.

"Cousin…" the man said.

"Sorry," Justice muttered. For some reason, this man having been in Iraq made Justice respect him some. But he reminded himself that this man would kill him if roles were reversed.

The man turned his dark brown almost black eyes on Justice. There seemed to be a softness about him. "S-sorry?" he said.

"Your cousin. They shouldn't treat him like that."

The man blinked a few times. "It's the way of the world. Why are you surprised? Americans like this, don't they?"

"We don't," Justice said. He didn't know how else to defend the country he loved. "Cigarette?" he asked.

The man choked, or laughed. A mixture of blood and saliva rose from his lips. "You always want to give things."

Justice flinched. He wasn't sure why, but those words, surely words of a mad man, stung.

"You're too nice," the man said, and turned his eyes back to the ceiling.

Something unwound in Justice's stomach. "Do you know anything about a Dr. Noklar?"

The man stopped blinking. Then he closed his eyes. "Dr. Noklar? You know?"

"You know? You know where he is?" he said his voice stretching. He wanted so badly to be done with this cruel part of the world.

The man closed his eyes.

"What is it?" Walid said, walking over. "He won't speak?"

Justice didn't want to say anything that might lead the doctor to suffer, but he needed this information. He stayed quiet.

Walid kicked the doctor's ribs. "Speak you filthy dog."

The man yelped, rocked his body and started to mumble.

"Don't make me," Walid said and placed a boot on a rib.

Just watching made Justice's skin crawl. He rubbed his own ribs.

"Dr. Noklar. Fight back..." the man said. It seemed like drawing breath was growing too hard for him.

"Is he here?" Justice asked.

"No..."

"What?" Justice said. For a second he thought that the doctor was fooling around with him, and for a split second he wanted to kick the man's ribs. He bit his inner cheek instead.

"Today. We hit back..." said the man.

"Hit? With the doctor?" Justice asked.

"US embassy..."

Justice looked up at Walid who nudged the doctor's ribs again.

The man screamed, and this time Justice didn't care.

"You're attacking the embassy today?" Justice said. His heart was rising to his throat. "Tell me!"

The man turned his now black eyes on Justice. "Too late."

Walid kicked the man's ribs. The man let out a scream that was cut midway through by a spasm, and the man fell quiet. Further kicks from Walid did nothing to rouse him. Justice leaned forward as Walid was busy kicking the man's ribs.

"He's dead," Justice said.

"Huh?" Walid said, exerting himself through another kick, this one snapping ribs.

Some blood flew into Justice's eye. "I said stop," Justice said in a loud voice. "He's dead."

"Oh," Walid said, looking a little disappointed. He kicked the man again, pulled out another cigarette and started smoking.

"What are we going to do?" Justice asked.

Walid shrugged. "He died with his secrets. If the boy knows anything, we'll beat it out of him soon enough."

"Isn't there anyone else? What about the women?" Justice asked.

Walid grinned. "Come now. We can't go beating women. That will really not go over well."

"Can't we ask?" Justice said, his eyes darting around the room. He wanted a clue.

"What do women know?" Walid said, looking at Justice through narrowed eyes. "The man died with his secrets." He pointed to the dead doctor. "Let him rest."

"There has to be something," Justice said. He pulled his cellphone out and dialed Rex. No answer. "Does this man have a cellphone?" he asked Walid.

Walid pulled out a bloody fat phone. "This was on the ground near him."

Justice ran outside. "Rex!" Justice yelled.

Rex was chatting to an old man who was sitting next to his donkey with his hands tied behind his back.

"What is it?" Rex asked, skewing his eyes at Justice as if he was losing his patience.

"Call the embassy. Tell them there's an attack."

"Right now?"

"I don't know when, but they need to know," Justice said.

"What sort of attack?"

"I don't know. The man down there." Justice pointed at the house. "Just said there was one."

"And?"

"He's dead."

"That's it? You know we need more than that."

"I know *that*," Justice said, "but we should let them know."

Rex looked over at Walid who was standing behind Justice.

"Do it, now!" Justice yelled.

"Fucking Tango-ones," Rex said, and walked off some ways and started to chat into his cellphone.

Justice pulled out the doctor's cellphone and handed it to Walid. He hoped that whoever the doctor had called would be fooled by the officer's voice.

"What?" Walid said, taking the phone.

"We've to figure out who he called before he died. All three calls from today were to one place. Call them back and ask to meet with them again," Justice said.

"You think that man's friends will want to meet with an officer?"

"No, not an officer," Justice said. "I want *you* to be the doctor. Pretend to have his voice." It was like the world was conspiring against him to solve this problem.

"Oh," the officer said. "Not terrorist."

"What?"

"My men... They get crazy thoughts if I am terrorist, then what?"

Justice stooped forward, eyeing Walid's face, trying to see if the man was joking. "Are you serious?"

"Yes," Walid said.

"I'm not asking you to become a mole in a cell. I just want you to sound like the doctor for a few seconds."

Walid shook his head.

"Listen, you have to," Justice said.

Walid's face hardened. "I am not an American dog. Go to hell if you think I listen. *You* are a guest."

"I know—"

"Anymore and you can go home."

Justice knew he was about to lose the officer. "No, I meant that it'll only help your promotion. Think about it. You help me, and I'll make sure your boss hears about it," said Justice. Walid's face didn't soften. "I can even get you side jobs at the embassy. Maybe a job in the States."

Walid's eyes widened. "A job in America?"

"Of course," Justice said.

"Can I live there?"

Justice didn't expect that. "N-Maybe. Yes. Sure, of course you can."

Walid nodded and looked at the bloody phone in his hand. "Okay."

Walid pressed a button on the phone and turned away to talk.

"Here," Rex said. He had his phone an inch away from Justice's face.

"What?" Justice asked, annoyed that Rex was now acting so uppity.

"The embassy wants to talk to you," he said.

"Hello?" Justice said.

"Justice? What the hell's going on there? I didn't send you out there to bark orders at us," Frank yelled through the phone; the phone's speaker spat static.

"Frank—"

"Don't Frank me you headquarters bitch. Who the hell do you think you are?"

Justice bit his tongue. He didn't like being talked to like this. And he really didn't like being talked to like this without knowing the reason. Was Frank really angry that he had warned them?

"Are you there?" Frank asked after pause.

"Yes," Justice said. "Why do you want me to talk when all you're doing is cutting me—"

"What? You still haven't learned any manners?"

"I—"

"You listen here, why the hell would you think it's important to call the embassy and tell us we have a threat?" Frank said, stopping to cough.

"I—"

"Especially without verification. Do you know how many threats we get in one day?"

"I would think no more than—"

"Ten a fucking day. And that's just on our Youtube channel," said Frank.

"You?—"

"Do you have any idea how much these people hate us? A threat is supposed to get us worked up?"

"I guess it sounds—"

"It just boggles the mind that you can't think beyond one dying man's wishes. What if he just wanted to watch us scramble from paradise?"

"A dying man? Don't you—"

"You don't even know how, do you? What if it's a computer attack?" Frank said. This time it sounded like he was spitting into the phone.

"I didn't know that they had those capabiliti—"

"So I'm supposed to get ready for anything? What the hell's keeping your eyeballs from falling back into your head?"

Justice's face glowed with warmth. "I'm not sure—"

"Of course you're not because you're an idiot."

Justice held the phone a few inches from his ear. He turned away from Rex's grinning face.

"This is the last insolence I'll put up with, got it?" Frank said.

"I'll let you know if we have anymore information to help you out," Justice said.

"Christ. I hope you do," Frank said, his voice softening somewhat.

"Justice!"

Justice turned to Walid's brown-yellow teeth.

"Yes?" Justice said.

"He thought I was the dead man," Walid said.

Justice stared at his teeth for a second. They seemed to have grown browner in the past few minutes, and he wasn't sure what Walid was talking about since his mind was still on the rebuke Frank had given him. "Huh?"

Walid's face, still happy, calmed down. "Don't you remember? You just told me to call the dead man's phone," Walid said, holding out the phone and pointing out the blood.

Justice put down the phone, though he could still hear Frank's yells punching through the air.

"You got him?" Justice said.

"Yes," Walid replied. "And he thought I was him. So I said the plan was not well."

"He believed you?"

"He said we should meet," Walid said, scrunching up his lower face as if to say he wasn't sure.

"Where?"

"I know the place. It's downtown. Great qat."

Justice smiled. He lifted the other phone with Frank still yelling. Now he would be able to shut the man up. "Frank?"

"What the hell?" Frank said. "Who the hell told you to call me Frank?"

Justice paused, holding back the information was making him giddy. "Listen to me," Justice barked down the phone. "I'm going to meet the guy and we'll have this attack all figured out." By this point Justice was really feeling good. He was certain that he could prove himself, and help all the people at the embassy.

"Are you still on this attack business?" Frank said.

"Yes, I am," Justice said. "I'm heading out to a qat cafe and I'll call you when we get more—"

"You really are dumb, aren't you?" Frank said.

Justice chewed his inner cheek. A memory of Frank being respectful to him crossed his mind, and that made him feel even smaller. "What?"

"No Americans in the qat bars. They're basically opium dens in this part of the world," said Frank, scoffing as he did so.

"What?" Justice said. Rex was grinning again, shaking his head. Justice turned away. But instead he was met by Walid's grinning face. Justice closed his eyes.

"I said you can't go into a qat bar just because you feel like it," Frank said. It sounded like he was eating food now. "Or because you want to get high on local fauna."

"I don't *feel* like it. And I definitely don't want to do it to get high,"

Justice said. Part of him was confused why Frank, or anyone, would be so against trying to gain more information about an impending attack. "I need to go there and see if what the doctor... the dead man said about an attack was right. And I think it might lead to Dr. Noklar."

"I know *your* reasons," Frank said. "I heard them just fine. I said no Americans, which I believe means you, is allowed. So unless you have a real strong desire to get high, I'd recommend you don't do anything stupid."

"Are you serious?" Justice asked. "Do you understand what a lead is?" He could feel Dr. Noklar falling out of his reach.

"Don't lecture me on leads," Frank said, gulping down some liquid. "I'm the lead master. I was pulling leads while you were a cocky zygote. Got it?"

"What?... Listen, we can't let this go. This is important to finding out what to do next. You get this, don't you?"

"I don't think you know what you're talking about, Justice. I do think you're in over your head."

Justice chewed his inner cheek even more. He could taste blood. "People might die, you know that, don't you?" He thought of the Freedom Tower, and how it was complacent bureaucrats who allowed that travesty to the previous twin towers to happen, and it would be the reason for another such travesty.

"People die every day. Actually one a second," Frank said. "And three born every second."

Justice paused, what was that supposed to mean? "Are you serious?" he said, though he felt like a recalcitrant child more so than a secret agent when he asked that question.

"Of course I am."

"And you think that me breaking a small rule to find out more information on an attack that might kill people is unacceptable?"

"Small rule?" Frank said. "You child. This is no small rule. If you go into a qat den there's a high chance that you'll be addicted to the stuff in no time. And that means you're no good to America anymore. And it means the enemy has an in."

"I'm not going to chew," Justice said, annoyed.

"Oh but you are. You see if there's one thing that get's your neck slit in a qat den quicker than insulting the Prophet, it's not chewing qat."

"Well once isn't going to hurt. This stuff is weak, from what I hear."

"Heard from who?" Frank said and let out a chortle. "Your friends? I'm sure you didn't include these illegal friends of yours in your entry questionnaire, and if so I'd really learn to shut up, if I were you."

"I—"

"And if you go into the den do you know what the chances are of you being put on video and thrown onto the internets?"

"I—"

"It's not a might, it's a fact. Then the blogs—God I hate those—and the twitters will start. I can't tell you how much of a pain those things are, can I?" Frank said.

"I—"

"And then there'll be pie all over our faces because you were a little too hyper."

"I'm not being—"

"So don't go. Besides let's forget about the man who died and spilled his heart," Frank said, and laughed again, as if this was a joke and his was too clever. "I think that he was full of shit anyways."

"*I* don't."

"Of course. You're an idiot."

Justice didn't answer.

Frank let out some air. "Listen, Justice, you're a good field agent. I know this. You just have to follow the rules sometimes, all right? They're made for a reason."

The sudden change in Frank's tone threw Justice off guard. He didn't know how to react. Was the man a psychopath? Or was Justice letting his emotions get the best of him? "All right," Justice said. "Sorry for my behavior." He wasn't certain if this was the right thing to say.

"Ahhh. I wouldn't be the boss if I wasn't used to it," Frank said. He sounded like a father now. Whose, Justice wasn't certain.

"Aren't you worried about an attack? That you won't be safe?"

"Me? Hell no. This room is in the middle of the embassy. Unless they have bunker busting technology I'm safe. It's the poor saps on the outer offices who'll be squealing," Frank said and let out a squeal of his own.

That didn't strike Justice as right. But before he could say anything Frank hung up.

"See?" Rex said.

"What, you heard?" Justice said.

"No, just that he'll be pissed about you, an outsider, starting to bark orders as soon you get incountry."

Justice felt like a child, watching adults do as they pleased. "This is madness. Who the hell got Youtubed in a qat bar?" Justice asked.

"No one from what I know," Rex said.

Walid stepped between. "The meeting is very soon. We should get going."

"Can I get inside without arousing suspicion?" Justice asked.

"Of course," Walid said. "Don't speak, and I'll say you're my bodyguard."

Justice glanced at Rex. "Can you keep a secret?"

Rex shook his head.

Justice took in a deep breath.

Rex grinned. "But I can come along."

"Really?" Justice said, not sure if Rex was joking.

"Of course. We're here to stop acts of terror from occurring, aren't we? Besides, we need more people for the prison. I think the old man who works there is getting antsy from all the spare time."

"Yessss," Justice said uncertainly. But Rex's beaming face was lifting his spirits.

Walid grinned and wrapped his arms around both their shoulders.

Walid commandeered a truck and drove them to a house on the outskirts of town. It was his house. Inside a woman cooked food, though she grimaced when she saw the two of them with Walid.

"Put on these clothes," Walid said. "They'll make you look more local."

Justice and Rex put on the dirty jeans and shirt that didn't quite look Western, yet didn't quite look local.

"They look Americanized," said Rex.

"Yes," Walid replied. "We're not fundamentalists."

They slept again on the side of the road, the incline so steep that Nasar nestled himself under the wheel well, not caring for the diesel and oil fumes that still wafted down from the cooling engine.

They were at a lower elevation now, and the hum of insects and mosquitoes darting into his ear kept him awake. He didn't mind. He wanted to dwell on the village he saw vaporized by the drones, the screams, the wailing. At least the drone's missile had hit Abdullah head on, he thought. There was no suffering. Was that it? Or was it because the living, like him, didn't have to deal with the memories of the screaming and wailing. Or perhaps he, a soft man who had never dealt with this kind of thing before, was not used to it. Death. How horrid.

And as the vision of the charred ruins that remained of the village floated into his mind and spewed toxic fumes at his heart, making him feel weak, he knew it was sad how people, Westerners in general, but people too, were able to come up with these horrific ways to kill each other. It was modern machineries that truly took death dealing to levels only previously available in imaginations about hell. Abdullah's corpse was only a small part of that, and Nasar's scientific mind knew that. The worst was firestorms of entire cities, eight hundred degree temperatures and a hundred and fifty mile an hour winds, bubbling asphalt and hundreds of thousands dead. A German professor had told him that one day as they passed a convoy of American Army Humvees near Friedberg.

Still, Nasar knew that that was the might of a very powerful country, and to be finally out of its influence Pakistan would have to create more weapons just like that.

After the mosquitoes buzzed in his ear for an hour straight, and had bitten every inch of exposed body, an itchy Nasar stepped into the truck. At first he thought there was a fire, but he was surprised to see Karim and the driver in leaned back front seats, incense burning.

"Close the door, you'll let more in," said the driver, angrily.

"Mosquitoes are bad," said Nasar, wondering why he felt guilty. He started to cough from the incense. "How can you breathe with this?" he asked.

"Leave if you don't like it," barked the driver.

Nasar peeked to see if Karim was going to take a side, but the young man's eyelids stayed closed, though his eyes were moving beneath.

Nasar couldn't stop coughing, so he left. A swarm of mosquitoes greeted him. He swatted for a few seconds and wondered what it was that made him now hate the driver and still feel like a child in front of him. He walked around the car and realized that he wouldn't be able to get away from the mosquitoes. Another one buzzed in his ear. He heard coughing from the truck and smiled to himself.

When the truck engine started up, Nasar hurried back inside.

They drove in silence, a window helped keep the incense' smoke to a minimum.

With the pitching and rolling of the truck, and the whine of its first and second gears, Nasar fell asleep.

He woke up when the truck lurched to a stop, the scream of the brakes cutting into his dreams.

"Shit," Karim said and turned.

"What is it?" Nasar asked. He could see a thread of gray in the horizon. It was almost daytime. For some reason that thought made him feel safe.

"Army trucks, up ahead," said the driver, backing up the truck.

"We can get past them," said Nasar. He assumed that this one would be like the previous times they'd come up against military vehicles.

"No," Karim said, sadly.

"These are smuggler roads," said the driver. "Now used by terrorists. Army arrests all here."

Nasar's throat tightened. He really just wanted to sleep. Why did this always keep happening? He was starting to think that maybe Karim wasn't the best person to have picked to lead him. But then who else was there?

The driver stopped the truck in between two boulders. "They might have seen us," he said. "They'll send a patrol back up the road or just start with mortars."

Nasar looked at the steep drop and rise to either side of the road. "And what do we do? We have to talk to them."

"We can't," Karim said. His voice sounded drained.

"There are old goat trails we can follow," said the driver and stepped out of the truck.

Nasar stepped out too and stared at the step incline before them. Surely this was madness. His hips and legs were stiff, tired from all the sitting. Now they wanted him to climb mountains?

The driver climbed up a rock and reached for Nasar's hand. Nasar shook his head.

"Here," said Karim. "Climb on me." He interlaced his hands.

Nasar used that to lift up and the driver pulled him. His shoulder joint popped; though there wasn't much pain, Nasar was sure that it would come sooner or later.

"Where's the goat trail?" asked Nasar.

The driver helped Karim up to the ledge and pointed at a place where the rocks were dusted off to each side. It was no more than a foot wide. Nasar's legs wobbled. He was way too old for this. His chest began to ache.

They walked on this razor-thin trail for a few minutes. Nasar kept his hand on the driver's back, and was glad that the man didn't shove him off. Darkness still made every step more precarious. They heard the bark of a dog and the tumult of boots and yells behind them. They kept walking.

Nasar's heart didn't want to relax. It kept beating and his head felt light. He stumbled on a rock, and when he saw the deep drop, he only felt more faint. Karim grabbed him.

"Be careful," Karim hissed. A rock bounced and sounded off below. "You'll give away our position.

Nasar hadn't heard anything for a few minutes, but he knew why Karim was nervous. Nasar took a few deep breaths and followed the driver. The air was thicker here, and he could swear that the smell of sea salt was buried somewhere between the dust and goat shit.

The sun rose and kissed the land with hazy light. The edges of

Nelson Lowhim

clouds swirled in half darkness, and Nasar tried to keep his eyes focused on the trail in front of him.

It was midday, the sun buffered by clouds, when Karim tapped Nasar's shoulder.

"Look, we're almost there."

The ridge they were on led down to a village with a handful of houses and a single minaret. There didn't seem to be a soul there.

When they arrived at the village, the driver led them to a group of shanties at the foot of the hill. He indicated that they should wait. The one room shanty, with corrugated sheet metal for walls and roof was empty with a smooth ground indicating that it had been slept in at one time or another.

Nasar collapsed. He'd never been this exhausted before, and he was overwhelmed by the wont to go home and lie on his soft bed and eat delicious meals. His muscles twitched as he drifted off.

Nasar opened his eyes. Karim's dark figure shook him. It was night again. Tired, his brain slapping against his skull. He turned, hoping to delay waking up.

"Wake up," Karim hissed and jerked him hard.

Nasar sat up, angry that the young man was being rude. "Wha—"

Karim covered his mouth. "No. They're near."

The footsteps of a group of people walking on gravel sounded out. Near. Nasar's body shrieked and woke up. He could smell something burning, and the grain sack that covered the front shack entrance was awash with the licks of an open fire's light. He watched as the light grew stronger. Whoever it was, they were coming right for them. Nasar had the sudden urge to pee, followed by a pang of pain in his bladder. He was definitely too old for this. He tried to move his feet, but his joints were too tight.

Karim tugged his shirtsleeve. There was a hole in the back of the shack. Karim pushed him towards it.

It smelled bad there, and as Nasar got down on all fours, the pain in his joints almost forcing tears into his eyes, he could smell the feces. Strong. A few flies rose up and flew into his face. He held his breath. But as his elbows pushed into the soft mush, and the aroma of feces crawled into his mouth, he dry heaved and stopped. Karim pushed him, punching his ass. Nasar remembered that someone was coming for them. He slid through the hole. He crouched outside and Karim slid through and held his shoulder.

"Wait, they have dogs," Karim said.

Nasar wasn't sure what that meant. His heart was about to break and was complaining about all it'd been put through lately. He clutched his chest. They were in the shadow of the shack, and the footsteps were closer now. The voices of the men were apparent, hurried, with a hint of martial crispness. The shadows danced and Nasar noticed that the other shacks had people in them, peering out, some yelled at the police.

Karim tugged him and they stepped over to the next shack. Then the next. Dogs barked. The little shantytown was alive with voices. The dogs barked louder. The men were walking right to the shack that they'd been sleeping in. Nasar remembered the driver and assumed that he'd turned them over. They skipped past a few more shacks. Nasar still didn't feel safe. They needed to run away and now, but he didn't want to speak.

The men were in the shack. In the flame of their torches, both fire and electrical, Nasar could see their uniforms. The dogs barked around the shack, then whined when the soldiers yelled at them.

Nasar, feeling his voice returning, and no longer wanting to vomit from the smell of feces, leaned into Karim. "The driver turned us in."

Karim shot him a look. "We don't know." He grabbed his sleeve and pulled him past a family who was staring at them and covering their noses.

They made it to a road that appeared to be the border between the shantytown and the start of regular buildings. "We need a boat."

A large military truck turned onto the road. Karim pulled, almost jerking Nasar's arm out of its socket. In the back of the truck, Nasar saw soldiers with guns. Was this really all for him? The truck turned and drove into the shantytown.

"Come," said Karim. "The dogs have lost the scent."

He was right, the dogs sounded weak, unsure, diffuse over the din of people yelling and soldiers barking orders. Nasar wondered why, then realized that it was the shit.

They stayed in an unlit road on the edge of the town. It was cloudy, so the darkness helped them stay hidden. But it also tripped up Nasar which sent debilitating pain through his body. When they reached the beach, Nasar was limping. His calves felt like they had shrunk into balls. The dark sea greeted them. In the distance he could see lights on the dock. That's where all the ships were.

"So we swim?" Nasar said, looking at Karim's face hidden in the dark, trying to see his eyes.

"No," said Karim, annoyed. He pointed to an outcrop of rocks.

"That's a good place to get smashed by the rocks and waves," said Nasar, angry that the young man didn't have any better ideas.

"No," Karim hissed. "That's where a smuggler might hide a boat."

Nasar followed the young man, though as his legs shrieked even more on the rocks, he wanted to hit the young man for putting him through this.

"There," said Karim with pride.

Indeed, a rowing boat, with two oars rocked but a few feet from the rocks. The waves were still, and only the only sound was a soft lapping of water on rocks. Karim lowered himself into the water, swam over to the boat and pulled up the anchor. Nasar stared at the water, knowing that he'd surely drown if he were to wade in.

With two swift rows, Karim pushed the boat against the rocks. Nasar jumped onto the boat. He landed on one foot. Pain shot up his leg rendering it numb. He collapsed on the boat, almost going over board. Karim held his shirt and pulled him back on.

"Quiet!" hissed Karim. "Stop moving, you'll overturn us."

Nasar rolled so that he was closer to the middle. He could hear Karim rowing, and the young man's feet pushed against his shoulders on each row. Nasar didn't dare move, as he was certain the young man had lost patience with him, and was close to pushing him overboard. He drifted off, his body trembling.

"Wake up," hissed Karim.

Nasar jolted up. "What?"

"Quiet. The sea carries sounds."

Again Nasar didn't dare move. His limbs were all too stiff to do so without upsetting the boat—and Karim. He wondered if this was the end of Karim's patience, and help.

"Get up," Karim said.

Nasar slowly started to move.

"If you overturn us the sharks will get us."

Nasar looked up. He could only see the outline of Karim. The young man was right. The sharks of the Red Sea were known to be bad. Thousands of years of feeding on the detritus of fishing boats had taught them to devour anything near a boat. That thought cleared Nasar's head and took away some stiffness in his bones.

"Hurry now. It's your turn to row. I can't do all the work all the time."

Nasar felt like whining, complaining that he was old and tired. But there was nothing he could do. He was at Karim's mercy. He moved his toes and fingers trying to limber up his joints. It worked and he slowly got up and reached out for the oars. Karim handed each one over to him.

"Which way are we going?" asked Nasar. All around them was darkness.

"Away from lights."

"I see no lights," said Nasar. Even the stars were hiding.

"Row there," said Karim and pointed.

Nasar didn't know how the young man could possibly have chosen any direction, so he just started to row. When he heard Karim's snores, he decided that it was right direction. His muscles limbered up even more with each row, but he knew that wouldn't last. Though he tried to get into a rhythm with each row, small pains exploded in his body, surprising him each time. Soon his back started to spasm. He wasn't going to be able to do this for long. He rowed less.

And then he saw a light. It was a boat in the horizon. He assumed that it was too far to matter, but soon it was no more then a few hundred meters away, the drone of its engine growing. Nasar tried to row away. But it didn't work. No matter what he did, it came at him. Soon it was close enough that its steel hull was apparent. He kicked Karim as a searchlight hit his face and he shielded his eyes. Their journey was finally at an end. He put down the oars and raised his hands. Karim did the same.

"Where?"

"Pakistan," Nasar said. The man, an American with a red face and thick mustache that reminded Nasar of the many officers in the Pakistani military, was kind, if a little ignorant. "You know, near India."

The man leaned back and let out a laugh. "What the hell were you doing in a row boat in the middle of the Red Sea? Did you think you'd make it to…" he said and looked over at Nasar, one eye narrowing, his bald head glistening in the room's white light.

Not wanting to give away everything, Nasar decided to give away something. "The Suez Canal."

The man roared with laughter again, spittle flying out of his mouth. He was a stout man, with a barrel chest and forearms that were suited for lifting cars. It was just him, Nasar, and a huddled Karim in the corner. They were in the Captain's quarters with a few plates of food on a table, a bed, and a desk on which there was a plethora of papers.

"You're a crazy bastard. How the hell did you think you were going to make it?" asked the Captain.

"Well. I…"

"Can't you afford a plane ticket? I mean, you seem smart."

"Maybe. But times are tough."

That seemed to sadden the captain. "They are," he said, stroking his chin. "Even back home things are going to hell. My cousin just got life for dealing meth. He was in IT before that." He stroked his chin some more. "And my parents can barely make ends meet. Thank God for Medicaid. Still, just to help all the relatives I have to do this damn gig." He pointed at the floor.

"And what, may I ask are *you* doing here?" asked Nasar.

In the corner, Karim snored.

"You sure your friend doesn't need a bed?"

"He prefers the floor," said Nasar, a little happy to get back at

Karim for his earlier intransigence. "And your reason for being—"

"Wait a minute. Are you a spy?" the captain said and leaned forward, that one eye narrowing.

"I-I," Nasar said.

The captain laughed again and slapped Nasar's thigh. "I'm just jostling you. I know you aren't. Unless..." Again he gave a silly suspicious look.

Nasar chuckled. He rather liked the captain.

"Well, you know how the Somalis are acting up."

"I've heard," said Nasar.

"Well, we're there to protect ships passing in that lane. Shoot up those pirates and all. You know how it is."

"That sounds noble," said Nasar. He thought about the fact that scores of Navies had come together to fight the pirates who were slowing down world trade with their antics. He'd never known Somalis, but he'd heard stories about how they stole no matter where they lived.

The captain looked disappointed. "Yeah. I guess if everyone agrees it's okay."

Karim snorted in his corner.

"What's wrong?" Nasar said. "They're attacking innocent ships. Of course some semblance of control must be shown."

The captain walked over to a bucket with ice. He pulled out a beer and walked back. The psst of the can opening was followed by the captain chugging.

Nasar thought he could actually see lines forming in the man's forehead. When the captain was done he let out a sigh and slammed down the can. "So you're with them?"

Nasar looked around him. Besides Karim in the corner, there was no one else around. The smell of beer hops settled in his mind for a second before he glanced back over at the captain who was looking at him with what could only be described as hate. Why would this American be against such a fight, especially when it was justified, unlike every other American transgression?

"You mean those who are fighting the pirates?" Nasar said, hoping to buy some time. He knew that he couldn't grow angry with the captain has he had saved them from the rowboat, and though nothing had been said, he did seem kind enough to be willing to drop them off where ever they wanted.

"Who else?" the captain said, his voice rising.

"Well, aren't the pirates breaking the law?"

The captain scoffed and rolled his eyes.

"What are your thoughts?"

"Laws are made by those in power, and are only meant to keep the powerless in place."

Nasar tried not to roll his eyes. Perhaps the captain was baiting him. "Is that right?"

"Come on. You know I'm right. How can you, a Pakistani, not see that?"

This had to be a test. Perhaps the captain was trying to see if he would say something unAmerican.

"How many wars have you been in?" Nasar asked, hoping to change the subject.

"All of them. I was in spec ops all over this goddamn region doing the bidding of our idiot masters."

The last word was so laden with contempt that Nasar couldn't maintain eye contact with the captain. He looked down at the crumbs on the table wondering if rats were still an issue on boats like these.

"I got out and had to do this."

"Had to?" asked Nasar.

"Yes. I had to. What else was I going to do after twenty years in? Get a job? Who'd hire me? Waste away? That might be the only true alternative."

"Perhaps if you hated such actions you could have legislated against them."

"It's a pay to play system."

"Come now," said Nasar. "It's still better than most other systems."

The captain rocked his head back and forth. "I guess. It's been perverted from its original intention."

Nasar's head warmed as he wondered if perhaps this man was one of those right-wingers he'd heard about. The ones who liked to fight and hated their black President. Yet if that was so, why was he taking the side of pirates? Then again, he'd always seen some of these extreme fundamentalists as the kind of people who couldn't truly see the world for the grays that it was and were thus forever lost intellectually.

"Did you try to make your voice heard?"

The captain stared down at his hands and rubbed them. His demeanor collapsed. "No."

"Why not?"

"I told you. The system's fixed. What are you going to do?"

"I don't know," Nasar said. "But is doing the same thing the right thing?"

"No," the captain said, shifting in his seat and rapping his knuckled on the table. "But I thought I could help save a few lives, then so be it."

"Of your men?"

The captain waved dismissively at the boat around them. "These aren't my men. They're mercenaries. Every last one of them."

"You mean…"

"Yes Somalis. And I did save 'em. Caught hell from these pipsqueaks. But they shut up in the end."

The drone of the boat sounded off and a foghorn broke the peace. Nasar wanted to badly sleep, but it looked as if the captain wanted to talk.

"How did you save them?" Nasar asked, hoping that the captain would be stoic enough to wave the question off.

"Let a few go. They weren't doing anything but patrolling their waters."

"But they've taken innocent yachters hostage. Hurt—"

The captain slammed his fist on the table. "Christ. You're a moron." His voice echoed off the steel walls.

For some reason the accusation hurt Nasar more than it should have. He was certain that he was smarter than this captain. "Excuse me?" he said with a squeak.

The captain massaged his temples. "I'm sorry. I've been under a lot of stress on this trip. These," he said and pointed upwards towards the deck. "Sailors of mine are a bunch of trigger happy fools. When I watched they didn't dare shoot a single boat. But they knew, as stupid as those meatheads were, they knew that higher and no one in the world cared if they shot up a few bastards. Who the hell's watching? The Chinese? Like they care if some third worlders get chopped up into shark food. All they care about is how far their stupid ship has managed to come without any mishaps."

Nasar didn't understand.

"Just shoot up the sand-niggers, no one will care."

Nasar cocked his head. "Would Somalis be considered—"

"Damn Chinese were just as bad as us. They're more than willing to kill a few. Hell, look what they did to their own people. Guess everyone wants to be like us," the captain said and looked at Nasar with disgust.

Nasar shifted in his seat, the captain's gaze burned through his skin. "Well. That's how the world works," he said. "Do you think letting the pirates go does any good?"

"I saved them for some amount of time." He held out his forefinger and thumb to indicate small. "Never said I was God."

Nasar shook his head. There was a philosophical riddle in here somewhere, he just wasn't sure where. The days when he'd mused such things were long past, though in the back of his head he knew this trip was an attempt to bring back some ideological certainty into his life; the scientific part of him was strong and it only saw the use for nuclear bombs, it had no care for the wreckage of human bodies, and smoked skin of the weak and unfortunate that came along with it. That, for some reason, tightened his head and his stomach rumbled.

He wasn't going to let the captain get away with this line of thinking. It was unbecoming of any leader and especially unbecoming of an American.

Nasar leaned in. "No one wants to be God. And that's fine. We'll probably all fail. But the thing is this: Sure the weak will suffer for some things. But there's a reason. Even the killing of *your* pirates. They don't matter. And why's that? They haven't built anything that matters. Look at their country."

"They had a choice?"

Nasar knew the logical conclusion of this was that even *his* country deserved its place, but he was certain of his own history's power. "Yes. They did. And the world, humans, all of us, want to build beautiful things. We can't have rebels blowing these things up."

"Even if they have the right."

"What right? There is none."

The captain leaned back. His face was pale, and he seemed to be breathing fast. "So you believe that might makes right?"

"What else? Might isn't just guns. It's museums. It's literature. What have the pirates done to that end?"

"They didn't have the chance," the captain said, murmuring to himself.

"Their fault. Even the Mongols, those barbarians, realized how much better the cities they ravaged were. In the end *they* knew what was better."

"Apes who like shiny things, eh?" said the captain, playing with the empty beer can.

"Whatever you call it. This is what we strive for. Those who don't are crushed," said Nasar. Though he had spoken, as the scientific him had always believed, there was a growing pain in his stomach. What was his body trying to say?

The captain shook his head. "Very well. But if that's the case, why don't those in power say that. Why don't they stop covering their blood with roses?"

Nasar tsked. "Come now, captain, you're not a child. Words were made to disguise what we do."

Another foghorn broke through the steel walls.

"Is *that* how you use words?" the captain asked. His head slumped into his hands.

Nasar paused to make sure the captain wasn't crying. "Sometimes."

The captain rapped his knuckles on the table. "And what's this trip of yours for?"

"To make peace with my past," said Nasar.

Nasar held the captain's stare and watched as the American's eyes licked up his face and hands.

"So you, Nasar, what blood have you ever seen?"

Abdullah came crashing into Nasar's head. The discontent in his bowels spread, and Nasar too placed his head in his hands. "Some," he croaked.

The captain cocked his head. "On this trip?"

"A few days ago. A companion," Nasar said, and when the word companion echoed off the steel walls he realized he'd called the boy a companion. Why? "He was mistaken for an enemy by one of your drones. And..." Nasar made a fist and then stretched out his fingers.

"Bombs are the worst," said the captain placing a hand on Nasar's shoulder. "The fragments they leave..."

"I know," said Nasar.

"And in your world this is okay? This was just an individual who didn't matter. I imagine he never created anything?"

That slapped Nasar. And now cold invaded his body. "No," Nasar whispered. His mind saw blood on a rock and an insect running over it like it was nothing. "I would never think that."

Ali rubbed the crust out of his eyes, and he stared at Saladin as the man stood up.

"The big hit goes down tomorrow, doesn't it?" Saladin asked.

"Yes. I'll—"

"You'll be nowhere near it, do you understand?"

Ali felt the sting of being talked down to. "I—"

"You're too important, Ali. We may have our disagreements, but I know your talent."

"And?"

"We can't use you on small attacks. Or any. You need to lead."

Ali chewed the inside of his cheek. In Iraq he'd seen some of the commanders do this and he'd hated them. And he realized that this was why he hated Saladin. But the man was the moneyman. "The men need to see their leader suffering with them," he said.

Saladin waved his hand. "What will it do if you're killed?"

"They'll understand the sacrifice."

"They're dogs!" yelled Saladin. His voice echoed and he looked around, as if scared that someone might have heard him. He lowered his chin and voice: "They'll listen to you. You can direct from a distance. They're ready, aren't they?"

Ali knew that this had been a very important part of AQ training recently: making independent cells. If he admitted that he couldn't do that, then he might lose his position. "Very well," he said.

Saladin placed his hand on Ali's shoulder. "It will go well, trust me."

Ali headed downstairs to the kitchen to get some breakfast. A phone on the kitchen counter started to ring. He stared at it and not recognizing the number decided to ignore it.

As he made his breakfast, the phone continued to ring, over and over. He turned it to silent, but the phone still lit up the kitchen, turning the ceiling white.

Saladin waddled into the kitchen. He seemed hungry. "You're not getting that?" he pointed at the phone's dancing lights.

Ali sighed and picked up the phone. It was the same unknown number. And for a split second his head whined and glowed with heat as he wondered who it could be, and he thought about the story he had heard about how Americans could listen through every phone, and if this was perhaps an attempt by them to zero in on him with a single phone call, and he was almost sure that there was a droning sound outside, and furthermore he was almost sure that perhaps it was the Israeli trick where they'd managed to stuff bombs into a phone and kill an agent of Hamas. "Hello?" he asked, put the phone on speaker, and threw it back on the kitchen table. Of course, he knew if there was a bomb in the phone he would be dead no matter what.

Saladin stared at him as if he were a fool.

"Hello?"

"Ali?"

Ali stared at the phone. He didn't recognize the voice, but whoever it was, they spoke in a hurried, scared fashion. "Yes?"

"They came. They're there," the man, maybe boy said.

"Who is this?"

There was a pause, some gunfire sounded over the phone. "The safe house outside the city. They came."

"Who is this?" Ali said, but when Saladin shot him another look, he knew that he'd have to act tougher.

"They're coming," the man whispered. The line went dead. In his chest, Ali's heart tripped into a sprint.

Ali looked at Saladin. His mind froze. Then a little voice reminded him that there was only one safe house on the outskirts of the city. "I know," he said before his voice cracked from his throat constricting.

He walked to the room where he'd seen the men sleeping the night before, but there was no one. Spilled coke cans and cigarette butts lay everywhere. Something was wrong. And for a second he was certain he could hear the swooshing of a rocket as it came towards the house.

He flinched. Nothing happened. A car drove by. He could hear birds chirping outside.

"What is it?" Saladin asked as he stepped into the room.

"Nothing," said Ali. He stared at a pile of blankets. "We should go."

"To the safe house?"

Ali didn't care to go where a raid was happening, but this house was giving him the chills. "Yes."

He walked outside, the blue sky pierced his retina, and he shielded his eyes.

"Come," Saladin said.

Ali watched the man lumber over to a rusted-out car. He could see his hairy ankles twitch, and he noticed that Saladin had no shoes on. Ali wanted to say something but didn't. Saladin opened the door; it screeched, and as Saladin sat in the driver's seat, the car rocked dangerously. The wheel hulls were eaten away, and a few chunks fell down, bounced off the tire, and fell to the ground and kicked up dust. "Is that your car?"

"Of course," Saladin said and turned the key. The engine turned and failed to start. Ali trotted over. He had the feeling that he'd be asked to push. And he wanted none of that. He sat down and relief splashed over him when the engine finally turned. Fumes filled the cabin and Ali rolled his window down.

Saladin let out a nasty laugh. "It helps keep my smoking down."

Ali stuck his head out. Behind the car a cloud of black smoke rose a few meters and settled around them. The car lurched forward with a loud grind. Ali couldn't believe that this was the car Saladin was now choosing to drive. "What happened to—"

"No more fancy cars. The Americans can see," Saladin said and pointed to the sky. "They know shiny cars, and they aim for them."

"Turn left," Ali said, smiling. So Saladin too was scared of being blown up. For some reason that made Ali feel better. He guided Saladin until they left the city and followed a winding road up a mountain. The car engine whined, and Ali could see smoke coming out from the top, but Saladin didn't seem perturbed, so Ali said nothing. Finally they came to an overlook. Ali pointed, and Saladin pulled over.

As soon as Ali stepped out he could hear yells and gunshots. But soon it was only yells. The yells of domination. He looked down the valley and could see the safe house surrounded by Army trucks. He saw a pink-skinned man walk out. The brown soldiers seemed to listen to him.

"American," Saladin said and spit off the edge. He pointed with his finger and pantomimed shooting.

"How do you think they found out?" Ali asked. He could see a few people staring from the outside. Any one of them could be eyes for the Army.

"Who knows? *This* is why it's good to scare the people. When they fear you, they don't tell anyone anything," Saladin said.

"But if you never attack the head of the snake it will never die."

Saladin grunted.

A few dead bodies were dragged out of the building. Ali trembled. "Did you know anyone there?" he asked.

"No," Saladin said. "But we have to get back at them."

"We can hit them today," Saladin said. "We know enough." He patted Ali's back.

"Do it. But watch from afar. We can't lose you."

Ali nodded. Staring at those dead bodies made him never want to become one, and Saladin's earlier argument seemed to have the weight. Ali kept his eye on the pink man as he chatted with an officer. There was something about the pick man that burrowed into Ali's skin, made the air feel oppressive. He turned to the car; right now he liked Saladin; right now he was ready to see something burn.

Nasar made his way up the steel steps of the boat. He saw a couple men, with full beards, tattoos on their arms and something in their mouths. They looked at him as if he were an insect to be stepped on. He didn't like that and walked on, though he stumbled now because he could feel their eyes upon him, and he felt sub human, but he told himself that this was silly, yet still he couldn't shake the feeling that something was horribly wrong with the way they looked at him. He hoped that Karim wouldn't step out, because the young man wouldn't take kindly to these looks.

As Nasar stepped up to the deck, the salty air relaxing him, he felt certain that he was in trouble, that these men wouldn't hesitate to throw him overboard if he dared to make a wrong move.

"There you are," the captain said and spread his arms out.

Nasar embraced the captain, though he felt foolish for doing so. Still, he realized the tenuous nature of his being allowed to stay on the boat. "How are you?"

The captain simply nodded. His hands swept to the sea. "See." His face glowed from the setting sun.

Nasar's body lost time before a breath brought him back. "It's amazing," he said. Several clouds burned in red and orange hues, covering the entire sky.

"You know what they say about an amazing sunset, right?" the captain said then laughed at his own joke.

Nasar glanced about to see a few of the bearded men staring at him. He wondered if they were Christian fundamentalists. "What do they say?"

The captain scrutinized his face. "Don't worry about them," the captain said, though his voice was low. "I told you…"

Nasar remembered their conversation. He really wanted to be at his destination. "Where are we?"

"We're close to the Suez. Don't worry, we'll get you there."

"Thank you."

"Of course." The captain dismissed this with a wave of his hand. "*This*, is what you should enjoy." He leaned over the railing.

Nasar mimicked him. The sea glowed, and a seagull, perhaps lost, squawked as it swooped by. "I will." He looked down and watched as the boat skimmed over the water, spitting white waves out. He could now feel the boat's rocking.

"Look up. You'll get sea sick," said one of the bearded, tattooed men who was walking by.

"He's right," the captain said.

Nasar looked up and felt woozy. He nodded his thanks to the man who stopped to stare at him.

"Of course," the man said. "What the hell were you doing in the middle of the red sea in that leak-ridden boat?"

"Getting someplace."

The man regarded him, regarded the captain, then walked away.

"Don't mind them," he said. "Mind the sun."

Nasar, feeling nauseous, stared hard at the horizon. If he turned sea sick, this trip was going to get much worse. "Why are your men so angry?"

"Iraq. Afghanistan. Too much war. You know."

"I don't," said Nasar.

"No? Don't you have your wars as well?"

"We do," Nasar said. He wasn't certain if they were that bad, or if the soldiers he'd met had been so angry all the time.

"Perhaps *our* wars are different," said the captain.

"Could be."

"They've seen a lot of blood and ripped flesh. They've caused it too."

"And the looks they give me?"

"Well," the captain said with a smile. "Combine that with their ability to think every darkie is a bad guy, and… that's what you get."

"They're racist."

"What do you expect, Mr. I like power?"

That stung Nasar harder than he'd expected. "I–"

"That's what power does. It makes people subhuman."

"Not always," Nasar said.

"No? Example."

Nasar couldn't think of one, but he was sure there was something. "There's plenty."

The captain laughed. "You're consistent. I'll give you that much."

"Thank you."

"And your explanation for why they're so racist to you?"

"Maybe they were that way to begin with."

"I'm sure they were."

The sun dipped below the horizon and froze the clouds in purple. "And what did *you* see in Iraq and Afghanistan?"

"Ripped flesh, blood, women screaming."

"Why didn't it change you?"

The captain shrugged. "Not sure."

"You're from a powerful country. So why?"

"I don't believe that power makes right."

"Might makes right." Nasar raised a finger in the air.

The captain laughed. "That's right."

"You lost friends in the war?" Nasar asked.

"Of course. But I can still see through things."

The sky grew darker. Nasar could feel the world closing in. He was sure there were words out there, somewhere, that would refute the captain. Another man, with beard and tats, walked by, staring at Nasar.

The captain lit up a cigarette. "So what are you doing when you get to land?"

"Nothing."

"Nothin? Seems pretty important for you get to your place."

"An old friend," said Nasar.

The captain nodded and stared off into the sea. After a few minutes of nothing but splashes and the boat droning, Nasar headed down.

In the captain's quarters, Karim arose. "Where were you?"

"On the deck," said Nasar. He was going to mention the sunset, but remembered that he wanted the young man to stay.

"How much longer do we have?"

"A couple days. Why?"

"The other men want us dead."

"How could you know?" Nasar asked, instinctively looking over his shoulder.

"I saw them, and saw the look they gave us. I know it. What happens when they find out who I am. Or you?" Karim said and rubbed his eyes.

"They won't," said Nasar.

"Can you trust the captain?"

"I hope."

Air wooshed by as the opening door missed Nasar's face by inches.

"Sorry," said the captain and locked the door behind him. "I…" he said and stared down at a piece of paper in his hand.

Nasar could see that it was a picture with words underneath. His heart froze and his throat tightened. "What?"

"Were you honest with me?" the captain asked.

"Some."

The captain cocked his head. "Well?"

"I'm a doctor."

"Noklar?"

"Yes."

The captain's shoulders fell. "No."

"Yes."

Karim took a step towards them, and Nasar held his hand out to stop the young man. "Why?"

The captain handed over the paper. It was a picture of Nasar, with a wanted sign below. He was accused of terrorism and other atrocities. His knees went weak and the room started to spin.

The captain caught him before he fell. Karim pulled out a chair.

"It's okay," the captain said, sprinkling some water on his face. "Don't worry."

Nasar sat up. "You knew."

"I suspected."

"Do they—"

"No," said the captain. "I got the bulletin before anyone else could see. Luckily. But I can't keep the information from everyone."

"No," said Nasar. He wasn't sure what was next. Even if the captain decided to let him leave, where would they go?

"You will have to stay here."

"Are you sure?" Nasar asked, giddy inside because he wanted nothing more than to stay. But his heart dropped as soon as he thought of the other men finding out.

"Yeah. I don't think they got a good look. And if I stay up there, I can keep them away from official comms. But you have to stay here."

"Why are you—"

"Remember what I said."

Nasar nodded. The captain straightened himself out, gave a half-nod and walked out of the room. Karim locked the door after him.

"We can't trust him," said Karim.

The young man was right.

They drove downtown in alleys which seemed the same as when Rex took him to the prison. Some old women grinned like skulls at Justice, and he could smell cumin. But when he stopped to meet their eyes, he was met with a vacant stare. He walked on. And soon they were standing outside the qat bar.

He could hear the chattering of men. And laughter that didn't seem to make sense. And the smell. He'd never smelled anything like it. Not like weed, not like anything. Just organic decay. They walked into a small room where two men were armed with AK-47s. Walid tipped his head and threw out a roll of money. The men grabbed the money and started to count. When they were finished, they handed Walid a plastic bag and nodded at a door, covered by a cloth.

They stepped into a dark room. Justice's heart raced. The room, full of chatter before, had fallen quiet. Too quiet for Justice's nerves. The men knew he didn't belong. They'd left all their guns in Walid's home. What could they do if the people decided to attack? Justice clenched his fists. Someone grab his wrist and he pulled away.

"It's me, friend," Walid said in his ear.

Justice allowed himself to be pulled by Walid. He was pulled off balance and landed, ass first, rather clumsily on a soft couch. He could hear the chatter rise up again. Everything was being said much too fast, and in too much of a dialect for him to follow. He decided to just let Walid do the talking.

"I don't know about this," Rex whispered into his other ear.

"Why?" whispered Justice.

"We're sitting ducks."

"We'll be fine. These are the risks of the game," Justice said.

The room was finally coming into view. Forms of men, all lying as far back as possible, and all sitting cross-legged, appeared. Justice saw that Walid was leaning over and whispering into a man's ear. The man regarded Justice with what seemed to be amusement. Walid leaned back to Justice.

"Our friend is a regular customer here," said Walid.

Justice didn't know what that meant. Walid looked at his phone, then looked up. The doorway sent blinding light into the room, and everyone stopped talking. A man, large and too well-built to be a local, shut the cloth behind him. The men went back to talking. Walid typed furiously into his phone.

The man walked towards them. Justice wondered what it was about these men that their eyes adjusted to the dark so quickly. He sat down besides Walid, away from Justice. The two men began talking. Justice tried his hardest to follow, but he couldn't keep up. He'd have to trust Walid completely.

They whispered for a few moments, then a pause. It shouldn't have meant anything, but Justice could feel the hairs on his arms rise. He realized that the man most likely knew what the doctor looked like. And that he'd smell that something was fishy, if he hadn't already heard about the raid on the doctor's house.

Now the words Walid and the man were exchanging sounded terse. Hushed, angry.

Justice leaned in, wondering what the right response was. The man could very well have friends in here or outside.

The man got up.

"What is it?" Justice asked in Walid's ear. "Walid?" Justice asked again. The man was making his way to the cloth. Justice grabbed Walid's shoulder and shook him. Walid didn't move. Justice reached across and touched something warm and wet. He pulled back for a second. He reached back in and felt the knife in Walid's chest. He realized that his head was at a slant.

"What the hell?" Rex asked. The man was moving the cloth.

"Stop him," Justice said and got up as quietly as he could. The man was out of sight. Justice started to run. There was no way he would let this killer out of sight. He could hear Rex swearing and moving behind him.

Justice made it to the cloth and saw the back of the man as he walked out of the building. The two men with AKs stared at Justice, but they didn't seem to notice his blood-drenched hands. Justice ran to the door and saw the man stop and turn. His hands were bloody too. His face was covered by a beard that almost engulfed his cheekbones. The look in his eyes was hollow, maybe evil. He saw Justice's red hands and turned, walking at such a slow pace that Justice had to wonder if this was in fact the man who'd just killed Walid.

But it had to be. Justice sprinted. The man took off as well. Justice, wearing sandals, knew that he wasn't going to win a foot race. He had to catch the man now.

The man disappeared around a corner. Justice came around the corner and was met with an empty alley. There were closed doors every three feet on either side.

"Shit, did we lose him?" Rex asked. He was panting.

Justice placed a finger on his lips to silence Rex. "I think so. Let's see if they know anything at the qat bar." He pointed in circular fashion at the other end of the alley. Rex nodded and trotted off.

Justice turned the corner he'd just come from. He could feel his heart beating fast. His throat was tight. And he wasn't certain if this was the right thing to do. What if the man was in a house and left out a window?

An old woman hobbled by, and stared at his hands. Justice wiped his hands on the sandy street runoff. It covered the blood. He didn't like to think that Walid died because Justice had promised something he could never have delivered on. Something wormed into his brain and he tried to stop thinking about that. He got down on his knees and peered around the corner from close to the ground. There was nothing.

"Chocolate."

Justice turned and saw a young boy in rags, his hand out. Justice reached in his pocket and pulled out some change. The boy looked at him with a sneer.

Justice shook his head. The boy smelled bad. Like he had crawled out of a sewer. Justice peeked back around the corner and saw the man stepping out of a door. Justice took off around the corner. The man jumped back, then ran down the alley. But Justice had closed the gap between them. He pumped his legs and arms as fast as he could. He moved them so fast he was certain they would tear out. One foot away from the man and he lunged.

He wrapped his arms around the man's ankles. The sound of the man falling, a combination of air being pushed and flesh smacking ground, filled Justice with glee. The adrenaline peaked. The man struggled and Justice climbed on top of him, placing his knees on the man's arms. The man squirmed.

"Stop moving," Justice said.

The man screwed up his face. "American?"

"Yes," Justice said. "You killed Walid, didn't you?"

The man was studying Justice's face.

"You got him," Rex said, as he stumbled in front of Justice. He placed his hands on his knees, doubled over.

"When's the attack taking place?" Justice asked.

"Attack?" the man said.

"Where's Dr. Noklar?"

The man seemed confused, then his face twisted into a smile. "The attack is called Dr. Noklar."

"You'd better be telling the truth," Rex said, having recovered his breath. "Or else we can tease it out of you."

The man seemed amused by them. "The men who tease secrets by

225

talking to the flesh of their victims. That's easy. Anyone can do it."

"And we'll do it to you," Rex said, kicking some dirt on the man's cheek.

"No. My friends, please. I work for you. Americans," he said. "Fifty-cent, Golden Gate, I love America."

"Shut up," Justice said, annoyed. "I want you to understand something, I'm trying to help you not feel pain. Tell me about this attack, tell me everything you know and we'll make sure you're treated properly."

"I work for Frank," the man said, grinning. "You can ask him."

Justice looked up at Rex. Rex didn't move.

"You just looked up some names on the embassy website, didn't you?" Justice said.

"I promise." The man said.

"That's why you killed the man back there?" Justice said.

"Walid's dead?" Rex asked, confused.

"Yes, killed by this bastard," Justice said. He held himself back from punching the man. He seemed like a weasel.

"Why?" Rex asked.

"He was trying to double-cross you two," said the man.

"Shut up," Justice said. Unfortunately part of his mind was already looking at some of the things Walid did, the way he smiled too much, and saw that perhaps this man was right. "Just shut up," he said again, but this time he whispered it.

"He was," the man repeated. "And if you think I don't work for Frank just call him."

Justice wanted to call to confirm, or see that the man was lying, but he also didn't want to call and be considered a fool by Frank once more. He looked up at Rex, who didn't seem to move. Justice shook his head, pretending to be disgusted by the man. Rex mimed him. Justice decided that if Rex wasn't going to call his boss, he wouldn't either.

"What about the attack? You're a friend of the doctor, aren't you?" Justice asked.

"Yes. He was the leader of the cell."

"He's dead," Justice said, trying to see if there would be a reaction in the man's face.

The man's eyes sunk into his skull. "Why?" he asked, his voice on the verge of breaking.

"He tried to kill us so we killed him."

The man shook his head.

"He was your friend, wasn't he?" Justice said.

"No," the man said. "It's just that he was the leader, and a very reasonable person."

"Bull," Rex said, rearing his head to cackle.

"I'm serious," the man said. "He was."

"Is that why he made bombs?" Justice asked. "To act as reasonable as possible?"

The man shook his head. "He rarely did any damage."

"He was in Iraq," Justice said, losing patience with the man's lies. "How little damage did he do there?"

"Okay," the man said. "But Iraq he was helping to protect neighborhoods."

"With bombs?" Justice said. "Listen, the sooner you can start with the truth, the better for all of us. But especially for you."

"This is truth," the man said.

"That a bomb-maker is reasonable?"

"He's the *most* reasonable. The next man, Khalid, won't be so reasonable. The doctor was holding him back."

Justice now knew that this man was full of shit. He looked around to make sure that no one was sneaking up on them. "What about the attack? You knew about that, didn't you?"

"Oh, the big attack?" said the man.

Justice was certain that this man was playing with him. "I'm going to lose my patience. And when I do, I'm going to hand you over to my friend here. He's not going to be so nice."

"I'm telling you," the man said, some nervousness returning to his actions. "We named the attack after the great Dr. Noklar. It's in protest of what the Americans and the puppet Pakistani government are doing to him."

Justice searched the man's eyes, but it seemed like he was telling the truth. "You don't know that he's escaped?"

"Pakistan? No…" the man said. Now he searched Justice's eyes to see if there was any indication that Justice was lying. "Is he here?"

"We're trying to find out," Justice said. "You don't know?"

"No."

"Christ," Justice said and leaned back.

"The attack," Rex said. Just then his phone rang and he turned away to take it.

"What about the attack?" Justice said.

"Tonight. We blow up part of the embassy," the man said.

"What?" Justice stared at the man.

"It's okay. We do it at night, and we try not to hurt anyone," said the man.

Something Frank said crossed Justice's mind, but he couldn't quite remember it. "And you want me to believe that?"

"Frank knows," the man said. "He said he needed an attack, but he doesn't want anyone to get hurt. So we'll plant one and everything will be all right. I get to take credit for it."

"I'm sure you will," Justice said.

"Justice," Rex said.

Justice looked up. Rex was holding out the phone, and he was shaking his head.

"Hello," Justice said.

"You really can't help fucking up, can you?" Frank said.

"What do you mean?"

"Do you have one of my agents on the ground?"

"I—"

"Does he have a star-shaped scar on his chest?"

Justice pulled down on the man's collar and saw a perfectly shaped star in the form of a scar. His heart dropped.

"Yes," Justice said.

"You moron. That's my man. Are you on top of him?" Frank said.

"That's right—"

"God, you're dumb. Stop harming him," Frank yelled. Again Justice had to hold the phone an inch away from his ear.

"I—"

"You're going to let him go right this minute."

"There's an attack. He knows—"

"Shut the hell up. This line isn't secure," Frank said.

"Then how come you just—"

"Didn't I say shut up? I know about their little attack. It's going to be fine. Don't meddle your nose in places it doesn't belong, got it?"

"Do you know the name?" Justice asked.

"How the hell should I know that?"

"I, I'll let him go."

"Listen, someone might be watching you. Don't just let him go," Frank said.

"What should I—"

"Give him the phone. Remember, you're not to hurt him," Frank said.

Justice placed the phone on the man's ear. Even though the phone was a few feet from his ear he could hear Frank yell: "Punch that idiot. Now!"

Justice heard the words, but he didn't comprehend them. He did, however, comprehend the punch that sent him reeling back. Another kick to the stomach sent him to the ground, and he opened his eyes to see the man dart around the corner. His mouth was filled with blood. He picked up the phone—Frank had hung up.

"Sorry about that," Rex said, leaning over him and dabbing the blood on his now swollen lip with a rag. "Frank's a prick sometimes."

"Christ, this place is fucked up," Justice said, resting his back on the wall.

"That it is," Rex said. "I can't wait till I get out."

"I can't either."

"Well. I guess you were following the wrong lead, right?" Rex said. He sat down next to him.

"I don't know," Justice said.

Rex pulled out a cigarette. "Didn't manage to grab any qat." He grinned sheepishly.

"Damn," Justice said. He meant that for the comment to be not about the qat, but rather about Walid.

"Well, it happens," said Rex. "We can always get you some. It's never too hard."

"In due time," Justice said. He took in a deep breath and let it out.

"It still stings?" Rex asked, moving his finger in to inspect the cut lip.

"It's not bad. And it'll heal," Justice said. Jerking his head away from the finger with more force than he intended. "I was thinking about Walid."

"Yeah. He seemed like one of the good ones."

"He had heart to him,"" Justice said. "Do you think he tried to sell us out?"

"Oh, what the rat said?"

"Yeah. I mean he works for Frank, doesn't he?"

"Yeah, but he's a rat. Why the hell believe anything that comes out of his face?"

Justice didn't know how to interpret that.

"It's better to believe in what you saw," Rex said.

"What do you mean?"

"That it's better to think about what you saw in front of you. You liked Walid, right?"

"That's right," Justice said.

"Then go with that. Don't trust what a rat said to save his hide."

"But Frank—"

"Fuck Frank," Rex said. He waved his cigarette in the air. "This is about you and making it through to another day with your soul intact." He pounded his chest and sucked down a hit of nicotine. "Fuck everyone else. You liked Walid. Then trust that. Otherwise you'll stop trusting your own instincts to be human and then what?"

Justice nodded his head not understanding. But he liked Rex now. "I suppose so." He thought about the prison. He'd judged Rex and the other men too harshly then. Or perhaps he didn't judge, but the tickle inside his belly *had* made him hate them all. That was one thing that he never learned in his life, that his parents never taught him: how to separate true wisdom from someone trying to influence you.

He realized then that he was smoking a cigarette. And he realized that this was a break with his promise to his girlfriend, and to himself, not to smoke. He sucked it in. The torched feeling ran through his throat. His extremities tingled. This was something he missed. He rubbed his lip.

"You going to be okay?" Rex asked.

"I think I will," Justice said. His phone vibrated in his pocket. He thought about the office. Where Drail was probably cracking his knuckles on a table that seemed impossibly polished in this dusty alley. Justice let out some air. "Why did you join?" he asked. As silence grew between them, he thought that perhaps he's stepped over a line, that perhaps he should figure a way to take it back.

"I think I joined for the reasons everyone joined. I was fifteen when the towers fell. But I saw how foolishly we'd been acting. So after protesting and complaining I decided that there was only one real way of solving the existential crisis I was in."

"To join?" Justice said. Rex's story sounded much like his. He inhaled another lungful of smoke. Why did health matter when somewhere in his bones he could hear the rumblings of discontent with what he had seen so far?

"Exactly," said Rex. He shook his head, somewhat in anger, and spat.

"How long you been here?"

"A couple years now. All in Yemen."

"They haven't moved you?"

"Only one willing to fight it out here. So I stay because I've learned the city and there's nothing else I would like better that the likes of Frank to give me a promotion."

"That happening soon?" Justice asked, wondering why Rex had said he wanted out a few minutes earlier.

"Who the hell knows?"

"I wish I knew," Justice said. "Then perhaps I'd get a promotion or stop stressing about it."

Rex let out a laugh. "Don't be modest. You're on a Tango-one. We all know that."

Justice, hearing the awe in Rex's voice, didn't want to burst that bubble or the cocoon it placed him in. He half closed his eyes as Rex's eyes looked at him and down at the ground. "Tango-one," Justice murmured. He wondered if this setback stopped any chance of him getting a promotion. He wondered why he cared. *That* feeling burst his cocoon.

"Christ," Justice said. "What will we do about Walid?"

"It's between them."

Justice nodded. He knew that wasn't the right attitude to have towards someone you were close to, but Rex was giving him an out.

"So Frank's cool with carrying out an attack on his own embassy?" Justice said, trying to speak so that the words of the reality that faced him could take a better form than the sick feeling, or a hatred to how the world worked that threatened to take over.

"It makes sense if you think about it."

"How?"

"The rat gets to carry out a harmless attack, and move up in the organization. Then Frank has a leader in the cell and can help catch other cells."

"Isn't the point to end all these cells?" Justice asked.

Rex glanced at him like that was a silly thing to say. "You're never going to get that. It's just a pipe dream," Rex said. "Most of them just hate our way of life. It's as simple as that."

Justice didn't reply because surely there were more. "Should we call Walid's wife and tell her?"

"No," Rex said and placed a hand on Justice's arm. "Just let it be."

Justice stood up, his lip still stinging. His phone vibrated again. He looked at it. It was Drail.

"Hello?" Justice said, taking a few steps from Rex.

"How's it going?" Drail asked.

The background noise was loud. Justice was certain he was the focal point of a conference call.

"Just used up a lead."

"Nothing?" Drail said, annoyed.

"Nope. Anything on your end?" Justice said, trying to find himself

232

some solid footing for the conversation. After being chewed out by Frank he was in no mood to deal with the same here with Drail.

"My end? Pretty sure I gave *you* this job, Tango-one," Drail said. Some chuckles in the background arose. Justice's skin warmed up. Was he the butt of a joke? After all he'd been through? He took a deep breath and reminded himself that he was in no position to argue with his boss.

"All right I'll call again in a few hours. By then I want a proper report put through and something we can discuss. That means you'd better have made some damn progress, got it?" Drail said. He was munching on food.

"Got it," Justice said.

"Wait," Drail said. "Your woman's been calling us, harassing us. I gave her your number so you can deal with her. Got it?" More chuckles came up.

Justice felt angry with the fact that they would chuckle about his personal life. "What—"

Drail had hung up on him. He'd been thinking about returning to the office, but now he decided that he'd be better off here.

"That the head honcho?" Rex asked. He was stretching out his muscles methodically.

Justice's muscles tightened. "Yeah, that was him."

And his phone started to vibrate again. Justice held up a finger and Rex nodded and turned away.

"Hi honey," Justice said.

"Where are you?" she asked.

Justice missed her voice and wanted nothing more in the world than to cuddle up with her and, with her head on his arm, pretend like the rest of the world didn't exist. "I'm sorry I didn't call earlier. I've been busy at work," he said.

"Where are you?"

"I'm out of the country," Justice said. He couldn't say much more. And his muscles tensed up, his mind preparing for a hit. Though this was a woman he loved, or at least did sometime in the past, he could sense a hostility in her voice that he'd never heard before. She was treating him like a stranger.

She let out air for what seemed to be a minute straight. It was loud enough that Rex cocked his head and raised an eyebrow. Justice walked a few more meters away and huddled over the phone. Was the truth even something he would tell her if he could?

"You're not going to tell me, are you? Are you at another woman's place?"

"No," he said, though it might have been better if he had said yes. And for a second he played it out in his head and got angry with her. Angry that she wouldn't give him the benefit of the doubt, and though she didn't know it she was trying to get him to put his job on the line by telling her some secrets.

"There you go again," she said.

There wasn't much to do with this. She seemed to have her mind made up. His anger dissipated at that thought, and his heart sank. "What do you mean?" he said, a crack in his voice.

"Never telling me, always pushing me away. If it's nothing why don't you tell me?"

"I can't. I've told you that before."

"You really expect me to believe you have a secret job? You don't even have enough money for a good place in the City."

Justice gently chewed on his tongue. He didn't want to argue about something they'd talked about many times before. "You know—"

"I know nothing. And this is all your doing. Don't you dare make me feel bad. Where are you?"

Now his heart splashed into his guts. Tears welled up. "I can't tell you. You know that."

"No I don't."

"I'm sorry," he said. He had an inkling of where this was going. He hoped, maybe prayed that this would be averted. Part of him considered telling the truth. But he knew that this call, like all calls in the agency, was being listened to.

"You're always sorry. Nothing changes."

"It doesn't," he said, agreeing with her. Seeing her side so clearly now that he knew it wasn't going to last.

"You don't seem to care," she said.

"I do," he replied, fighting back the tears from overwhelming him.

"Good-bye Justice."

He thought about how they met. He thought about how lonely it would be in the City without her. Static rose up. Then the line went dead.

He took a few minutes fighting what seemed to be a heart attack. There was a job to do.

"The old lady?" Rex said when Justice turned.

Justice took a few breaths. "You know how it is."

"Damn, that bad?"

"We're done," Justice said. "Fucking done."

Rex wrapped his arm around Justice again. "The hits keep coming, don't they?"

"They certainly do."

"Can't expect much from the girls at home, though. Not with as long as we're gone."

"You have one back home?" Justice asked.

"Had," Rex said with a raised index finger. "Was gone too long without enough answers and she dumped me."

"Yeah…" Justice said, feeling better knowing that he wasn't the only one.

"Best thing is to get one from inside."

"All the ones in my agency are taken."

"Well, I've yet to meet one," Rex said. "And half the reason I signed up for this job was for the chicks. Christ, right now I'll jump into a honey trap without reservations."

Justice laughed as Rex chuckled.

"I think I could go for a honey trap myself," Justice said.

"Yeah," Rex said, shaking his head. "Before this, I was certain that secret agent was a perfect pickup line at a bar."

"That's what they told me when they recruited me," Justice said, sighing out loud.

They lumbered out of the alley, paying no attention to the ambulance outside the qat bar.

Not sure where Rex was taking him, Justice followed, keeping an eye on his rear. He noticed a young man following for a few too many blocks.

"We're being followed," Justice said.

"You certain?" Rex said. "We're almost a few blocks from the prison."

Justice's muscles clenched.

"What's wrong? If it's someone following us he'll never go near there." Rex said.

"Why not?"

"Oh, all the locals know it as a place to avoid. It's being included in some of the local folklore as a place for hell," Rex said, grinning.

"How do you know that?" Justice asked, keeping an eye on the young man who was now pretending to be extremely interested in the rooftops around him.

"An anthropologist works for the embassy. He tells us all these effects."

"That's good," Justice said, though he still didn't want to go to the prison.

"Let's catch him," Justice said after a few seconds of thinking of other excuses to stay away from the prison.

"How?"

"You stay here. I'll go forward and double back from another alley."

"Sure you won't get lost?"

"No," Justice said. "But we need to try. I need answers to some questions I have."

"And a random guy following us has that?" Rex said.

Justice didn't reply. He picked up his pace and made a turn. He turned into another alley, but it slanted at an angle from the previous one. He wasn't going to be able to double back. There was an old man selling what appeared to be old dusty brass wares of varying sizes and in different conditions of wear. He looked up, a white cloak over him and eyed Justice.

The world stopped and Justice stared back at the old man, almost helpless to turn away. The old man raised a teapot and beckoned, with his head, for Justice to come over. Justice walked over to the man, against his will. His brain was telling him to run off. That he needed to head off the man who was following them, but he couldn't help it.

"American?" the man asked, in a heavy, rusty, British-tinged voice.

"Yes," Justice said. his hands were sweaty.

The man handed him the teapot. It was brown, old. Justice looked at it. It smelled like his parent's attic, a place where time no longer mattered.

"It's a gift," the man said. "You look like you've been through a lot. Don't let it get to you."

Justice didn't know how the man knew what was weighing down on him, but he wasn't surprised either. "Thanks," Justice said.

The man handed him a bottle. "This is for polishing it. It's ugly, but underneath it's beautiful. A little like this country."

"You from here.... originally," Justice said. He gulped when a ray of light highlighted the fact that the man only had one eye. The dark socket stared at him.

"Born and raised," the man said. "Don't let my accent fool you. I went to college at Oxford," he said and winked.

"What're you doing here?" Justice asked. He liked the old man, sensing a connection to the glint in his eyes.

"I'm happy here," the man said. He grinned. He had perfect teeth, though the ones in the back, in the shadows of his mouth, glinted with gold.

Justice held on to the teapot, the recesses of his brain screaming that he had to turn and find the man who was chasing Rex and him. "Thank you," Justice said, wondering if he had anything to give the man.

"Don't worry," the man said. "Just do your job." His voice rattled Justice's chest.

And Justice's mind remembered the smell of the prison. "What do you think of us coming here?" Justice asked. He knew that the man wasn't going to mistake him for some tourist.

This question pushed a whole lot of air leaked out of the man. His breath smelled like cloves.

"There is evil in the world, is there not? And here, in this country we have a lot of our young men finding solace in these… extreme ways. We don't want it, but we can't explain away the things that make them so. And because of these men you're coming here, and you're figuring out how to take them away because otherwise these words of theirs, these promises of attacks on your land will drive you insane."

The man stopped, looked down on his hand and rubbed his knuckles. He looked back up at Justice.

Justice wasn't certain if that was a question or a statement. He didn't know. And he really didn't like not knowing. He had the feeling that this lack of knowledge was the reason he was here. Was the reason he was in some back-alley in Yemen, with a man following him, and without a clue as to how to solve the mission before him. When the old man patted his shoulder, Justice gazed down. A very small part of him wanted to sit here and drink tea until his days passed.

"And perhaps this is the only way. If one looks at history the only ones who go crazy are the ones who look for empires or nations or rebellions to act with kindness. So you will come here as long as our young men yell loud threats, and they will yell loud threats for as long as you are here," said the old man. Again he stopped to massage his knuckles.

"I take it you don't like us here?" Justice said. He spoke not because he thought that was what the old man was saying, but because the old man's words were making him uncomfortable and that was really making him doubt something about himself. He just couldn't tell what that was.

"It's not a matter of liking. Not anymore at least. I'd never say that revolutions are worthless. Much of what we know in the world wouldn't have come around if not for the revolutions. But I am wary… I am old…" the old man said and closed his eye.

Justice glanced around and realized that he was surrounded by a few men, mostly young, who seemed to understand the old man's words. They muttered amongst themselves and eyed Justice. Justice held his breath. The other men had cut off any chance of him leaving. He could feel his balls shrinking.

"What do you mean?" Justice finally said. He wanted the old man to open his eye. Perhaps he hadn't noticed the newcomers.

The old man opened his eye and nodded at the other men. "I mean that the revolutions happen for a reason. They are reactions to too much injustice. Right?"

"Right," Justice said, weary of speaking his true beliefs on revolutions. Or at least any revolution besides the American one.

"From evil there will arise a violent reaction. A will to change that evil. And also seeing that those who wield the evil won't give it up easily. They're too conniving, too smart, too cunning for that. And to overthrow them you must, on the rebels side, have someone who's more cunning, more treacherous than those already in power. And then what?"

"I don't know," Justice said. The men'd moved in closer.

"You don't know? And you're here?" the old man said. His voice louder now. His back straight and his eye poking into Justice.

Justice tried to say something, but no words came out. He had to get going.

"I'll tell you what," the old man said, holding up a silver dagger. "It's the same cycle. We can't live like that. But what else is there?"

Justice wasn't certain what the man was trying to say. "I have to go," Justice said. "Thank you." He held up the bottle the old man had given him. For some reason this old man reminded Justice a lot of the old man at the prison.

"Fine, fine," the old man said, sitting back and casting his dagger aside. "Go then. You don't want to see and you'll die being a fool for others."

With the bottle and teapot in hand, Justice pushed his way past the men. They didn't seem hostile now. Justice bemoaned his luck to meet the crazy people in this world. He ran to the alley, wanting to talk to Rex. A conversation with someone sane would help him erase the memory of this old man.

He turned back to the alley where he'd left Rex and found it empty. No one to be seen in either direction. His heart dropped. Was he too late? Did he make Rex needlessly risk his life? Would he find Rex dead? These series of thoughts forced his legs into action and he ran down the alley in the direction Rex had been heading. He could smell an open sewage. He wondered if he'd be able to find his way to the prison if that was needed. He looked down a side alley; it looked exactly like all the others. Sweat poured down his face.

He swore under his breath and kept on running. Up ahead he saw a young man walking. He had a black shirt and blue jeans on. His hair shone from grease. It didn't occur to him that this might have been the man following him earlier until he was only a few yards away. He slowed down to a saunter and his senses heightened when he realized that the young man was staring intently ahead of him.

When the alley straightened out, Justice saw that the young man was following Rex. Justice was surprised that the young man hadn't seen him or heard him yet. By now Justice was only a few steps away. The young man smelled ambitiously like cologne. There was the small chance that this young man was just a common crook looking for a mark. Justice ignored his brain's pleas and grabbed the man's elbow, squeezing tight on his funny bone.

The young man spun around. Justice didn't mean to, but the man's face scared him. It was scarred with part of his lip torn off, leaving a half-skull grin that pinched Justice's eyes.

Rex spun around and came running. The young man pulled out a knife. "You die," he said.

Justice stared at the knife. The young man swiped at him. Justice jumped back out of pure instinct. The knife grazed the skin on his left hand. A knuckle protested with sharp pain. When he looked down at his hand he saw a red hand. Drops of blood formed on his fingertips.

The young man was lunging at him again. Justice pulled out the small teapot the old man had given him and deflected the knife. The collision rang in a high pitch, forcing him to cock his head. The man stared at the teapot like it was some talisman sent to end him.

Justice took this pause to throw his bottle at the young man. The young man ducked and the bottle flew by his head and broke on the mud wall behind. Keeping his eye on the knife, Justice came at him with the teapot. This seemed to surprise even the young man. He took a step back then slashed his knife at Justice.

But Justice was ready for this moment. He moved the teapot, handle first, at knife. He had the plan, but there wasn't much room for error. And he knew Rex wasn't close enough to help yet. Handle first he deflected the knife and grabbed the man's wrist. He straightened the arm and punched the man hard in the nose. The man's head flew back. Justice punched the man on his elbow and watched with relief as the knife clattered harmlessly to the ground.

Rex arrived just then and grabbed the man from behind.

There were a few children watching from a window. Justice waved them away, but they stared on, wide-eyed and uncertain.

"Who do you work for?" Justice asked, pulling the man close to him.

The man smiled. "You're cut bad. You'd better tend to that first."

Rex nodded.

Justice stepped back and stared at his hand. It was dripping. Bad. He didn't have anything to wrap it with. One of the children from the window threw him a rag. Justice smiled at the children. Now, however, they ran away. He wrapped the wound. The blood soaked the rag right through.

The young man laughed. Rex tweaked his arm and he shut up.

Justice stared at his hand, willing it to stop bleeding, but it wouldn't. Angry he held it above his head. He needed answers, and he needed them now. Besides, this wasn't a deep wound.

"Answer me," Justice said.

The man smiled. The only thing odd was that his teeth were in a perfect straight line.

"Or what?" the man said.

Rex pulled on the man's arm. "We can make it hurt even worse," Rex said.

That didn't seem to make the man talk. Instead he stared out to a point between the two men. Justice remembered some of his interrogation training telling him that when a person did this, they were visually holding on to something so that they steady themselves. So that they wouldn't blurt out truths.

Justice placed his non-bleeding hand on the man's shoulder. "We're trying to help you out, you know that?"

The man didn't move. Justice thrust his head into the man's line of sight.

"We already have your friends, and they told us everything."

The man didn't move.

"At Jebel Nabi Suyad," Justice continued. "Surely you knew about this?"

The man blinked. It was hard to tell whether this line of questioning was getting him to open or not.

"You know where we'll take you," Rex said, pushing the man.

Justice wanted to raise his hands to his partner, but decided not to. "We know about the Dr. Noklar plan," Justice said. "We know all about that. We also know about the other attack. Your friends all blamed you. One friend of yours was especially talkative," he said.

"You're lying," the man blurted out. "And you can put me under whatever pain. Allah will give me the strength to carry on."

"If I was lying," Justice said, keeping his cool. "How would I know about the Dr. Noklar plan?"

The man flinched; his eyes searched Justice's face for a moment. Overhead a jet pierced the sky. Justice looked up, the white plume it left behind on the blue sky somehow seemed out of place in this country. And he looked at the man, caught his eye and smiled. "And how would I know that your friend has a scar like a star on his chest?" He maintained eye contact with the man.

The man looked down, then up at the jet plume. "Dr. Noklar isn't my group's plan. We don't really believe in hitting innocents. We believe that the Quran forbids that."

Justice nodded. And again he was starting to like someone who was a sworn enemy.

"And our group plans on hitting the people who really cause the pain in this world."

Justice looked up at the jet plume, now disintegrating into nothing. He knew this news was bad, that he should do something, but he didn't much feel like moving. He felt like sitting down and talking to this man.

"What the hell are you doing?" Rex whispered.

Justice, startled, looked over at Rex who had a furious face on.

"What?"

"He's going to hit Frank, you just heard what I heard, right?" Rex asked.

"Yeah, let's get going," Justice said. He let go of the man. The man looked at them both. It was obvious from his glare that he didn't like Rex, but he liked Justice.

"What do we do with him?" Justice asked, half-hoping that Rex would want him to be released.

"I'll call for backup," Rex said, pulling out his phone and dialing a number.

A mosquito whined into Justice's ear. That snapped him out of his stupor. "*I'll* call Frank," Justice said.

He dialed a number. He wanted to smoke. He felt like he was hitting a wall. "Frank?"

"What the hell are you doing calling me again shit head?" Frank yelled. In the background a feminine voice spoke up. "Get the hell out of here Mary," Frank said.

"We have reason to believe that your life's in danger," Justice said. He should have let the bastard face the terrorists on his own. He really didn't want to put up with anymore of Frank's bullshit.

"Are you still going on about that attack?" Frank said, laughing, then breaking into a cough. "I told you that it was—"

"Listen Frank, this is a verified source, and it's about an attack on your persons. So if you like those small balls and brains of yours you'll increase your security detail and make sure your family's safe. Got it?" Justice smirked.

There was a pause, like the phone might have gone dead. Justice even checked it to make sure that it wasn't a lost connection, but the call was still going.

"You really have pair on you, don't you Tango-one?" Frank said. "Well listen up hot shot, this is my country and ain't no skinnies trying to kill me."

Before Justice could answer, the line went dead.

"Damn," Rex said with a grin. "You really unloaded on him."

Justice detected a certain awe in Rex's tone, but there was no time for that. Now that the thrill of telling Frank off was wearing thin, he knew that he may very well have put his entire career in jeopardy. "Help coming?"

"They'll be here soon," Rex said.

"Can you call Frank?" Justice said. Rex nodded and dialed into his phone. He gave up after a few minutes.

"He's not answering," Rex said. His voice squeaked.

Ali stared forward at the two cars ahead of him. Saladin was in the driver's seat of his smoking mobile. For some reason the big man had left it idling. The alleyway they were parked in, filled with smoke. The men in the two cars ahead of him looked back, they seemed annoyed. Ali rolled his eyes.

"Do we need to leave the car running?" asked Ali.

"Of course. What if we get the word?" Saladin shifted to one side and let out a huge fart and grunted.

Ali was really growing annoyed with Saladin's habits.

They had managed to put together everyone for the hit. They had a vendor outside the embassy who would tell them when the target had left.

When Saladin's sulfuric smell grew too powerful to allow breathing, Ali stepped out of the car and walked to the men in the car. He tried to remember their names, but instead was visited with flashes of Laith's face. Then the warmth of Nadia close by. He didn't want to go another night without her, but he had a sinking feeling that things were not going to end well with her. She was right: he was a targeted man, and being close to anyone was an attempt to kill them.

"You doing all right?" he asked as he peered into the first car. The four men, each with magazines and RPG rocket heads at their feet, nodded their heads. They were sweating.

"Can you ask the idiot to turn off his car? He'll run out of gas before this mission is over," the driver, a young man with gleaming eyes said.

Ali smiled and raised his eyebrows. "He's the boss."

The others scoffed.

"You need to focus on what's ahead. Everyone knows what they have to do?" Ali asked.

"We do, boss."

They seemed to want something more from him.

"Remember why we're doing this. All the people who have died. This is for them," said Ali, trying to smile. A fly bounced off his face. The diesel fumes were making him dizzy.

The men nodded.

"This is for Allah. You will be scared. But remember your jobs. Pray and this will go well," said Ali.

"You ever do this?" asked a young man in the back seat. His body trembled, though he flexed to cover it up.

"Yes," Ali said, smiling; inside he grimaced at the thought of sending so young a man into a fight like this. Then again, wasn't he that young when he first snuck across the border between Syria and Iraq?

All the faces looked at him with a level of awe. There was tension in the air, though Ali wasn't quite certain why. He decided to say something to help squash it. "It's always tough, your first coordinated hit. It takes…" He took a deep breath trying to think of his first time.

It had been near the Green Zone. He'd been riding on the back of a dirt bike, two other dirt bikes behind him. And a van in front to do the blocking. This was early in the war, when no one expected such attacks, and thus there wasn't much security. The hit was on an ambassador's aide, though he hadn't asked from which country, and he certainly had no more information than the color of the car they were looking for. His nerves before the hit almost incapacitated him; praying to Allah had helped soothe his nerves. In the end, after the van had blocked the aide's car from escaping, Ali had barely been able to squeeze the trigger, and the dead body, spreading blood on the dusty road was something he'd never forget. Nor would he forget how the others dragged the Iraqi driver out and taunted him before they shot him. But he also remembered that after that day he swore to never be an assassin again. This was before the days when kidnapping became a form of currency.

He simply didn't want to not know who he was attacking, and why. Luckily, being one of the first fighters there, and one who survived, afforded him many perks.

A fly buzzed into his face. The men, or boys, in the car were staring at him.

"We're going after someone bad. Very bad. You can believe that. This man has blown our children and women apart. Innocents who've done nothing. And yet they still drive around our country with impunity," Ali said. He could feel his voice growing stronger, a bass coming somewhere from depths he never knew he had. "But today you will show them. And it will be hard. But pray, believe. Nothing they have can compare to your belief in Allah. Remember that. And remember how your training. All of these things will guide you." He tipped his head forward. And the men nodded. Confidently, or so Ali thought.

He repeated a similar speech to the other car before the two men on motorcycles, near the embassy, cackled on the radio that the ambassador was leaving. He ran to Saladin's car.

"You talk to the soldiers?" Saladin said. His face, scrunched up, almost disgusted, seemed to say that he found this odd.

"Yes," Ali said, hissing and thinking that perhaps dealing with someone like Saladin was not what he wanted to do in life, but he didn't want to say anything because, well, Saladin still provided the money for everything. Ali sniffed, but resorted to breathing through his mouth when he realized that the moneyman had farted again.

The cars moved out and Ali turned up the volume on his radio. They were on shortwave.

They drove close behind the other cars, Ali's head buzzing. When they split, Saladin drove them up to an overlook in a poor neighborhood. Ali stepped out. He sensed a sudden urge to beat Saladin down. He was remembering how such men had always looked afar as flesh was churned in Iraq. And now Ali felt dirty because he was finally one of these men. But he was also relieved. He stared at the section of the highway. He could hear Saladin walking towards him. To feel cleaner, Ali imagined the men in the car, nerves tingling, guns in hand. Over the radio the men said they had the ambassador's car in sight.

Ali glanced about the neighborhood. A handful of old women stared at them, but they didn't seem to care beyond staring.

"Almost," Saladin said.

Ali nodded and stared at the stretch of highway. His heart jumped when he saw the distinct shape of the ambassador's car. This was it. All the training and time he'd put into his men. His vision would be proven today.

Saladin pulled out his cell phone and started to chatter into it. Ali balled his hands up. He would not, could not, hit this man. At least he wasn't talking about the operation. Ali stepped away from him and watched, his heart bouncing around in his chest.

"Do you think he's heading home?" Justice said. Even though Frank had just cussed him out, and a more juvenile part of him wanted Frank to suffer, if only to prove himself right, Justice knew they were going to have to save Frank.

"I think so," Rex said.

Just then a black SUV screeched to a halt in front of them.

"Can we drive that?" Justice asked.

"Of course," one of the men in a polo shirt and khakis said.

Justice and Rex handed over the terrorist and drove off.

"Who were they?" Justice asked. "They work for the agency?"

"Mainly contractors," said Rex, swerving the car to avoid a pedestrian, and pressing down on the horn. "All ex-SF guys."

Justice nodded, not sure what to make of it. The inside of the SUV smelled of canned tobacco and everything was covered in black leather. He reminded himself that he had to go and save Frank right now. "How far away from his route are we?"

"We should be there in a few seconds," said Rex. With that he pulled the handbrake and turned the SUV into a highway. Other cars screeched and honked their horns.

Justice, feeling his heart in his mouth took deep breaths. He realized that the SUV's radio was playing some country music. He turned it off.

"There!" Rex yelled.

Justice saw a black SUV drive by the opposite way. He only noticed that there was one person in it. "He drives alone?"

"That's right. He thinks security details are for pussies."

Justice shook his head. Rex slowed down and turned the SUV over a small berm that divided the two sides of the highway. Soon they were driving as fast as they could down the highway. As Rex weaved between the cars on the highway, honking his horn, Justice could sense the roll of the truck making him ill.

The SUV hit a pothole and the back fishtailed. The rising feeling of flying hit Justice's stomach and he held on to the handle beside him. By some fortunate turns of the steering wheel, Rex managed to get the SUV under control.

"There," Justice said. Several cars ahead, and barely in dusty sight, was a black SUV. "That his license plate?"

"Not sure," said Rex, honking his horn at a two cars blocking his way.

"He looks fine, though," said Justice. He squinted to see what was going on, and it appeared as if Frank's SUV was alone. Justice relaxed. They'd come on time.

And as Rex sped past more cars, closing the distance to Frank's truck, Justice saw two motorcycles and two cars moving in unison towards Frank's car. At first he thought that it was a mirage. Perhaps a freak coincidence. But as the cars approached Frank's, it was obvious that they were coordinating.

"Shit," said Justice, pulling out his handgun. He rolled down his window.

"What? Rex asked.

They were two hundred yards away from Frank. The two motorcycles and cars were about fifty.

"Those cars, they're moving to Frank," Justice said. He pulled out his phone, but there was no reception. Justice could feel his chest tighten and his bladder filled with piss.

"They are?" Rex asked.

"Faster," Justice said. He leaned out of the window and pointed his gun. But he couldn't see down his sights, let alone get a decent shot off. The SUV was moving too fast, and the road too bumpy to be able to aim. Not from this far at least. He inhaled dust into his lungs and coughed.

The other cars and motorcycles were almost upon Frank.

"Dammit," Justice said. They were going down a hill on the highway, a long straight stretch with houses on either side. Justice saw the semi-truck barreling down at the highway from a perpendicular side road. And he saw one of the motorcycle passengers pull out a gun. One car was in front of Frank and the other behind. The two motorcycles were beside Frank.

"Fuck," Justice said. He looked down his sights again. They were fifty yards away. And the semi truck slammed into the highway, blocking it. Frank's SUV squealed and the back fishtailed. Justice saw the motorcycle raise his gun. There was no choice, even if he risked hitting Frank, Justice had to fire a shot. He fired twice.

He couldn't see where he hit. He hoped it was on the road and not the houses. He aimed again. And fired. This time he saw the road beside the motorcycle with the raised gun kick up dust. And the rider swerved the motorcycle. And as the passenger fired a three round burst, his aim was off and his barrel flung towards the sky.

By now Frank was at a complete stop. It was hard to say what was going on inside his SUV. Its wheels spun.

"Hold on," said Rex.

Justice gripped the handle on the door and hoped that he remembered to buckle up.

It happened fast. And all Justice could do was tense up. And hope that he didn't wet his pants. Their SUV plowed into a motorcycle. The rider and the passenger of the cycle both crashed into the windshield, sending spider cracks all across it. Their SUV hurtled past Frank and into the car in front of him. The airbags deployed.

Justice had his seatbelt on. He could feel it dig into his torso. He could also feel his head lurch forward and hit the airbag. The sound of metal grinding filled his head.

And as the SUV came to a complete stop, he peeled himself off the airbag and looked over. The men in the car they hit, four of them, all seemed knocked out. Justice could smell gasoline, shit and pared steel.

"Let's go," Rex said. Justice didn't look over, but could hear Rex's door open. All of Justice's joints felt out of place. He blinked, then wondered where his handgun was. He saw it on the floor, looking right at him. He shook his head and grabbed it. His door wouldn't open, so he kicked down his window and crept out.

Still dazed, Justice walked over to the men in the car they hit. The two in the front sat with bent necks. The two in the back were barely stirring. Justice opened their door and rummaged through each man's pockets. He found a one handgun amongst the four, and took it.

"Justice!"

Justice turned his head and looked over. For some reason he forgot about the other car and motorcycle. Two shots pushed him out of his cocoon.

"Coming," he said and stepped past their SUV to survey the situation. The car was still behind Frank, though now there were two men leaning out of the back seat. One had an RPG and the other had an AK-47. The motorcycle with two people was shooting at Frank's car.

Rex crouched in front of Frank's hood, trying to keep the SUV between him and the attackers. And Frank was squealing his SUV back and forth. Justice wasn't sure where Frank thought he was going. The road had barriers on either side, and was blocked going both ways.

Another burst of shots went off, and Justice saw Frank's front tire pop, the tire turning into strands of rubber in a second. Justice, his heart now catching up to the situation, held his breath and fired at the man on the motorcycle. He hit the driver. The passenger turned his gun to Justice. But Justice squeezed off another round and watched as the man's head snapped back as he went flying to the ground.

A swoosh went off and Justice turned to see the RPG with a trail of smoke behind it. It was too fast to react to. The RPG head went flying at Frank. Rex hit the ground. The RPG warhead skipped off the hood and came at Justice. Justice froze. He could feel his brain yelling for him to move, but his insides were jelly.

The RPG's warhead whistled above Justice. He dove at the ground.

The explosion filled his chest with a punch, and turned his world black for a second. Metal whistled through the air. Justice looked up to see that the RPG had hit the car with the four men. It was burning. The flames licked Justice with their heat. The smell of gasoline now mixed with fire. The car was now a burned hulk with charred bodies inside, flames still leaping out from it.

A hail of bullets whistled above Justice. The car with the RPG and AK came at him. He could see Frank shooting out of his sunroof, and Rex firing at the car too. Justice raised his gun and fired several times. The man with the AK twisted back and his assault rifle flew from his hands. His body hung from the window.

But the car was still coming at Justice. He dove to the ground and rolled under their SUV.

The car scraped by. One of the SUV's tire almost grazed Justice's head. And as shots filled the air. Justice rolled to try to stay out of the bullets' paths.

The whine of the car as it sped away filled Justice with some calm.

"Incoming!"

Justice rolled out from under the SUV, looked up and saw the RPG warhead coming at them. He dove behind the burned car.

The warhead hit their SUV directly. The explosion cracked open Justice's eardrums and he screamed.

His world went black and he looked up to see Frank and Rex smiling down on him.

"You sonofabitch," Frank said, and stretched out his hand.

Justice took the hand and pulled himself up.

"He's a tough one, ain't he?" Frank said, patting Justice on the back.

The pats were like punches, and Justice held himself together long enough so that he didn't wince. "Thanks," he managed to say.

Rex grinned and handed Justice a cigarette.

Justice took it and inhaled long and hard.

"Beats any woman, any day, don't it?" Rex said.

Justice forced a grin.

Frank gave an odd look.

"His woman broke up with him," said Rex.

"Ah," Frank said waving his hand at Justice. "Women come and go. Just look on to the next one."

"Thanks," Justice said. He wasn't sure what else to say.

"Well, how about you come over for dinner?" Frank said. "The wife's cooking some shish-kebabs."

"Yeah, come on over," Rex said, beaming.

"Unless double-O here has more leads to follow," Frank said, again patting Justice hard on the back.

Justice couldn't help but wince this time. And he coughed as the smell of burning plastic hit his nostrils. "No. I need a breather."

Frank chuckled. "Your parents really knew what they were doing when they named you. You know that?"

They waited until the police arrived and filled out a report. Then they went on to Frank's house only a few minutes away. There was a security detail outside the house.

"Guess I need them now," Frank said.

A small woman with brown skin and curly hair came running out of the house.

"Frank! Are you all right?" She ran into him and hugged him.

"Of course honey. They were no match for me," Frank said, pushing out his chest.

Justice stepped forward, expecting to be introduced, but Frank turned with the woman and walked inside.

Justice glanced at Rex who shrugged. "They're close, from what I hear."

"You've never been here?" Justice asked. His mind focused on how green and lush the lawn was. It was a bright contrast to the rest of the dried up country. And for some reason it didn't feel right. And it also made him think about the doctor. He was going to have to find out where he was.

"No, first time," Rex said.

Justice crouched and rubbed grass between his fingers. He could smell the moist soil here. It made his mouth water.

"Yeah, only goddamn place you can grow grass in this country," Rex said.

"Here?"

"No, in embassy row. This street is for foreign diplomats. And they're the only lawns in the country where you can get enough water to grow grass. The rest of the monkeys in this place are too stupid to know how to grow grass," Rex said and shook his head.

"Yeah," Justice said. "Or they can't afford water in a desert."

Rex narrowed his eyes. "You're not going native on me, are you, Justice? Not after these bastards just tried to kill us all."

"No," Justice blurted out. "I'm just saying…" and he hoped that Rex wouldn't ask anything more because Justice did feel something odd growing inside him. Something that made grass like this infuriated him. He shook his head as Rex stared. "I'm just thinking about getting that damn doctor," he said.

"Damn. You never stop working, do ya?" Rex said smiling and shaking his head.

"What about—"

"The man we got information from? They've taken him to the five star resort," Rex said.

"The prison?"

"Yeah. We'll find out everything he knows. If there's a doctor around we'll find out about that too."

"Dinner, boys!" Frank yelled from inside the house.

"Come on. His wife cooks some great food," Rex said.

Justice, hearing the ringing in his ears wasn't sure he heard that right, didn't Rex say that he hadn't been here before? But he decided not to worry. His stomach grumbled and he walked in, the smell of grilled beef calling him.

At the table sat Frank, his wife and a girl and boy.

"Sit down fellas. Let's fill our bellies," Frank said and let out a laugh.

"I've no fork," Rex said as he sat down.

"Me either," said Justice. Though he was prepared to eat with his hands, he didn't want to after Rex's earlier accusation.

But before anyone could answer, Rex got up and came back from the kitchen with a pair of forks.

Frank narrowed his eyes. "A more suspicious man than myself

would say that you knew where those were," said Frank.

Rex let out a half-grin. "Of course. The kitchen's layout makes sense."

Justice thought he caught a look between Frank's wife and Rex, but the smell of meat pulled him to his meal. He took one bite of the fatty juicy grilled meat, along with some grilled onions, and he closed his eyes. He was pretty sure this was the best meal he had had in quite some time.

"Good, isn't it?" Frank asked.

"Great," Justice said. He opened his eyes and noticed the two kids, both with collared shirts on, and both looking too blonde to be the children of either Frank or his wife, staring at him.

"Don't stare, it's not polite," said the wife.

Justice realized that he didn't know what her name was. But his mouth was too full to rectify that right away.

"Children," Frank growled. "Don't let them bother you," he said to Justice.

"It's fine," Justice said. He also noticed that both children had green eyes. Not just any green, but a glowing-green.

"Is it true they call you Justice?" asked the girl. She had shark teeth.

"That's what my parents called me," Justice said.

"Are you sure you're not an emblem for the long arm of American law?" asked the boy.

The way the kids talked wasn't how Justice thought kids talked. He shifted in his seat, realizing that the adrenaline from the firefight was still in his blood and if the boy asked another silly question he was probably going to *do* something silly. Justice stared at his drink. If he drank he would definitely do something.

The kids seemed to sense his unease and they went back to their food.

"Well, hero, do you have something to say?" Frank asked.

"Well—" Justice started to say when his phone began ringing. He looked down. It was Drail. "Have to take this. Sorry."

"Of course," said Frank.

Rex shook his head, looking amazed. "Always working."

Frank nodded with approval, and as Justice walked into the kitchen, he swore that Frank's wife gave him a suggestive look mixed with the lick of her finger.

"Hello?"

"Justice. I heard what you did. Congrats!"

It was Drail, though there was enough of a seashell sound for Justice to know he was on speakerphone. He wondered who else was listening. Then he decided that he really hated his boss too.

"Thank you," he said and a round of murmurs went up.

"Who else is there?" Justice asked.

"No one," said Drail.

Justice realized that Drail's voice dropped low, angry even, whenever he lied. That was most of the time.

"Any information on your end?" Justice asked.

"What? You mean to tell me that the doctor wasn't involved in this?"

"No," said Justice, flinching a little, as if his body knew a barge of comments was about to be launched in his direction.

"No?" Drail said, scoffing. A round of chuckles went up in the background. Drail shut them up. "Then what the hell are you doing playing the hero, Justice?"

Justice felt guilty for what he'd done, and hearing the round of laughter coming from the living room, he wondered why he had saved a man's life. That thought only lasted a second before his body revolted. He was right, and he shouldn't let a pissant like Drail, no matter how threatening, tell him otherwise. "I was saving someone's life. Perhaps that desk has skewed your view of what's what." The words came out before Justice could think about them, and he was only surprised that his voice was so low. He realized his hands were sweating and that the phone was silent on the other side. He wondered if he'd been cut off and if his sentence had been thrown into a digital void.

Drail chuckled. "Watch what you say." His voice almost cracked.

"I'm trying. It's hard without a mirror."

More silence.

"You there?"

"Yes," Drail said.

"Well?"

"I'm absorbing this."

"Are you?" Justice knew he was about to cross a line, so he drew a deep breath and held it.

"Christ, Justice." Drail paused and blew air into the phone. "What's gotten into you?"

"Just saying, I'm not going to apologize for saving a man's life."

"I didn't say that. Just know what side you're on."

"I'm sure *I* do," Justice said. He knew what Drail meant, that he needed to keep his own agency and unit in mind at all times, after all that's how money flowed, but he was still thinking about the grass, about the bureaucratic idiocy that he'd been dealing with. "Do you?"

Drail laughed. "All right. I'll lay off."

"Why thank you, kind sir," said Justice. He did indeed still have adrenaline pumping through his veins. "So you're telling me you've found nothing on your end?"

"No," Drail said, his voice sad. "We've found nothing."

"Have th—"

"Nothing, Justice. Sorry. We've combed through every single phone and email and blog and Facebook update and twitter feed and comments and lord knows what else these kids use these days and we've found nothing. First we looked for all instances of doctor or escape or synonyms thereof. Nothing. And we further more looked for any with even part of those words."

"Part?"

"The letter d and so forth."

"Nothing?"

"That's right."

"Christ," said Justice.

"I know. Nothing on your end?"

"Just some insurgents. One claimed there was a doctor around, but I'm not so sure anymore."

"Well, we'll keep an eye out and let you know if something comes up."

"Okay," said Justice.

"And have you found any other leads?"

"What do you mean?" Justice asked. There was a scorning chuckle in the background.

"I'm talking about drone targets, Justice. We haven't received a single one from you."

"Oh, I wasn't aware that—"

"Christ, Justice. Just when I think that you've learned something… You're a Tango-one, you know that, right?"

"Well, not in pay grade."

Silence, the phone ticked in digital-speak.

"Was that a joke?"

"Yes," Justice said. How could he be defeated so quickly?

"Good. So you have at least a few targets, then right? Because your mission's no joke."

"I'll get a few targets," Justice said, trying to think of how he was going to do that.

"A few?"

"A lot," Justice said. "I have a few in custody, we'll get something out of them."

A voice on the phone, though not Drail, whispered something. Drail laughed.

Justice pulled the phone away from his ear.

"Yeah, well get whatever you can."

"Uh-huh," said Justice. He knew what that meant. A tremor ran through his body. He remembered what the old man at the prison had said. Justice's balls shrivel.

Drail laughed again. "You know what they say? You can tell an Arab, but you can't tell him much."

"Of course," said Justice.

"So get it out of 'em. I want targets in a few hours."

"I'll try," said Justice, torn now between hurting the men and his job.

"Try? You'll *get* them. You know we've had twenty drones flying in your vicinity for just this reason? This is what it means to be a Tango-one. Don't be the cog that breaks down."

Nelson Lowhim

"I know," said Justice, feeling bad for letting Drail down. There was a real sense that Drail was saddened by Justice's failure, and he was simply trying to help him get back up.

"I hope so. You know how much waste there is when they don't have any targets? Not just the money, think about the pollution in the air."

"Yeah," said Justice feeling sad for contributing to something so sinister.

"Good. Well go get them soldier."

Before he could say anything, the phone line died.

Justice walked back to the dining room. The family and Rex looked at him expectedly.

"Rex, you have the number for the five star hotel?"

"Why? Eat, enjoy some time off."

"No time," said Justice, feeling a little more important now that he had to go and do something of importance.

"Always working. Tango-one," said Rex with a grin. "I'll call them. I'm sure they have information for us by now." He glanced at his watch. "We've broken down breaking down a suspect to a science. It's a bell curve that sits with thirty minutes at the center. No one's done longer than an hour. Never. Right?"

Frank nodded his head and wiped his lips with his napkin. He swallowed. "Right. We have a unit near Wall Street, pulling all the best big data guys from the banks, and they've been helping us with this. It's beautiful stuff, really. You can see the formula for breaking down a person is quite easy. And not just breaking him down as a man, but really getting inside his head. And remember we never use barbaric methods—"

Rex coughed.

"Well," Frank continued, "except for the electrical burns. But this is nothing like..." He seemed to stare at the table.

"That's good," said Justice not wanting to hear more.

"Well, the formula or model for breaking down a man is almost the same as that for finding out what a customer will like on a music streaming site, or how a twitter farming algorithm can predict the oil prices. Amazing, right?"

"Very," Justice said loudly. A horrid feeling wormed its way into his guts and up to his heart. He started shaking. He tried to fight it off. That didn't help, so he tried to think of the money they'd been pouring into the African continent for AIDS. He felt better. Everyone was staring at him. He needed to pull his thoughts together, or he'd never leave this place alive.

Frank's wife coughed, and Frank seemed to snap out of his smile. "Oh, kids, you should leave." The kids and wife shuffled out of the dining room.

Rex dialed a number. He barked a hello, then uh-huhed.

"Brilliant," Rex said as he hung up.

"What?" asked Justice.

"We have a few leads from the man."

"Targets?" Justice asked.

Rex grinned. "Tango-one, chomping at the bit."

When he got the coordinates, Justice stared at the numbers, then at the bird's eye view of the map. It didn't seem right. But the local Yemeni liaison at the embassy clapped with glee when they showed him the houses to be hit. They'd been waiting all year to hit those places, but some judge—Justice was surprised they had judges in this country—had stopped them. Now there was no way they could be stopped.

Justice smiled, feeling his stomach grumble, and wondered if it was the food he had at Franks. When he asked for the liaison to hand over some intel on the houses and occupants, the man tapped his head with his finger. One thing that Justice could always appreciate was cultural differences, so he left it at that. Besides, he liked the liaison. And the sick feeling left his body.

An hour later, in a helicopter with some large men with beards with even larger rifles tied to bungee cords, Justice called in the targets. They were high enough that they could see each swath of city and mountain sides below. It was night, but Justice had a pair of night vision goggles on. The helicopter hovered a mile outside each target. When the air collapsed and exploded to each missile, and Justice's face glowed with heat, his chest filled with fear and weakened concussion waves, the helicopter would swoop in and the men would shoot all people aiding and abetting the terrorist hideouts, and he'd watch as they took out young men with burning backs.

"Get 'em all," said one of the gruff men.

Justice had to agree. Better now than later.

Justice was dropped off at the five-star hotel—the bearded gruff lumberjacks seemed to laugh too long about it—and he walked in, after Apropos allowed him inside.

"Busy night?" the old man asked.

Justice paused, Apropos seemed cheery. "You have the prisoners from tonight's hits?"

"Of course," said the old man. His clothes smelled of weed, and his breath smelled of garlic. He wobbled for a few seconds. The sound of a pipe dripping in the building somewhere. Then a muffled scream.

"Will you take me to them?" asked Justice.

"They're being worked on," said the old man.

The old man's eyes licked Justice's face. He was being judged; he shifted his feet. "What?"

"You were in New York, weren't you?"

"I don't know you," said Justice.

"I didn't say that. You bring in a couple of boys, college boys?"

Justice flinched. The painting in Drail's office, the uncle's suicide.

"They're here. They're being softened as well."

"Here?" Justice said, his throat constricting, his voice cracking. He felt light headed, and the room spun half a degree. Trying to flex and stay strong he drew deep breaths.

"Yup. Their family, or members of the family called. Don't ask me how they found us."

"Here?" Justice said, feeling better, since the ridiculousness of family members calling made him want to laugh. For some reason his mind grasped memories of mothers in a plaza in Argentina, with faces of young men on posters. He brushed that off. This wasn't that, he scolded himself.

"That's right, here. Cousins, or people married in. One sounded smart."

"They were all smart," said Justice.

The old man cocked his head. "The man said he worked as a contractor for DOD."

"Doing what?"

"Some research or another. Crowd control."

"Oh?"

"I looked it up. His company has a computer that figures out ways to find the loudest in a crowd that's protesting, then it heats them up with microwaves. It only touches one person, causes stroke or heart attacks and there's no collateral."

"Oh?" Justice said. It sounded amazing. No more fires on the backs of children. Whole anti-American movements could be stopped before they killed people.

"You like this, don't you?" said the old man.

"It'd make many parts of my job easier."

The old man laughed. "God, you are a loyal dog, aren't you?"

"The better choice being?"

The old man shook his head. "You do have another choice, and you know it."

Justice reminded himself that the old man was probably broken. "You need to know which side *you're* on." Another memory drifted into his mind: he was a child, playing in snow and he asked his father a question about the flag. His father explained the colors, and explained how the red represented the blood that had been spilled to create and keep the nation free. His heart—then and now—swelled with pride at the thought. And here he was fighting the good fight.

The old man spat on the ground. "I know plenty. Do you?"

That angered Justice. "I know damn well." Another muffled scream echoed. Justice wanted to change the subject. "What did the relative say?"

"That he wanted a reason, that he had done a lot for the country and that his family didn't deserve such things."

"Did you report him?"

"Why? And allow another man to be ruined?"

Now Justice knew that this old man was a coward. "Take me to the prisoners," he said. That smell, of pine cleaners and blood, wormed its way into his head as the old man led him in.

Drail gave him a clap when he called with the results, but Justice didn't feel well at all. He wondered if it was something in the water.

The men with beards went in with the local police force and swapped up everything that the houses held. Intel for the large machine in the desert. Sooner or later a supercomputer was going to spit out another place to hit.

"Good job,"

Drail said on the phone. He was no longer clapping, and even though Justice needed sleep more than anything, he knew that he was going to be asked to do more.

"Thanks," said Justice. He was in a room in the embassy, and he was starving, but at this time of night no one was around. He could smell himself, his farts, his body odor stinking up the room's paper and jet ink smell. His mind was shrinking with the sleep deprivation, but every few seconds a new update on the information farmed from all the hit sites would pop up and he would comb through it: comments denouncing the United States and its drone policy; comments claiming that the government was filled with Western stooges.

Drail tapped his fingers. "Where're my reports?" He'd put Justice on speakerphone again, and this time Justice was certain he could hear a woman's voice whispering and giggling in the background. *Her?* He remembered his now ex-girlfriend and all his pain was compounded with the fact that he didn't have a woman, and he desired a woman he couldn't have. He was immensely sad and lonely. He reminded himself that he would only get a woman like that if he worked harder at his job.

Justice hit his head, and remembered the reports. "I—"

"You're a Tango—"

"I know," Justice said, angry with himself for slacking. "I'll get them."

"For everything, Justice. Everything since the moment you landed there. Hell, since this mission started."

"I'll," he said and drifted off, almost falling asleep.

"You tired, Justice? Didn't you get some pills?"

"I—"

"You understand how important this is, right? You haven't lost sight?"

"I know."

"You do? A nuke, Justice. These crazies get a nuke and it's good-bye to New York City. Millions will die. We have increased chatter on all our sensors. It's the doctor, we know it. But we need you to get him before they do. Before he blows up the entire world."

Justice grunted, heard the whispers and giggles in the background and hung up. He pulled out the pills, tossed a handful at the back of his throat, and pulled up the report writing program.

Two days later he had written all the reports. Each hour was accounted for and Drail called him to approve. Justice refused to answer the phone. He was crashing, and hard. He downed the last of his pills and started to read all the information from the destroyed houses. He collapsed on his keyboard.

Rex woke him up.

"Shit! What day is it?" Justice asked. His vision blurred and he couldn't make out where he was.

"Man, you were out," said Rex. "You taking pills?"

"Of course," Justice said, shaking his head, then rubbing his eyes. It didn't help.

"A few days. Your boss back home's been calling."

Justice should've been jolted by that, but he wasn't. All he wanted was more sleep.

"Why?" Justice asked.

"Well first to say your reports were top notch."

"Uh-huh."

"There's something else."

"What?" Justice said. His head pounded, and he really was hoping for a terrorist attack to end all his pain.

"They found the doctor," said Rex.

Justice sat up straight. "Don't fuck with me."

"I'm not," Rex said holding up his hands to his chest to signal his innocence. "In France. I got you your tickets."

"Paris?"

"No. Nice."

Justice nodded and wondered how he was going to find the doctor in that city. "I've heard the women there are nice."

Rex laughed. "Exactly. Get back on the horse with a French."

Justice smiled and the pounding in his head subsided.

"To kill."

"What?" asked Justice, as he saw a brown bag that smelled like shawarmas in Rex's hand. Justice's stomach started to growl. He was starving. Rex smiled and handed the bag over.

"Your orders are to shoot to kill."

"No need for nukes in our cities, eh?"

"That's right," said Rex, patting Justice on his back.

There was tension in the air, and Justice knew that this latest order meant things were really getting serious.

Justice dove into the chicken, roasted to a perfection and didn't think about the doctor until he was on the plane out. A civilian plane with quiet Arabs all around him.

Ali watched as another car came into view. A firefight broke out. Ali flinched as his men were mowed down. The sounds of gunfire and explosions pulled out a few children from the corners of the houses nearby. They stayed away from Ali and Saladin.

The scene ended before Ali realized he'd been holding his breath. He inhaled, and stared. The pink man. It was the same pink-skinned man from the raid. How could *he* have known? He glanced up to the sky.

And he stared at the bodies of his men. They'd looked to him for hope, and he'd let them down.

"See?" Saladin said pointing to the wreckage. "You can't train them to do this."

Ali clenched his jaw and walked to the car.

Saladin chuckled and got in as well. He patted Ali's shoulder. "Not to worry. You tried. I'll make sure to let everyone know that."

"Thanks," said Ali; he noticed kids pointing at them.

"But there's good news," said Saladin, with another chuckle.

Ali didn't answer. The moneyman was grating on his nerves, so he looked out to the city, going about its business as it always did. He hated that it would do it after what had just happened. And for a second Ali's heart was lightened. But Saladin's voice brought him back down.

"We know where the doctor is going to be."

"You do?" Ali asked. He wanted to forget the doctor.

"Yes. And I'm going there, to make sure that he helps us. We're going to plan a huge attack to convince him."

Ali stared at a bead of sweat underneath Saladin's lips. "We?"

"Well. I am. I'll head out there tomorrow. We'll find him, convince him, and show him our abilities. I think he'll be impressed. Or scared."

Ali didn't nod. He had a clear vision of what he had to do, and he knew that involved leaving this place. He looked at some people milling about. Up in the sky he wondered if he could hear a drone.

"Do you hear that?" he asked Saladin.

"What?" Saladin asked, cocking his head. He gave off a nasty chuckle, food flying from his mouth, some landed on Ali's hand. "Don't be scared because of this one thing."

Ali's mind, throttled with thoughts about how many times he'd to put up with incompetent leaders, moneymen, like Saladin—which wasn't his real name which only infuriated Ali more. Besides, what had the fat man ever done in battle? Ali ground his teeth. Now he was sure he heard something in the sky. He grabbed Saladin's wrist. For as big as the man was, he wasn't very strong. He didn't say anything as Ali pulled him to the shacks. Ali looked at a kid in front of a shack. "Can I go in?" Ali asked.

"Maybe something in this hand will help," the kid said, holding out his hand.

"You little—"

"Hey," the boy said, frowning and a sneer developing on his face, making him seem wiser than his years would have suggested. "That's the price for getting in."

Ali, in no mood to be told what to do by a child took a step forward, raising his free hand. "Maybe you—"

"No. I'll stick you," said the boy, puffing out his chest. "Then you'll see how tough you are. Or maybe you like little boys?"

Ali, taken aback, shook his head, pulled out some money and handed it to the kid. He walked in and blinked a few times as his eyes adjusted to the darkness. He could hear the boy behind him. "I need another exit and clothes for us."

He could feel the boy jab him with his hand.

Ali pulled out more money and handed it to him. The boy ran off, though Ali couldn't see where.

"He's gone off," Saladin said. "What are you thinking?" There was fear in the man's voice.

That made Ali feel better. "Nothing. It's just that... I've been in drone attacks before."

"And?"

"I know they're watching. I can hear it."

Saladin let out another nasty laugh. "You are getting scared. Don't let this break you, Ali. You're useless then."

Ali grabbed Saladin's phone and threw it on the ground, smashing it. "This is why they're following us," said Ali. And he brought his face inches away from Saladin's. He could smell the garlic, and the man's breathing almost stopped. Ali bit his tongue to stop from smiling.

"Okay," said Saladin, trying to break free from his grip. Ali held on tighter.

"Here," said the boy. He had a candle now, and shoved some clothes into Ali's hand. Ali looked at them.

"What are these?" Ali asked.

"Hey," said the boy. "You should be glad I found anything at all."

"This is almost nothing. It won't fit."

"Is that your mess outside? Those dead men?" the boy asked, the candle lighting up the smirk on his face.

Ali's heart sank. Those men were dead. It was never easy.

"The police will soon be looking everywhere," said the boy.

Ali wondered what he would do with this young boy if he were to turn them in.

"Don't get smart," Saladin said. "We're fighting for you people."

"Well don't fight for me," said the boy, that sneer creeping across his face.

Ali wondered where he learned it from, if perhaps all the street kids knew how to sneer, because Ali was certain that he'd never sneered as a child.

"All you bring are more bombs on people like us," said the boy. And he spat on the ground. Ali heard it smacking the dirt floor.

"Let us change," said Ali.

"I'm not wearing this," said Saladin as the boy and his candle walked away.

"Yes you are. What if they're above watching us?"

"They'd have hit this house already. Do you hear missiles?" Saladin said, pantomiming cocking his head, and cupping his ear with his hand. Saladin shook his head, then pulled some of the clothes from Ali's hands. "These are some fine clothes," he said, then held out a finger. "I'm only doing this because I have so much respect for you."

"Thank you," said Ali. They both squeezed into the orange suits the boy had brought them. Saladin's was especially tight, and his arms lifted off to each side.

Ali laughed at him. "It'll be worth it, trust me." He stopped when he saw a hurt look on Saladin's face. "What?"

"What the kid said."

"About the bombs?" Ali asked, sighing. "Maybe..." and he tried to think of what to say. After all, what *were* they doing?

"It makes me sad. Such dogs. Do they think that America thinks this way? No. They go out and kill." Saladin's held out a fist. "Why do we cow instead of fighting back?"

Something strange pulled in his guts. "Let's get out of here."

The boy came back with the candle and led them through a series of rooms, with children and old men. After a few minutes, they were in another part of the city. And they stepped out, feeling all the stares on their suits. The boy was gone as fast as he had come.

Ali looked up to the sky. "That's how we will defeat them."

"How?" asked Saladin.

"We stay away from the sky. We build tunnels."

"You think that will help us?"

"We control our environment, we light tires and let the smoke engulf the city." Ali was hoping to do anything to stop that nagging feeling that he was being watched.

"You really have lost it, haven't you? Who is going to live underground? How do you get the people to do so? How will anyone live with smoke in their eyes? Sometimes, Ali, you don't seem so smart."

That stung, but Ali knew he was right. They couldn't keep fighting the way they were, and they couldn't stop fighting, not when they were being crushed by a boot. No, they had to think of new ways, perhaps hacking into drones, perhaps never wearing the same thing, or driving the same car. And he remembered what the boy had said. What was he doing to his people? Was he merely bringing them pain? "I'm coming with you," Ali said. The pain, sooner or later, had to be spread out.

Saladin hailed a taxi. "What?" he said as he opened the door.

"I want to help." Ali thought about the boy again. This was going to be his gift to his people. A foreigner like Saladin could never understand.

Nasar stared at the door as the soft tapping continued. Karim was shaking his head, whispering that they shouldn't open the door for anyone. Of course, Nasar knew that this was foolish. If the captain was against them, he'd have thrown them overboard, or turned them over without saying anything. And yet, in the back of his head, Nasar knew that there was plenty of time for the captain to change his mind. He had been a soldier, and he was a mercenary, and not a normal heartless mercenary, but one still doing the work of his country, and his country alone. That had to count for something, didn't it? The captain had to feel some trepidation, some sense that he was betraying his country. His country of birth. And in the end, Nasar almost hated the captain for taking his side. After all, though he'd escaped without the authorities knowing, Nasar would never have even entertained the idea of *betraying* his country. And he could never see or hope that someone else would for their country. It was the ultimate representation of biting the hand that fed you, wasn't it? An act of cowardice.

He strained to hear anything, then swore that it was the captain. He opened the door.

The captain snuck in and locked the door behind him.

Karim held a knife behind his back.

The captain grinned. "Gonna stick me, eh? Well wait until we're off the boat."

"Why?"

"I think the men know. Or they suspect."

"Oh," said Nasar, his heart dropping. "Where are we?"

"We're there," the captain said and punched Nasar. A sharp pain shrieked through his body.

"Nice?"

"Of course. We just need to leave without these idiots hearing us."

"Call a meeting," said Nasar. Karim was edging closer, nervous because he didn't understand. Nasar waved him away with his hand. The young man stepped back. There was a smell, of diesel, on the captain. Nasar sniffed out loud.

"Sorry, was getting the extra boat ready. Though we need to paddle away," said the captain as he sniffed his own clothes.

"Yes," said Nasar, though he didn't want to hold a pair of oars so long as he lived.

"A meeting's a good idea," said the captain.

"Can we bar the door?"

"Maybe, but how to do it without them knowing? I'm not big on meetings."

Nasar glanced over at Karim and explained the situation. The young man had been feeling seasick for the past few hours. Or perhaps he too was missing home. There appeared to be no end to what they were going to be put through.

"We should leave by boat when we can," said Karim. "How far from land are we?"

Nasar translated for the young man.

The captain looked at Karim for a second, then grinned. His teeth were more yellow-brown than Nasar remembered. "Ata boy. He's a thinker. Street style, eh?" He patted Karim, who looked at Nasar with a confused face. Nasar wasn't sure how to translate that, so he kept quiet.

"Well," the captain said, after the awkward silence was broken with some yells above on the ship. "I think we need to get going."

Nasar's body froze. As if it didn't want to go through this torture anymore. He hated being old.

"How far are we?" Nasar repeated Karim's question. He didn't want to deal with water. Not directly at least.

"We're near the port. Just outside. It's getting dark," said the captain.

"Will they go onshore?" Nasar asked. He translated for Karim as the captain hummed and hawed.

"They might. But their papers have to be in order. I can use that..." the captain said and looked at Nasar.

That look jolted Nasar's momentary hope, and he wondered if the captain had something else up his sleeve. "What?" he said, knowing full well that he didn't have much of a choice but to trust the captain, and that worrying would only make the growing tremors in his guts worse.

The captain smiled. "I've a plan. You're going to be my escorts, and... wait here," said the captain and he darted out of the room before Nasar could say anything. As the echo of the door slamming ringed in Nasar's ears he drew in deep breaths trying to assuage his thoughts.

The captain was a traitor at heart, wasn't he? He didn't like whatever it was his own country was doing, and even went so far as to back his nation's own enemies. Surely a man like that was never to be trusted? Wasn't it proof that he would be willing to turn them in for any flimsy reason? There was, after all, a reason for nations, and the wars they fought. And yet Nasar couldn't trust anyone else. Nor could his mind reconcile the two thoughts: the captain being a traitor and being the only way Nasar was going to get help. He started shaking.

"Well?" Karim asked, locking the door.

"He said he has a plan," Nasar said, his voice cracking, echoing in his skull.

"What's wrong?"

"I don't trust him."

Karim tilted back and laughed. "Of course you don't."

That didn't help. Nasar would have liked to hear Karim bad mouth the captain. "You trust him?"

Karim shrugged. "What choice do we have?"

"Do you trust him?" Nasar said, hearing his voice drop low and growl. A clairvoyant feeling overcame him, followed by a brief flash where he saw his body, face down on the port in Nice, his eyes dull, blood spreading. Another piece of flesh, just like any other. Like Abdullah. And the shaking grew worse.

Karim grabbed his shoulders and squeezed. "Doctor," said the young man. "Not now. We're close."

Nasar sat down. "Are we? You yourself said it: the captain…"

"He's fine," said Karim, waving his hand at the door. "He's going to help us. If he wanted to turn us in, he would have."

"He may have other plans," said Nasar. He stopped as a herd of footsteps stomped by and his heart nearly collapsed. He held his breath. He could see that Karim did as well.

"He's a good man," said Karim. "You yourself said he actually cares for people and not just for his laws."

"Is that a good thing?" Nasar asked.

"I think it is," Karim said. His eyes filled with recognition and he stepped back.

Someone knocked on the door. Nasar stepped up to it and placed his ear there, but he jumped back when whoever was on the other side kicked the door. Not thinking, and half scared, Nasar opened the door.

It was a bearded man, with tattoos all over his arms. The man narrowed his eyes. "Where's the captain?"

"He's on the deck," Nasar said. He surprised himself with how quickly he lied. "Why?"

"Who told you to lock the door?" the man said, sneering.

There was twang to his voice which Nasar had only ever heard in the movies. It sounded exotic, if not a little threatening now. "The captain said we could." He hoped that Karim was staying out of sight.

He was certain that the two young men would get at each other's throats.

"What's the message?" Nasar asked, when he saw the bearded man hesitating.

The man shook his head and fumed off. Nasar took a quick look up and down the hallway. There was no one else. Then the captain appeared from one of the doors. Nasar could see the surprise on his face when he bumped into the bearded man. The two conferred, the bearded man pointing at Nasar. His initial reaction was to duck into the room, but he decided that doing that would only make him look even more guilty. He smiled and waved. The captain placed a hand on the bearded man's shoulder and glanced, if only for a fraction of a second, and whispered into his ear. Nasar flinched. The bearded man looked over at Nasar, gave a nasty smile, and walked off.

The captain walked by Nasar. "What's gotten into you? Let's get going, shall we?" He had a large backpack slung over one shoulder, and he stunk of cologne. Strong cologne like a bazaar's barrel. Nasar tried to see if the wrinkles in his smile had any tell to what had just conspired. All he saw was kindness, and that made him feel bad and duped at the same time. He followed the captain into the room, locking the door.

"What was that?" Nasar asked. He looked down, feeling lightheaded. He was getting old: any confrontation was an ache in his bones now.

"Oh, don't worry," the captain said, he was shuffling through a draw beneath the table that Nasar hadn't seen before. He pulled out several bags of food and nodded and threw them into his bag.

"He won't care when we leave?"

"You're going to help me get their passport issue resolved so that they can go on land," the captain said, winking. "And we'd better go quickly before they figure out the real story."

"Will they?" Nasar asked.

"If we wait on board they'll get a message soon." Captain grinned. "Let's go."

He led them out and to the deck. On every corner stood massive tattoos, and Nasar did his best, fiddling with his hands, not to stare at them and crumble. The air was warm, soft, and kissed him on the heart when he got up to the deck. The city of Nice stood in front of him, smooth, gliding, though standing still. For a second he smelled a million perfumes and kisses in the air. The captain snapped him out of the stupor with a tug on his arm. Nasar realized that the captain was holding his wrist very tightly. It hurt, in fact, but Nasar didn't dare say a word. On the deck stood all the ship's crew. All their faces lit by the glow of the city. All their eyes piercing Nasar.

The captain gripped his arm as they made their way down a ladder. They were on a small boat now, the captain starting the motor. A bead of sweat rolled off the man's forehead. Karim sat still on one end. Nasar sat in the middle looking at the captain. He was shrouded in darkness, his grin gleaming in the boat's lights. A foghorn sounded. More lights twinkled. The captain pushed the boat away and they were in complete darkness. They glided over the water, the pulsing of the sea soothing Nasar's nerves.

There was a cry from the deck: "Stop!"

The boat pushed away from the ship. Nasar's heart was in his throat. The captain pushed him down to the ground. Something splashed the sea around him. It couldn't have been bullets; he hadn't heard any shots. But the captain held him down. There was a sound like a ball dropping in a liquid that was heavily viscous. Nasar felt something warm. He wiped it. He looked up at the captain; he was no longer smiling.

The captain's eyes fell on Nasar. He pulled them both over the side. Nasar tried to say something but then there was the water in his throat and he held his breath, just in time because the captain wouldn't let go and was rolling him underwater, and Nasar thought of crocodiles and knew that this was how the captain had planned to kill him along, who knows, maybe it was a fetish of his, to kill men like him underwater, and why had he, Nasar, trusted this man? Nasar tried to fight back, to struggle, because his lungs were burning and it was as if the water was trying to seep in, and he didn't want to die underwater, but the captain held him tight and rolled. It took a second for Nasar to realize that they weren't rolling, and instead swimming.

They were in darkness now, but Nasar could see a search light probing the darkness, and there was their rowing boat in the light, and trajectories of bullets piercing that. Now he could see blood clouding the light out.

And directly above them were more boats, but they were in darkness, and then rocks were around and the captain pulled them up. Nasar gasped, sucking in smooth pure air, like he had never tasted something so beautiful in his life. But the captain placed his finger on Nasar's lips and leaned into his ear.

"Let's move. They'll be coming for us now. *Everyone*."

"Karim," Nasar said. But again the captain had a vice grip on his wrist, almost close to breaking it, and they were running. Nasar looked back, and couldn't see the ship anymore, just an array of boats in a C shape. The port, he imagined. He tripped and a sharp pain traveled up his arm as the captain dragged him. Nasar righted himself only when they came to a large road, taxis zooming by, and the captain looked both ways. They crossed the street, and entered a dark alley.

There were a few people at doorways here, staring, angry that strangers were here. Nasar remembered Iran and the people on the fringes of society. He would be safe here. The captain knocked on a door as a gang of youths glanced over and stood up, burning red dots to mark their cigarettes. One came up to the captain. He was young, wiry, a wolf's walk and eyes. The captain nodded. The man stood and judged, with a cloud of smoke as his friend. Nasar looked at him, wanted to say something, but when he made eye contact with the youth, the young man looked down at Nasar's clothes and cocked his head. Nasar wanted to hide.

The smell here, away from the sea and breeze, was dank: cigarettes and urine. A woman, old, dressed in black, opened the door. Her eyes lit up with hate when she saw the captain.

Sirens blared in the background.

The old woman cocked her head and stepped aside. The sirens were louder now. Nasar couldn't feel his arm, his legs, but fear was coursing through his veins. The captain pulled him inside. The sirens louder than ever now, and the door slammed shut. The sirens nearer. How did they know to follow? More sirens. Everywhere.

They moved up a flight of stairs, to a window with wooden shutters. The captain peered down. Nasar moved, broke the grip on his wrist and looked down. Police were out of their cars. The youth raised his hands and threw something at the police. The other youths did the same. Beer bottles as artillery now, and the cops backed away, sirens blaring and they drove off. Still the city was abuzz with death in the air. Nasar stared at his clothes and realized he was drenched in blood and bone fragments.

They were in a bedroom. Nasar took off his shoes and placed his feet on the cool cement. The bed he sat on creaked; he could smell the rust from its headrest. The only light was in the hallway. The captain sat down in an equally creaky wicker chair next to him. The place smelled like faint perfume and clean everything. He could die there and not care; he'd come far enough, yet everything in his body didn't care for another step, another moment of darkness. He could feel the cool of his drenched clothes morph into something hard. His skin started to chafe. He wanted to say something to the captain. He opened his mouth and just drew in more air. To live, even like an animal, was all he cared for.

He looked down at his shirt. The blood. Karim's.

"Two head shots. He was caught in the light," the captain said. He seemed very sorry. "Luckily I locked up all the night vision, or else we would have been ground up." He shook his head. "Bastards were always good shots." He now sounded proud.

"Will…" Nasar couldn't think of anything appropriate. So another human was dead because of him. He started to convulse.

"Easy now," the captain said and sat next to Nasar, holding his shoulders. "There's nothing to do."

Of course there was nothing to do. Nasar wanted to shake off the American's touch, but couldn't. His eyes stung and tears rolled down his cheek.

"He was a good man. Taking care of you, wasn't he?" the captain said.

Nasar nodded. He wondered if he should have ever started on this journey of death and destruction. When his tears stopped, his brain relaxed. He leaned back and positioned himself to rest his shoulders on the metal headrest. It was uncomfortable. He remembered the original reason for this trip. There was a reason. He had to finish it now. There was no going back. Do what you came to do. The final meet. He wondered if he was too late. "Why?" he asked, surprising himself.

"They're just pit bulls. They're used to shooting to kill. I told you that," said the captain.

Nasar stared at the lit hallway. A shadow appeared and the old lady parked herself in the doorway. She muttered a few things. Nasar didn't understand her, but he was sure it was vehement. The captain simply hung his head. A door somewhere slammed and sharp heels echoed softly, then grew louder.

A svelte female figure appeared next to the old woman, and leaned in. Some whispers, almost Arabic, though Nasar wasn't sure, sent the old woman away. The captain stood up.

The woman was quick. In two steps she was in front of the captain, who now hung his head again. The woman's face was still in the shadows, though she seemed to brim with anger. Nasar could smell the woman's sweat. It lulled him half asleep.

The first slap jolted Nasar wide-awake. The next two were just as hard, and seemed to echo across the room. The captain kept his hands by his side and didn't look up. Three more slaps and Nasar stood up.

"You can't blame him," said Nasar. He was trying to think what could have possibly been done by the captain to elicit such a reaction. "He means well."

The woman turned to Nasar. Her eye caught some light from the hallway and the ferocity forced Nasar to jump back. She raised her hand. Nasar flexed, fully expecting a slap. He sighed with relief when she lowered her hand.

"I'll get you some clothes. Food too," she said. Her voice, soul had been cut somewhere. Nasar assumed the captain would know about that.

She turned and walked out. Nasar sat down. The aura of the woman was still in the room. She was beautiful. And having just seen her ached Nasar's heart. "What have you been doing, captain?"

The captain sat back on his chair.

Sleep was now worming its way back into Nasar's nose. And so was the memory of Karim. The blood on his shirt. He took it off. And still he couldn't shake off the image. He shook as tears poured down. He heard the captain start to move over, then stop and hold his breath. Nasar fell back on the bed, his feet on the floor and closed his eyes. He wanted anything but this life.

The red-faced man next to Justice ordered another scotch.

"The problem with these Arabs," said the man, loud enough for everyone in the cabin to hear. "Is that they don't know how to enjoy a drink," he said and raised his glass.

Justice stared with as much intensity as he could at the airplane magazine.

"Or like women enough. That's what ends up leading to all the killing."

Justice closed his eyes. Normally a polite nod of the head would be all he'd attempt. "So what's our excuse?"

The man's eyes widened a slight fraction of an inch.

"Say," said the man, spilling some of his drink on Justice's shirtsleeve. "You're not one of those liberal pansies, are you?"

Justice leaned forward and pantomimed bashing his head against the seat in front.

"Oh, I get it," the man continued. "You're one of those people who loves them and hates his own kind. Is that it?"

"I'm not," said Justice.

"I'm not saying that I hate all Arabs," the man said, ordering another scotch. "I'm a huge fan of the Omanis, for example. I think they know what's up."

"They do?"

The man looked at Justice like he was crazy. "Of course. The Syrians, now. They're a whole different lot. I mean, what did anyone expect?"

"I suppose," Justice said and held his tongue.

"Suppose? It's their minds," said the man tapping his head. "I should know. I've worked with them for ages, and I've never seen one with their head on straight. If they do, they move over to our side."

"Is that so?" Justice looked at the man's khaki pants and tucked in black polo shirt and wondered who this man was. No one went to Yemen for vacation, so that ruled out a tourist. "You work for the embassy?" Justice asked, leaning in and speaking in a low tone.

"What?" the man yelled, a mist of scotch hitting Justice's face. He leaned away.

Justice turned to look at all the people turned his way. The last thing he needed was more attention. He murmured his consent to the man who was leaning in, and stared at the airplane magazine with an intensity he didn't know possible.

"Sorry," the man mumbled.

Justice could feel his warm breath on his ear.

"I know you, Justice. I work the embassy. I'm with the X-agency."

Justice flinched. He'd heard about the X-agency. All private, all with amazing pay and retirement packages. "You're at the embassy?"

"At first they had me in that dinky motel." The man shook. He didn't appear drunk anymore. "Then I ended up sleeping in the embassy. I prefer to be surrounded by concrete barriers. Was busy enough as it was."

"Oh, what was your job?"

The man's lips were almost touching Justice's ear lobe now, and it sent a chill down his spine.

"I was the man helping you clean up that mess. You are a busy bastard. Cold too."

Justice both liked and hated being called cold. He wondered if this man had any pull. "What were you doing, exactly?"

"I help cover it all up. Painful in some other countries. But here they have Sharia law, so it ends up being cheap."

"That always does," said Justice. "I suppose that they've been helpful to me."

"Of course. The other countries get you lost in a million other bureaucratic mazes and their rights and all." The man waved his hand in the air dismissively. "That's what you get, they never get their shit together."

"And yet look at the Yemenis," said Justice. He hailed over a stewardess and ordered a water. She handed him a cup full of ice, water at the bottom. Justice sipped the water and stared at the droplets forming and dripping down on the outside. The LCD screens in front of everyone else were blaring a plethora of movies and TV shows.

"Sure you don't want a scotch?" the man asked.

"Have to stay clear," said Justice.

The man gave him an odd look. "You can do all that and not drink? Not human," he said, now looking scared of Justice and shifting away.

"I have more to do," Justice said. He liked that someone was scared of him, though he immediately regretted it. And now the memory of the moments on top of the helicopters, and how he preferred to stare at tattoos of skulls rather than the burning people or the blooded shoes and pieces of people. He ordered a scotch.

"They're really working you, aren't they?"

"Well. It's the same mission," he said. Now he wondered if he was saying too much. He forced his mouth shut.

"Ah, they got you on pills, don't they?"

Justice stayed silent.

"Well, Mr. Justice," the man said, leaning in super close again. There was, beneath the scotch, the stench of sweat, fear even. "How long have you been in this line of work?"

"A few."

"Let me tell you something. The only ones who survive and get promoted are those who survive. You either learn to live off the sweat of others, taking credit for their work, or you will burn yourself out. And," he said, raising his thick, red finger in the air. "The only other thing you must do is point out the other employees who are about to burn out. Those two things are the reason I can work one week out of the month and pull in a quarter million a year, tax free."

Justice didn't like this talk. It was people like this that made his work a nightmare. "You—"

"Listen to me, Justice. I know your type. All American. Hell, I'm all about America and this is the way to help. Not slaving away."

Justice ordered another scotch. He didn't like talking to the man, even if he was being helpful. He closed his eyes, leaned far back in his chair and tried to think about catching the Doctor.

Justice was jolted awake by the ding of a bell. He looked up and saw that they were landing, the plane tilting at a sharp angle. The blue sea was cut with a glimmer, and the land seemed fertile as the plane lurched forward.

The scotch drinking man was observing him. "You missed out on our fly by Syria."

"That's allowed?"

"It is now."

"What about the—"

"We could see flashes of artillery in the horizon. Pretty cool."

"Shame."

The man's look seemed full of disgust. "I guess," he said.

Justice tried to avoid the man as best he could, and ran for the airport entrance. He was surprised to see Drail and a local man standing there. Behind them stood Natalie and Sasha. Justice remembered his girlfriend, or ex, and his heart dropped then swooned when Natalie smiled at him. Then he saw their hands intertwined and he remembered the cafeteria. His heart dropped, and he tried to remember the mission at hand. Catch the doctor and you'll be able to sleep.

Drail said something to the French man next to him and nodded at Justice, his fingers on his lips to silence any comment. Justice followed Drail to where two black SUVs, with at least ten antennas pointing out. In front of each sat bullet-headed men with large aviator glasses, grim jaws, and thick forearms.

Natalie and Sasha stepped into the second car behind them.

As soon as they were in the back seat, the SUV squealed away.

"We in a rush?" Justice asked.

"Have to at least look it," said Drail. He seemed sterner than Justice had ever seen him.

"I wasn't expecting you here. You should have told me."

"We have information, on the doctor. We couldn't send it to you inflight, so…"

"We have a location?" said Justice.

"Not yet. They came in a couple nights ago. A whole lot of shooting at the port. Le Port," he said with emphasized accent on the French. "Our friends here aren't too happy. So we're here to help, but that means we stand by for any major event, but we let them handle it."

"They want all of us?" Justice asked. He liked having backup, but having everyone here couldn't be good.

"Of course not. But how are we going muscle out for more of the budget next year?"

"I didn't—"

"You didn't learn anything new?"

"You saw the reports," Justice said, a little annoyed now. He didn't want his boss breathing down his back, but if he was, Justice at least expected help to do what they had to finish.

"Easy," Drail said, smiling now and he slapped Justice on the shoulder. "You get some sleep on that flight?"

"I managed. Met a guy from Agency X."

"Is that a fact?" Drail said. "They're a bunch of yahoos. Don't deserve a single crumb from the pie, they don't."

"Yeah. I didn't like him much."

"Good," said Drail. "What he say?"

"Nothing," said Justice. "Just how to work as an operator."

Drail didn't answer, and the two men in front had turned up some AC/DC, and though Justice hated that band, he liked the wall it placed between him and Drail. He pressed his face to the window. The town seemed to be, like many European cities, of two parts. The gorgeous centers with pedestrian ways and facades of yore, made for tourists, and the newer bland city made to be lived in by the locals.

He realized then that he may not have missed New York once. And that, in fact, he didn't care for any city, dusty or sea-kissed, or skyscraper addled. Was he turning bitter? Slowly becoming the old man outside the five star hotel in Yemen? Slowly becoming nothing more than a man screaming at the incoming tide, but without any power to stop it. He ground his mind shut. He didn't want to keep thinking in these terms. And he wouldn't become the old man. There was a terrorist to be stopped somewhere in the city. And for a second he watched the people strolling the sidewalks, standing around speaking, and he imagined a missile hitting them, or a car bomb, or perhaps the dirty bomb maker that they were hunting at that moment. He felt energized. So many innocent people dead, and *he* had to make sure it wouldn't happen. If it took all his energy, maybe even his life, there was no way that he was going to allow people of the civilized world to live in fear like he had seen the people of Yemen.

The music was turned down as the SUV drove through an automatic gate, and it shook as it drove onto a cobblestone driveway.

Drail leaned in. "Any ideas?"

"Why?" asked Justice. "The local police have none?"

"Well, we'll first have to start talking to them."

"Who was the guy at the—"

"Don't let me down," Drail said and gripped Justice's shoulder hard.

"I'm sorry," Justice said as they came to a halt in front of a white walled villa. Roman arches and columns rose up to greet them, and he noticed that the courtyard they were in was empty. He opened the door and stepped out. A slight sea breeze greeted him, and palm trees danced. It smelled like heaven. Justice forgot about his sudden hatred for Drail and remembered what was needed.

Drail came to stand by him.

"Let's get a constant line to the liaison," said Justice.

"We've got that."

"But nothing else?" asked Justice.

"You know the drill, we're helping our French friends comb every cell phone conversation, on and off line, as well as the internets and what have you."

"And their sources? And what about their reaction times?" Justice asked.

"All being squeezed. Several QRFs are being placed around the city. They're ready," said Drail with heavy approval in his voice. "A lot of people call the French pussies, but remember they fought some great wars in Algeria and Indochina. Tough."

Justice turned when he heard slight shuffle and the smell of fruit perfume.

"So what did you learn in Yemen?" asked Natalie.

Sasha grinned beside her. Their hairs were tussled, and their lipstick smeared.

Drail seemed dazed. He kicked the top of the cobblestones with his shoes and stared down at a loose pebble. "We should fix that," he muttered.

"Not much, I'm afraid," said Justice.

"Oh come now," said Natalie, poking his arm. "We heard about how big of a hero you were out there, big tango." She winked and touched his arm again. Sasha did the same.

Justice swore he could feel his balls grow and his fists hit the ground. "Yeah," he said, his voice box low and near his balls. There was nothing more to do than to try and smile. "It wasn't too tough."

"Big tango," Sasha said.

For a second, Justice sensed that perhaps they were mocking him. But suddenly the guilt from all that he'd done in Yemen evaporated. "The thing is to find the doctor and bring him in, right?"

"No," said Drail.

"Kill him on sight?" Justice asked, half-joking.

"That's right," Drail said and slapped Justice's back again. The hand remained and pushed Justice inside. It was a cool lobby, domed with a Michelangelo painting and a fountain in the middle. But Justice could smell pine cleaners here, and he was brought back to the torture chamber in Yemen. A shiver ran up his spine. Another smile and wink from Natalie and Sasha helped to calm him down. Two Marines stood by another door and they walked past the Marines into a hallway. Several doors later, they entered a room, with screens and a table.

"Your office," said Drail. "Big tango."

Justice didn't reply.

The ceiling had cracks, and it smelled like a gypsy's car in here—better than pine cleaners. "Thank you," said Justice.

He sat down on a chair and they all stood around him. A tension filled his chest. He had to tell them something. But wasn't that Drail's job? The drone of a printer made itself known.

"I'll be back," said Drail and left.

"Well?" Sasha said. There was no more kindness or flirtatiousness in her eyes. Nor Natalie's. Kill the doctor. He supposed that there wasn't a choice. As long as there was the specter of a smoldering city, then killing would be fine. He repeated that to himself. He remembered how easy things were with the drones and the bearded men in the helicopters. If only they had that here. Or even at home. They would be able to crush any enemy.

"Well, I was hoping that you'd find something out," Justice said.

Natalie and Sasha exchanged looks. "We have nothing," said Sasha.

"Well, let's start looking," said Justice, feeling freed suddenly. "Keep your ear to the email and cell phone farming," he said to Sasha. "But both of you go out, talk to the liaison and find out what the—"

"We're close," said Drail, bursting into the room. "They have one of the leaders of AQ coming through."

"Where?" Justice asked. If the head of AQ was here, then it really meant that this was going to be a huge ordeal. He started to sweat.

"We're not sure. But they've arrived. Cell traffic points to it, and we're sure that they're here, though. You know that whenever these people land here they will leave death in their wake. That's more reason to shoot anything that we deem suspicious."

Justice paced the room. "We have to find out where he is, or where he's going." Something in his gut was telling him to get away and think on his own. There was no way that he was going to be able to think of a plan when Drail, Sasha, and Natalie were standing here. Just their presence constricted his thought, made him think of how not to be wrong, the required protocol, instead of just solving the problem at hand. He moved to the door.

"And where are you going?" asked Drail. Sasha and Natalie gave him odd looks.

Uncomfortable, he shuffled his feet. "I need to get out of here," he said. His word seemed to startle the others.

"Wait a second," said Drail. He too seemed uncertain.

Almost a minute passed and no one said anything. Justice's mind fell blank.

"How's the painting?" asked Justice.

Drail gave him an odd look.

"I think Justice has had a rough time of it in Yemen," said Natalie.

"I'm fine," he said. It was now as if the energy bubbling off the three people, people he'd worked with, was suffocating him. Perhaps Yemen *had* been too much.

"If you need to take a walk—"

"I do," Justice said, cutting off Drail's sentence. And before anything could be said he walked out. Down the hallway, holding his breath so the smell wouldn't remind him of the torture chambers and the old man and his foul complaints. Right now he was afraid of being that old man guarding a place like this, worried about the young men brought in and sliced apart in the name of good. Justice pounded his chest and brushed by the grim jawed drivers from earlier. They seemed to be laughing about something, but stiffened up when they saw him.

"Need anything sir?" one of them asked.

Justice walked on. He was out in the cobblestone courtyard now. He sucked in the sea breeze and expanded. He walked to the gate. More guards. They stared at him, and he wanted to challenge them. He brushed past them and through a narrow side door. After a few more minutes of walking he was alone in a narrow street; he calmed down. There was no room for anything but people and a few brave scooters. He walked on. Cement and perfume smells calmed him further.

A man, longhaired, lanky, calm and collected sat on some stairs in front of a door. The sweet smell of weed wafted off his clothes, and his eyes, surprisingly white, took in Justice. A group of tourists, smelling of beer and heavy Ozzy accents walked by. And again Justice's mind wandered and tried to comprehend the old man's disgust with torture and the need to save a city from destruction. He started to shake.

"You all right?" the man asked.

The English wasn't perfect, but Justice couldn't place where it was from. "I'm fine," he said.

"American," the man said. Smiling and nodding.

Justice felt uncomfortable that the man knew more, and thus had the upper hand for the moment. Then he reminded himself that there was no reason for him to feel so off. That was his training speaking. And right now he was suspicious of his training. "Who are you?" he asked. The man seemed too smart and collected to be a homeless man. But he also seemed like the kind of man who would be fine without a place to live.

The man, eyes black, moved a strand of hair from his face. Justice jumped back. The hand was metallic, robotic. Connections made to be oiled. He stared. The other hand was fine. As was the rest of the man's body.

"Where's that from?" Justice asked.

The man again considered the question with much too much time. This kind of collected reaction could only come from training. Again he pushed that aside. He wanted to make a connection and kick his training to the side.

"A failed bet," said the man. He smiled and several gold teeth glinted in a sunray.

"Is that right?" Justice said. A warmth filled his heart, and he squatted next to the man.

Again the man observed him. "You're not a tourist," he said.

"Nor you."

The man laughed. There was something for all humans in his laugh. "I'm from this town."

"Oh? And what is it you do?" asked Justice.

"I find things for people."

"Like what?" asked Justice.

"Bad things," said the man. He fell silent, staring at his arm, moving the robotic fingers, as the whir of small hydraulics whined in Justice's ear.

"You don't seem happy about it."

"Who would be?" the man said. "It pays the bills, but I'd rather not help people die quicker."

"What do you find?"

"Hope in the most hopeless form, love in the most loveless form. That's me. The wizard who brings all of those forth."

Justice stared at the man's metallic hand. "You're a drug dealing pimp?"

The man stared at his normal hand, moving it, running a metallic finger over the wrinkles. "I believe you do something similar," he said in a hurt voice.

Justice cocked his head. Normally, and by any society's convention he would've disagreed. But now his mind was certain this was right. "How did you know?"

"You seem like that kind of man. I can smell it," the man said and sniffed.

Justice now noticed a cane lying by the man's side. It was studded with jewelry, and a metallic angry moon face. "Do you know what I do?" he asked. He wasn't allowed to tell anyone, but he was ready to throw overboard most of his training and at least allow someone to guess.

"We both know what you are," the man said and looked up and down the alley.

He said it with confidence though Justice wasn't certain if the man knew anything, or if he was bluffing.

After a minute of silence and a handful of drunk tourists stumbling by, the man pointed to the sky and pantomimed praying.

It could have meant anything, really, but Justice took it to mean the man knew what Justice was going through and had been through.

"What do you know of the darkness of life?" asked the man.

"I am it," Justice said. He was thinking of a teen with burning clothes running from rubble. He also thought of the wind in his face and the smell of pine cleaners overwhelming dead souls. He also saw the painting. And he imagined those innocent college boys in a torture chamber. "Too much darkness."

"But sometimes darkness is needed. To confront and change and move forward."

"That's always the excuse, though. There has to be something else."

"I too help the darkness," said the man.

"At least you give people what they want," said Justice.

The man shook his head, but didn't say anything else. He pulled out a joint that had been packed too loosely. A nugget of weed fell to the ground. "This might help."

"No," Justice said. "My mind has to be clear. Darkness is afoot here as well," he said this even though he wasn't sure if he knew what darkness was anymore. Was it just a country code? Or was it actual actions?

"Oh." A light of recognition fluttered through the man's eyes. "That."

"Do you know?"

"I'm also an informant," said the man. "They told me to keep an eye out."

Justice looked up and down the alley. "For what?"

"You know." The man grabbed his cane with such force, that Justice jumped back, expecting an attack.

"The doctor?"

"Of course. But I won't help them. Not for this."

"And why not?" asked Justice.

The man, stood up, wobbling on his cane. Even though he stooped, he was a good head taller than Justice. "I thought you were of the same mind," said the man.

"We have to stop them," Justice said, though he wasn't sure if he had meant to say that.

"There are times to take sides," said the man. "Make sure you know which side you're on."

"I don't even know what the sides are." Justice could feel himself pleading.

"Of course you don't," said the man. "That's the nature of the game."

A plane flew overhead. A woman, walking like she was balancing a book on her head, floated by on stilettos. They watched her smile, bright, and disappear around the corner.

"What are the sides?" asked Justice. His phone started to vibrate. He pulled it out. It was Drail. He wondered if his boss had been listening to all of this. He answered it, listened, hung up, then threw the phone with all his might at the ground. The shattered and the sim-card gleamed in a ray of light, the battery laughing at Justice, with its Latin and Chinese letters.

"Your boss?" asked the man as he kicked the battery. It skidded and bounced up before settling some yards away from them.

"They found him," said Justice. He realized that he had lost *something*. The doctor's near the Promenade." The lost feeling turned into something worse, and his intestines crawled. Justice tried to tell himself that it was having not found the doctor himself that irked him, but he knew it wasn't true.

"He's not," said the man.

Justice's heart froze. "You know where he is?"

"I always did."

"And you won't tell?"

"I'll tell you, but you have to promise to make the right decision."

Not sure what that meant, Justice nodded his head.

The man stared at Justice for a few seconds then jerked his head and started to walk. Justice followed. The tapping of the man's cane echoed through the alleys. It seemed that all the storekeepers were wary of the man, and it was only the small gangs of youth who seemed to give him cheerful nods. They walked until they crossed a wide road. Here the sun tore open the avenue with light. They stopped in front of an apartment door. The man's cane touched Justice's chest.

"You'll make the right decision?"

Justice smiled.

Arriving by boat, a small boat that lurched at any sniff of the sea, hadn't been what Ali expected, but he had managed it somehow. And now they were in an apartment, in a tall building, on the outskirts of Nice. Saladin was outside talking to 'his people' trying to find where the good doctor was. The apartment, with a new kitchen and sparkling floors, was devoid of any furniture. Crates were used as seats, and wrappers of all kinds of junk food littered the floor. Ali thought he saw some beer cans, and he wanted to yell at these young bearded fools who spoke Arabic in halting manners, but he kept silent, preferring to catch up on his sleep and telling anyone with a cellphone to use it elsewhere. At first they'd looked at him with challenging eyes, but when he stood up, they'd backed down. He heard Saladin telling them what he'd been through and done, and they seemed to give him a wide berth since.

Apparently these were the new fighters in the war against the infidel, and Ali hated them. They all sprayed themselves with enough canned cologne that Ali kept the windows wide open, even when they complained about the street noise. There was one TV and one computer, though both were constantly being used to play video games. What Ali couldn't believe was that these men had been through training, and that they'd somehow proven themselves to be violent.

At the moment, Ali was enjoying a rare calm. He thought about Nadia and Laith and hoped that they were doing all right back home. He hated the sterile smell of the apartment and the city. If it weren't for the sea, this town wouldn't smell of life at all. And something in that lack of smell seemed to speak volumes about the Westerners' ways of killing and sterilizing the world of everything they didn't believe in, and also how far removed they were from organic humans.

Two of the young men walked back in the apartment. They were laughing and chuckling about women. Ali's stare shut them up, and one, with a brown bag oiled at the bottom, pointed at it and Ali. Ali nodded. He was starving, and perhaps they'd something more than candy bars or baguettes. He walked to the kitchen. The one with a limp pointed out a gyro sitting on the counter. Ali grabbed it and bit into the soft bread. The sauce was fine if a little sugary, but the meat tasted sterile. He ate it anyways.

When the stares of the two men got to be too much, he looked up, licking his fingers.

The one with a limp gave a tepid smile. "We heard that another cell like this was just broken up," the man said. His voice cracked, and Ali could see that he was scared. Ali suppressed a grin.

"Here?"

"In this town. The cops are everywhere," said the limp man, widening his eyes as if that made his story more believable.

Ali hadn't heard anything about that from Saladin. "Looking for?"

"For us. The doctor. It's all over the news. You should watch it sometime," replied the limp man.

Anger bubbled up so quickly that Ali couldn't stop himself from grabbing the man by his orange polo shirt and slamming him against the wall.

"Watch your attitude," Ali said. He could feel his grip tightening around the young man's shirt, the sound of fabric ripping, and the limp man's wide-open eyes.

Ali saw a movement from the other young man, a chubby one, behind him. "He didn't mean anything, sir."

Ali turned his head; the young man was stilled with fear. Ali released his grip on the limp man. He was sick and tired of all these people. He wanted to see Saladin, though at this point in time Ali wasn't sure what he was going to do with that boss of his.!@#

"So what is the TV saying?" Ali asked, after a long silence, filled with an odd ammonia-like smell filled the room. He glanced at each of the young men, both staring at their feet. Ali followed their eyes and realized he'd dropped his food. He stared at it. He hated wasting food. All he could think about was those kids on the streets of his hometown. He felt sad, contemplating how food here was so plentiful as to be wasted without care. It was the Westerners, he knew it. A few men who managed to work, or know Iraqis working in American bases had told him about the tons of food thrown away and the waddling soldiers everywhere.

He could still feel the stares of the two young idiots, and thankfully the sadness was replaced with more anger. There was a distance with them that he could never bridge. Being nice was not going to help. It was the same in Iraq. People who first arrived believed, like he did, that the struggle was more important than any differences in background. But time, oh time, always forced a drift of some sort. Sure there were exceptions here and there, but in the end most cells cracked and reformed along national or even regional lines. Algerians hated Saudi accents and so forth. It was the same here. These men were aliens to him, and Ali couldn't stand them even breathing near him. And he definitely couldn't stand that they were staring unsure of what to say when a Yemeni would know exactly what to say. Ali drew in a deep breath. Perhaps he'd never be a leader of large organizations.

"Well?" asked Ali.

The two men jumped. The limp one, still staring at his feet, spoke: "They are trying to find us and the doctor. They think we're working together. The French and Americans are working together. They even gave them drones." His voice wavered on the last word, and his face quivered, but as if he remembered his company, he straightened out. "They're scared," he said pounding his chest.

Ali stared at the limp man's reaction. He wanted to ask him his name, but didn't care to. He'd seen the same kind of bravado in men in Iraq. He saw it often in the words of Saladin. He was not a fan. "Are you certain?" Ali asked, trying to see how the limp one would react.

"Of course," said the limp one.

"Oh?" Ali said. And with that his desire to put these men straight and perhaps even teach them something died. Not that he'd given up, but rather that he knew that the men were too dumb and thick skulled to change their minds.

"What do you think?" asked the chubby one.

Ali ignored him. Another silence fell upon the room. Flies were buzzing around the fallen food. The chubby one scooped it up and threw it into the overflowing garbage can.

"What was Iraq like?" asked the limp one. He was staring a hole into Ali's cheek.

Ali wondered what Saladin could have possibly told this young men. He knew, however, that he had no inclination to answer these men's questions on that period of his life. In fact, as he drifted back to fighting in Iraq, and he remembered Nadia's words, he knew that he'd try his hardest to forget everything about that period of his life. But how was a man to erase his past? How was a man to make amends for mistakes of that magnitude? His head and his chest filled with warmth from contemplating this.

"Saladin," the limp one continued. "Said that you were a leader of a cell which snatched up diplomats near the Green Zone. You made Iraq hell for any one who dared to work with the infidels." The young man grinned, as if he could ever imagine doing such things.

Ali frowned as hard as he could at the limp one. "What do you know of such things?"

The young man shrank back. "N-Nothing. I was hoping you would tell us. Saladin said you were brought here for that reason."

Ali glanced at the young man's eyes, which were darting from Ali to the other man. A bead of sweat dripped down, passed a slight scar and slowed down on his brow.

Ali thought about Saladin's words. So *this* was Ali's legacy? Fear drawn from the land. Left there. And now those men's ghosts would whisper into the ears of the remaining Iraqis and terrorists and drive more blood into the land. Ali knew he would never want that for his land, so why want it for other lands?

"You will help us with snatching the doctor. Then we can show these Infidels what exactly power is," the limp one said. And he gave off a cackle; the chubby one joined.

Ali stared at them, at history repeating. How many men had he talked to in Iraq, the ones who wanted nothing more than to make a city's sidewalk weep with blood, and be able to count bodies on their kill list, and how many managed to do that then start to fall apart, memories of too many women's screams? Those same men who would start to lose touch with reality of being a human and they would lose touch with wanting to live, would place too much emphasis on the words of false imams and soon would throw themselves on the gears of war—always cloaked in martyrdom and Islam, but Ali knew what they were trying to forget. Of course there were ones who reveled in the dance of blood; those were the men Ali hated with a passion. But in the end, was he, Ali, any better? He two saw fountains of blood. Saw life reduced to nothing but smells and slippery asphalt. And again he thought about what it was that he had to do to make amends for that. To stop the anger, the murders, and start with something that could be built for the likes of Laith and Nadia. He had to stop thinking about what the other side was doing. One could, with anger bubbling, justify anything. What mattered now was that he as a man, as one who submitted to Allah, had to make the amends. It was time to stop making excuses. He had to stop fearing. And he had to move forward.

"I will get the doctor," Ali said.

The two men grinned, and just then Saladin burst into the

apartment. His heavy feet fell and he turned the corner into the kitchen. "Salaam alaiykum," he said, his arms outstretched.

Ali knew what that meant. "You found the doctor?"

"I know *exactly* where he is," said Saladin. "We had to pay off hundreds of people, but we found out."

"Where is he?" Ali asked. His throat tightened.

"Where are the others?" Saladin asked.

"They're coming back," said the limp one, seeming even more sheepish than before.

"Are they at the beach?" Saladin asked. Ali was glad to see the boss get angry about something Ali hated seeing these so called mujahedeen do.

"They're trying to fit in. Look like the locals," said the chubby one, his voice squeaky. "You said to do everything to look like the locals. Just like our manual says." Out of his pocket he pulled out a folded and crumpled manual. It was a manual that Ali himself had read once and held in almost as high esteem as the Quran.

"I know," Saladin said, his eyes narrowing. "But do they have to seem so happy when they do it and ogle the local women?"

The two young men grinned and stared down.

"Well, go get them, we need to get going."

"I can call…" the limp man said, staring at Ali.

Ali gave a sound that could only have been a growl. The two young men left, running.

Saladin grinned and patted Ali's shoulder. "We're finally going to get him. And when we do," Saladin said and stopped to mimic an explosion with his hands. "I have a car. Let's get inside."

It took until evening to find the others in the group. They weren't at the beach, but rather at a nearby bar, talking up American tourist girls, trying to get them drunk. They stayed in a windowless van as the three young men sobered up.

Ali, close to bursting, had to be held back by Saladin.

"We need them," whispered Saladin.

Ali knew better but kept quiet.

The five men sat on the metal-ridged floor of the van, the drunk ones exhaling liquor until Ali was almost sick. Saladin kept the young men motivated with stories of winning gun battles and bombings that Ali was certain the man had never participated in. Saladin went on about what they were going to do with the doctor's knowledge. How they were finally going to pay back the Imperial West for every single wrongful death and slight with a nuclear bomb in a city of theirs.

"What if the doctor doesn't want to help us?" asked the limp one.

Silence fell. It was dark outside, and a few headlights drove by their parked van. In front was the two-door hatchback, rusted to the gills, that Saladin and Ali would drive to the doctor's place. Ali stared on. The lights, the artificially lit night sky, everything was different from home. Even Baghdad hadn't been that different.

"Well, we'll squeeze him. Such are the ways of these doctors. They are strong in ways, but sometimes they require men of vision, men like us," Saladin pounded his chest. "To tell them what they have to do. They require a strong hand."

Everyone except Ali murmured their agreement. The young men started to joke about the ruins in which they would leave every Western city.

"Are you ready?" Saladin asked. "Let's go then."

When Ali was alone in the hatchback with Saladin, he finally spoke: "Those men aren't ready."

"Oh, don't be such a worrier," said Saladin. He pulled out a handgun and handed it to Ali. "Besides. With you leading, what could go wrong? Aren't you the best one to pull something like this? Isn't this what you wanted?"

"They haven't even been trained for this."

"Of course they have. In the Pakistani camps. I told you this," Saladin continued without a worry.

"What training? Monkey bars?"

"You're making fun of our training?"

"I've seen what it produces," said Ali, truly angry now, though he knew this wasn't what he wanted to argue about.

Saladin let out a sigh. "All Western intelligence services fear our training and hope to never face it. They consider any Muslim who's gone through it to be dangerous. Yet you mock this training?"

The headlights of the van behind them turned on sent shafts of light through the hatchback. "Then they are fools too. Besides, all they care about is money. Better to fear monkey bars than to be a pauper," said Ali.

Saladin shook his head slowly now, and with so much sadness, that Ali wondered if he was wrong for thinking this way.

"You need a rest," Saladin said.

"I don't. These men might be able to do good if they were good Muslims with discipline. They brandish that manual like it's an excuse. Yet they cannot manage a single prayer on their own." He rolled down his window and spat out.

Saladin placed his hand on Ali's shoulder. "Can you lead these men or not?"

"I can," Ali said, holding back a snide remark. As Saladin pulled out into the main road, Ali checked the handgun. The bullets were tipped with stripes. They were meant to shred whoever they hit. Ali made sure a round was chambered and gripped the handle tight. His heart started to pump furiously. A police car, its sirens blaring, sped by them. Ali focused on what he would have to do next. His soul required nothing but the utmost concentration.

Saladin grinned and honked his horn at a double-parked truck holding up traffic.

The captain shuffled around as Nasar slipped into the clothes given to him the previous night. The captain looked utterly defeated. It was almost funny in a way. Nasar had seen him rail against an entire Empire, and he seemed to have the energy to continue that fight until the end. Yet all it took was a slap and a look from a woman to crumple his spirit.

Nasar stepped in front of the closet mirror and stared at his khaki pants and black polo which seemed to fit perfectly. His shoes, brown wingtips, also seemed to fit. The chances of this was close to nil, but he accepted it as a sign.

The captain, lit a cigarette and stared at the street. Sirens wailed in the distance. A sea breeze, addled with diesel blew in. The captain's eyes were shining with potential tears.

Nasar peered over the captain's shoulder. There wasn't much going on in the street. The youth were gone, and a few old women with shopping bags shuffled on the sidewalk. When it was apparent that the sirens weren't going to stop, Nasar's chest tightened. He had felt young when he woke up, but now his age, and the deterioration of his heart, was apparent as flashes of pain ran from his chest to his neck.

"Who is she?" Nasar asked, hoping to see a little more humanity in the captain's eyes.

The captain shook his head.

Nasar remembered what the driver on the trip from Oman to Yemen had said. Nasar realized that perhaps that uneducated man had known something he, the good doctor, hadn't. And he realized that there and then, he wanted, hoped, prayed for the captain to give up his lofty goals of staining or slinging a futile rock at the Empire, and figured out how to stay with the woman. Or perhaps that was the captain's problem. He was too proud and he would fight on for something in his mind rather than what was right in front of his face.

"Come on," said Nasar, not used to cajoling and not knowing what to say to such a rough man. "She seems to really like you."

The captain released a puff of a laugh. "Right."

"No. A woman slaps you like that, then you must have something."

The captain shook his head chuckling. "I would only hope."

"What happened?"

The captain shook his head.

"Well, she's letting you stay here."

"That's because she's better than me."

Those words floated up in the air before settling slowly. Nasar signaled for a cigarette and drew in some nicotine, releasing a plume of smoke into the sea breeze. He knew when a man refused to open up and when it was useless to pry. Only alcohol would work now.

The captain lumbered over to a shirt hanging from the closet. He stripped. Nasar stared at the tattoos and scars. It always reminded him of men trying to be bigger than they were, these tattoos, but he remained silent.

A rap on the door startled them both. The captain pulled on the new shirt, pants, and opened the door. The old woman was there. She said something sharp and pointed downstairs. She stared so hard at the captain that he was forced to look down and stoop. The old woman grunted and walked downstairs, as if the captain's wilting was the only thing that satisfied her.

Downstairs, on the wobbling kitchen table, lay two plates with eggs and a croissant. Coffee steamed next to the plates. They sat and ate, under the piercing gaze of the old woman. Any crumble out of place was met with her grunt. Each man cleaned up anything that dropped. When they were finished, the captain placed the dishes in the sink. Another grunt and he was soon washing them. Nasar tried to say something to the old woman, but she waved him away, her eyes never leaving the captain. Nasar knew better than to ask where the young woman was. All that remained of her was her perfume that drifted in corners like a ghost, and he sniffed at it, its sadness, trying to take in her essence.

When they were done, the captain showed Nasar a map. It seemed almost like a foreign city. They finally found the neighborhood that Nasar vaguely remembered. They waited until dusk before moving out. Nasar was glad to be out of the apartment's oppressive tension and the old woman's gaze.

Arriving in the vicinity of the neighborhood, Nasar's mind started to click. "I remember this," he said. Not all the buildings were different, and things seemed busier, but the air, and the way elders loitered like they were tough, struck him as the same. They walked in to the apartment building, Nasar's heart beating fast. This lobby was the same. The walls were cracked, moist with water and it smelled of roses and bath water.

"All this look right?" the captain asked. He was eyeing two men. One seemed like a drifting pimp, the other like an American. They didn't seem to be paying Nasar any attention, but something pricked his skin, they didn't belong, and he reminded himself that there were men out there to get him. Spies, assassins even. They would all have a price on his head. Hell, knowing the way the Americans worked, they'd probably put out a wanted poster and let the free market work itself out. And that meant almost every gangster in the world would be after him. His skin tightened, and he started to feel dizzy.

"Come on," said the captain, grabbing him by the armpits and pulling him up to the stairwell. "Third floor right?"

The steps seemed a foreign concept, and Nasar tried to keep an eye on the two men. He lost sight of them on the second floor, and by the time they rounded up to the third, Nasar chided himself for overreacting to the appearance of strangers. Then he realized that the third floor's hallway was unlit. The captain paused, sniffing the air and swiveling his head around. The air felt heavy here; Nasar stooped and started to sniff too. There were cigarettes here, as the butts that littered the stairwell attested to their most used place. But there was no one, no voices, nothing.

Nasar tried to peer into the dark hallway. It was the same T-shaped one he remembered from before. They'd have to make a left turn. But the darkness would not reveal a thing.

They stepped forward, Nasar behind the captain. Now he was wondering why there was no sound at all. The other floors seemed to have some slight drift of music, or children playing, or arguments in the breeze. But on this floor there was nothing.

Nasar cocked his head. There was a whining sound in his ears. They were halfway down to the intersection in the hallway. Cloaked in darkness, Nasar could now hear dripping. It sounded like it was coming from somewhere in the hallway. Glass crunched underneath their shoes, loudly, it echoed down the hallway. They froze, and Nasar could hear the captain breathing, his forearm, which Nasar was holding, was tense. Nasar wished his hearing was better, because right now it sounded like someone else was in the hallway. The slight ruffling of clothes. He tapped the captain, but the American didn't seem to react.

Nasar could feel his heart pumping faster, blood pressure rising. Then he noticed that all the doorways they'd passed didn't have any light leaking out from underneath. How was that? He wanted to say something to the captain about this, to tell him this had to be wrong in some way, but he knew that a whisper would be a shout in this quiet hallway. And as they moved, the crunch sound changed, was less confined, and Nasar breathed a sigh of relief as he knew they'd reached the intersection. It was only two more doorways and to the left. His journey was almost over.

The blinding light curdled Nasar's pupils. He raised his hands, and closed his eyes. His eyelids were no help, though, and white-hot rods appeared in his vision.

"Put the gun down," said a very British accent. It wasn't perfect, though, and Nasar could tell the intonations that most Arab speakers of English tended to have.

He heard the captain's gun rattle to the floor. Nasar's heart dropped. He looked back to the stairway, but there was only darkness there. So this was how it would end. From what country were these assassins?

"Doctor," said the voice. "It's an honor to meet you."

There was something about the voice that made Nasar's heart lurch into his guts. He doubled over.

"Who is this American?" asked the voice.

The light still shone in their faces and the captain seemed to have given up.

"He's a friend," said Nasar. Then realized that he had just signed the captain's death warrant. Best not to tell these kinds of people anything. The captain flinched. "Who are *you*?" asked Nasar.

"We talked on email," said the voice. "I'm the representative for Al Qaeda."

Now Nasar's head was in a whirlwind. "I never emailed you," he said.

"Come now, doctor. No need to deny it. You're in safe hands. Trust me."

Nasar knew what that meant. He heard a rougher voice yell in Arabic, and when the first shot—muffled, yet still loud and echoing— was fired, he screamed and lurched himself to the ground. And as the shots continued to fire, Nasar curled into the fetal position, his fingers in his ears, and all he could pray for was that he wouldn't end up like Abdullah and be nothing but paint for the walls. And he screamed. And he prayed. But the shots didn't seem to stop.

When the two men moved up the stairs, Justice stared at the man as he read a piece of paper lodged between the door edges of the post boxes. The man rapped his cane on the floor. The echo of the cane dissipated and gave way to the sound of the two men walking up the stairs.

"Third floor," said the man. He followed Justice's eyes to the stairwell. Then he cocked his head and furrowed his forehead. "Those men were not of this city, were they?"

Justice shook his head. He heard a flock of cars outside, and when one peeled out, he froze. He'd forgotten that the others were looking for this building too. And even though he knew that less than an hour ago the people he worked with, for, had no clue, now that he was in the building, he felt nervous and assigned them super powers. What if they were to break in right at this moment?

The man seemed to read Justice's thoughts. "Not to worry. Only *I* know the men who know this. And only I they talk to. And now, only I and I," the man said and jutted his bony finger into Justice's chest. "Know this."

The accent change didn't surprise Justice. The man seemed to be the kind of person who would change accents naturally. He seemed at this point a prophet.

The sound of the glass crunching trickled down the stairwell. Something was up; Justice knew it. His breathing grew shallow and he took a step forward. The man placed his cane in Justice's way.

"Not yet," said the man. "Even when the path is known, you must be clear of heart before setting upon the journey."

Justice stared at the man; he was obviously mad.

"What's in your heart, I?"

More glass crunched. It sounded distant. Justice knew that his window to act was narrowing. Was this man here to delay him? He stared into the man's black eyes.

No, Justice told himself, this was his training speaking up, telling him to mistrust another human. He didn't want that anymore. Justice allowed his mind to consider the man's question, to turn in its folds, what it was that had been bothering him lately. "I don't know," he said.

The man's head jerked back. He seemed confused, and he leaned into Justice's face. His body moved with his breaths. The smell of garlic and cloves, underneath smoked flesh, hit Justice's nostrils. But just like the eyes, there was something clean, pure underneath that breath. The man placed his hand on Justice's heart. "You don't know your own heart?" he asked, sounding genuinely concerned. There was talking drifting down the stairs now.

"No," Justice said. He was thinking now of burned rubble. The smell of flesh, the smell of plastic burnt, the smell of concrete powder. The screams. And that tearing feeling in his heart. And the equally harsh feeling in his mind as he tried to remind himself about his job, his allegiances, and the weakness he'd been told since a child was endemic of anyone thinking as he was. "You go through certain things and you don't know."

"But you do. It's only listening to those who don't know that makes you think that you don't. But stop, listen to that heart of yours. Know what you feel is true. What you've seen is true. Know it all ends in dust. But while the flesh is animate it can only trust itself. Not the words of fools."

Justice wasn't sure what that meant, though it struck him deep in his heart. The man's hand was warming his chest and that too was helping the spiritual feeling Justice sensed in his bones. "I know," said Justice. There were many things he could be making that point in regards to. Perhaps his heart, and that odd feeling this entire time, and even his desire to get away from Drail and Natalie and Sasha was the truth.

"Good," said the man. "Then—"

His words were cut, and both of them froze, when popping sounds, subdued, but with enough of a crack to let Justice know shots were being fired. Many shots. Justice ran up the stairs, the man was behind him, his cane not making a sound. When they came to the third floor, the hallway echoed in silence. There was the sound of crawling.

Justice imagined that this might be assassins, and that perhaps his government hired private contractors for such an act. His guts shriveled at the thought, he a man with a heart so pure. He almost laughed.

Turning on the third floor, he noticed that a tarp blocked a hallway. He tore it down, then remembered the shots, and ducked out from the dark hallway. He crouched and peered around the corner. There was a distant body on the floor, and a flashlight lighting a strip of the floor and it disappeared around the corner of another intersection. There was no sound.

Justice, still not thinking, and still only sensing that lucid feeling from his pure heart, ran towards the intersection. He could hear the man with his cane behind him. Glass crunched. Justice stopped for a second; he couldn't hear anything but his heart pumping in his ears and temples. At the intersection, almost sliding in the blood, he stepped over a body and froze. A man, tattooed to the gills, stood awash in an open doorway's light. The man raised a gun at Justice. Justice instinctively raised his hands above his head and walked to the man.

"Stop," said the man. He was American. "You OGA?"

Justice, though he knew better, nodded.

The man tilted his head, sizing him up. He looked over Justice's shoulder. "And him?"

"He's a local."

With a tip of his gun, the man indicated that the local should scram. Before Justice could say anything the man with the cane was walking away. For a few moments there was the sound of the man's footsteps-cane, crunching glass, then footsteps-cane, then the sound dwindled as it echoed from the stairs and dissipated. Justice felt betrayed. Perhaps the man's words were as fickle as him.

"You here for the doctor?" asked the man with the gun. "To take him away to your... masters?"

Justice thought for a second. The man's voice was disrespectful, but also knowledgeable. "No. I just want to see him."

The man studied Justice for a few seconds.

"Who were they?" Justice asked, pointing at the corpses on the floor.

"Al Qaeda," said the man.

"And you?" Justice asked, though he knew it would make the man defensive.

"Ex-military."

"SOF?"

"Yup."

Justice thought for a second. "You're not an assassin?"

The man's face turned sad. He lowered his gun, and tucked it into his pants and shrugged. "I am what I am."

"I wasn't trying to say anything bad. Hell, as much as I want to think I'm a spy, I'm no better than an assassin, or an assassin's spotter."

Talking drifted out of the open apartment. There was some laughter.

The man, staring at the floor in front of his feet nodded. "I guess that's the fate of a pawn."

"Well, no longer," Justice blurted out, then felt sheepish. What *was* he going to do?

The man cocked his head at Justice. "Easy, now. There are easier ways to commit suicide."

Justice took a step forward. The man didn't move. "What about knowing what's right?"

The man nodded. "I've always known what's right. Still I'm helping the machine. Sometimes I think that the little things help my conscience out. But I'm probably fooling myself."

"Starve or obey."

The man looked up. Justice held his breath.

"But it's better to be on the right side than not," said the man.

"Indeed," said Justice. Perhaps this man was crazy. He entered the apartment. It was overly decorated with a flower theme.

The talking from another room grew louder. There seemed to be crying. An Arabic man came out and closed the door behind him. He stared at them both. He was covered with blood, though he'd tried to wash it off.

"This is Ali," said the American.

"I'm Justice." He put out his hand and shook the Arab's hand. "Those men?" He jerked his thumb back at the hallway.

The man nodded. He had a relaxed demeanor.

"And you?" Justice asked the American.

"Call me captain."

"Where's the doctor?" Justice asked. He flinched when he recognized the Arab man. He'd seen his wanted poster in the embassy in Yemen. "They were your friends," he said. He meant to whisper it, but it came out louder.

"Not mine," said Ali. The look of worry growing on his face, however, said otherwise.

"What were you doing here?" Justice asked.

"Easy now," said the captain.

"The doctor wasn't here for you," said Justice, mouthing the words, though something deep inside him said that he already knew this.

Ali shook his head.

"You can go inside," the captain said and nodded at the closed door inside the apartment from where talking and sobbing was continuing.

Justice walked up to the door and opened it. The smell of iodine and bodily fluids overwhelmed him. He saw a brown man, in his fifties, hunched over a woman, who looked shriveled up, and ill.

The man stared at Justice, both frightened and defiant.

"Doctor?"

The man studied him. He was holding the woman's hand. "You here for me?" His lower lip quivered. "You are always shredding the humanity of others while claiming your own—"

"I'm just checking," Justice said and raised his hand to assuage the doctor. "How are things?"

"Fine." The doctor patted the woman's forehead as she groaned. He looked back up. "You're not here to take me away?"

"No," said Justice. For some reason it was easy to fight off the overwhelming feelings of being a traitor—he knew better now. The heart, his heart, was strong. "You came here for her?"

The doctor nodded.

"Will she be okay?"

The doctor shook his head. His free hand stroking the woman's cheek. There were tears forming in the doctor's eyes. The woman started to cough, weakly, but consistently. Justice backed out of the room.

The captain and Ali looked up at him.

"You'll take him back home when all this is over?" Justice asked. Both men nodded. "You're from Yemen?"

Ali stared at him, almost grimacing. "I am."

"Al Qaeda?"

Ali didn't answer.

"I guess I'll see you back there one day," said Justice.

"It's home," said Ali.

Justice wasn't certain what that meant.

The captain seemed disgusted with Justice, but Justice decided to pay no one any heed. He walked out of the apartment, crunched the now almost dusty glass, and left the building. The man with the cane was gone.

When he saw Natalie and Sasha, his head felt light. He was happier than he'd been in a long time. Their stares didn't affect him anymore.

"Anyone find anything?" he asked.

Sasha, looking down at her tablet, glanced up. "We're tracking all cell phone calls. There might be some luck. It's hard since there're so many damn Arabs here."

Drail burst in, red eyed and sweaty. "Christ, we've information that AQ has enough uranium to send thousands of civilians to their fiery deaths. If we don't find the doctor, we'll be nothing but shadows in an hour."

Justice's heart spiked as he wondered if he had made a mistake, before he realized that he'd *just* seen the sinister doctor. The thought of Ali and the captain double-crossing him crossed his mind again, but he remembered the words he was going to try living by. "Is that a fact?" he asked.

Drail paused. The others paused. "It is, Justice. Don't misunderestimate these people. I know I have before, you reading all these reports and you think nothing will happen. And then."

"9-11," said Justice. He couldn't hide his disdain.

"That's right," said Drail. "You joined because of that, right?"

"Of course I did," Justice said. He was angry.

Drail stared hard, then walked out the room.

"You okay?" Natalie asked.

Justice, not looking up, nodded. They knew his secret. What could he do to hide it?

"*Something* seems different about you." It was Sasha talking this time, and she kept an eye him while pinching her tablet's screen.

"Nothing. I hope we find him," said Justice.

"So do I," Natalie said. "I hope we get to finish him off. Such people cause too much pain in the world." She said this with such a nonchalant and cheery way that the room almost brightened.

He grit his teeth and looked up. It was funny; after all, he'd been through Natalie didn't hold any sway over him. And now hearing her say this only made him feel completely disgusted with her. Seeing Sasha nod with fury only added to his hate for her. He thought about his now ex-girlfriend. There was no remorse. She'd been right to leave him.

"So do I," said Justice. He stood up. "I'll go pound the streets some more and see if there's any word." His knees were shaking because he knew what his treason meant. Before his cracked and tightened throat could betray him, he left.

Justice managed to control the search so that it never went near the apartment building, and when they didn't find any doctor it was only a week before the entire operation was called off. The bodies of the Al Qaeda soldiers were found soon after.

Justice took a week off as soon as they touched down in New York. Drail didn't seem to mind. Though it was great to breath air that had none of the toxic fumes of pressure that his job usually forced into his lungs, the vacation was not the catharsis he'd expected. He drove around the Midwest looking for a piece of America. But all he found was dull stares and people who couldn't even name a country where America was still murdering innocents. But he did find plentiful food and distractions in the form of sports or gatherings. There was some innocence to that. So he laughed and cheered. Driving back to New York, he received a text from Drail: Urgent.

Justice headed to the building, without any sleep, and after the usual security checks, found himself in Drail's office with an urge to piss his pants. Treason hung above his head and made him sweat too. He could feel a noose around his neck, and he tried to remind himself about the words of the man with the cane. It helped. A little. But it was the memories of the rubble and powdered concrete, though not of his city, that brought him strength and he stood tall waiting for the punch.

The painting from the uncle's house was still up on the wall. Drail noticed him staring at it.

"Yeah. I might get rid of it. You know the newest rage is robot paintings? They randomly place strokes on a canvas. Might have to check it out," said Drail.

"You wanted to see me?" Justice said, annoyed. The high of his disobedience long over, he felt like he was down in a dark pit. There was fear in his stomach as he imagined that he was about to be crushed. But he would go out swinging; he returned Drail's stare.

"The doctor is back in Pakistan," said Drail.

He relaxed. "Good."

"But *you* didn't find him."

Here it comes, thought Justice. The ax.

"Good job."

Justice bit his tongue. "Excuse me? For what?"

Drail opened a manila folder and browsed through it. "For increasing our drone attacks ten fold in Yemen. For getting us a 6% boost in our budget. That's what. We'll each have several private contractors helping us. No more trips to the badlands." Drail closed the folder, cracked his knuckles and grinned. "Big Tango."

Justice, more confused than ever, felt warm, but he couldn't help smiling. "That's great." He was choking up.

"Congratulations," said Drail, sticking out his hand. "We'll have a party for you in a week. Natalie and Sasha wanted to surprise you, but I figure, what the hell."

Justice left. The feeling of elated confusion was a high he kept until he reached his car. He stared up at the Freedom Tower feeling powerful. There would be more work coming up, but for now he was going to absolve his soul with liquor.

THE END

About the Author:

Nelson Lowhim was born in Tanzania where he lived for the first decade of his life. He then lived in India for a year before finally settling in the U.S. in the state of Michigan. He spent some of his formative years hitchhiking and hiking around the great state of Alaska. From there he joined the Army and served for seven years as an Infantryman in 1st AD then as an Engineer in Fifth Group. After his time in the Military—which included many travels through Europe and the Middle East—he came to New York and earned an undergraduate degree from Columbia University. He currently lives with his girlfriend in the Bronx.